HARRAP'S

Th

Wrong

of

Goodbye

MICHAEL

CONNELLY

This educational edition of *The Wrong Side of Goodbye* by Michael Connelly is published by arrangement with the Orion Publishing Group Limited, London.

Orion Publishing Group
Carmelite House
50 Victoria Embankment
London EC4Y ODZ
An Hachette UK company
www.orionbooks.co.uk

21, rue du Montparnasse
75283 Paris Cedex 06

HARRAP'S® est une marque de Larousse SAS
www.harrap.com

ISBN 978 2 81 870667 1

About the author

Michael Connelly is the author of thirty-two novels. His very first novel, *The Black Echo*, won the prestigious Mystery Writers of America Edgar Award[1] for Best First Novel in 1992. His books, which include the bestselling Harry Bosch series and Lincoln Lawyer series, have sold[2] more than fifty-eight million copies[3] worldwide[4].

Connelly is a former[5] newspaper reporter who has won numerous awards[6] for his journalism and his novels. He spends his time in California and Florida.

1. prix
2. se sont vendus à
3. exemplaires
4. dans le monde
5. ancien
6. couronné par de nombreux prix

DIRECTION DE LA PUBLICATION : Carine Girac-Marinier

NOTES EN MARGE : Delphine Nègre-Bouvet

RÉVISION DES NOTES : Marianne Mouchot

RELECTURE : F. Le Dantec

INFORMATIQUE ÉDITORIALE ET MISE EN PAGES :
Philippe Cazabet, Marie-Noëlle Tilliette

CONCEPTION GRAPHIQUE : Uli Meindl

FABRICATION : Rebecca Dubois

Mot de l'Éditeur

Vous aimeriez lire en langue originale, mais le vocabulaire, les expressions figurées ou la syntaxe vous arrêtent parfois ?

Cette collection est faite pour vous !

Vous trouverez en effet, en note dans la marge, une traduction de certains mots et expressions qui vous permettra d'avancer facilement dans votre lecture.

Nous n'avons pas cherché à vous donner une traduction littéraire de l'ouvrage et nous nous sommes parfois écartés du sens littéral pour vous fournir le sens qui convient le mieux à l'histoire. Aussi les mots sont-ils traduits dans le contexte du texte original.

Les expressions figées anglaises sont, bien entendu, rendues par une expression équivalente en français.

Les allusions à des réalités culturelles du monde anglo-saxon sont expliquées également dans la marge, pour vous aider à mieux comprendre la trame de l'histoire.

Vous aurez ainsi, en regard du texte original, tout le savoir-faire d'un dictionnaire rien que pour vous et adapté à ce livre !

Notre objectif est de vous mener jusqu'au mot FIN en vous donnant les clés nécessaires à la compréhension du récit.

Laissez-vous gagner par l'angoisse, l'humour et le suspense qui règnent chez les maîtres de la littérature anglo-saxonne.

Lire en VO ? You can indeed!

For Vin Scully
With many thanks

Acknowledgments

All novels are the product of research and experience, some more than others. This book relied heavily[1] on the help of others. The author gratefully acknowledges them[2] for their contributions and for sharing their memories.

Many thanks to John Houghton, former Navy corpsman who served in Vietnam. His experiences on the *Sanctuary* and with Connie Stevens many years later became Harry Bosch's experiences and the emotional core of the novel. Many thanks to Dennis Wojciechowski, the author's researcher and a Vietnam vet as well[3].

The "blue" team was invaluable as usual. A great big thank you to Rick Jackson for being there from the start, opening doors and providing the kind of direction that could only come from a detective who spent more than twenty-five years tracking down murderers. Former and current[4] LAPD homicide detectives Mitzi Roberts, Tim Marcia, and David Lambkin provided outstanding[5] advice and contributions to this story as well.

The San Fernando Police Department opened its doors to the author and embraced him with open arms[6]. Many, many thanks to Chief Anthony Vairo and Sergeant Irwin Rosenberg. The author hopes the novel does the department proud[7] (because Harry Bosch wants to come back).

Thank you to Terrill Lee Lankford, Henrik Bastin, Jane Davis, and Heather Rizzo for reading early drafts[8] and providing exceptional advice.

1. s'est beaucoup appuyé
2. leur adresse un grand merci
3. également vétérinaire au Viêt nam
4. anciens ou en service
5. d'une exceptionnelle qualité
6. l'ont accueilli les bras ouverts
7. fait honneur à la police de San Fernando
8. les premières versions

A tremendous amount of help also came from attorney Daniel F. Daly, photographer Guy Claudy, and NCIS investigator Gary McIntyre. The author also gratefully acknowledges the help of Shannon Byrne, and many thanks go to Pamela Wilson and artist Stephen Seemayer, who have been documenting[9] L.A.'s Arts District for many years through films like *Young Turks* and *Tales of the American*.

Last but not least are[10] the editors who helped sculpt a coherent story from an unwieldy block of[11] a manuscript. Asya Muchnick and Bill Massey are the best any writer could ask for. Copyeditor Pamela Marshall knows more about Harry Bosch than the author and is always there to fix things.

The author gratefully acknowledges all who contributed to this book.

9. décrivent

10. Enfin, et non des moindres :

11. la grosse masse que constitue

Coup de pouce pour vous aider à bien comprendre le début de l'histoire...

Le lieu : une rizière au Viêt nam.

L'année : 1969.

C'est bientôt la quille pour ce jeune soldat. Sauf que son hélicoptère est tombé dans une embuscade.

They charged from the cover of the elephant grass toward the LZ[1]*, five of them swarming the slick*[2] *on both sides, one among them yelling, "Go! Go! Go!"—as if each man needed to be prodded and reminded*[3] *that these were the most dangerous seconds of their lives.*

The rotor wash[4] *bent the grass back and blew the marker smoke*[5] *in all directions. The noise was deafening*[6] *as the turbine geared up for a heavy liftoff*[7]*. The door gunners*[8] *pulled everyone in by their pack straps*[9] *and the chopper*[10] *was quickly in the air again, having alighted*[11] *no longer than a dragonfly*[12] *on water.*

The tree line could be seen through the portside[13] *door as the craft*[14] *rose and started to bank*[15]*. Then came the muzzle flashes*[16] *from the banyan trees. Somebody yelled, "Snipers!"—as if the door gunner had to be told what he had out there.*

It was an ambush[17]*. Three distinct flash points, three snipers. They had waited until the helicopter was up and flying fat*[18]*, an easy target from six hundred feet*[19]*.*

The gunner opened up his M60, sending a barrage of fire into the treetops, shredding them with lead[20]*. But the sniper rounds*[21] *kept coming. The slick had no armor plating*[22]*, a decision made nine thousand miles away to take*[23] *speed and maneuverability over the burden of weight and protection.*

1. zone d'atterrissage
2. se précipitant sur l'hélico
3. qu'on lui martèle
4. souffle de l'hélice
5. fumée de balisage
6. assourdissant
7. vrombit en prévision d'un lourd décollage
8. mitrailleurs de porte
9. les bretelles de leur sac à dos
10. l'hélico
11. s'étant posé
12. libellule
13. à bâbord
14. l'appareil
15. virer de bord
16. clignotement des tirs
17. embuscade
18. en plein vol
19. à env. 200 m [d'altitude]
20. les criblant de balles
21. tirs
22. blindage
23. privilégier

1. capot moteur
2. gros « braoum »
3. hors jeu
4. capot
5. brisé
6. improbable
7. plaqua
8. se mit à tournoyer
9. avant de piquer en vrille
10. s'éloigna en tourbillonnant
11. rizières
12. soute
13. flèche
14. en reconnaissance
15. bientôt la quille
16. s'en sortir
17. Agrippez-vous !
18. puisse espérer
19. sans parler du

One shot hit the turbine cowling[1]*, a* thock *sound*[2] *reminding one of the helpless men on board of a fouled-off*[3] *baseball hitting the hood*[4] *of a car in the parking lot. Then came the snap of glass shattering*[5] *as the next round tore through the cockpit. It was a million-to-one*[6] *shot, hitting both the pilot and co-pilot at once. The pilot was killed instantly and the co-pilot clamped*[7] *his hands to his neck in an instinctive but helpless move to keep blood inside his body. The helicopter yawed into a clockwise spin*[8] *and was soon hurtling out of control*[9]*. It spun away*[10] *from the trees and across the rice paddies*[11]*. The men in the back started to yell helplessly. The man who had just had a memory of baseball tried to orient himself. The world outside the slick was spinning. He kept his eyes on a single word imprinted on the metal wall separating the cockpit from the cargo hold*[12]*. It said* Advance*—the letter* A *with a crossbar that was an arrow*[13] *pointed forward.*

He didn't move his eyes from the word even as the screaming intensified and he could feel the craft losing altitude. Seven months backing recon[14] *and now on short time*[15]*. He knew he wasn't going to make it back*[16]*. This was the end.*

The last thing he heard was someone yell, "Brace![17] *Brace! Brace!"—as if there was a possibility that anybody on board had a shot at*[18] *surviving the impact, never mind the*[19] *fire that would come after. And never mind the Vietcong who would come through with machetes after that.*

While the others screamed in panic he whispered a name to himself. "Vibiana …"

He knew he would never see her again. "Vibiana …"

The helicopter dove into one of the rice paddy dikes[1] *and exploded into a million metal parts. A moment later the spilled fuel caught fire and burned through the wreckage*[2]*, spreading flames across the surface of the paddy water. Black smoke rose into the air, marking the wreckage like an LZ marker*[3]*.*

The snipers reloaded and waited for the rescue choppers to come next.

1. digues

2. l'épave

3. fumigène de balisage

1

Bosch didn't mind the wait. The view was spectacular. He didn't bother with the waiting room couch[1]. Instead he stood with his face a foot[2] from the glass and took in[3] the view that ranged from the rooftops of downtown[4] to the Pacific Ocean. He was fifty-nine floors up in the U.S. Bank Tower, and Creighton was making him wait because it was something he always did, going all the way back to his days[5] at Parker Center, where the waiting room only had a low-angle view of the back of City Hall. Creighton had moved a mere[6] five blocks west since his days with the Los Angeles Police Department but he certainly had risen far beyond that to the lofty heights of[7] the city's financial gods.

Still[8], view or no view, Bosch didn't know why anyone would keep offices in the tower. The tallest building west of the Mississippi, it had previously been the target[9] of two foiled terrorist plots[10]. Bosch imagined there had to be a general uneasiness[11] added to the pressures of work for every soul who[12] entered its glass doors each morning. Relief[13] might soon come in the form of the Wilshire Grand Center, a glass-sheathed spire[14] rising to the sky a few blocks away. When finished it would take the distinction of tallest building west of the Mississippi. It would probably take the target as well.

1. canapé
2. à 30 cm
3. admirait
4. du centre-ville
5. déjà du temps où il était
6. d'à peine
7. grimpé très haut, jusque chez
8. N'empêche
9. cible
10. attentats terroristes déjoués
11. malaise
12. quiconque
13. Un sentiment de soulagement
14. gratte-ciel de verre

Bosch loved any opportunity to see his city from up high. When he was a young detective he would often take extra shifts[1] as a spotter[2] in one of the Department's airships[3]—just to take a ride above Los Angeles and be reminded of its seemingly infinite vastness.

He looked down at the 110 freeway[4] and saw it was backed up[5] all the way down through South-Central. He also noted the number of helipads[6] on the tops of the buildings below him. The helicopter had become the commuter vessel[7] of the elite. He had heard that even some of the higher-contract basketball players on the Lakers and Clippers[8] took helos[9] to work at the Staples Center.

The glass was thick enough to keep out any sound. The city below was silent. The only thing Bosch heard was the receptionist behind him answering the phone with the same greeting over and over: "Trident Security, how can I help you?"

Bosch's eye held[10] on a fast-moving patrol car going south on Figueroa toward the L.A. Live district. He saw the *01* painted large on the trunk[11] and knew that the car was from Central Division. Soon it was followed in the air by an LAPD airship that moved at a lower altitude than the floor[12] he stood on. Bosch was tracking it[13] when he was pulled away by a voice from behind.

"Mr. Bosch?"

He turned to see a woman standing in the middle of the waiting room. She wasn't the receptionist.

"I'm Gloria. We spoke on the phone," she said.

"Right, yes," Bosch said. "Mr. Creighton's assistant."

"Yes, nice to meet you. You can come back now."

"Good. Any longer[14] and I was going to jump."

1. faisait souvent des heures sup
2. guetteur
3. dirigeables
4. autoroute
5. embouteillée
6. d'hélistations
7. moyen de transport quotidien
8. équipes de basket [rivales] de Los Angeles
9. l'hélico
10. se fixa
11. coffre
12. l'étage
13. le suivait du regard
14. Encore un peu

She didn't smile. She led Bosch through a door into a hallway with framed watercolors[1] perfectly spaced on the walls.

"It's impact-resistant glass," she said. "It can take[2] the force of a category-five hurricane."

"Good to know," Bosch said. "And I was only joking. Your boss had a history of[3] keeping people waiting—back when he was a deputy chief with the police department[4]."

"Oh, really? I haven't noticed it here."

This made no sense to[5] Bosch, since she had just fetched him from the waiting room fifteen minutes after the appointed meeting time[6].

"He must've read it in a management book back when he was climbing the ranks[7]," Bosch said. "You know, keep 'em waiting even if they're on time. Gives you the upper hand[8] when you finally bring them into the room, lets them know you are a busy man."

"I'm not familiar with that business philosophy."

"Probably more of a cop[9] philosophy."

They entered an office suite. In the outer office, there were two separate desk arrangements[10], one occupied by a man in his twenties wearing a suit, and the other empty and, he assumed[11], belonging to Gloria. They walked between the desks to a door and Gloria opened it and then stepped to the side[12].

"Go on in," she said. "Can I bring you a bottle of water?"

"No, thanks," Bosch said. "I'm fine."

Bosch entered an even larger room, with a desk area to the left and an informal seating area[13] to the right, where a couple of couches faced each other across a glass-topped coffee table[14]. Creighton was sitting behind his desk, indicating Bosch's appointment was going to be formal[15].

1. des aquarelles sous cadre
2. supporter
3. était connu pour
4. directeur adjoint de la police [de Los Angeles]
5. parut absurde à
6. l'heure du rendez-vous
7. échelons
8. l'avantage
9. de flics
10. coins bureau
11. supposa-t-il
12. s'écarta
13. salon
14. table basse
15. avoir un caractère officiel

It had been more than a decade[1] since Bosch had seen Creighton in person. He could not remember the occasion but assumed it was a squad meeting[2] where Creighton had come in and made an announcement concerning the overtime[3] budget or the department's travel protocols. Back then[4] Creighton was the head bean counter[5]—in charge of budgeting for the department among his other management duties. He was known for instituting strict policies[6] on overtime that required detailed explanations to be written on green slips[7] that were subject to supervisor[8] approval. Since that approval, or disapproval, usually came after the extra[9] hours were already worked[10], the new system was viewed as an effort to dissuade cops from working overtime or, worse yet, get them to work overtime and then deny authorization or replace it with comp time[11]. It was during this posting[12] that Creighton became universally known as "Cretin" by the rank and file[13].

Though Creighton left the department[14] for the private sector not long after that, the "greenies"[15] were still in use. The mark he left on the department had not been a daring rescue[16] or a gun battle[17] or the takedown of an apex[18] predator. It had been the green overtime slip[19].

"Harry, come in," Creighton said. "Sit down."

Bosch moved to the desk. Creighton was a few years older than Harry but in good shape. He stood behind the desk with his hand held forward. He wore a gray suit that was tailor-cut to his taut frame[20]. He looked like money. Bosch shook his hand and then sat down in front of the desk. He hadn't gotten dressed up[21] for the appointment. He was in blue jeans, a blue denim shirt[22], and a charcoal corduroy[23] jacket he'd had for at

1. dix ans
2. réunion d'équipe
3. d'heures supplémentaires
4. À l'époque,
5. tenait les cordons de la bourse
6. des règles
7. bordereaux
8. de votre supérieur
9. supplémentaires
10. effectuées
11. par des heures de récupération
12. en occupant ce poste
13. les flics de base
14. la police
15. fameuses petites vertes
16. sauvetage héroïque
17. fusillade
18. prise d'un grand
19. fiche verte des heures sup
20. taillé sur mesure pour sa solide carrure
21. ne s'était pas mis sur son trente et un
22. chemise en jean
23. en velours anthracite

least twelve years. These days Bosch's work suits from his days with the department were wrapped in plastic. He didn't want to pull one of them out just for a meeting with Cretin.

"Chief, how are you?" he said.

"It's not 'chief' anymore," Creighton said with a laugh. "Those days are long ago. Call me John."

"John, then."

"Sorry to keep you waiting out there. I had a client on the phone and, well, the client always comes first. Am I right?"

"Sure, no problem. I enjoyed the view."

The view through the window behind Creighton was in the opposite direction, stretching[1] northeasterly across the Civic Center and to the snow-capped[2] mountains in San Bernardino. But Bosch guessed that the mountains weren't the reason Creighton picked[3] this office. It was the Civic Center. From his desk Creighton looked down on the spire of City Hall, the Police Administration Building, and the Los Angeles Times Building. Creighton was above them all.

"It is truly spectacular seeing the world from this angle," Creighton said.

Bosch nodded[4] and got down to business.

"So," he said. "What can I do for you … John?"

"Well, first of all, I appreciate you coming in[5] without really knowing why I wished to see you. Gloria told me she had a difficult time[6] persuading you to come."

"Yeah, well, I'm sorry about that. But like I told her, if this is about a job, I'm not interested. I've got a job."

"I heard. San Fernando. But that's gotta be part-time, right[7]?"

He said it with a slightly mocking tone and Bosch remembered a line[8] from a movie he once

1. et s'étendait
2. enneigées
3. avait choisi
4. acquiesça
5. que vous soyez venu
6. du mal à
7. c'est forcément un temps partiel, non
8. réplique

saw: "If you're not cop, you're little people[1]." It also held[2] that if you worked for a little department, you were still little people.

"It keeps me as busy as I want to be," he said. "I also have a private ticket[3]. I pick up stuff[4] from time to time on that."

"All referrals[5], correct?" Creighton said.

Bosch looked at him a moment.

"Am I supposed to be impressed that you checked me out[6]?" he finally said. "I'm not interested in working here. I don't care what the pay is, I don't care what the cases are."

"Well, let me just ask you something, Harry," Creighton said. "Do you know what we do here?"

Bosch looked over Creighton's shoulder and out at the mountains before answering.

"I know you are high-level security for those who can afford it[7]," he said.

"Exactly," Creighton said.

He held up three fingers on his right hand in what Bosch assumed was supposed to be a trident.

"Trident Security," Creighton said. "Specializing in financial, technological, and personal security. I started the California branch ten years ago. We have bases[8] here, in New York, Boston, Chicago, Miami, London, and Frankfurt. We are about to open in Istanbul. We are a very large operation with thousands of clients and even more connections in our fields of expertise."

"Good[9] for you," Bosch said.

He had spent about ten minutes on his laptop[10] reading up on Trident before coming in. The upscale security venture[11] was founded in New York in 1996 by a shipping magnate[12] named Dennis Laughton, who had been abducted and ransomed[13] in the Philippines. Laughton first hired a

1. Si t'es pas flic, t'es pas grand-chose

2. sous-entendait

3. travaille aussi dans le privé

4. fais des missions

5. Toutes par relations

6. par le fait que vous vous soyez renseigné sur moi

7. en ont les moyens

8. des succursales

9. Tant mieux

10. ordinateur portable

11. l'entreprise de sécurité haut de gamme

12. magnat du transport maritime

13. enlevé et mis à rançon

former[1] NYPD police commissioner to be his front man[2] and had followed suit[3] in every city where he opened a base, plucking[4] a local chief or high-ranking commander[5] from the local police department to make a media splash[6] and secure the absolute must-have[7] of local police cooperation. The word was[8] that ten years ago Laughton had tried to hire L.A.'s police chief but was turned down[9] and then went to Creighton as a second choice.

"I told your assistant I wasn't interested in a job with Trident," Bosch said. "She said it wasn't about that. So why don't you tell me what it is about so we can both get on with our days[10]."

"I can assure you, I am not offering you a job with Trident," Creighton said. "To be honest, we must have full cooperation and respect from the LAPD to do what we do and to handle the delicate matters that involve our clients and the police. If we were to bring you in[11] as a Trident associate, there could be a problem."

"You're talking about my lawsuit[12]."

"Exactly."

For most of the past year Bosch had been in the middle of a protracted[13] lawsuit against the department where he had worked for more than thirty years. He sued[14] because he believed he had been illegally forced into retirement[15]. The case had drawn ill will toward Bosch from within the ranks[16]. It did not seem to matter that during his time with a badge[17] he had brought more than a hundred murderers to justice. The lawsuit was settled[18] but the hostility continued from some quarters of the department, mostly the quarter at the top[19].

"So if you brought me into Trident, that would not be good for your relations with the LAPD,"

1. ancien
2. en guise de directeur
3. fait de même
4. piochant
5. un haut gradé
6. coup médiatique
7. s'assurer l'indispensable
8. La rumeur voulait
9. avait essuyé un refus
10. retourner à nos occupations
11. on devait vous prendre
12. procès
13. interminable
14. avait intenté le procès
15. à prendre sa retraite
16. On lui en voulait dans la police
17. ses années de service
18. Il avait gagné le procès
19. de la direction

Bosch said. "I get that[1]. But you want me for something. What is it?"

Creighton nodded. It was time to get down to it[2].

"Do you know the name Whitney Vance?" he asked.

Bosch nodded.

"Of course I do," he said.

"Yes, well, he is a client," Creighton said. "As is his company, Advance Engineering."

"Whitney Vance has got to be eighty years old."

"Eighty-five, actually[3]. And ..."

Creighton opened the top middle drawer of his desk and removed[4] a document. He put it on the desk between them. Bosch could see it was a printed check with an attached stub[5]. He wasn't wearing his glasses and was unable to read the amount or the other details.

"He wants to speak to you," Creighton finished.

"About what?" Bosch asked.

"I don't know. He said it was a private matter and he specifically asked for you by name[6]. He said he would discuss the matter only with you. He had this certified check drawn for ten thousand dollars. It is yours to keep[7] for meeting him, whether or not the appointment leads to further work[8]."

Bosch didn't know what to say. At the moment he was flush[9] because of the lawsuit settlement, but he had put most of the money into long-term investment accounts designed to carry him comfortably into old age[10] with a solid stake left over[11] for his daughter. But at the moment she had two-plus years of college[12] and then graduate school tuition ahead of her[13]. She had some generous scholarships[14] but he was still on the hook[15] for

1. comprends
2. d'en venir au fait
3. en fait
4. en sortit
5. un chèque avec son talon
6. en personne
7. Vous pourrez le garder
8. que votre entrevue mène à une mission ou non
9. en fonds
10. lui assurer une retraite confortable
11. et il en resterait une bonne marge
12. il lui restait encore plus de deux ans d'études
13. les frais du troisième cycle à payer
14. bourses
15. serait quand même un peu à court

the rest of it in the short term. There was no doubt in his mind that ten thousand dollars could be put to good use.

"When and where is this appointment going to be?" he finally said.

"Tomorrow morning at nine at Mr. Vance's home in Pasadena," Creighton said. "The address is on the check receipt. You might want to dress a little nicer than that."

Bosch ignored the sartorial jab[1]. From an inside jacket pocket he took out his eyeglasses. He put them on as he reached across the desk and took the check. It was made out[2] to his full name, Hieronymus Bosch.

There was a perforated line running across the bottom[3] of the check. Below it were the address and appointment time as well as the admonition[4] "Don't bring a firearm." Bosch folded the check along the perforation and looked at Creighton as he put it into his jacket.

"I'm going to go to the bank from here," he said. "I'll deposit this, and if there is no problem, I'll be there tomorrow."

Creighton smirked[5].

"There will not be a problem."

Bosch nodded.

"I guess that's it, then[6]," he said.

He stood up to go.

"There is one more thing, Bosch," Creighton said.

Bosch noted that he had dropped[7] from first name to last name status with Creighton inside[8] of ten minutes.

"What's that[9]?" he asked.

"I have no idea what the old man is going to ask you, but I'm very protective of him," Creighton said. "He is more than a client and I don't want to

1. la pique sur sa tenue vestimentaire
2. libellé
3. une ligne en pointillé en bas
4. l'avertissement
5. eut un petit sourire narquois
6. Bon, je suppose que c'est tout
7. était passé
8. en l'espace
9. Laquelle

see him taken for a ride[1] at this point in his life. Whatever the task is that he wants you to perform, I need to be in the loop[2]."

"A ride[3]? Unless I missed something, you called me, Creighton. If anybody's being taken for a ride, it will be me. It doesn't matter how much he's paying me."

"I can assure you that's not the case. The only ride is the ride out to[4] Pasadena for which you just received ten thousand dollars."

Bosch nodded.

"Good," he said. "I'm going to hold you to that[5]. I'll see the old man tomorrow and find out what this is about. But if he becomes my client, then that business, whatever it is, will be between him and me. There won't be any loop that includes you unless Vance tells me there is. That's how I work. No matter who the client is."

Bosch turned toward the door. When he got there he looked back at Creighton.

"Thanks for the view."

He left and closed the door behind him.

On the way out he stopped at the receptionist's desk and got his parking receipt validated. He wanted to be sure Creighton ate the twenty bucks for that[6], as well as the car wash he agreed to when he valeted the car[7].

1. je n'ai pas envie qu'on le mène en bateau
2. boucle
3. En bateau
4. seul voyage est en voiture, jusqu'à
5. vous croire sur parole
6. se farcisse les 20 $ de parking
7. avait confié sa voiture au voiturier

2

The Vance estate[1] was on San Rafael near the Annandale Golf Club. It was a neighborhood of old money[2]. Homes and estates that had been passed down[3] through generations and guarded behind stone walls and black iron fences. It was a far cry from[4] the Hollywood Hills, where the new money went and the rich[5] left their trash cans[6] out on the street all week. There were no For Sale signs here. You had to know somebody, maybe even share their blood, to buy in[7].

Bosch parked against the curb[8] about a hundred yards[9] from the gate that guarded the entrance to the Vance estate. Atop it were spikes[10] ornately disguised as flowers. For a few moments he studied the curve of the driveway[11] beyond the gate as it wound[12] and rose into the cleft of[13] two rolling green hills and then disappeared. There was no sign of any structure, not even a garage. All of that would be well back from the street, buffered[14] by geography, iron, and security. But Bosch knew that Whitney Vance, eighty-five years old, was up there somewhere beyond those money-colored[15] hills, waiting for him with something on his mind. Something that required a man from the other side of the spiked gate.

Bosch was twenty minutes early for the appointment and decided to use the time to review several stories he had found on the Internet and downloaded to his laptop that morning.

1. propriété
2. fortunes
3. transmises
4. n'avait rien à voir avec
5. le quartier des nouveaux riches qui
6. poubelles
7. acheter dans le coin
8. le long du trottoir
9. mètres
10. La grille était hérissée de pointes
11. l'allée
12. serpentait
13. entre
14. protégé
15. couleur de dollars [vert]

The general contours[1] of Whitney Vance's life were known to Bosch as they were most likely known to[2] most Californians. But he still found the details fascinating and, even admirable, in that Vance was the rare recipient of a rich inheritance who had turned it into something even bigger[3]. He was the fourth-generation Pasadena scion[4] of a mining family that extended all the way back to[5] the California gold rush[6]. Prospecting was what drew Vance's great-grandfather west[7] but not what the family fortune was founded on. Frustrated[8] by the hunt for gold, the great-grandfather established the state's first strip-mining operation[9], extracting multi-tons of iron ore[10] out of the earth in San Bernardino County. Vance's grandfather followed up[11] with a second strip mine farther south, in Imperial County, and his father parlayed that success into[12] a steel mill[13] and fabrication plant[14] that helped support the dawning[15] aviation industry. At the time, the face of that industry belonged to[16] Howard Hughes, and he counted Nelson Vance as first a contractor[17] and then a partner[18] in many different aviation endeavors[19]. Hughes would become godfather to[20] Nelson Vance's only child.

Whitney Vance was born in 1931 and, as a young man, apparently set out to blaze a unique path for himself[21]. He initially went off to the University of Southern California to study filmmaking[22] but he eventually dropped out[23] and came back to the family fold[24], transferring to[25] the California Institute of Technology, in Pasadena, the school "Uncle Howard" had attended. It was Hughes who urged[26] young Whitney to study aeronautical engineering at Caltech.

As with the elders[27] of his family, when it was his turn Vance pushed the family business in new

1. grandes lignes
2. comme elles l'étaient sans doute pour
3. une exception, un riche héritier qui fait fructifier son héritage
4. descendant
5. remontait jusqu'à
6. ruée vers l'or
7. ce qui avait attiré à l'Ouest l'arrière-grand-père de Vance
8. Déçu
9. exploitation à ciel ouvert
10. minerai de fer
11. avait poursuivi
12. avait fait de cette réussite
13. aciérie
14. une fabrique
15. naissante
16. le visage connu en était
17. d'abord comme entrepreneur
18. associé
19. contrats
20. le parrain de
21. entreprit de suivre sa propre voie
22. le cinéma
23. finit par abandonner
24. giron familial
25. pour intégrer
26. incita
27. anciens

and increasingly successful directions, always with a connection to the family's original product: steel[1]. He won numerous government contracts to manufacture aircraft parts[2] and founded Advance Engineering, which held the patents on[3] many of them. Couplings[4] that were used for the safe fueling of aircraft[5] were perfected in the family steel mill and were still used today at every airport in the world. Ferrite extracted from the iron ore at Vance mining operations was used in the earliest efforts[6] to build aircraft that avoided radar detection. These processes were meticulously patented[7] and protected by Vance and they guaranteed his company's participation in the decades-long development of stealth technologies[8]. Vance and his company were part of the so-called military-industrial complex, and the Vietnam War saw their value grow exponentially. Every mission in or out of that country over the entire length[9] of the war involved equipment from Advance Engineering. Bosch remembered seeing the company logo—an *A* with an arrow through the middle of it—imprinted on the steel walls[10] of every helicopter he had ever flown on in Vietnam.

Bosch was startled[11] by a sharp rap[12] on the window beside him. He looked up to see a uniformed Pasadena patrol officer, and in the rearview[13] he saw the black-and-white[14] parked behind him. He had become so engrossed[15] in his reading that he had not even heard the cop car come up on him.

He had to turn on[16] the Cherokee's engine to lower the window[17]. Bosch knew what this was about[18]. A twenty-two-year-old vehicle in need of paint parked outside the estate of a family that helped build the state of California constituted a suspicious activity. It didn't matter that the car was

1. l'acier
2. pièces détachées
3. possédait les brevets pour
4. Des couplages
5. l'avitaillement sécurisé des avions
6. lors des premières tentatives
7. brevetés
8. long développement des technologies furtives
9. pendant toute la durée
10. parois
11. tiré de ses pensées
12. petit coup sec
13. rétroviseur
14. voiture de police
15. était tellement plongé
16. démarrer
17. baisser la vitre
18. ce qu'on lui voulait

freshly cleaned or that he was wearing a crisp suit and tie[1] rescued from a plastic storage bag. It had taken less than fifteen minutes for the police to respond[2] to his intrusion into the neighborhood.

"I know how this looks[3], Officer," he began. "But I have an appointment across the street in about five minutes and I was just—"

"That's wonderful," the cop said. "Do you mind stepping out of the car?[4]"

Bosch looked at him for a moment. He saw the nameplate above his breast pocket said[5] Cooper.

"You're kidding, right[6]?" he asked.

"No, sir, I'm not," Cooper said. "Please step out of the car."

Bosch took a deep breath, opened the door, and did as he was told. He raised his hands to shoulder height[7] and said, "I'm a police officer."

Cooper immediately tensed, as Bosch knew he would.

"I'm unarmed," Bosch said quickly. "My weapon[8]'s in the glove box."

At that moment he was thankful for the edict typed on the check stub telling him to come to the Vance appointment unarmed.

"Let me see some ID[9]," Cooper demanded.

Bosch carefully reached[10] into an inside pocket in his suit coat[11] and pulled his badge case[12]. Cooper studied the detective's badge and then the ID.

"This says you're a reserve officer," he said.

"Yep," Bosch said. "Part-timer[13]."

"About fifteen miles off your reservation[14], aren't you? What are you doing here, Detective Bosch?"

He handed the badge case back and Bosch put it away.

"Well, I was trying to tell you," he said. "I have an appointment—which you are going to make

1. costard-cravate impeccable
2. réagir
3. que ça n'en a pas l'air
4. Veuillez sortir du véhicule !
5. indiquait
6. C'est une blague
7. en l'air
8. arme
9. Montrez-moi vos papiers
10. glissa la main
11. veston
12. l'étui
13. à temps partiel
14. Vous êtes à 25 km de votre périmètre

me late for[1]—with Mr. Vance, who I'm guessing you know lives right over there."

Bosch pointed toward the black gate.

"Is this appointment police business[2]?" Cooper asked.

"It's actually none of your business[3]," Bosch replied.

They held each other's cold stares[4] for a long moment, neither man blinking[5]. Finally Bosch spoke.

"Mr. Vance is waiting for me," he said. "Guy like that, he'll probably ask[6] why I'm late and he'll probably do something about it. You got a first name, Cooper?"

Cooper blinked[7].

"Yeah, it's fuck you," he said. "Have a nice day."

He turned and started back toward the patrol car.

"Thank you, Officer," Bosch called after him.

Bosch got back into his car and immediately pulled away from the curb[8]. If the old car still had had the juice to leave rubber[9], he would have done so. But the most he could show Cooper, who remained parked at the curb, was a plume[10] of blue smoke from the ancient exhaust pipe[11].

He pulled into the entrance channel at the gate[12] to the Vance estate and drove up to a camera and communication box[13]. Almost immediately he was greeted by a voice.

"Yes?"

It was male, young,[14] and tiredly arrogant. Bosch leaned out[15] the window and spoke loudly even though he knew he probably didn't have to.

"Harry Bosch to see Mr. Vance. I have an appointment."

1. pour lequel vous allez me mettre en retard
2. Est-ce un rendez-vous dans le cadre de vos fonctions
3. Ça ne vous regarde pas
4. se dévisagèrent froidement
5. sans sourciller ni l'un ni l'autre
6. C'est le genre de type à demander
7. cilla
8. s'éloigna du trottoir
9. avait encore la capacité de laisser des traces de pneus
10. panache
11. antique pot d'échappement
12. sas d'entrée
13. Interphone
14. la voix d'un homme jeune
15. passa la tête par

After a moment the gate in front of him started to roll open.

"Follow the driveway to the parking apron[1] by the security post," the voice said. "Mr. Sloan will meet you there at the metal detector. Leave all weapons and recording devices[2] in the glove compartment of your vehicle."

"Got it[3]," Bosch said.

"Drive up[4]," the voice said.

The gate was all the way open now and Bosch drove through. He followed the cobblestone driveway[5] through a finely manicured set of emerald hills[6] until he came to a second fence line[7] and a guard shack[8]. The double-fencing security measures here were similar to those employed at most prisons Bosch had visited—of course, with the opposite intention of keeping people out instead of in[9].

The second gate rolled open and a uniformed guard stepped out of a booth[10] to signal Bosch through[11] and to direct him to the parking apron. As he passed, Bosch waved a hand and noticed the Trident Security patch[12] on the shoulder of the guard's navy blue uniform.

After parking, Bosch was instructed to place his keys, phone, watch, and belt in a plastic tub[13] and then to walk through an airport-style metal detector while two more Trident men watched. They returned[14] everything but the phone, which they explained would be placed in the glove box of his car.

"Anybody else get the irony here[15]?" he asked as he put his belt back through the loops[16] of his pants[17]. "You know, the family made their money on[18] metal—now you have to go through a metal detector to get inside the house."

Neither of the guards said anything.

1. l'aire de stationnement
2. enregistreurs
3. Entendu
4. Avancez
5. l'allée pavée
6. série de collines vert émeraude parfaitement entretenues
7. clôture
8. guérite
9. d'empêcher les gens d'entrer plutôt que de sortir
10. guérite
11. faire signe à Bosch de passer
12. insigne
13. bac
14. lui rendirent
15. Vous ne trouvez pas ça ironique, vous
16. passants
17. pantalon
18. a fait fortune dans le

"Okay, I guess it's just me, then," Bosch said.

Once he buckled[1] his belt he was passed off to the next level of security, a man in a suit with the requisite earbud and wrist mic[2] and the dead-eyed Secret Service stare[3] to go with them. His head was shaved just so he could complete the tough-guy look[4]. He did not say his name but Bosch assumed he was the Sloan mentioned on the intercom[5] earlier. He escorted Bosch wordlessly through the delivery entrance[6] of a massive gray-stone mansion that Bosch guessed would rival anything the Du Ponts or Vanderbilts had to offer. According to Wikipedia, he was calling on[7] six billion[8] dollars. Bosch had no doubt as he entered that this would be the closest to American royalty he would ever get.

He was led to a room paneled in dark wood with dozens of framed 8 × 10[9] photographs hung in four rows across one wall. There were a couple of couches and a bar at the end of the room. The escort in the suit[10] pointed Bosch to one of the couches.

"Sir, have a seat, and Mr. Vance's secretary will come for you[11] when he is ready to see you."

Bosch took a seat on the couch facing the wall of photos.

"Would you like some water?" the suit asked.

"No, I'm fine," Bosch said.

The suit took a position next to the door they had entered through and clasped one wrist with the other hand[12] in a posture that said[13] he was alert and ready for anything.

Bosch used the waiting time[14] to study the photographs. They offered a record of[15] Whitney Vance's life and the people he had met over the course of it[16]. The first photo depicted[17] Howard Hughes and a young teenager he assumed was[18]

1. eut bouclé
2. les inévitables oreillette et micro de poignet
3. regard indéchiffrable du mec des services secrets
4. pour compléter son look de gros dur
5. l'Interphone
6. l'entrée des livraisons
7. mettait les pieds dans
8. milliards
9. de 20 × 25 cm
10. en costume
11. vous chercher
12. se tint le poignet de l'autre main,
13. en un geste montrant qu'
14. profita de l'attente
15. retraçaient
16. au cours de son existence
17. montrait
18. qu'il supposa être

Vance. They were leaning against the unpainted metal skin of a plane. From there the photos appeared to run[1] left to right in chronological order. They depicted Vance with numerous well-known figures[2] of industry, politics, and the media. Bosch couldn't put a name to every person Vance posed with but from Lyndon Johnson to Larry King he knew who most of them were. In all the photos, Vance displayed[3] the same half smile, the corner of his mouth on the left side curled up, as if to communicate to the camera lens[4] that it wasn't his idea to pose for a picture. The face grew older photo to photo, the eyelids more hooded[5], but the smile was always the same.

There were two photos of Vance with Larry King, the longtime interviewer of celebrities and newsmakers[6] on CNN. In the first, Vance and King were seated across from each other[7] in the studio recognizable as King's set[8] for more than two decades. There was a book standing upright[9] on the desk between them. In the second photo Vance was using a gold pen to autograph the book for King. Bosch got up and went to the wall to look more closely[10] at the photos. He put on his glasses and leaned in close to the first photo so he could read the title of the book Vance was promoting on the show[11].

STEALTH[12]: The Making of the Disappearing Plane
By Whitney P. Vance

The title jogged loose a memory[13] and Bosch recalled something about[14] Whitney Vance writing a family history that the critics trashed[15] more for what was left out[16] than for what it contained. His father, Nelson Vance, had been a ruthless[17] businessman and controversial political figure in his

1. se lire
2. personnalités
3. affichait
4. à l'objectif
5. les paupières de plus en plus tombantes
6. vedettes de l'actualité
7. l'un en face de l'autre
8. plateau TV
9. posé à la verticale
10. de plus près
11. pendant l'émission
12. Avions furtifs
13. réveilla un souvenir
14. se souvint vaguement de
15. avaient décriée
16. ce qui avait été omis
17. impitoyable

day. He was said, but never proven, to be a member of a cabal of wealthy industrialists who were supporters of eugenics[1]—the so-called[2] science of improving the human race through controlled breeding[3] that would eliminate undesirable attributes. After the Nazis employed a similar perverted doctrine to carry out[4] genocide in World War II, people like Nelson Vance hid their beliefs and affiliations.

His son's book amounted to little more[5] than a vanity[6] project full of hero worship[7], with little mention of the negatives[8]. Whitney Vance had become such a recluse in his later life[9] that the book became a reason to bring him out into public light and ask him about the things omitted.

"Mr. Bosch?"

Bosch turned from the photos to a woman standing by the entrance to a hallway on the other side of the room. She looked to be almost seventy years old[10] and had her gray hair in a no-nonsense bun[11] on top of her head.

"I'm Mr. Vance's secretary, Ida," she said. "He will see you now."

Bosch followed her into the hallway. They walked for a distance that seemed like a city block[12] before going up a short set of stairs[13] to another hallway, this one traversing a wing[14] of the mansion built on a higher slope[15] of the hill.

"Sorry to keep you waiting[16]," Ida said.

"It's okay," Bosch said. "I enjoyed checking out the photos."

"A lot of history there."

"Yes."

"Mr. Vance is looking forward to[17] seeing you."

"Great. I've never met a billionaire before."

His graceless[18] remark ended the conversation. It was as though his mention of money was

1. en faveur de l'eugénisme
2. pseudo
3. procréation
4. commettre leurs
5. n'était guère plus
6. à compte d'auteur
7. culte du héros
8. aspects négatifs
9. s'était tellement isolé dans son âge mûr
10. semblait avoir près de 70 ans
11. chignon strict
12. aussi longue qu'un pâté de maisons
13. volée de marches
14. aile
15. versant
16. vous avoir fait attendre
17. impatient de
18. inélégante

entirely crass and uncouth[1] in a mansion built as a monument to money.

Finally they arrived at a set of double doors and Ida ushered[2] Bosch into Whitney Vance's home office.

The man Bosch had come to see was sitting behind a desk, his back to an empty fireplace big enough to take shelter in[3] during a tornado. With a thin hand so white it looked like he was wearing a Latex glove, he motioned for[4] Bosch to come forward[5].

Bosch stepped up to the desk, and Vance pointed to the lone leather chair[6] in front of it. He made no offer to shake Bosch's hand. As he sat, Bosch noticed that Vance was in a wheelchair[7] with electric controls extending from the left armrest[8]. He saw the desk was clear of work product[9] except for a single white piece of paper that was either blank[10] or had its contents facedown[11] on the polished dark wood.

"Mr. Vance," Bosch said. "How are you?"

"I'm old—that's how I am," Vance said. "I have fought like hell to defeat[12] time but some things can't be beat. It is hard for a man in my position to accept, but I am resigned, Mr. Bosch."

He gestured with that bony white hand again, taking in all of the room with a sweep[13].

"All of this will soon be meaningless[14]," he said.

Bosch glanced around in case there was something Vance wanted him to see. There was a sitting area to the right with a long white couch and matching[15] chairs. There was an office bar that a host could slip behind[16] if necessary. There were paintings on two walls that were merely splashes of color.

1. la pire des grossièretés
2. fit entrer
3. servir d'abri
4. fit signe à
5. s'avancer
6. l'unique fauteuil en cuir
7. fauteuil roulant
8. accoudoir de gauche
9. dépourvu de tout document de travail
10. vierge
11. posée face cachée
12. lutté de toutes mes forces pour vaincre le
13. embrassant la pièce d'un geste
14. n'aura bientôt plus de raison d'être
15. assortis
16. derrière lequel on pouvait se glisser

Bosch looked back at Vance, and the old man offered the lopsided smile[1] Bosch had seen in the photos in the waiting room, the upward curve on only the[2] left side. Vance couldn't complete a full[3] smile. According to the photos Bosch had seen, he never could.

Bosch didn't quite know how to respond to the old man's words about death and meaninglessness. Instead, he just pressed on[4] with an introduction he had thought about repeatedly since meeting with Creighton.

"Well, Mr. Vance, I was told you wanted to see me, and you have paid me quite a bit of money to be here. It may not be a lot to you, but it is to me. What can I do for you, sir?"

Vance cut the[5] smile and nodded.

"A man who gets right to the point[6]," he said. "I like that."

He reached to his chair's controls[7] and moved closer to the desk.

"I read about you in the newspaper," he said. "Last year, I believe. The case[8] with that doctor and the shoot-out[9]. You seemed to me like a man who stands his ground[10], Mr. Bosch. They put a lot of pressure on you but you stood up to it[11]. I like that. I need that. There's not a lot of it around anymore[12]."

"What do you want me to do?" Bosch asked again.

"I want you to find someone for me," Vance said. "Someone who might never have existed."

1. sourire de travers
2. la commissure relevée juste du
3. n'était pas capable de faire un vrai
4. se contenta de poursuivre
5. ravala son
6. va droit au but
7. allongea le bras vers les manettes de son fauteuil
8. L'affaire
9. fusillade
10. ne cède pas
11. avez tenu bon
12. C'est rare, de nos jours

3

After intriguing Bosch with his request, Vance used a shaky left hand to flip over[1] the piece of paper on his desk and told Bosch he would have to sign it before they discussed anything further.

"It is a nondisclosure form[2]," he explained. "My lawyer said it is ironclad[3]. Your signature guarantees that you will not reveal the contents of our discussion or your subsequent investigation to anyone but me. Not even an employee of mine, not even someone who says they have come to you on my behalf[4]. Only me, Mr. Bosch. If you sign this document, you answer only to me. You report any findings of your investigation only to me[5]. Do you understand?"

"Yes, I understand," Bosch said. "I have no problem signing it."

"Very good, then. I have a pen here."

Vance pushed the document across the desk, then drew a pen from an ornate gold holder[6] on his desk. It was a fountain pen[7] that felt heavy in Bosch's hand because it was thick and made of what he presumed was real gold. It reminded Bosch of the pen Vance used in the photo to sign the book for Larry King.

He quickly scanned[8] the document and then signed it. He put the pen down on top of it and pushed both back across the desk to Vance. The old man placed the document in the desk drawer

1. de sa main gauche qui tremblait, retourna
2. accord de confidentialité
3. D'après mon avocat, c'est du béton
4. de ma part
5. ne confierez qu'à moi les résultats de votre enquête
6. porte-stylos en or ouvragé
7. stylo-plume
8. parcourut des yeux

1. pour que Bosch puisse l'observer
2. terrains aurifères
3. qui s'y est développée
4. le signe d'un esprit défaillant
5. données
6. étudiées
7. résumés
8. sous-entendaient
9. pris
10. entretenir une relation stable
11. encore moins fonder
12. On lui attribuait quelques brèves idylles
13. peut-être juste pour les photographes,
14. et mettre fin aux conjectures

and closed it. He held the pen up for Bosch to study[1].

"This pen was made with gold my great-grandfather prospected in the Sierra Nevada goldfields[2] in 1852," he said. "That was before the competition up there[3] forced him to head south. Before he realized that there was more to be made from iron than from gold."

He turned the pen in his hand.

"It was passed on from generation to generation," he said. "I've had it since I left home for college."

Vance studied the pen as if seeing it for the first time. Bosch said nothing. He wondered if Vance suffered from any sort of diminished mental capacity and if the old man's desire to have him find somebody who may never have existed was some sort of indication of a failing mind[4].

"Mr. Vance?" he asked.

Vance put the pen back into its holder and looked at Bosch.

"I have no one to give it to," he said. "No one to give any of this to."

It was true. The biographical data[5] Bosch had looked up[6] said Vance was never married and childless. Several of the summaries[7] he had read suggested obliquely[8] that he was homosexual but there was never confirmation of this. Other biographical extracts suggested that he was simply too driven[9] by his work to keep up a steady relationship[10], let alone establish[11] a family. There were a few brief romances reported[12], primarily with Hollywood starlets of the moment— possibly dates for the cameras[13] to put off speculation[14] about homosexuality. But for the past forty years or more, Bosch could find nothing.

"Do you have children, Mr. Bosch?" Vance asked.

"A daughter," Bosch answered.

"Where?"

"In school[1]. Chapman University, down in Orange County."

"Good school. Is she a film student?"

"Psychology."

Vance leaned back in his chair and looked off[2] into the past.

"I wanted to study film when I was a young man," he said. "The dreams of youth ..."

He didn't finish his thought. Bosch realized he would have to give the money back. This was all some kind of derangement, and there was no job. He could not take payment from this man even if it was only an infinitesimal drop from Vance's bucket[3]. Bosch didn't take money from damaged[4] people, no matter how rich they were.

Vance broke away from his stare into the abyss of memory and looked at Bosch. He nodded, seeming to know Harry's thoughts, then gripped[5] the armrest of his chair with his left hand and leaned forward.

"I guess I need to tell you what this is about," he said.

Bosch nodded.

"That would be good, yes."

Vance nodded back and offered the lopsided smile again. He looked down for a moment and then back up at Bosch, his eyes deeply set[6] and shiny behind rimless glasses[7].

"A long time ago I made a mistake," he said. "I never corrected it, I never looked back. I now want to find out[8] if I had a child. A child I could give my gold pen to."

1. À la fac
2. se plongea
3. ça nétait qu'une goutte d'eau pour le richissime Vance
4. dérangés
5. saisit
6. enfoncés
7. des lunettes sans monture
8. savoir

Bosch stared at him for a long moment, hoping he might continue. But when he did he seemed to have picked up another string of memory[1].

"When I was eighteen years old I wanted nothing to do with my father's business," Vance said. "I was more interested in being the next Orson Welles. I wanted to make films, not airplane parts. I was full[2] of myself, as young men often are at that age."

Bosch thought of himself at eighteen. His desire to blaze[3] his own path had led him into the tunnels of Vietnam.

"I insisted on film school," Vance said. "I enrolled[4] at USC in 1949."

Bosch nodded. He knew from his prior reading[5] that Vance had spent only a year at USC before changing paths[6], transferring to Caltech and furthering the family dynasty[7]. There had been no explanation found in his Internet search. Bosch now believed he was going to find out why.

"I met a girl," Vance said. "A Mexican girl. And soon afterward, she became pregnant[8]. It was the second worst thing that ever happened to me. The first was telling my father."

Vance grew quiet[9], his eyes down on the desk in front of him. It wasn't difficult to fill in the blanks[10] but Bosch needed to hear as much of the story from Vance as he could.

"What happened?" he asked.

"He sent people," Vance said. "People to persuade her not to have the child. People who would drive her to Mexico to take care of it."

"Did she go?"

"If she did, it was not with my father's people. She disappeared from my life and I never saw her again. And I was too much of a coward[11] to go find her. I had given my father all he needed to

1. ravivé un autre souvenir
2. imbu
3. tracer
4. me suis inscrit
5. récentes lectures
6. de voie
7. reprendre le flambeau familial
8. tombée enceinte
9. se tut
10. compléter l'histoire
11. trop lâche

control me: the potential embarrassment and disgrace. Even prosecution[1] because of her age. I did what I was told[2]. I transferred to Caltech and that was the end of it[3]."

Vance nodded, as though confirming something for himself.

"It was a different time then … for me and for her."

Vance looked up now and held Bosch's eyes[4] for a long moment before continuing.

"But now I want to know. It's when you reach the end of things that you want to go back …"

A few heartbeats went by[5] before he spoke again.

"Can you help me, Mr. Bosch?" he asked.

Bosch nodded. He believed the pain in Vance's eyes was real.

"It was a long time ago but I can try," Bosch said. "Do you mind if I ask a few questions and take some notes?"

"Take your notes," Vance said. "But I warn you again[6] that everything about this must remain completely confidential. Lives could be in danger. Every move you make, you must look over your shoulder. I have no doubt that efforts will be made to find out why I wanted to see you and what you are doing for me. I have a cover story for that[7], which we can get to[8] later. For now[9], ask your questions."

Lives could be in danger. Those words ricocheted inside his chest as Bosch took a small notebook[10] from the inside pocket of his suit coat. He pulled out a pen. It was made of plastic, not gold. He'd bought it at a drugstore.

"You just said lives could be in danger. Whose lives? Why?"

1. des poursuites judiciaires
2. ce qu'on m'a dit de faire
3. ce fut terminé
4. soutint le regard de Bosch
5. secondes s'écoulèrent
6. vous préviens à nouveau
7. un scénario de remplacement
8. dont on pourra parler
9. Pour l'instant
10. calepin

"Don't be naive, Mr. Bosch. I am sure you conducted[1] a modicum[2] of research before coming to see me. I have no heirs[3]—at least, known heirs. When I die, control of Advance Engineering will go to a board of directors[4] who will continue to line their pockets with millions[5] while fulfilling government contracts. A valid heir could change all of that. Billions[6] could be at stake[7]. You don't think people and entities would kill for that?"

"It's been my experience that[8] people will kill for any reason and no reason at all," Bosch said. "If I find you have heirs, are you sure you want to possibly make them targets[9]?"

"I would give them the choice," Vance said. "I believe I owe them that. And I would protect them as well as is possible."

"What was her name? The girl you got pregnant."

"Vibiana Duarte."

Bosch wrote it down on his pad[10].

"You know her birthdate by any chance?"

"I can't remember it."

"She was a student at USC?"

"No, I met her at the EVK. She worked there."

"EVK?"

"The student cafeteria was called Everybody's Kitchen. EVK for short[11]."

Bosch immediately knew this eliminated the prospect[12] of tracing[13] Vibiana Duarte through student records, which were usually very helpful, since most schools kept close track of their alums[14]. It meant the search for the woman would be more difficult and even more of a long shot[15].

"You said she was Mexican," he said. "You mean Latina? Was she a U.S. citizen?"

"I don't know. I don't think she was. My father—"

He didn't finish.

1. mené
2. minimum
3. d'héritiers
4. conseil d'administration
5. s'en mettre plein les poches
6. Des milliards de dollars
7. en jeu
8. D'après mon expérience,
9. en faire des cibles potentielles
10. carnet
11. en abrégé
12. perspective
13. chercher
14. suivaient leurs anciens étudiants de près
15. incertaine

"Your father what?" Bosch asked.

"I don't know if it was the truth but my father said that was her plan," Vance said. "To get pregnant so I would have to marry her and she would become a citizen. But my father said a lot of things to me that weren't true and he believed a lot of things that were ... out of step[1]. So I don't know."

Bosch thought about what he had read about Nelson Vance and eugenics. He pressed on.

"By any chance, do you have[2] a photograph of Vibiana?" he asked.

"No," Vance said. "You don't know how many times I've wished for a[3] photograph. That I could just look at her one more time."

"Where did she live?"

"By the school. Just a few blocks away. She walked to work."

"Do you remember the address? The street, maybe?"

"No, I don't remember. It was so long ago and I spent so many years trying to block it out[4]. But the truth is, I never really loved anybody again after that."

It was the first time Vance mentioned love or gave an indication of how deep the relationship had been. It had been Bosch's experience that when you looked back at a life[5], you used a magnifying glass[6]. Everything was bigger, amplified. A college tryst[7] could become the love of a lifetime in memory. Still, Vance's pain seemed real so many decades after the events he was describing. Bosch believed him.

"How long were you together with her before all of this happened?" he asked.

"Eight months between the first and last times I ever saw her," Vance said. "Eight months."

1. hors de propos
2. Auriez-vous par hasard
3. j'ai regretté de ne pas avoir de
4. le refouler
5. on se retourne sur sa vie
6. on la voit comme sous une loupe
7. amourette d'étudiant

"Do you remember when she told you she was pregnant? I mean, what month or time of year?"

"It was after the start of the summer session. I had enrolled[1] just because I knew I would see her. So late June 1950. Maybe early July."

"And you say you met her eight months before that?"

"I had started in September the year before. I noticed her right away working at the EVK. I didn't get the courage to talk to her for a couple[2] months."

The old man looked down at the desk.

"What else do you remember?" Bosch prompted. "Did you ever meet her family? Do you remember any names?"

"No, I didn't," Vance said. "She told me her father was very strict and they were Catholic, and I was not. You know, we were like Romeo and Juliet. I never met her family and she never met mine."

Bosch seized on the one piece of[3] information in Vance's answer that might advance the investigation[4].

"Do you know what church she went to?"

Vance looked up, his eyes sharp[5].

"She told me she was named after[6] the church where she was baptized. St. Vibiana's."

Bosch nodded. The original St. Vibiana's was in downtown[7], just a block from the LAPD headquarters, where he used to work. More than a hundred years old, it was badly damaged in the 1994 earthquake[8]. A new church was built nearby and the old structure was donated to the city and preserved. Bosch wasn't sure but he believed it was an event hall[9] and library[10] now. But the connection to Vibiana Duarte was a good one. Catholic churches kept records[11] of births and baptisms. He felt this bit of good information countered[12]

1. m'y étais inscrit
2. avant deux
3. releva la seule
4. susceptible de faire avancer l'enquête
5. pénétrants
6. qu'on lui avait donné le nom de
7. en centre-ville
8. tremblement de terre
9. salle de spectacle
10. une bibliothèque
11. des registres
12. Pour lui, cette bribe d'information compensait

the bad news that Vibiana had not been a USC student. It was also a strong indication that she might have been a U.S. citizen, whether or not her parents were. If she was a citizen, she would be easier to track through public records.

"If the pregnancy was carried to full term[1], when would the child have been born?" he asked.

It was a delicate question but Bosch needed to narrow the timing down[2] if he was going to wade into records[3].

"I think that she was at least two months pregnant when she told me," Vance said. "So I would say January of the following year would be the birth. Maybe February."

Bosch wrote it down.

"How old was she when you knew her?" he asked.

"She was sixteen when we met," Vance said. "I was eighteen."

It was another reason for the reaction of Vance's father. Vibiana was underage[4]. Getting a sixteen-year-old pregnant in 1950 could have gotten[5] Whitney into minor but embarrassing legal trouble[6].

"Was she in high school[7]?" Bosch asked.

He knew the area around USC. The high school would have been Manual Arts—another shot at traceable records[8].

"She had dropped out[9] to work," Vance said. "The family needed the money."

"Did she ever say what her father did for a living[10]?" Bosch asked.

"I don't recall[11]."

"Okay, going back to her birthday, you don't remember the date but do you remember ever celebrating it[12] with her during those eight months?"

1. elle a mené à terme sa grossesse
2. limiter la fourchette
3. se plonger dans des archives
4. mineure
5. aurait pu valoir à
6. de gênants, bien que légers, soucis judiciaires
7. Allait-elle au lycée
8. possibilité de retrouver sa trace
9. arrêté l'école
10. comme métier
11. ne m'en souviens pas
12. l'avoir fêté

Vance thought a moment and then shook his head.

"No, I can't remember a birthday occurring[1]," he said.

"And if I have this right[2], you were together from late October till June and maybe early July, so her birthday would have likely been somewhere in July to late October. Roughly[3]."

Vance nodded. Narrowing it[4] to four months might help at some point when Bosch was going through records[5]. Attaching a birth date to the name Vibiana Duarte would be a key starting point. He wrote the spread of months down[6] and the likely[7] birth year: 1933. He then looked up at Vance.

"Do you think your father paid her or her family off?" he asked. "So they would keep quiet and just go away?"

"If he did, he never told me that," Vance said. "I was the one[8] who went away. An act of cowardice[9] I have always regretted."

"Have you ever looked for her before now? Ever paid anybody else to?"

"No, sadly, I have not. I can't say if anyone else has[10]."

"Meaning what?"

"Meaning that it is quite possible such a search was conducted as a preemptive move in preparation for[11] my death."

Bosch thought about that for a long moment. He then looked at the few notes he had written. He felt he had enough to start.

"You said you had a cover story for me?"

"Yes, James Franklin Aldridge. Write it down."

"Who is he?"

"My first roommate[12] at USC. He was dismissed[13] from school in the first semester."

1. ne me souviens pas d'un anniversaire
2. j'ai bien compris
3. Grosso modo
4. Limiter le champ des recherches
5. éplucherait des archives
6. nota la fourchette de mois
7. probable
8. C'est moi
9. lâcheté
10. Et je ne sais pas si quelqu'un d'autre l'a fait
11. en prévision de
12. camarade de chambre
13. s'est fait renvoyer

"For academics[1]?"

"No, for something else. Your cover is that I asked you to find my college roommate because I want to make amends for[2] something we both did but he took the blame for[3]. This way[4], if you are looking at records from that time, it will seem plausible."

Bosch nodded.

"It might work. Is it a true story?"

"It is."

"I should probably know what it is you both did."

"You don't need to know that to find him."

Bosch waited a moment but that was all Vance had to say on the subject. Harry wrote the name down after checking the spelling[5] of Aldridge with[6] Vance and then closed his notebook.

"Last question. The odds are[7] Vibiana Duarte is dead by now. But what if she had the child and I find living heirs[8]? What do you want me to do? Do I make contact?"

"No, absolutely not. You make no contact until you report to me[9]. I'll need thorough confirmation[10] before any approach will be made[11]."

"DNA confirmation[12]?"

Vance nodded and studied Bosch for a long moment before once more going to the desk drawer. He removed a padded[13] white envelope with nothing written on it. He slid it across the desk to Bosch.

"I am trusting you[14], Mr. Bosch. I have now given you all you need to trick[15] an old man if you want. I trust you won't[16]."

Bosch picked up the envelope. It wasn't sealed[17]. He looked into it and saw a clear glass test tube[18]

1. Pour sa scolarité
2. réparer
3. c'est lui qui a tout pris
4. Comme ça
5. avoir vérifié l'orthographe
6. auprès de
7. Vraisemblablement,
8. des descendants vivants
9. avant de m'en parler
10. de preuves concrètes
11. qu'ils soient contactés
12. Des preuves ADN
13. matelassée
14. vous fais confiance
15. escroquer
16. Mais j'espère que vous ne le ferez pas
17. cachetée
18. tube à essai transparent

1. bâtonnet
2. prélever
3. échantillon
4. j'avais effectué le prélèvement moi-même
5. parole
6. J'y étais
7. Deux fois
8. est-ce que je vous contacte

containing a swab[1] used to collect[2] saliva. It was Vance's DNA sample[3].

"This is where you could be tricking me, Mr. Vance."

"How so?"

"It would have been better if I had swabbed you, collected this myself[4]."

"You have my word[5]."

"And you have mine."

Vance nodded and there did not seem to be anything else to say.

"I think I have what I need to start."

"Then I have a final question for you, Mr. Bosch."

"Go ahead."

"I'm curious because it wasn't mentioned in the newspaper stories I read about you. But you appear to be the right age. What was your status during the Vietnam War?"

Bosch paused a moment before answering.

"I was over there[6]," he finally said. "Two tours[7]. I probably flew more times on the helicopters you helped build than you ever did."

Vance nodded.

"Probably so," he said.

Bosch stood up.

"How do I reach you[8] if I have more questions or want to report what I find out?"

"Of course."

Vance opened the desk drawer and removed a business card. He handed it to Bosch with a shaking hand. There was a phone number printed on it, nothing else.

"Call that number and you will get to me. If it's not me, then something is wrong. Don't trust anyone else you speak to."

Bosch looked from the number on the card to Vance, sitting in his wheelchair, his papier-mâché skin and wispy[1] hair looking as frail as dried leaves. He wondered if his caution[2] was paranoia or if there was a real danger to the information he would be seeking[3].

"Are you in danger, Mr. Vance?" he asked.

"A man in my position is always in danger," Vance said.

Bosch ran his thumb along the crisp edge[4] of the business card.

"I'll get back to you[5] soon," he said.

"We have not discussed payment for your services," Vance said.

"You've paid me enough to start. Let's see how it goes."

"That payment was only to get you to come here."

"Well, it worked and it's more than enough, Mr. Vance. All right if I find my way out[6]? Or will that set off[7] a security alarm?"

"As soon as you leave this room they'll know it and come to meet you."

Vance registered[8] Bosch's puzzled look.

"This is the only room in the house not under camera surveillance," he explained. "There are cameras to watch over me even in my bedroom. But I insisted on privacy here. As soon as you leave, they will come."

Bosch nodded.

"I understand," he said. "Talk to you soon[9]."

He stepped through the door and started down the hallway. Soon enough Bosch was met[10] by the man in the suit and escorted wordlessly through the house and out to his car.

1. filasse
2. prudence
3. qu'il allait tenter d'obtenir
4. bord bien net
5. Je vous rappelle
6. Je peux sortir tout seul
7. déclencher
8. remarqua
9. À bientôt
10. rejoint

4

Working cold cases[1] had made Bosch proficient in time travel[2]. He knew how to go back into the past to find people. Going back to 1951 would be the farthest and likely[3] the most difficult trek he had ever made but he believed he was up to it[4] and that made him excited about the challenge.

The starting point was finding the birth date of Vibiana Duarte and he believed he knew the best way to accomplish that. Rather than go home after his meeting with Vance, Bosch took the 210 freeway[5] across the northern rim[6] of the Valley and headed toward the city of San Fernando.

Barely[7] bigger than two square miles[8] in size[9], San Fernando was an island city within the megalopolis of Los Angeles. A hundred years earlier all of the small towns and cities that comprised[10] the San Fernando Valley were annexed into Los Angeles for one reason: the newly built Los Angeles Aqueduct offered bountiful supplies of[11] water that would keep[12] their rich agricultural fields from drying up and blowing away[13]. One by one they were added and Los Angeles grew and spread north, eventually taking in the area's entire sprawl[14]. All except for the 2.3 square miles of the Valley's namesake[15], the city of San Fernando. The little town didn't need L.A.'s water. Its ground supplies[16] were more than adequate. Avoiding the overture[17] of the big city that now surrounded it, it stayed independent.

1. sur des affaires non résolues

2. expert en voyages dans le temps

3. probablement

4. pensait en être capable

5. autoroute

6. bordure nord

7. À peine

8. 5 km^2

9. de superficie

10. constituaient

11. un abondant approvisionnement en

12. protègerait

13. de la sécheresse et du vent

14. intégrant peu à peu toutes les agglomérations de la vallée

15. la vallée du même nom

16. nappes phréatiques

17. les avances

A hundred years later it remained so. The Valley's agriculture pedigree[1] may have long ago given way[2] to urban sprawl and urban blight[3], but the city of San Fernando remained a quaint throwback to small-town sensibilities[4]. Of course, urban issues[5] and crime were unavoidable[6] but they were nothing the tiny town's police department couldn't routinely take care of.

That is[7], until the financial crash of 2008. When the banking crisis happened and economies constricted and spiraled downward[8] around the world, it was only[9] a few years before the tidal wave of financial pain hit[10] San Fernando. Deep budget cuts occurred and then occurred again. Police Chief Anthony Valdez saw his department drop from forty sworn officers[11], including himself, in 2010 to thirty officers by 2016. He saw his detective squad of five investigators shrink[12] to just two—one detective to handle property crimes[13] and one to handle crimes against persons. Valdez saw cases start to pile up unsolved, some not even initially investigated fully and properly.

Valdez was born and raised in San Fernando but was seasoned as a cop[14] with the LAPD, putting in[15] twenty years and rising to the rank of captain before taking his pension and checking out[16], then landing the top spot at[17] his hometown's department[18]. His connections to the bigger department that surrounded his own ran deep, and his solution to the budget crisis was to expand SFPD's[19] reserve program and bring in more officers[20] who worked part-time hours but for free[21].

And it was this expansion that led Chief Valdez to Harry Bosch. One of Valdez's early assignments[22] when he was with the LAPD had been in a gang-suppression unit in the Hollywood Division. There he ran afoul of[23] a lieutenant named

1. passé agricole
2. cédé le pas
3. à l'expansion urbaine et à ses fléaux
4. gardait un côté désuet et provincial
5. problèmes
6. inévitables
7. Enfin
8. avaient sombré
9. il n'avait fallu que
10. la crise n'atteigne de plein fouet
11. ses effectifs passer de 40 agents assermentés
12. équipe de 5 enquêteurs se réduire
13. chargé des atteintes aux biens
14. avait fait ses armes
15. effectuant
16. de prendre sa retraite
17. et d'atterrir à la direction de
18. la police de sa ville natale
19. de la police de San Fernando
20. policiers
21. gratis
22. premières missions
23. s'était mis à dos

Pounds, who filed an internal complaint[1] and unsuccessfully attempted to have[2] Valdez demoted[3] or even fired[4].

Valdez avoided both and just a few months later heard about a detective named Bosch who himself got into an altercation with Pounds and ended up throwing him through a plate-glass window at[5] Hollywood Station. Valdez always remembered that name, and years later when he read about a now-retired Harry Bosch suing[6] the LAPD for forcing him out of his job on the cold case squad[7], he picked up the phone.

Valdez couldn't offer Bosch a paycheck[8], but he could offer him something Bosch valued more[9]: a detective's badge and access to all of the tiny city's unsolved cases. The SFPD's reserve unit had only three requirements[10]. Its officers had to maintain their state training standards[11] as law enforcement officers[12], qualify[13] once a month at the department's shooting range[14], and work[15] at least two shifts[16] a month.

It was a no-brainer[17] for Bosch. The LAPD didn't want or need him anymore but the little town up in the Valley certainly did. And there was work to be done and victims waiting for justice. Bosch took the job the moment it was offered. He knew it would allow him to continue his life's mission, and he needed no paycheck for that.

Bosch easily met[18] and surpassed the reserve officer minimums[19]. It was rare that he didn't put in[20] at least two shifts a week, let alone a month, in the detective bureau. He was there so often that he was permanently assigned[21] one of the cubicles[22] that had been left open when the squad was trimmed in the budget crunch[23].

1. avait déposé une plainte en interne
2. faire
3. rétrograder
4. renvoyer
5. qui avait fini par l'envoyer valser contre une vitre de
6. poursuivre
7. brigade
8. salaire
9. appréciait plus encore
10. exigences
11. respecter les principes qu'ils avaient en tant que fonctionnaires
12. dans la police
13. valider leurs compétences
14. champ de tir
15. effectuer
16. services de garde
17. Ça allait de soi
18. remplissait
19. conditions minimums
20. ne fasse
21. qu'on lui avait définitivement attribué
22. box
23. le coup de vis budgétaire avait touché l'équipe

Most days he was working in the cubicle or across First Street from the police station in the old city jail[1] where the cells[2] were repurposed[3] as storage rooms. The former drunk tank[4] now housed three rows of standing shelves[5] stocked with open case files going back decades[6].

Because of the statute of limitations[7] on all crimes but murder[8], the great majority of these cases would never be solved or even examined. The small city didn't have a lot of murders, but Bosch was meticulously going through them[9], looking for ways to apply new technologies to old evidence[10]. He also took on[11] a review of all sexual assaults[12], nonfatal shootings, and attacks resulting in major injuries[13] within the statute of limitations[14] for those crimes.

The job had a lot of freedom to it. Bosch could set his own hours and could always take time away[15] if a case came up for him[16] in private investigation. Chief Valdez knew he was lucky to have a detective with Bosch's experience working for him, and he never wanted to impinge on[17] Bosch's ability to take on[18] a paying job. He just stressed to[19] Bosch that the two could never mix. Harry could not use his badge and access as a San Fernando cop to facilitate or further[20] any private investigation. That would be a firing offense[21].

1. l'ancienne prison

2. cellules

3. réaménagées

4. ancienne cellule de dégrisement

5. bibliothèques

6. remplies de dossiers en cours depuis des dizaines d'années

7. prescription

8. sauf les homicides

9. les parcourait minutieusement

10. indices

11. entreprit

12. agressions

13. blessures graves

14. avant qu'il y ait prescription

15. se mettre en absence

16. lui était soumis

17. entraver

18. d'accepter

19. avait juste insisté auprès de

20. faire avancer

21. motif de renvoi

5

Murder knows no bounds[1] or city limits. Most of the cases Bosch reviewed and pursued took him into LAPD turf[2]. It was only expected[3]. Two of the big city's police divisions shared borders with San Fernando: Mission Division to the west and Foothill Division to the east. In four months Bosch had cleared[4] two unsolved gang murders—connecting them through ballistics to murders in L.A. for which the perpetrators[5] were already in prison—and linked a third to a pair of suspects already being sought[6] for murder by the larger department[7].

Additionally, Bosch had used MO—modus operandi[8]—and then DNA to connect four sexual assault cases in San Fernando over a four-year period and was in the process[9] of determining whether the attacker was responsible for any rapes[10] in Los Angeles as well.

Driving the 210 away from Pasadena allowed Bosch to check for a tail[11]. Midday[12] traffic was light[13] and by alternately driving five miles below the speed limit and then taking it up[14] to fifteen above it, he could check the mirrors[15] for vehicles following the same pattern. He wasn't sure how seriously to take Whitney Vance's concerns[16] about the secrecy of his investigation but it didn't hurt to be alert to a tail[17]. He didn't see anything on the road behind him. Of course, he knew that his car could have been tagged

1. de frontières
2. territoire
3. C'était prévisible
4. élucidé
5. dont les auteurs
6. recherchés
7. police de la grande ville
8. le mode opératoire [du criminel]
9. essayait
10. de viols commis
11. vérifier s'il était filé
12. À midi,
13. il y avait peu de circulation
14. en faisant des pointes
15. dans ses rétroviseurs
16. ne savait pas s'il fallait prendre au sérieux les inquiétudes de Whitney Vance
17. à l'affût d'une éventuelle filature

with a GPS tracker[1] while he was in the mansion with Vance, or even the day before while he met[2] with Creighton at the U.S. Bank Tower. He would need to check for that later.

In fifteen minutes he had crossed the top of the Valley and was back in L.A. He took the Maclay Street exit and dropped down into San Fernando, where he turned onto First Street. The SFPD was located in a single-story[3] building with white stucco walls and a red barrel-tile roof[4]. The population of the tiny town was 90 percent Latino and its municipal structures were all designed with a nod to[5] Mexican culture.

Bosch parked in the employee lot[6] and used an electronic key to enter the station through the side door. He nodded to[7] a couple of uniform cops through the window of the report room and followed the back hallway past the chief's office toward the detective bureau.

"Harry?"

Bosch turned and looked through the door to the chief's office. Valdez was behind his desk, waving him in[8].

Harry stepped into the office. It wasn't as big as the LAPD chief's suite but it was comfortable and had a sitting area for informal discussions. Hanging from the ceiling[9] was a black-and-white toy helicopter with SFPD painted on its body.

The first time Bosch had been in the office Valdez had explained that this was the department's helicopter—a joking reference[10] to the fact that the department didn't have its own bird[11] and had to call in air support when needed from the LAPD[12].

"How's it going?" Valdez asked.

"Can't complain," Bosch said.

1. on avait pu coller une balise GPS sur sa voiture
2. pendant son entretien
3. de plain-pied [USA]
4. toit de tuiles rouges
5. rappel de
6. parking réservé aux employés
7. salua de la tête
8. et lui faisait signe d'entrer
9. Suspendu au plafond
10. allusion plaisante
11. hélico
12. faire appel à ceux du LAPD en cas de besoin

1. Coupeur de portes à moustiquaire
2. l'enquête sur le violeur en série
3. la suite
4. j'ai validé
5. Il faut qu'on le chope, ce type
6. ne veux pas te retenir
7. à quelques mètres dans le couloir
8. Par rapport au LAPD ou même d'autres services de police,
9. plutôt
10. était sous-louée
11. Service médico-légal
12. entassés
13. pour le chef un cagibi
14. Le box
15. des cloisons de 1,50 m
16. occupé par un lieutenant à plein temps
17. coup de vis budgétaire
18. actuellement
19. unique
20. jusqu'à présent
21. dans les locaux
22. le tenait à l'œil

"Well, we certainly appreciate what you're doing around here. Anything happening on the Screen Cutter[1]?"

It was a reference to the serial rapist case[2] Bosch had identified.

"I'm about to go check on responses to our e-mail. After that I'll get with Bella to talk about next moves[3]."

"I read the report from the profiler when I approved[4] the payment. Interesting stuff. We gotta get this guy[5]."

"Working on it."

"Okay, well, I won't hold you up[6]."

"Okay, Chief."

Bosch glanced at the helicopter for a moment and then left the office. The detective bureau was just a few paces down the hall[7]. By LAPD or any standards[8], it was quite[9] small. It had once consisted of two rooms, but one room had been subleased[10] to the County Coroner's Office[11] as a satellite office for two of its investigators. Now there were three detective cubicles crammed[12] into one room with a closet-size supervisor's office[13] adjoining.

Bosch's cubicle[14] had five-foot walls[15] that allowed him privacy from three sides. But the fourth side was open to the office door of the squad's supervisor. That post was supposed to be a full-time lieutenant's slot[16], but it had been vacant since the budget crunch[17] and the supervisor was currently[18] the department's only[19] captain. His name was Trevino and he had so far[20] not been convinced that having Bosch on the premises[21] and handling cases was a good thing. He seemed suspicious of Bosch's motives for working so many hours for no pay and kept a careful watch over him[22]. For Bosch, the only thing that alleviated[1] this unwanted attention was that Trevino wore multiple hats[2] in the department, as is often the case with small agencies. He was running[3] the detective bureau and was also in charge of interior operations in the station[4], including the dispatch center[5], the indoor firing range[6], and the sixteen-bed jail built to replace the aging facility[7] across the street[8]. These responsibilities often drew Trevino out of the detective bureau and off Bosch's back[9].

Bosch checked his mail slot[10] upon entering and found a reminder notice[11] that he was overdue[12] qualifying this month on the range[13]. He moved into his cubicle and sat down at his desk.

Along the way he saw that Trevino's door was closed and the glass transom[14] above it was dark. The captain was most likely in another part of the building carrying out one of his other duties. Bosch thought he understood Trevino's suspicion and lack of welcome[15]. Any success he had in clearing cases could be seen as a failing[16] on Trevino's part. After all, the detective bureau was currently his domain[17]. And it didn't help when word got around[18] that Bosch had once thrown his LAPD supervisor through a plate-glass window.

Still, there was nothing Trevino could do about Bosch's placement in the office, because he was part of the police chief's effort to overcome personnel cuts[19].

Bosch turned on his computer terminal and waited for it to boot up[20]. It had been four days since he was last in the office. A flyer[21] for a department bowling night[22] had been left on his desk and he immediately transferred this to the recycle bin[23] beneath it. He liked the people he

1. pouvait atténuer
2. casquettes
3. dirigeait
4. au sein du commissariat
5. centre de communication
6. champ de tir
7. structure vieillissante
8. d'en face
9. Bosch ne l'avait plus sur le dos
10. case au courrier
11. rappel
12. en retard
13. pour sa validation mensuelle de tir
14. l'imposte vitrée
15. sa froideur
16. échec
17. sous sa direction
18. on avait raconté
19. faire face aux réductions d'effectifs
20. qu'il démarre
21. prospectus
22. soirée bowling au commissariat
23. corbeille à papiers

worked with in the new department, but he wasn't much of a bowler[1].

Using a key to open a locked file cabinet[2] in his desk, he pulled out a few folders[3] pertaining to open cases he was working and spread them on his desk so it would appear[4] he was engaged in SFPD business. He noticed when he reached for[5] his Screen Cutter folder that it wasn't there. He found it in the wrong spot in the drawer. It had been misfiled[6] under the first victim's name rather than under the unknown suspect's moniker[7]: Screen Cutter. This immediately alarmed and annoyed[8] Bosch. He didn't believe he could have misfiled the case. All of his career he had carefully managed his case files. The file—whether it was a murder book[9] or a manila folder[10]—was the heart of the case and it always needed to be neatly and thoroughly put together and safely stored.

He put the folder on his desk and considered[11] that someone with a duplicate key[12] might be reading his files and checking his work. And he knew exactly who that might be. He reversed himself[13] and returned all his files to the drawer, then closed and locked it with his key. He had a plan for smoking out[14] the intruder.

He sat up straight[15] to look over the partitions[16] and saw that both of the other detective cubicles were empty. Bella Lourdes, the CAPs[17] investigator, and Danny Sisto, who handled property crimes, were probably out in the field[18] following up on crime reports. They often went out to handle much of their fieldwork together.

Once he was logged into the[19] department's computer system, Bosch opened up the law enforcement databases[20]. He got out his notebook and began the search for Vibiana Duarte, knowing he was breaking[21] the one rule the police

1. un passionné de bowling
2. caisson
3. dossiers
4. pour donner l'impression qu'
5. voulut sortir
6. classé par erreur
7. surnom
8. contraria
9. que ce soit un registre d'enquête criminelle
10. une sous-chemise en papier kraft
11. envisagea l'hypothèse
12. double de sa clé
13. pivota
14. débusquer
15. bien droit
16. cloisons
17. chargée des atteintes aux personnes
18. sur le terrain
19. Une fois connecté au
20. bases de données policières
21. enfreignait

chief had given him: using his SFPD access to supplement[1] a private investigation. Not only was it a firing offense[2] at SFPD but it was a crime[3] in California to access a law enforcement database for information not pertaining[4] to a police investigation. If Trevino ever decided to audit Bosch's use of the computer, there would be a problem. But Bosch figured[5] that would not happen. Trevino would know that if he made a move against Bosch, he was making a move against the police chief, and that was most likely career suicide.

The search for Vibiana Duarte was short. There was no listing of her ever having a driver's license in California, no record of her ever committing a crime or even getting a parking ticket[6]. Of course, the digital databases were less complete the farther back the search went[7] but Bosch knew from experience that it was rare not to find any reference to an entered name. It supported the possibility[8] that Duarte had been an illegal and possibly returned to Mexico in 1950 after becoming pregnant. Abortion[9] in California was against the law back then[10]. She might have crossed the border to have her baby or to have the pregnancy terminated[11] in one of the backroom clinics[12] in Tijuana.

Bosch knew the law on abortion back then because he had been born in 1950 to an unmarried woman[13] and, soon after becoming a cop, he had looked up the laws[14] so that he would better[15] understand the choices his mother had faced[16] and made.

What he was not familiar with[17] was the California penal code in 1950. He accessed it next[18] and checked the laws about sexual assault. He pretty[19] quickly learned that in 1950 under penal code section 261, sexual intercourse[20] with a female under

1. faire avancer
2. motif de renvoi
3. délit
4. ne se rapportant pas
5. pensait
6. ni même qu'elle ait reçu une contravention
7. à mesure qu'on remontait dans le temps
8. était compatible avec le fait
9. L'avortement
10. à l'époque
11. mettre fin à la grossesse
12. cliniques clandestines
13. d'une mère célibataire
14. était allé vérifier les textes en vigueur,
15. pour mieux
16. affrontés
17. ce qu'il connaissait mal
18. y accéda
19. très
20. les rapports sexuels

age eighteen was considered a chargeable offense of rape[1]. Consensual relations[2] were not listed as an exclusion to prosecution[3]. The only exclusion offered[4] was if the woman was the wife of the offender[5].

Bosch thought about Vance's father believing the pregnancy was a trap set[6] by Duarte to force a marriage that would bring her citizenship[7] and money. If that was the case, the penal code gave her a solid piece of leverage[8]. But the lack[9] of any record[10] of Duarte in California seemed to belie[11] that angle[12]. Rather than use her leverage, Duarte had disappeared, possibly back to Mexico.

Bosch switched the screen[13], went back to the DMV[14] interface, and typed in "James Franklin Aldridge," the cover name Vance had given him.

Before the results came up[15], he saw Captain Trevino enter the squad room, carrying a cup of coffee from Starbucks. Bosch knew there was a store located a few blocks away on Truman. He often took a break from computer work in the bureau and walked over himself. This was not only to give his eyes a rest[16] but to indulge in a[17] recent addiction to iced lattes that had developed[18] since he began routinely meeting with his daughter at various coffee shops near her school campus.

"Harry, what brings you in today?" Trevino said.

The captain always greeted him cordially and by his first name.

"I was in the neighborhood," Bosch said. "Thought I'd check e-mail and send out a few more alerts on the Screen Cutter."

As he spoke, he killed[19] the DMV screen and pulled up[20] the e-mail account he had been given by the department. He didn't turn around as Trevino went to the door of his office and unlocked it.

1. viol au regard de la loi
2. Un rapport consenti
3. n'empêchait pas les poursuites
4. seule exception admise
5. contrevenant
6. piège monté
7. la citoyenneté [américaine]
8. bon moyen de pression
9. l'absence
10. trace officielle
11. démentir
12. hypothèse
13. changea d'écran
14. des Cartes grises et permis de conduire [Department of Motor Vehicles]
15. ne s'affichent
16. se reposer les yeux
17. s'offrir
18. un de ces cafés au lait frappés auxquels il était accro depuis peu,
19. éteignit
20. afficha

Bosch heard the door open but then felt Trevino's presence behind him in the cubicle.

"In the neighborhood?" Trevino said. "All the way up here? And all dressed up in a suit[1]!"

"Well, actually, I was in Pasadena seeing somebody and then I just took the Foothill across[2]," Bosch said. "Thought I'd just send out a few e-mails, then get out of here."

"Your name's not on the board[3], Harry. You have to sign in to get credit for[4] your hours."

"Sorry, I was only going to be here a few minutes. And I don't have to worry about making my hours. I put in[5] twenty-four last week alone[6]."

There was an attendance board[7] by the entrance to the detective bureau on which Bosch had been instructed to sign in and out[8] so Trevino could chart[9] his hours and make sure he hit[10] the reserve officer minimum.

"I still want you signing in and out," Trevino said.

"You got it[11], Cap," Bosch said.

"Good."

"By the way …"

Bosch reached down and rapped his knuckles[12] on the file drawer.

"I forgot my key," he said. "You have a key I can open this with? I need my files."

"No, no key. Garcia turned in[13] the only one. He said that was all he got from Dockweiler."

Bosch knew that Garcia was the last detective to occupy the desk and that he had inherited it from Dockweiler. Both were casualties[14] of the budget crunch. He'd heard in the office scuttlebutt that[15] both men left law enforcement[16] after being laid off[17]. Garcia became a schoolteacher and Dockweiler saved his city paycheck and pension by transferring to the Public Works[18]

1. en costard, en plus
2. j'ai juste bifurqué par la vallée
3. tableau
4. vous y inscrire pour qu'on vous compte
5. J'en ai fait
6. rien que la semaine dernière
7. tableau de présence
8. d'inscrire ses arrivées et départs
9. compter
10. qu'il atteignait bien
11. Entendu
12. toqua
13. a rendu
14. des victimes
15. D'après les ragots du bureau,
16. la police
17. avoir été licenciés
18. de la Voirie et Travaux publics

Department, where they had an opening[1] in code enforcement[2].

"Anybody else have a key around here?" Bosch asked.

"Not that I know of," Trevino said. "Why don't you just open it with your lock picks[3], Harry? I heard you're good with those[4]."

He said it with a tone that implied that Bosch was somehow skilled in the dark arts[5] because he knew how to pick a lock[6].

"Yeah, I might do that," Bosch said. "Thanks for the idea."

Trevino stepped into his office and Bosch heard the door close. He made a mental note to[7] check with Dockweiler about the missing key. He wanted to make sure the former detective didn't have it before he took any steps toward proving[8] Trevino was the one secretly checking his files.

Bosch reopened the DMV portal to run[9] Aldridge's name. He soon pulled up a history[10] that showed Aldridge had a California driver's license from 1948 until 2002, at which point it was surrendered[11] when the license holder moved to Florida. He wrote down Aldridge's date of birth and then entered it with his name on a check[12] of the Florida DMV database. This determined that Aldridge had surrendered his license in Florida at age eighty. The last address listed was in a place called The Villages.

After writing down the information, Bosch checked for a website[13] and found that The Villages was a massive retirement community[14] in Sumter County, Florida. Further searching of online records[15] found an address for Aldridge and no indication of a death record or obituary[16]. He had likely surrendered[17] his driver's license be-

1. offraient un poste
2. application de la réglementation
3. crochets à serrure
4. Il paraît que vous savez bien les manier
5. avait des dons de magicien
6. crocheter une serrure
7. se dit qu'il ne faudrait pas oublier de
8. d'entreprendre quoi que ce soit pour prouver que
9. entrer
10. un historique
11. date à laquelle le permis avait été rendu
12. consultation
13. chercha leur site
14. vaste complexe pour retraités
15. Poursuivant ses recherches en ligne, il
16. avis de décès ou d'une notice nécrologique
17. sûrement rendu

cause he no longer could or needed to drive, but it appeared that James Franklin Aldridge was still alive.

Curious about the incident that supposedly got Aldridge kicked out[1] of USC, Bosch next ran[2] the name through the crime database, doubling down on[3] his firing offenses for the day. Aldridge had a DUI[4] on his record from 1986 and that was it. Whatever had happened back in his freshman year of college[5] remained hidden from Bosch.

Content that he had sufficiently chased down the name as needed for a possible cover story[6], Bosch decided to check through the e-mail that had accumulated on the Screen Cutter case. It was the investigation that had consumed most of his time since he had joined the ranks of the San Fernando Police Department. He had worked serial murder cases before during his time with LAPD and most, if not all, had a sexual component to them, so the territory was not new to Bosch. But the Screen Cutter case was one of the more puzzling cases[7] he had ever encountered.

1. avait soi-disant fait renvoyer Aldridge

2. entra alors

3. portant au nombre de deux

4. condamnation pour conduite en état d'ivresse [= driving under the influence]

5. pendant sa première année de fac

6. Estimant qu'il avait assez pisté comme ça le nom fixé pour sa couverture

7. affaires les plus déconcertantes

6

Screen Cutter was the case name for the serial rapist[1] Bosch had identified among the department's open[2] sexual assault reports. Combing through[3] the files in the old city jail, Bosch had found four cases since 2012 that were seemingly related by MO[4] but previously[5] not seen as connected.

The cases shared five suspect behaviors[6] that alone were not unusual but when taken as a whole[7] indicated the strong possibility of one perpetrator at work. In each case the rapist had entered the victim's home through a rear[8] door or window after cutting the screen[9] rather than removing it. All four assaults occurred during the day and within fifty minutes before or after noon. The rapist used the knife to cut the victim's clothes off rather than ordering her to remove them. In each case the rapist wore a mask—a ski mask[10] in two attacks, a Freddy Krueger Halloween mask in a third, and a Mexican Lucha Libre wrestling mask[11] in the fourth. And finally, the rapist used no condom[12] or other method to avoid leaving his DNA behind.

With these commonalities in hand[13], Bosch focused[14] an investigation on the four cases and soon learned that while the suspect's semen[15] had been collected in rape kits[16] in three of the four cases, only in one instance had the material actually been analyzed in the L.A. County Sheriff's crime lab[17] and submitted for comparison to state

1. nom donné au violeur en série que
2. en cours
3. En épluchant
4. le mode opératoire
5. jusqu'alors
6. avaient en commun cinq comportements suspects
7. ensemble
8. à l'arrière
9. grillage [anti-moustiques]
10. cagoule
11. masque de lutte mexicaine
12. préservatif
13. Fort de ces points communs
14. mena
15. bien que le sperme du suspect
16. dûment recueillis
17. labo de la police du comté

and national DNA databases, where it found no match[1]. Analysis in the two most recent cases was delayed because of a backlog of[2] rape kits submitted to the county lab for examination. In the fourth case, which was actually the first reported rape, a rape kit was collected but no DNA from the rapist was found on the vaginal swab[3] because the victim had showered and douched[4] before calling police to report the assault[5].

The county lab and the LAPD lab shared the same building at Cal State L.A., and Bosch used his connections from his cold case days[6] to speed up[7] analysis of the two recent cases. While he awaited the results he thought would solidly connect[8] the cases, he began requesting follow-up interviews of[9] the victims. Each of the victims—three women in their twenties and a now-eighteen-year-old—agreed to meet with the detectives. On two of the cases he would have to turn over the questioning[10] to Bella Lourdes because it was noted that the victims preferred to do the interviews in Spanish. It underlined the one drawback[11] for Bosch in working cases in a city where nine out of every ten citizens[12] were Latino and had varying capabilities when it came to English. He spoke Spanish passably, but for an interview with a crime victim, where subtle nuances of storytelling[13] might be important, he needed Lourdes, who understood it as a first language[14].

To each meeting Bosch brought a copy[15] of a victim questionnaire[16] used by LAPD investigators who worked violent crimes. It was nine pages of questions designed to help identify habits[17] of the victim that might have drawn the attention of the offender[18]. The questionnaires were helpful in serial investigations, particularly in profiling[19] the offender, and Bosch had cadged[20] a copy from a

1. correspondance
2. retard dans les
3. prélèvement
4. s'était fait une douche vaginale
5. signaler l'agression
6. années passés aux Affaires non résolues
7. faire accélérer
8. qui, d'après lui, établiraient un rapport irréfutable entre
9. des entretiens complémentaires avec
10. devrait confier l'interview
11. l'unique inconvénient
12. neuf citoyens sur dix
13. récit
14. langue maternelle
15. exemplaire
16. questionnaire destiné aux victimes
17. les habitudes
18. agresseur
19. pour dresser le portrait de
20. réussi à obtenir

Hollywood Division sex crimes investigator who was a friend.

The questionnaire became the stated purpose[1] of the new round of interviews, and the stories that emerged were equal parts sad and[2] terrifying. These were undoubtedly stranger rapes[3] and the attacks had left each woman recovering both mentally and physically as long as four years after the crime[4]. They all lived in fear of their attacker returning and none had recovered the confidence they once had[5]. One of them had been married and at the time was trying to conceive a child. The attack changed things in the marriage and at the time of the follow-up interview, the couple were in the midst of divorce proceedings[6].

After each interview Bosch felt depressed and couldn't help but[7] think about his own daughter and what sort of impact such an assault would have on her. Each time, he called her within the hour to check that she was safe and okay, unable to tell her the true reason he was calling.

But the follow-up interviews did more than reopen wounds for[8] the victims. They helped focus[9] the investigation and underlined the urgent need to identify and arrest the Screen Cutter.

Bosch and Lourdes adopted a conversational approach to each victim that started with assurances that the case was still being investigated as a priority by the department.

They scheduled[10] the interviews in chronological order of the assaults. The first woman was the victim from whom no DNA evidence had been collected. The initial report on the crime explained that the woman had taken a shower and douched immediately after the attack out of fear that she would become[11] pregnant. She and her husband at the time were trying to conceive a child and she

1. prétexte
2. aussi tristes que
3. des viols commis par un inconnu
4. chaque femme avait mis jusqu'à quatre ans pour se remettre mentalement et physiquement du viol
5. leur confiance d'autrefois
6. en plein divorce
7. ne pouvait s'empêcher de
8. des plaies chez
9. à resserrer
10. avaient organisé
11. par crainte de tomber

knew that the day of the attack was also the day that she was most fertile in her ovulation cycle.

The victim was still separated by almost four years from the attack, and while the psychological trauma persisted, she had found coping mechanisms[1] that allowed her to talk more openly about what was the worst single hour of her life.

She described the attack in detail and revealed that she had attempted to dissuade the suspect from raping her by lying[2] and saying she was having her period[3]. The woman told Bosch and Lourdes that the man replied, "No, you're not[4]. Your husband's coming home early to fuck you and make a baby."

This was new information and it gave the investigators pause[5]. The woman confirmed that her husband was scheduled[6] to come home early that day from the bank where he worked so that they could have an evening of romance[7], with the hope that it would result in her pregnancy. The question was, how did the Screen Cutter know that?

Under questioning from[8] Lourdes the victim revealed that she had an app[9] on her cell phone[10] that tracked[11] her menstrual cycle and told her the day of the month when she was ovulating and most likely to conceive. It was then her practice[12] to transfer this information to a calendar kept on the refrigerator door. Each month she marked the day with red hearts and phrases like "Baby Time!" so her husband would be reminded of its significance.

On the day of the attack the woman had gone out to walk[13] her dog in the neighborhood and was away from her home no more than fifteen minutes. She had her phone with her. The Screen Cutter had gained entrance to[14] the house, and when she returned, he was waiting for her.

1. des stratégies d'adaptation
2. en mentant
3. ses règles
4. c'est pas vrai
5. donna à réfléchir aux enquêteurs
6. avait prévu
7. soirée romantique
8. Interrogée par
9. appli
10. téléphone portable
11. permettait de suivre
12. Elle avait alors pris l'habitude
13. promener
14. réussi à entrer dans

At knifepoint[1] he made her lock[2] the dog in a bathroom and then took her into a bedroom, where the assault took place.

Bosch wondered whether those fifteen minutes she was walking the dog were enough time for the Screen Cutter to break[3] into the house, see the calendar on the refrigerator, and understand its meaning to the point that he could make the comment to her about knowing what she and her husband had planned for the day.

Bosch and Lourdes discussed this and both felt it was more likely[4] that the rapist had been in the house previously, either as part of stalking[5] the victim, or because he was a family friend or relative or a repairman or someone who'd had some other business there.

This theory was supported[6] when the other victims were interviewed and an eerie new component to the[7] Screen Cutter's MO was established. In each case, there were indicators inside the victim's home that revealed details of her menstrual cycle. In each case as well, the assault had taken place during what would have normally been the ovulation phase of each woman's cycle.

The second and third victims revealed during the interviews that they used birth control pills[8] that were dispensed from push-through pill cards[9]. One of the women kept her pill card[10] in a medicine cabinet, and the other in her bedside table. While the pills suppressed the ovulation cycle, the cards and color-coding of the pills could be used to chart[11] when that five-to-seven-day phase would normally occur.

The last victim had been attacked the February before. She was sixteen years old at the time and home alone on a school holiday. The girl report-

1. Sous la menace d'un couteau,
2. enfermer
3. s'introduire
4. trouvaient plus plausible
5. parce qu'il avait suivi
6. corroborée
7. nouvel et sordide élément relatif au
8. prenaient un contraceptif oral
9. sous la forme de plaquettes de pilules
10. plaquette
11. déterminer

ed that at fourteen she had been diagnosed with[1] juvenile diabetes and her menstruation cycle affected her insulin needs. She tracked her cycle on a calendar on the door of her bedroom so she and her mother could prepare the proper[2] insulin dosage.

The similarity in the timing of each of the attacks was clear. Each victim was assaulted during what would normally be the ovulation phase of their cycle—the time when a woman is most fertile. For this to have occurred in four out of four cases[3] seemed beyond coincidence to Bosch and Lourdes. A profile began to emerge. The rapist had obviously carefully chosen the day of each attack. While[4] information about each victim's cycle could be found inside her home, the attacker had to know this information beforehand[5]. This meant he had stalked[6] his victims and likely had previously been in their homes[7].

Additionally, it was clear from descriptions of the attacker's body that he was not Hispanic. The two victims who spoke no English said he gave them orders in Spanish but it was clearly not his first language[8].

The connections between the cases seemed stunning[9] and raised[10] serious questions about why the cases had not been linked before Bosch arrived as a volunteer[11] investigator. The answers were rooted[12] in the department's budget crisis. The assaults occurred while the detective bureau was shrinking in size[13] and those left in the squad had more cases to work and less time to work them. Different investigators initially handled each of the four rapes. The first two investigators were gone when the second two cases occurred. There was no cohesive understanding

1. on lui avait diagnostiqué un
2. adéquat
3. Le fait que cela soit vrai des 4 cas
4. Même si les
5. à l'avance
6. suivi
7. était sûrement déjà entré chez elles
8. langue maternelle
9. stupéfiants
10. soulevaient
11. bénévole
12. résidaient
13. réduisait ses effectifs

of what was going on[1]. There was no constant supervision in the squad either[2]. The lieutenant's position[3] was frozen[4] and those duties were assigned[5] to Captain Trevino, who had responsibilities in other areas of the department as well.

The connections Bosch identified between the cases were confirmed when the DNA results came back linking[6] the three cases in which semen had been collected. There was now no doubt that a serial rapist had struck at least four times in four years in tiny San Fernando.

Bosch also believed that there were more victims. In San Fernando alone, there was an estimated population of five thousand illegal immigrants, half of them women and many who would not call the police if victimized by crime[7]. It also seemed unlikely[8] that such a predator would operate only within the bounds[9] of the tiny city. The four known victims were Latinas and had similar physical appearances: long brown hair, dark eyes, and a slight build[10]—none of them weighed more than 110 pounds[11]. The two contiguous LAPD geographic divisions had majority Latino populations, and Bosch had to assume[12] that there were more victims to be found there.

Since discovering the connection between the cases, he had been spending almost all of his time on the SFPD job making contact with investigators from LAPD's burglary[13] and sexual assault squads throughout the Valley as well as in the nearby departments in Burbank, Glendale, and Pasadena. He was interested in any open cases involving screen cutting and the use of masks. So far nothing had come back but he knew it was a matter of getting detectives interested and looking[14],

1. aucune vue synthétique quant à l'interprétation des faits
2. non plus
3. poste
4. bloqué
5. ses tâches étaient confiées
6. et permirent de relier
7. en cas d'agression
8. peu probable
9. dans les limites
10. menues
11. 50 kg
12. supposait donc
13. des cambriolages
14. qu'il s'agissait simplement d'attendre que les enquêteurs s'y intéressent et se penchent dessus

maybe getting[1] the message to the right detective who would remember something.

With the police chief's approval[2], Bosch had also contacted an old friend who had been a senior profiler[3] with the FBI's Behavioral[4] Analysis Unit. Bosch had worked with Megan Hill on several occasions when he was with the LAPD and she was with[5] the Bureau[6]. She was now retired from the FBI and working as a professor of forensic[7] psychology at the John Jay College of Criminal Justice in New York. She also kept her hand in profiling as a private consultant[8]. She agreed to look at Bosch's case for a discounted rate[9] and he sent her a package[10] on the Screen Cutter. He was keenly[11] interested in knowing the motivation and psychology behind the attacks. Why did the Screen Cutter's stalking pattern include[12] determining his intended victim's ovulation phase? If he was trying to impregnate[13] his victims, why did he choose two women who were taking birth control pills[14]? There was something missing in the theory, and Bosch hoped the profiler would see it.

Hill took two weeks to get back to Bosch, and her assessment[15] of the cases concluded that the perpetrator was not choosing the attack dates because he wished to impregnate his victims. Quite the opposite. The details of the stalking[16] and subsequent attacks[17] revealed a subject with a deep-seated hatred of[18] women and disgust toward[19] the bodily ritual of bleeding[20]. The day of the attack is chosen because the victim is considered by the offender to be at the cleanest part of her cycle. For him, psychologically, it is the safest moment for him to attack. Hill added to[21] the profile of the rapist by describing him as a narcissistic predator with above-average intelligence[22]. It was likely,

1. ou peut-être de passer
2. accord
3. profileuse chevronnée
4. comportementale
5. quand elle travaillait pour
6. FBI
7. médico-légale
8. était aussi consultante en profilage, ce qui lui permettait de ne pas perdre la main
9. prix d'ami
10. dossier
11. vivement
12. avait-il pour habitude de
13. féconder
14. la pilule
15. évaluation
16. des traques
17. des agressions consécutives
18. qui haïssait profondément
19. que dégoûtaient
20. saignements menstruels
21. complétait
22. doté d'une intelligence au-dessus de la moyenne

however, that he had a job that did not involve intellectual stimulus[1] and allowed him to fly below the radar when it came to the assessment[2] of his employers and coworkers[3].

The offender also had a high degree of confidence in his skill at[4] eluding[5] identification and capture. The crimes involved careful planning and waiting and yet were marked by what seemed to be a critical mistake in leaving his semen in the victim. Discounting[6] that this was part of an intention to impregnate, Hill concluded that it was intended to taunt[7]. The offender was giving Bosch all the evidence he needed to convict him[8]. Bosch just had to find him.

Hill also focused on the seeming[9] incongruity of the offender leaving probative evidence[10] of identity behind—his semen—and yet committing the crimes while masking his visual identity. She concluded that the offender might be someone the victims had previously met or seen, or he intended to make[11] contact with them in some manner[12] following[13] the attacks, possibly deriving[14] some of his satisfaction from getting close to the victims again.

Megan Hill's profile ended with an ominous warning[15]:

> If you eliminate the idea that the perpetrator's motive is to give life (impregnate) and realize[16] that the attack is urged[17] by hate, then it is clear that this subject has not concluded[18] his evolution as predator. It is only a matter[19] of time before these rapes become kills[20].

The warning resulted in[21] Bosch and Lourdes upping the game[22]. They started by sending out

1. peu stimulant intellectuellement
2. passer inaperçu aux yeux
3. collègues
4. grande confiance dans ses talents pour
5. se soustraire à
6. Balayant l'hypothèse
7. cela visait à narguer la police
8. faire condamner
9. l'apparente
10. des preuves probantes
11. d'entrer en
12. d'une manière ou d'une autre
13. après
14. tirant
15. inquiétant avertissement
16. si on comprend
17. motivée
18. terminé
19. question
20. des meurtres
21. poussa
22. à passer à la vitesse supérieure

another set of e-mails to local and national law enforcement agencies with Hill's assessment attached. On the local level, they followed up[1] with phone calls in an effort to break through the typical law enforcement inertia[2] that descends on[3] investigators who have too many cases and too little time.

The response was close to nothing[4]. One burglary detective from LAPD's North Hollywood Division reported that he had an open burglary case involving a screen cutting but there was no rape involved. The detective said the victim was a male Hispanic twenty-six years old. Bosch urged[5] the investigator to go back to the victim to see if he had a wife or girlfriend who might have been attacked but was afraid or embarrassed to report the assault. A week later the LAPD detective reported back and said there was no female living in the apartment. The case was unconnected.

Bosch was now playing a waiting game[6]. The rapist's DNA was not in the databases. He had never been swabbed. He had left no fingerprints or other evidence behind other than his semen. Bosch found no other connecting cases in San Fernando or elsewhere. The debate over whether to go public with the case[7] and ask for the help of citizens was simmering on the back burner[8] in the office of Chief Valdez. It was an age-old[9] law enforcement[10] question: Go public and possibly draw a lead[11] that breaks the case open[12] and leads to an arrest? Or go public and possibly alert the predator, who changes up his patterns[13] or moves on and visits[14] his terror on an unsuspecting community somewhere else?

In the Screen Cutter case Bosch and Lourdes had conflicting views. Lourdes wanted to go public, if only to chase[15] the rapist out of San Fernando

1. enchaînèrent
2. briser l'inertie, caractéristique dans la police,
3. s'empare des
4. réaction fut presque nulle
5. pressa
6. à un jeu de patience
7. sur la pertinence ou non de rendre l'affaire publique
8. couvait dangereusement
9. l'éternelle
10. pour la police
11. trouver une piste
12. soit le tournant décisif
13. complètement de schéma
14. parte exercer
15. au moins pour chasser

if the move produced no leads[1]. Bosch wanted more time to quietly look for him. He felt that going public would indeed chase him out of town but that it would not stop the victim count[2]. Predators didn't stop—until they were caught. They just adapted and continued, moving like sharks[3] to the next victim. Bosch didn't want to move[4] the threat to another community. He felt a moral obligation to chase the suspect down here[5] where he was active.

But there was no right answer, of course, and the chief appeared to be waiting, hoping that Bosch would come through and break[6] the case before another victim was attacked. Bosch was ultimately relieved[7] not to have the decision on his shoulders. He figured[8] this was why the chief made the big bucks and he made none[9].

Bosch checked his e-mail now and saw he had no new messages in his queue with[10] *Screen Cutter* in the subject line. Disappointed, he shut down the computer. He put his notebook back in his pocket and wondered if Trevino had looked down on it[11] while hovering[12] in the cubicle. It had been opened to the page with James Franklin Aldridge's name written on it.

He left the squad room without bothering[13] to say good-bye to Trevino or write his time down[14] on the board at the front door.

1. l'initiative ne donnait rien
2. nombre de victimes
3. des requins
4. déplacer
5. le traquer ici même,
6. parviendrait à résoudre
7. En définitive, Bosch était soulagé
8. se disait que
9. était grassement payé, et pas lui
10. liste ayant
11. y avait jeté un œil
12. pendant qu'il rôdait
13. prendre la peine
14. d'inscrire son heure de départ

7

After leaving the station Bosch got on the 5 freeway and turned back to the Whitney Vance case. Not coming up with any[1] birth date or other information on Vibiana Duarte on the DMV database was disappointing but no more than a temporary setback[2]. Bosch was headed south to Norwalk, where the time-travel gold mine was housed[3]: the Los Angeles County Department of Public Health, the place he spent so much time as a cold case investigator in the Vital Records[4] office that he knew exactly how the clerks[5] liked their coffee. He felt confident[6] he would be able to answer some questions about Vibiana Duarte there.

Bosch put a CD in the Jeep's music slot[7] and started listening to a young horn player[8] named Christian Scott. The first track up[9], "Litany Against Fear," had a relentless sound and drive to it[10] and that's what Bosch felt he needed at the moment. It took him an hour to get down to Norwalk after a slow crawl[11] around the east edge[12] of downtown. He pulled into the lot[13] fronting the seven-story county building and killed[14] the engine while Scott was in the middle of "Naima," which Bosch thought compared favorably with[15] John Handy's classic version recorded fifty years earlier.

Just as he stepped out of the car his cell phone chirped[16] and he checked the screen. It said Unknown Caller but he took it anyway. It was John Creighton and the call was not a surprise.

1. Le fait de n'avoir trouvé aucune

2. ce n'était qu'un contretemps

3. se trouvait la mine d'or des voyages dans le temps

4. de l'état civil

5. employés

6. était sûr

7. lecteur

8. trompettiste

9. morceau

10. un son et une dynamique implacables

11. ralentissement

12. frange

13. se gara dans le parking

14. éteignit

15. qui, d'après Bosch, était meilleure que

16. gazouilla

"So, you saw Mr. Vance?" he asked.

"I did," Bosch answered.

"Well, how did it go?"

"It went fine."

Bosch was going to make Creighton dig for it[1]. It might be considered passive-aggressive behavior on his part but he was keeping the wishes of his client in mind. "Is there anything we can help with?"

"Uh, no, I think I can handle it[2]. Mr. Vance wants it kept confidential, so I'll just leave it at that[3]."

There was a long silence before Creighton spoke next.

"Harry," he said, "you and I go way back to the department[4], and of course Mr. Vance and I go way back as well. As I said yesterday before hiring you, he's an important client of this firm and if there is anything wrong regarding his comfort and security, then I need to know it. I was hoping as a former brother in blue[5] you might share with me what is going on. Mr. Vance is an old man, I don't want him taken advantage of[6]."

"By 'taken advantage of,' are you talking about me?" Bosch asked.

"Of course not, Harry. Poor[7] choice of words. What I mean is if the old man is being extorted[8] or otherwise facing any sort of trouble[9] involving the need for a private detective, well, we are here and we have enormous resources at our fingertips[10]. We need to be brought in[11]."

Bosch nodded. He expected this sort of play from Creighton after the demand in his office to be looped in[12].

"Well," he said. "All I can tell you is that first of all, you didn't hire me. You were the bagman[13]. You delivered money to me. Mr. Vance hired me

1. n'allait pas lui faciliter la tâche
2. gérer tout seul
3. je vais m'en tenir à ça
4. on se connaît depuis nos années dans la police
5. qu'en tant qu'ancien collègue,
6. qu'on profite de lui
7. Mauvais
8. soumis à un chantage
9. exposé à tout autre problème
10. portée de main
11. Il faut qu'on soit dans la boucle
12. tenu au courant
13. l'intermédiaire

and that's who I work for. Mr. Vance was very specific and even had me sign a legal document agreeing to follow his instructions. He told me not to share with anyone what I'm doing or why I'm doing it. That would include you. If you want me to break from that, I need to call him back and ask for his per—"

"That won't be necessary," Creighton said quickly. "If that's how Mr. Vance wants it, that's fine. Just know, we are here to help if needed."

"Absolutely," Bosch said in an upbeat but phony[1] voice. "I'll call you if needed, John, and thanks for checking in[2]."

He disconnected the call before Creighton could respond. He then headed through[3] the parking lot toward the massive rectangular building that contained the records[4] of all official births and deaths in L.A. County. All records of marriage and divorce were recorded here as well. The building always reminded Bosch of a giant treasure chest[5]. The information was in there if you knew where to look—or knew somebody who did. For those who didn't, the front steps of the building were where hawkers[6] stood by, ready to counsel the uninitiated on how to fill out request forms[7]—all for the price of a few dollars. Some of them already had the forms in their briefcases. It was a cottage[8] industry built on the naïveté and fear of those who find themselves venturing into the maw[9] of government bureaucracy.

Bosch jogged up the steps[10], ignoring those who came at him asking if he was applying[11] for a fictitious business name or a marriage license. He entered and walked past the information booth[12] and then toward the stairs. Knowing from experience that waiting for an elevator in the building could suck the will to live out of a person[13], he

1. enjouée mais fausse
2. de prendre des nouvelles
3. traversa
4. archives
5. coffre au trésor
6. des démarcheurs
7. remplir des formulaires
8. artisanale
9. gueule
10. gravit prestement les marches
11. venu faire une demande
12. guichet
13. pouvait être désespérant à en mourir

took the stairs down to the basement level[1] where the BDM[2] section of the Register-Recorder's Office was located[3].

As he pushed through the glass door, there was a shriek[4] from one of the desks lining[5] the wall on the other side of the public counter[6] where birth, death, and marriage records could be requested. A woman stood up and smiled broadly[7] at Bosch. She was Asian and her name was Flora. She had always been most helpful to Bosch when he had carried a badge[8].

"Harry Bosch!" she called out.

"Flora!" he called right back.

Along the counter, there was a window for law enforcement requests[9], which were always given priority, and two windows for citizen requests. There was a man standing at one of the citizen windows looking at copies of records. Bosch stepped up to the other. Flora was already heading to the law enforcement window.

"No, you come down here," she instructed.

Bosch did as instructed and then leaned over the counter for an awkward embrace[10].

"I knew you'd come back to us here," Flora said.

"Sooner or later[11], right?" he said. "But, hey, I'm here as a citizen right now. I don't want to get you in any trouble[12]."

Bosch knew he could pull the[13] San Fernando badge, but he didn't want a move like that to possibly track back to[14] Valdez or Trevino. That would cause problems he didn't need. Instead, he started back[15] to the citizen's window, choosing to keep his private and public detective work separate.

"It no trouble[16]," Flora said. "Not for you."

He ended the charade[17] and remained at the LE[18] window.

1. sous-sol
2. état civil [Birth, Death and Marriage]
3. située
4. exclamation
5. bordant
6. guichet
7. adressa un grand sourire
8. était dans la police
9. les requêtes policières
10. l'embrasser tant bien que mal
11. tôt ou tard
12. causer d'ennuis
13. sortir son
14. que son geste puisse remonter jusqu'à
15. entreprit de retourner
16. Pas problème
17. mit fin à la comédie
18. pour flics [Law Enforcement]

"Well, this one might take a while[1]," he said. "I don't have all the information and I need to go way, way back[2]."

"Let me try it. What you want?"

Bosch always had to guard against chopping his language the way she did[3]. His natural inclination was to start leaving out words[4] when he spoke to her. He had caught himself doing it in the past and he tried to avoid doing it now.

He pulled out his notebook and looked at some of the dates he had written down that morning in Vance's office.

"Looking for a birth record[5]," he said while reading. "Talking about[6] 1933 or '34. What do you have going that far back?"

"Not on database," Flora said. "We have film here only. No hard record anymore[7]. Let me see name."

He knew she was talking about records transferred to microfilm in the 1970s and never updated to the computerized database. He turned his notebook around so she could see the name and spelling[8] of Vibiana Duarte. Bosch hoped that he would catch a break with the unusualness of it[9]. At least it wasn't a common Latino surname[10] like Garcia or Fernandez. There probably weren't too many Vibianas around either.

"She old," Flora said. "You want death too?"

"I do. But I have no idea when and if she died. Last time I have her alive for sure is June 1950."

She made a frowning face[11].

"Ooh, I see, Harry."

"Thanks, Flora. Where is Paula? She still here?"

Paula was the other clerk he remembered from his frequent forays[12] to the basement while a detective[13]. Locating witnesses[14] and families of

1. risque de prendre du temps
2. remonter très loin dans le temps
3. s'empêcher de parler comme elle
4. Il avait tendance à adopter un langage télégraphique
5. acte de naissance
6. Vers
7. Plus rien sur papier
8. l'orthographe
9. aurait de la chance avec un nom si peu courant
10. patronyme
11. fronça les sourcils
12. incursions
13. du temps où il était inspecteur
14. Retrouver les témoins

victims was a key part of cold case investigation, usually the foundation[1] of any case. The first thing you did was alert the family that the case was back under active investigation[2]. But murder books from old cases rarely contained updates[3] on deaths, marriages, and the migration of people. Consequently, Bosch did some of his best detective work in the halls of records and libraries.

"Paula out today," Flora said. "Just me. I write down now and you get coffee. This take time."

Flora wrote down what she needed.

"Do you want a coffee, Flora?" Bosch asked.

"No, you get," she said. "For waiting."

"Then I think I'll just stick around[4]. I filled up[5] this morning and I have stuff[6] to do."

He pulled his phone out and held it up by way[7] of explanation. Flora went back into the microfilm archives to hunt. Bosch sat down on one of the plastic seats in an unused microfilm cubicle.

He was thinking about next moves[8]. Depending on what he came up with[9] here, his next step was to go to St. Vibiana's to see if he could get a look at baptismal records[10], or to the main library downtown, where they kept phone directories going back decades[11].

Bosch pulled up his phone's search app[12] and typed in[13] *USC EVK* to see what might come up. It got a hit right away[14]. The EVK[15] was still operating[16] on the campus and was located in the Birnkrant Residential College on 34th Street. He pulled[17] the address up on his maps app and was soon looking at an overview[18] of the sprawling[19] campus just south of downtown. Vance said Vibiana had lived only a few blocks from the EVK and walked to work. The campus ran along[20] Figueroa Street and the Harbor Freeway corridor[21]. This limited the number of residential streets in the

1. base
2. enquête était rouverte
3. une mise à jour
4. Dans ce cas, je vais rester là à attendre
5. J'ai fait le plein
6. des trucs
7. en guise
8. réfléchissait à ce qu'il allait faire ensuite
9. obtiendrait
10. registres de baptême
11. des annuaires téléphoniques vieux de plusieurs décennies
12. appli
13. tapa
14. La réponse s'afficha aussitôt
15. cafétéria universitaire
16. toujours en activité
17. rentra
18. vue générale
19. immense
20. longeait
21. autoroute

area with direct access to the EVK. Bosch started writing them down along with address spans[1] so he might be able to place the Duarte house when he checked[2] the old phone directories at the central library.

It soon occurred to him[3] that he was looking at a 2016 map of the campus and its surroundings and that the Harbor Freeway might not even have existed in 1950. That would give the neighborhood around USC a completely different make-up[4]. He went back to the search app and pulled up the history of the freeway, also known as the 110, which slashed an eight-lane diagonal across[5] the county[6] from Pasadena down to the harbor[7]. He soon learned that it was built in sections in the 1940s and '50s. It was the dawn[8] of the freeway era in L.A. and the 110 was the very first project. The section that edged[9] the east side of the USC campus was begun in 1952 and completed two years later, both dates well after the time Whitney Vance attended[10] the school and met Vibiana Duarte.

Bosch went back to his mapping and started including streets that in 1949 and 1950 still provided walking access to the northeast corner of campus, where the EVK was located. Soon he had a list of fourteen streets with a four-block range of address numbers[11]. At the library he would first look up the name Duarte in the old directories[12] and see if any were located on the streets and blocks[13] on the list. Back then[14] almost everybody was listed in the phone book—if they had a phone.

He was leaning over his phone's small screen, checking the map for side streets[15] he might have missed, when Flora came back from the bowels[16] of the record center. She was carrying one spool[17] for the microfilm machine triumphantly up in

1. avec leurs fourchettes de numéros,
2. chercherait dans
3. Il songea alors
4. configuration
5. dont les 8 voies traversaient en biais
6. le comté,
7. jusqu'à la baie
8. les débuts
9. longeait
10. eut fréquenté
11. assorties de tous les numéros, sur 4 pâtés de maisons
12. annuaires
13. dans toutes les rues
14. À l'époque,
15. des rues transversales
16. des profondeurs
17. bobine

her hand and that immediately put a charge[1] in Bosch's bloodstream. Flora had found Vibiana.

"She not born here," Flora said. "Mexico."

This confused Bosch. He stood up and headed to the counter.

"How do you know that?" he asked.

"It say on her death certificate," Flora said. "Loreto."

Flora had pronounced the name wrong but Bosch understood it. He had once traced a[2] murder suspect to Loreto, far down the inner coast of the Baja peninsula[3]. He guessed if he went there now he would find a St. Vibiana's Cathedral or Church.

"You already found her death certificate?" he asked.

"Not taking long," Flora said. "Only look to nineteen and fifty-one."

Her words sucked the air out[4] of Bosch. Vibiana was not only dead, but dead so long. He had heard her name for the first time less than six hours ago but already he had found her—in a way. He wondered how Vance would react to the news.

He held his hand out for the microfilm reel[5]. As Flora handed it to him she told him the record number he should look for: 51-459. Bosch recognized it as a low number[6], even for 1951. The four hundred and fifty-ninth death recorded in L.A. County that year. How far into the year could that be? A month? Two?

A fleeting[7] thought came to him. He looked at Flora. Had she read the cause of death when she found the document?

"She died in childbirth[8]?" he asked.

Flora looked puzzled.

"Uh, no," she said. "But you read. Make sure."

1. envoya une décharge d'adrénaline
2. jadis suivi la trace d'un
3. bien au sud sur la péninsule de Basse-Californie [au Mexique]
4. coupèrent le souffle
5. bobine
6. nota qu'il s'agissait d'un chiffre peu élevé
7. fugace
8. en couches

Bosch took the spool and turned back to the machine. He quickly threaded the film through[1] and turned on the projection light. There was an automatic feed[2] controlled with a button. He sped through[3] the documents, stopping every few seconds to check the record number stamped[4] at the top corner. He was halfway through[5] February before he got to the four hundred and fifty-ninth death. When he found the document, he saw that the State of California certificate of death had not changed much over the decades. It might have been the oldest such document he had ever looked at but he was intimately familiar with it. His eyes dropped down to the section the coroner[6] or attending physician[7] filled in. The cause of death was handwritten: strangulation by ligature (clothesline[8]) due to suicide.

Bosch stared[9] for a long time at the line without moving or breathing. Vibiana had killed herself. No details were written beyond what he had already read. There was just a signature too scribbled to decipher[10], followed by the printed words *Deputy*[11] *Coroner.*

Bosch leaned back and took in air[12]. He felt immense sadness come over him. He didn't know all the details. He had heard only Vance's view of the story—an eighteen-year-old's experience filtered through the frail[13] and guilty memory of an eighty-five-year-old. But he knew enough to know that what happened to Vibiana wasn't right[14]. Vance had left her on the wrong side of goodbye, and what happened in June brought about[15] what happened in February. Bosch had a gut feeling[16] that Vibiana's life was taken from her[17] long before she put the rope around her neck.

The death certificate offered details that Bosch wrote down. Vibiana took her life[18] on

1. inséra le film dans le projecteur
2. entraînement
3. fit rapidement défiler
4. tamponné
5. en était à la moitié du mois de
6. que l'expert médico-légal
7. le médecin présent
8. corde à linge
9. fixa
10. trop griffonnée pour être lisible
11. adjoint
12. inspira longuement
13. fragile
14. était mal
15. avait entraîné
16. sentait tout au fond de lui-même
17. l'avait quittée
18. s'était donné la mort

February 12, 1951. She was seventeen. Her next of kin[1] was listed as her father, Victor Duarte. His address was on Hope Street, which had been one of the streets Bosch had written down after studying the map of the USC neighborhood. The street name seemed like a sad irony now.

The lone curiosity[2] on the document was the location[3] of death. There was only an address on North Occidental Boulevard. Bosch knew that Occidental[4] was west of downtown near Echo Park and not at all close to[5] Vibiana's home neighborhood. He opened his phone and typed the address into the search app. It came back as the address of St. Helen's Home for Unwed[6] Mothers. The search provided several websites associated with St. Helen's and a link to a 2008 story[7] in the *Los Angeles Times* marking the[8] one-hundredth anniversary of the facility[9].

Bosch quickly pulled up the link[10] and started reading the story.

Maternity Home Marks 100th Birthday
By Scott B. Anderson, Staff Writer[11]

St. Helen's Home for Unwed Mothers is marking its 100th birthday this week with a celebration that honors its evolution from a place of family secrets to a center for family life.

The three-acre[12] complex near Echo Park will be the site of a full week of programs, including a family picnic and featuring an address[13] from a woman who more than 50 years ago was forced by family to give up her newborn for adoption at the center.

Just as social mores[14] have changed in the last few decades, so has St. Helen's. Getting prematurely pregnant once resulted in the mother

1. plus proche parent
2. L'unique énigme
3. l'endroit
4. ce boulevard
5. proche de
6. célibataires
7. article
8. à l'occasion du
9. l'établissement
10. cliqua sur le lien
11. rédacteur
12. d'env. 1 ha
13. un discours
14. mœurs

being hidden away, delivering[1] a child in secret and then having that child immediately taken away for adoption

...

Bosch stopped reading as he came to understand what had happened sixty-five years ago to Vibiana Duarte.

"She had the baby," he whispered. "And they took it away from her."

1. accouchant

8

Bosch looked over at the counter. Flora was looking at him strangely.

"Harry, you okay?" she asked.

He got up without answering and came to the counter.

"Flora, I need birth records for the first two months of 1951," he said.

"Okay," she said. "What name?"

"I'm not sure. Duarte or Vance. I'm not sure how it would be listed. Give me your pen and I'll write it down."

"Okay."

"The hospital will be St. Helen's. In fact, I want to look at all births at St. Helen's the first two—"

"No, no St. Helen Hospital in L.A. County."

"It's not exactly a hospital. It's for unwed mothers."

"No record here, then."

"What are you talking about[1]? There has to be a—"

"Records secret. When a baby is born, get adopted. New certificate come in and no mention of St. Helen. You see?"

Bosch wasn't sure if he was tracking[2] what she was trying to tell him. He knew there were all kinds of privacy laws protecting adoption records.

"You're saying they don't file the birth certificate until[3] after the adoption?" he asked.

"Exactly," Flora said.

1. Qu'est-ce que tu racontes

2. de suivre

3. qu'ils n'enregistrent l'acte de naissance qu'

"And it only has the names of the new parents on it?"

"Uh-huh[1]. True."

"And the baby's new name?"

Flora nodded.

"What about the hospital? They lie about that?"

"They say home birth[2]."

In frustration Bosch slapped his hands down flat on the counter[3].

"So there is no way I can find out who her child was?"

"I'm sorry, Harry. Don't be mad[4]."

"I'm not mad, Flora. At least not at you[5]."

"You good detective, Harry Bosch. You figure it out[6]."

"Yeah, Flora. I'll figure it out."

Hands still on the counter, Bosch leaned down and tried to think. There had to be a way to find the child. He thought about going to St. Helen's. It might be his only shot[7]. He then thought of something else and looked back up at Flora.

"Harry, I never see you this way[8]," she said.

"I know, Flora," he said. "I'm sorry. I don't like dead ends[9]. Can you bring me the reels with births in January and February 1951, please?"

"You sure? You got a lot a[10] births in two month."

"Yes, I'm sure."

"Okay, then."

Flora disappeared again and Bosch went back to the microfilm cubicle to wait. Checking his watch, he realized that it was likely he would be looking through microfilm until the office closed at 5:00. He would then face a brutal rush-hour drive through[11] the heart of downtown and up into Hollywood to get home, a slog[12] that could take two hours. Since he was closer to Orange County than home, he decided to text[13] his

1. C'est ça, oui

2. accouchement à domicile

3. donna une grande claque sur le guichet

4. Ne te fâche pas

5. contre toi

6. trouver

7. chance

8. comme ça

9. les impasses

10. [=of]

11. Il lui faudrait ensuite affronter les embouteillages de l'heure de pointe pour traverser

12. trajet pénible

13. d'envoyer un SMS à

1. au cas où

daughter on the off chance[1] she'd have time for dinner away from the Chapman University student cafeteria.

2. Maddie

Mads[2], I'm in Norwalk on a case. I could come down for dinner if you have time.

3. tout de suite

She texted back right away[3].

Where is Norwalk?

Down near you. I could pick you up at 5:30 and have you back doing homework by 7. What do you say?

4. en train de peser le pour et le contre
5. contraintes
6. par rapport à l'année précédente
7. ravi
8. morose
9. lui rappelait
10. juste

Her decision did not come quickly and he knew she was probably weighing her options[4]. She was in her second year, and social and school demands[5] on her time had grown exponentially from the previous year[6], resulting in Bosch seeing her less and less. It was a development that occasionally left him feeling sad and alone, but delighted[7] for her at most other times. He knew that this would be one of the nights he would feel gloomy[8] if he didn't get to see her. The story of Vibiana Duarte, what little he knew of it, depressed him. She had been just a few years younger than his own daughter and what happened to her was a reminder[9] that life is not always fair[10]—even to the innocent.

11. visionna
12. à éplucher péniblement

While he was waiting for his daughter's decision Flora came out with two reels of microfilm for him. He put his phone down on the table next to the machine and spooled[11] the reel marked January 1951. He started wading through[12] hundreds of birth records, checking the hospital line on each and printing out every certificate recorded as a home birth.

Ninety minutes later Bosch stopped at February 20, 1951, having extended[1] his search a week past Vibiana's death to account for the[2] delay in the filing[3] of a birth certificate under the names of the new parents. He had printed out sixty-seven birth certificates in which there was a home birth and the child's race was listed as either Latino or white. He had no photo of Vibiana Duarte and he did not know how dark or light her complexion had been[4]. He could not rule out[5] the possibility that her baby was adopted as white, even if just to match[6] the race of the adoptive parents.

As he squared up the stack of printouts[7] he realized he had forgotten about dinner with his daughter. He grabbed[8] his phone and saw that he had missed her final text on his offer[9]. It had come in more than an hour earlier and she had accepted, as long as they were finished eating and she was back studying by 7:30. This year she was sharing a house with three other girls a few blocks from campus. Bosch checked his watch and saw he'd been correct in predicting he would finish up as the records office was closing. He shot[10] a quick text[11] to Maddie saying he was heading her way[12].

Bosch brought the microfilm copies to the counter and asked Flora what he owed[13] for sixty-seven birth certificates.

"You law enforcement," she said. "No charge[14]."

"Yeah, but I'm not saying that, Flora," he said. "This is private."

Again he refused to play the San Fernando card where it was not necessary. He had no choice when it came to running names through[15] law enforcement databases, but this was different. If he accepted free copies under false pretenses[16],

1. prolongé
2. tenir compte du
3. enregistrement
4. si elle avait été claire ou foncée de peau
5. exclure
6. ne serait-ce que pour que cela coïncide avec
7. Alors qu'il ordonnait le tas de feuilles imprimées,
8. saisit
9. réponse à sa proposition
10. envoya
11. SMS
12. se mettait en route
13. combien il lui devait
14. Gratuit
15. s'agissait d'entrer des noms dans
16. prétextes

then there would be financial gain to his bending the rules[1] and the blowback[2] could be extreme. He pulled out his wallet.

"Then you pay five dollar for every copy," Flora said.

The price shocked him, even though he had made ten thousand dollars that very morning[3]. It must have shown on his face. Flora smiled.

"You see?" she said. "You are law enforcement."

"No, Flora, I'm not," Bosch said. "Can I pay with a credit card?"

"No, you pay cash."

Bosch frowned and looked through his billfold[4] to get the secreted[5] hundred-dollar bill[6] he always carried for emergencies. He combined it with the cash he carried in a fold in[7] his pocket and made[8] the $335 copy bill[9] with six bucks left over[10]. He asked for a receipt even though he didn't think he would be filing an expense report with[11] Vance.

He waved the stack of printouts[12] as a farewell[13] and thank-you to Flora and left the office. A few minutes later he was in his car, lining up[14] to get out of the parking lot with everybody else leaving the government building at five o'clock sharp[15]. He put the CD player on and switched things up a bit, listening to[16] the latest album from Grace Kelly, the saxophonist.

She was one of the few jazz musicians his daughter liked and appreciated. He wanted to have the disc playing in the car in case Maddie chose a restaurant they had to drive to.

But instead his daughter chose a place in the Old Towne circle that was walking distance[17] from her house on Palm Avenue. Along the way she explained how much happier she was renting[18] a house with three girls than she'd been sharing a two-room, one-bathroom dorm[19], as she did her

1. cela voudrait dire tirer un bénéfice financier de son entorse au réglement
2. répercussions
3. ce matin même
4. portefeuille
5. caché
6. billet
7. repli de
8. réussit à payer
9. de sa facture
10. dollars de reste
11. demanderait un défraiement à
12. agita le paquet de feuilles
13. pour dire au revoir
14. faisant la queue
15. tapantes
16. pour changer un peu, écouta
17. où l'on pouvait se rendre à pied
18. de louer
19. chambre universitaire

freshman year[1]. She was also much closer to the satellite campus where the psychology school was located. All in all[2], life seemed good for her, but Bosch worried about security at the private house. There was no campus police patrol. The four girls were left on their own in the jurisdiction[3] of the City of Orange Police Department. The drop-off in response time[4] between the campus and the municipal law enforcement was[5] minutes, not seconds, and that bothered Bosch too.

The restaurant was a pizza joint[6] where they stood in line to each order[7] a customized pie[8] that they took to their table hot from the oven. Sitting across from her, Bosch was distracted by the neon-pink highlights[9] accenting his daughter's hair. Finally he asked why she had gone and done that to herself.

"Solidarity," she said. "I have a friend whose mom has breast cancer."

Bosch didn't get the connection[10] and she easily read him[11].

"Are you kidding?" she said. "October is breast cancer awareness[12] month, Dad. You should know that."

"Oh, yeah, right. I forgot."

He had recently seen on TV some football players from the Los Angeles Rams wearing some pink equipment. Now he understood. And while it made him happy that Maddie had dyed her hair[13] for a good cause, he was also secretly pleased that it was probably only a temporary thing. In a few weeks the month would be over[14].

Maddie ate exactly half of her pizza and put the other half in a cardboard to-go box[15], explaining that the remainder[16] would serve as breakfast.

1. en première année
2. En somme
3. secteur
4. temps de réaction
5. se comptait en
6. pizzeria
7. pour que chacun commande
8. pizza personnalisée
9. mèches rose fluo
10. ne saisit pas le rapport
11. le vit tout de suite
12. de sensibilisation
13. se soit teint les cheveux
14. terminé
15. boîte à emporter
16. reste

"So what case are you on?" she asked when they were walking back down Palm to her house.

"How do you know I'm on a case?" he asked.

"You said in your text, plus you're wearing a suit. Don't be so paranoid. You're like[1] a secret agent or something."

"I forgot. It's just an heir-hunting[2] case."

"'Air hunting'? What is that?"

"*Heir*[3] like in heir to the throne."

"Oh, got it[4]."

"I'm trying to find out if an old man up in Pasadena with a lot of money has an heir out there[5] that he can give it all to[6] when he dies."

"Wow, cool. Did you find anybody yet?"

"Well, I have sixty-seven possibilities at the moment. That's what I was doing in Norwalk. Looking at birth records."

"Cool."

He didn't want to tell her about what happened to Vibiana Duarte.

"But you can't tell anyone about this, Mads. It's top secret, whether I'm a secret agent or not."

"Like, who am I going to tell[7]?"

"I don't know. I just don't want you putting it out there on MyFace or SnapCat[8] or something."

"Funny[9], Dad, but my generation is visual. We don't tell people what other people are doing. We show what we're doing. We put up photos. So you don't need to worry."

"Good."

Once back at the house, he asked if he could come in to check the locks and other security measures. With the landlord[10]'s permission he had added extra[11] locks on all doors and windows back in September. He checked everything and couldn't avoid thoughts of the Screen Cutter as he moved about the house. He finally stepped

1. On dirait
2. de chasse aux héritiers
3. [se prononce sans h aspiré]
4. j'ai pigé
5. un quelconque descendant dans la nature
6. à qui il pourra tout donner
7. Genre, à qui voudrais-tu que je le dise
8. [réseaux sociaux, sur internet]
9. Très drôle
10. propriétaire
11. supplémentaires

into the small backyard[1] to make sure the wooden fence[2] that ran the perimeter[3] was locked from the inside. He saw that Maddie had done as he had advised and bought a dog bowl[4] for the back step even though the girls didn't have a dog and the landlord didn't allow it.

Everything seemed in order and he reminded his daughter once again not to sleep with any windows open. He then hugged her and kissed the top of her head before leaving.

"Make sure there's water in the dog bowl," he said. "Right now it's dry[5]."

"Yes, Dad," she said in that tone she had[6].

"Otherwise it doesn't sell it[7]."

"Okay, I get it."

"Good. I'll pick up a couple Beware of Dog[8] signs at Home Depot[9] and bring them down next time."

"Dad."

"Okay, I'm going."

He gave her another hug and headed back to his car. He had not seen any of the roommates[10] during his brief stop-off. He wondered about this but didn't ask for fear Maddie would accuse him of invading the privacy of the other girls. She had already told him once before that his questions about them bordered on being creepy[11].

Once he got in the car he wrote a note to himself about the Beware of Dog signs and then put the key into the ignition[12].

The traffic had thinned[13] by the time he headed north for home. He felt good about the accomplishments[14] of the day, including having dinner with his daughter. The next morning he would work on narrowing[15] the search for Vibiana Duarte and Whitney Vance's child. The child's name had

1. jardin arrière
2. clôture en bois
3. en faisait le tour
4. avait acheté une écuelle pour chien
5. vide
6. qu'il connaissait si bien
7. ça ne sert à rien
8. Chien méchant
9. [grands magasins d'articles pour la maison]
10. colocataires
11. frisaient l'indécence
12. démarra le moteur
13. Il y avait moins de circulation
14. était content de ses réussites
15. essaierait d'avancer sur

to be somewhere in the stack[1] of birth certificates on the seat next to him.

There was something comforting[2] about making progress on the Vance case, but a low-grade dread[3] was building inside of him about the Screen Cutter. Something told him that the stalking rapist[4] was watching another victim and preparing for his next assault. There was a clock ticking up[5] in San Fernando. He was sure of it.

1. la pile
2. de réconfortant
3. sourde appréhension
4. ce violeur [qui avait suivi ses victimes]
5. Un compte à rebours était lancé

9

In the morning Bosch made coffee and had it out on the rear deck[1], where he sat at the picnic table with the copies of the birth certificates he had printed the day before. He studied the names and dates on the documents but quickly came to the conclusion that he had nothing with which to narrow the focus[2]. None of the certificates were dated in a timely way[3]. Each was issued[4] at least three days after the birth and this precluded him[5] from looking at delayed issuance[6] as an indicator of adoption. He decided his best bet[7] was to somehow go through[8] St. Helen's.

He knew this would be a difficult path. Privacy laws governing adoptions[9] were difficult to break through, even with a badge and authority. He considered[10] calling his client Vance and asking if he wanted to get a lawyer involved in a request[11] to open up the adoption records regarding the child born to Vibiana Duarte but he decided it was a nonstarter[12]. That move[13] would most likely announce Vance's plans to the world and he had been vehement about secrecy.

Bosch remembered the *Times* story on St. Helen's and went inside to get his laptop[14] so he could finish reading it. He brought the stack of birth certificates inside so they wouldn't blow away and paper[15] the canyon below his house.

The *Times* story recounted[16] the transformation of St. Helen's from a place where mother and child

1. le prit sur la terrasse de derrière
2. qui lui permette de limiter son champ de recherche
3. n'avait une date assez précoce
4. avait été établi
5. l'empêchait
6. considérer ces certificats tardifs
7. que le mieux
8. trouver un moyen d'accéder à
9. En matière d'adoption, les lois sur la protection de la vie privée
10. envisagea
11. mandater un avocat
12. voué à l'échec
13. initiative
14. ordinateur portable
15. pour éviter qu'ils s'envolent et tapissent
16. relatait

were quickly separated when adoption occurred[1], to a place in more recent decades where many mothers kept their children after birth and were counseled on[2] returning to society with them. The social stigma[3] of unwed pregnancy[4] in the 1950s gave way to the acceptance[5] of the 1990s, and St. Helen's had a number of successful programs designed to keep fledgling families together[6].

The story then branched out to a section[7] containing quotes[8] from women who had been clients of St. Helen's saying how their lives were saved by the maternity center that took them in[9] when they were banished in embarrassment by their own families. There were no negative voices here. No interviews with women who felt betrayed[10] by a society that literally snatched their children away from them[11] and gave them to strangers.

The final anecdote of the story drew Bosch's rapt attention[12] as he realized it gave his investigation a new angle. It began with a number of quotes from[13] a seventy-two-year-old woman who had come to St. Helen's in 1950 to bear a child and then stayed for the next fifty years.

Abigail Turnbull was only fourteen when she was left with a suitcase on the front steps of St. Helen's. She was three months pregnant and this deeply humiliated her fervently religious parents. They abandoned her. Her boyfriend abandoned her. And she had nowhere else to go.

She had her child[14] at St. Helen's and gave her up for adoption[15], spending less than an hour with the infant girl[16] in her arms. But she had nowhere to go afterward. No one in her family wanted her back. She was allowed to stay on at St. Helen's and was given menial jobs[17] like mopping floors[18] and doing laundry[19]. Over the years, however, she

1. au moment de l'adoption
2. bénéficiaient d'une aide psychologique pour
3. stigmatisation sociale
4. filles-mères
5. avait cédé le pas à la tolérance
6. empêcher que ne se disloquent ces très jeunes familles
7. menait alors à un encadré
8. des paroles
9. les avait accueillies
10. trahies
11. leur volait littéralement leurs enfants
12. fascina Bosch
13. avec des propos recueillis auprès d'
14. avait accouché
15. l'avait fait adopter
16. nouveau-née
17. de simples tâches
18. passer la serpillière
19. les lessives

attended night school[1] and eventually earned[2] both high school and college degrees[3]. She became a social worker[4] at St. Helen's, counseling those who had been in her position and staying until her retirement, a half century in all.

Turnbull gave the keynote speech[5] at the one-hundred-year celebration and in it she recounted a story that she said showed how her dedication to[6] St. Helen's paid off[7] in immeasurable ways.

"One day I was in the staff lounge[8] and one of our girls came in with a message that there was a woman at the entrance lobby who had come because she was tracing[9] her own adoption. She wanted answers about where she had come from. Her parents had told her she was born here at St. Helen's. So I met with her and right away a strange feeling came over me. It was her voice, her eyes—I felt as though I knew her[10]. I asked her what her birthday was and she said April 9, 1950, and then I knew, I knew she was my child. I put my arms around her and everything went away. All my pain, every regret I ever had. And I knew it was a miracle and that was why God had kept me at St. Helen's."

The *Times* report ended with Turnbull introducing her daughter, who was in attendance[11], and described how Turnbull's speech had left not a dry eye in the house[12].

"Jackpot," Bosch whispered as he finished reading.

Bosch knew he had to speak to Turnbull. As he wrote her name down he hoped that she was still alive eight years after the *Times* story was published. That would make her[13] eighty years old.

He thought about the best way to get to her quickly and started by putting her name into the

1. avait suivi des cours du soir
2. avait fini par obtenir
3. diplômes
4. assistante sociale
5. discours principal
6. dévouement envers
7. avait été récompensé
8. salle du personnel
9. enquêtait sur
10. j'avais l'impression de la connaître
11. présente
12. avait fait pleurer toute la salle
13. Elle aurait maintenant

1. moteur de recherche
2. réponses
3. payants
4. n'étaient que des publicités-leurres
5. faire sans l'univers numérique
6. le composa sur
7. cher monsieur
8. nous survivra
9. lueur
10. persévéra
11. c'est à quel sujet
12. vient de décéder

search engine[1] on his laptop. He got several hits[2] on pay-to-enter[3] search sites but he knew most of these were bait-and-switch jobs[4]. There was an Abigail Turnbull on LinkedIn, the business-oriented social-networking site, but Bosch doubted it was the octogenarian he was looking for. Finally he decided to put the digital world aside[5] and try what his daughter called social engineering. He pulled up the website for St. Helen's, got the phone number, and punched it into[6] his phone. A woman answered after three rings.

"St. Helen's, how can we help you?"

"Uh, yes, hello," Bosch started, hoping to sound like a nervous caller. "Can I please speak to Abigail Turnbull? I mean, if she's still there."

"Oh, honey[7], she hasn't been here in years."

"Oh, no! I mean, is she—do you know if she is still alive? I know she must be very old now."

"I believe she is still with us. She retired a long time ago, but she didn't die. I think Abby will outlive us[8] all."

Bosch felt a glimmer[9] of hope that he would be able to find her. He pressed on[10].

"I saw her at the anniversary party. My mother and I spoke to her then."

"That was eight years ago. Who, may I ask, is calling, and what is this regarding[11]?"

"Uh, my name is Dale. I was born at St. Helen's. My mother always spoke of Abigail Turnbull as being such a friend and taking such good care of her during her time there. Like I said, I got to finally meet her when we went back for the anniversary."

"How can I help you, Dale?"

"Well, it's sad, actually. My mother just passed[12] and she had a message she wanted me to give to

Abigail. I also wanted to tell her when the services[1] were in case she wanted to attend. I have a card. Do you know what would be the best way for me to get it to her?"

"You could send it here addressed to her in care of St. Helen's. We'll make sure she gets it."

"Yes, I know I could do that but I'm afraid it might take too long. You know, going through a third party[2]. She might not get it until after the services this Sunday."

There was a pause, and then:

"Hold on and let me[3] see what we can do."

The connection went silent and Bosch waited. He thought he had played it just about right. Two minutes later the voice came back on the line.

"Hello?"

"Yes, I'm still here."

"Okay, we don't normally do this but I have an address here that you can use to mail[4] a card to Abigail. I can't give out her phone number without her permission and I just tried[5] and couldn't reach her[6]."

"The address will be fine, then. If I put it in the mail[7] today, she should get it in time."

The woman proceeded to give[8] Bosch an address on Vineland Boulevard in Studio City. He wrote it down, thanked her, and quickly got off the phone.

Bosch looked at the address. It would be a quick drive from his house down into the Valley and Studio City. The address included a unit number[9], which made him think it could be a retirement home[10], considering Turnbull's age. There might be real security involved[11] beyond the usual gates and buttons found at every apartment complex in the city.

1. funérailles

2. le fait de passer par une tierce personne

3. Ne quittez pas, je vais

4. poster

5. je viens d'essayer

6. mais je ne l'ai pas eue

7. au courrier

8. donna alors à

9. numéro de bâtiment

10. maison de retraite

11. un vrai dispositif de sécurité

Bosch grabbed a rubber band[1] out of a kitchen drawer and stretched it around the stack of birth certificates. He wanted to take them with him, just in case. He grabbed his keys and was heading toward the side door when there was a hard knock at the front of the house[2]. Changing course[3], he went to the front door.

The unnamed security man[4] who had escorted Bosch through the Vance house the day before was standing on the front step.

"Mr. Bosch, I'm glad I caught you," he said.

His eyes fell on the banded stack of birth certificates and Bosch reflexively[5] dropped the hand that held them down and behind his left thigh[6]. Annoyed that he had made such an obvious move to hide them, he spoke abruptly.

"What can I do for you?" he said. "I'm on my way out."

"Mr. Vance sent me," the man said. "He wanted to know if you have made any progress."

Bosch looked at him for a long moment.

"What's your name?" he finally asked. "You never said it yesterday."

"Sloan. I'm in charge of security at the Pasadena estate."

"How did you find out where I live?"

"I looked it up[7]."

"Looked it up where? I'm not listed anywhere and the deed[8] to this house isn't in my name."

"We have ways of finding people, Mr. Bosch."

Bosch looked at him for a long moment before responding.

"Well, Sloan, Mr. Vance told me to talk only to him about what I was doing. So if you'll[9] excuse me."

1. élastique
2. lorsqu'il entendit frapper brusquement à la porte
3. de direction
4. L'agent de sécurité au nom inconnu
5. instinctivement
6. cuisse
7. J'ai cherché
8. l'acte de vente
9. vous voulez bien

Bosch started to close the door and Sloan immediately put his hand out and stopped it.

"You really don't want[1] to do that," Bosch said.

Sloan backed off[2] and held his hands up.

"I apologize," he said. "But I must tell you, Mr. Vance took ill[3] yesterday after speaking with you. He sent me this morning to ask you if you've made any headway[4]."

"Headway with what?" Bosch asked.

"With the job you were hired to do."

Bosch held up a finger.

"Can you wait here one minute?" he asked.

He didn't wait for an answer. He closed the door and put the stack of birth certificates under his arm. He went to the dining room table, where he had left the business card with the direct number to Vance printed on it. He punched in the number on his phone and then went back to the front door, opening it while listening to his call ringing.

"Who are you calling?" Sloan asked.

"Your boss," Bosch said. "Just want to make sure he's okay with our discussing the case."

"He won't answer."

"Yeah, well, we'll just—"

The call clicked over to[5] a long beep without an outgoing message[6] from Vance.

"Mr. Vance, this is Harry Bosch. Please call me back."

Bosch recited his number, disconnected[7], and then spoke to Sloan.

"You know what I don't get[8]? I don't get Vance sending you here to ask that question without first telling you what the job is he hired me to do."

"I told you, he has taken ill."

"Yeah, well, then I'll wait until he's better. Tell him to call me then."

1. Je ne vous conseille pas
2. recula
3. s'est trouvé mal
4. avancé
5. La sonnerie fut suivie d'
6. message personnalisé
7. raccrocha
8. je pige pas

Bosch read the look of hesitation on Sloan's face. There was something else. He waited and Sloan finally delivered[1].

"Mr. Vance also has reason to believe the phone number he gave you has been compromised[2]. He wants you to report through me[3]. I've been in charge of his personal security for twenty-five years."

"Yeah, well, he'll have to tell me that himself. When he gets better, you let me know and I'll come back out there to the palace."

Bosch swung the door closed[4] and it caught Sloan by surprise. It banged loudly in its frame[5]. Sloan knocked on it again but by then Bosch was quietly opening the side door to the carport[6]. He exited the house, then stealthily[7] opened the door of his Cherokee and got in. The moment the engine turned over he dropped the vehicle into reverse[8] and backed out quickly into the road. He saw a copper-colored sedan[9] parked pointing downhill[10] across the street. Sloan was walking toward it. Bosch turned the wheel[11] and backed out to his right[12], then gunned the Cherokee uphill[13], speeding by Sloan at the door to his car. He knew Sloan would have to use the carport to turn around in the narrow street, a maneuver that would give Bosch enough time to lose him.

After twenty-five years of living there, taking the curves[14] of Woodrow Wilson Drive came as second nature to Bosch. He quickly arrived at the stop sign at Mulholland Drive and banged a hard right[15] without pausing. He then followed the asphalt snake along the mountain ridgeline[16] until he reached Wrightwood Drive. He checked his mirrors and saw no sign of Sloan or any other follow car[17]. He took the sharp right[18] onto Wrightwood and quickly descended the northern slope

1. finit par lâcher le morceau
2. n'est plus fiable
3. que vous passiez par moi
4. claqua la porte
5. claqua violemment contre le chambranle
6. donnant sur l'allée du garage
7. furtivement
8. passa en marche arrière
9. berline cuivrée
10. dans le sens de la descente
11. volant
12. recula vers la droite
13. accéléra pour monter la côte
14. tournants
15. vira à droite
16. crête
17. voiture susceptible de le suivre
18. à droite toute

into Studio City, hitting the Valley floor[1] at Ventura Boulevard.

A few minutes later he was on Vineland, parked against the curb in front of an apartment complex[2] called the Sierra Winds. It was built next to the 101 freeway overpass[3] and looked old and worn[4]. There was a twenty-foot concrete sound-barrier wall[5] running along the curve of the freeway but Bosch imagined that the sound of traffic still swept across[6] the sprawling two-story[7] complex like a sierra wind.

The important thing was that Abigail Turnbull was not living in a retirement center after all. Bosch would have no trouble getting to her door and that was a good break[8].

1. pour atteindre le fond de la vallée

2. résidence

3. pont autoroutier

4. décrépit

5. mur de béton antibruit haut de 6 m

6. balayait tout de même

7. à un étage [USA]

8. appréciable

10

Bosch loitered[1] near the gated entrance[2] to the apartment complex and acted like he was[3] on a phone call[4], when all he was really doing was replaying a year-old message his daughter had left him after she had accepted admission to Chapman University.

"Dad, it's a really exciting day for me and I want to thank you for all your help in getting me to this point. And I am so glad I won't be too far away from you and that whenever we need each other we will only be an hour away. Okay, well, maybe two because of traffic."

He smiled. He didn't know how long messages would be retained on his phone but he hoped he would always be able to listen to the pure joy he heard in his daughter's voice.

He saw a man approaching the gate from the other side and timed[5] his approach to reach it at the same time. He acted like he was trying to carry on[6] a phone conversation while digging[7] his key to the gate out of his pocket.

"That's great," he said into the phone. "I feel the same way about it too."

The man on the other side pushed open the gate to exit. Bosch mumbled a thank you and entered. He preserved[8] the message from his daughter one more time and put his phone away.

Signs[9] along the stone pathway directed him to the building he was looking for and he found

1. traîna
2. grille d'entrée
3. fit semblant d'être
4. en train de téléphoner
5. minuta
6. poursuivre
7. tout en cherchant
8. sauvegarda
9. Des panneaux

Abigail Turnbull's apartment on the first floor. As he approached he saw that the front door was open behind a screen door[1]. He heard a voice from within the apartment.

"All done[2], Abigail?"

He stepped closer[3] without knocking and looked through the screen. He could see down a short hallway into a living room, where an old woman was sitting on a couch[4] with a folding[5] table in front of her. She looked old and frail and had on thick glasses and an obvious wig[6] of brown hair. Another woman, much younger, was clearing[7] a dish off the table and gathering silverware[8]. The woman Bosch assumed was Abigail was just finishing a late breakfast or early lunch.

Bosch decided to wait to see if the caregiver[9] would be leaving after cleaning up. The apartment fronted[10] a small courtyard where the water tumbling down a[11] three-level fountain masked most of the freeway noise. It was most likely the reason Turnbull was able to leave her door open. Bosch took a seat on a precast concrete bench[12] in front of the fountain and put the stack of birth certificates down next to him. He checked his phone for messages while he waited. No more than five minutes later he heard the voice from the apartment again.

"You want the door left open, Abigail?"

Bosch heard a muffled reply[13] and watched as the caregiver stepped out of the apartment, carrying an insulated[14] bag for transporting meals. Bosch recognized it as belonging to a charitable meal delivery service[15] for shut-ins[16] that his daughter had volunteered for[17] while she was a senior in high school[18]. He realized that she might have delivered meals to Abigail Turnbull.

1. porte grillagée

2. Vous avez fini

3. s'approcha

4. canapé

5. pliante

6. perruque

7. débarrassait

8. prenait les couverts

9. l'aide ménagère

10. donnait sur

11. qui se déversait d'une

12. banc en béton préfabriqué

13. réponse étouffée

14. isotherme

15. service caritatif de livraison de repas

16. les personnes incapables de se déplacer

17. pour laquelle sa fille avait travaillé comme bénévole

18. en terminale

The woman followed the path toward the front gate. Bosch waited a moment and then approached the screen door and looked in. Abigail Turnbull was still seated on the couch. The folding table was gone and in its place in front of her was a walker[1] with two wheels. She was staring across the room at something Bosch could not see but he thought he could hear the low murmur of a television.

"Ms. Turnbull?"

He said it loudly in case she had hearing loss[2]. But his voice startled her[3] and she looked fearfully toward the screen door.

"I'm sorry," Bosch said quickly. "I didn't mean to startle you. I'm wondering if I could ask you a few questions."

She looked around her as if to see if she had anyone with her as backup if needed[4].

"What do you want?" she said.

"I'm a detective," Bosch said. "I want to ask you about a case I'm working on."

"I don't understand. I don't know any detectives."

Bosch tried the screen door. It was unlocked. He opened it halfway so that she could see him better. He held his SFPD badge up and smiled.

"I'm working on an investigation and I think you could help me, Abigail," he said.

The woman who had delivered her meal had called her by her full first name[5]. He thought he would try. Turnbull didn't reply but Bosch could see her hands ball[6] into nervous fists.

"Do you mind if I come in?" he said. "This will only take a few minutes."

"I don't have[7] visitors," she said. "I don't have any money to buy anything."

1. déambulateur
2. des problèmes d'audition
3. la fit sursauter
4. qui pourrait l'aider en cas de besoin
5. prénom
6. se serrer
7. ne reçois pas de

Bosch slowly entered the hallway. He kept the smile on his face even though he felt bad[1] about scaring the old woman.

"I'm not trying to sell you anything, Abigail. I promise."

He stepped down the hallway and into the small living room. The TV was on and Ellen DeGeneres was on the screen. There was only the couch and a kitchen chair set in the corner of the room. Behind it there was a small kitchenette with a half-size refrigerator. He put the birth certificates under one arm and pulled his SFPD ID[2] out of his badge wallet[3]. She reluctantly took it from him and studied it.

"San Fernando?" she said. "Where is that?"

"Not too far," he said. "I—"

"What are you investigating?"

"I'm looking for someone from a long time ago."

"I don't understand why you want to talk to me. I've never been to San Fernando."

Bosch pointed to the chair against the wall.

"Do you mind if I sit down?"

"Go ahead. I still don't know what you want with me."

Bosch pulled the chair over and sat down in front of her, her walker between them. She wore a loose-fitting housedress[4] with a faded pattern of flowers[5] on it. She was still looking at his ID card.

"How do you say this name?" she asked.

"Hieronymus," Bosch said. "I was named after a painter."

"I've never heard of him."

"You're not alone[6]. I read the article that was in the paper a few years ago about St. Helen's. It had the story you told at the anniversary party. About your daughter coming there for answers and finding you."

1. coupable
2. carte
3. porte-badge
4. robe d'intérieur large
5. motif floral un peu passé
6. la seule

1. Et alors

"What about it[1]?"

"I'm working for a man—a very old man—who is looking for answers. His child was born at St. Helen's and I'm hoping you could help me find him or her."

2. comme pour s'écarter

She leaned back as if to remove herself[2] from the discussion and shook her head.

"So many children were born there," she said. "And I was there for fifty years. I can't remember all of the babies. Most of them got new names when they left."

Bosch nodded.

3. Ça remonte à

"I know. But this I think was a special case. I think you'd remember the mother. Her name was Vibiana. Vibiana Duarte. I'm talking about[3] the year after you got to St. Helen's."

4. se défendre d'une

Turnbull closed her eyes as if to ward off a[4] great pain. Bosch knew instantly that she knew and remembered Vibiana, that his journey back through time had found a destination.

"You remember her, don't you?" he said.

Turnbull nodded once.

"I was there," she said. "It was an awful day."

"Can you tell me about it?"

"Why? It's a long time ago."

Bosch nodded. It was a valid question.

"Remember when your daughter came to St. Helen's and found you? You called it a miracle. It's like that. I'm working for a man who wants to find his child, the child he had with Vibiana."

5. lui monter au visage

Bosch could see the anger work into her face[5] and immediately regretted his choice of words.

6. d'abandonner

"It's not the same," she said. "He wasn't forced to give up[6] his baby. He abandoned Vibby and he abandoned his son."

Bosch quickly tried to repair the damage, but he noted that she had said the child was a boy.

"I know that, Abigail," he said. "Not the same at all. I know that. But it's a parent who is looking for his child. He's old and he's going to die soon. He has a lot to pass on[1]. It won't make up for things[2]. Of course not. But is that our call or the son's call to make[3]? Do we not even allow the son to make that choice?"

She remained quiet while considering Bosch's words.

"I can't help you," she finally said. "I have no idea what happened to that boy after the day they took him."

"Just, if you can, tell me what you do know," Bosch said. "I know it's an awful story, but tell me what happened. If you can. And tell me about Vibby's son."

Turnbull cast[4] her eyes down toward the floor. Bosch knew she was seeing the memory and that she was going to tell the story. She reached out both hands and gripped her walker as if reaching for support[5].

"He was frail[6], that one," she began. "Born underweight[7]. We had a rule, no baby could go home until it weighed at least five pounds[8]."

"What happened?" Bosch asked.

"Well, the couple that was there to take him couldn't. Not like that. He needed to be healthier and heavier."

"So the adoption was delayed[9]?"

"Sometimes it happened like that. Delayed. They told Vibby she had to get weight on him[10]. She had to keep him in her room and feed him with her milk. Feed him all the time to get him healthy and get his weight up.

"How long did that last?"

1. transmettre
2. Ça ne compense rien
3. est-ce à nous ou à son fils de juger
4. baissa
5. comme pour chercher un soutien
6. n'était pas bien costaud
7. Poids insuffisant à la naissance
8. s'il ne pesait pas au moins 2,2 kg
9. retardée
10. lui faire prendre du poids

"A week. Maybe longer. All I know is that Vibby got that time with her baby that nobody else ever got with theirs. That I never got. And then after that week it was time for the switch[1]. The couple came back and the adoption proceeded. They took Vibby's baby."

Bosch glumly[2] nodded. The story got worse from every angle.

"What happened to Vibby?" he asked.

"My job back then was in the laundry[3]," she said. "There wasn't a lot of money. There were no dryers[4]. We hung everything on the clotheslines in the field behind the kitchen. Before they built the addition[5] there.

"Anyway, the morning after the adoption, I took sheets out to hang and I saw that one of the clotheslines was missing."

"Vibiana."

"And then I heard. One of the girls told me. Vibby had hanged herself. She had gone into the bathroom and tied the rope to one of the shower pipes[6]. They found her in there but it was too late. She was dead."

Turnbull looked down. It was as if she didn't want to make eye contact with[7] Bosch over such a horrible story.

Bosch was repelled[8] by the tale. It sickened him[9]. But he needed more. He needed to find Vibiana's son.

"So that was it[10]?" he asked. "The boy was taken and never came back?"

"Once they were gone, they were gone."

"You remember his name? The name of the couple who adopted him?"

"Vibby called him Dominick. I don't know if that name stayed with him[11]. They usually didn't.

1. de donner l'enfant
2. tristement
3. buanderie
4. de sèche-linge
5. l'annexe
6. tuyaux
7. croiser le regard de
8. horrifié
9. Ça l'écœurait
10. c'est tout
11. lui est resté

I called my daughter Sarah. When she came back to me her name was Kathleen."

Bosch pulled up the stack of birth certificates. He was sure he remembered seeing the name Dominick when he had gone through the documents that morning on the back deck. He started quickly moving through the stack again, looking for the name. When he found it, he studied the full name and date. Dominick Santanello was born on January 31, 1951. But his birth wasn't registered with the recorder's office[1] until fifteen days later. He knew the delay was probably caused by the baby's weight postponing the adoption[2].

He showed the sheet to Turnbull.

"Is this him?" he asked. "Dominick Santanello?"

"I told you," Turnbull said. "I only know what she called him."

"It's the only birth certificate with Dominick on it from that time period. It's got to be him. It's listed as a home birth, which was how they did it back then."

"Then I guess you found who you're looking for."

Bosch glanced at the birth certificate. In the boxes[3] denoting the race[4] of the child, "Hisp." was checked[5]. The Santanello family's address was in Oxnard in Ventura County. Luca and Audrey Santanello, both of them twenty-six years old. Luca Santanello's occupation was listed as appliance salesman[6].

Bosch noticed that Abigail Turnbull's hands tightly gripped the aluminum tubes of her walker. Thanks to her, Bosch believed he had found Whitney Vance's long missing child, but the price had been high. Bosch knew he would carry the story of Vibiana Duarte with him for a long time.

1. portée à l'état civil

2. dû à l'adoption, elle-même repoussée en raison du poids du bébé

3. cases

4. l'origine ethnique

5. coché

6. vendeur d'appareils électroménagers

11

Bosch drove west from the Sierra Winds until he hit[1] Laurel Canyon Boulevard and then pointed the car north. It might have been quicker to jump on a freeway but Bosch wanted to take his time and think about the story Abigail Turnbull had told him. He needed to grab[2] something to eat as well and went through an In-N-Out drive-thru[3].

After eating in his car on the side of the road, he pulled out his phone and hit redial on[4] the last number he had called—the number Whitney Vance had given him. Once again the call went unanswered[5] and he left a message.

"Mr. Vance, Harry Bosch again. I need you to call me back. I believe I have the information you've been looking for."

He disconnected, put the phone in the center console's cup holder[6], and pulled back into traffic.

It took him another twenty minutes to finish crossing the Valley south to north on Laurel Canyon. At Maclay he turned right and drove into San Fernando. Once again the detective bureau was empty when he entered, and he went directly to his cubicle[7].

The first thing he checked for was e-mail to his SFPD account. He had two new messages and he could tell from the subject line that they were both returns on his inquiries regarding[8] the Screen Cutter case. The first was from a detective in the LAPD's West Valley Division.

1. jusqu'au
2. de se prendre
3. passa par un fastfood In-N-Out [avec service « drive-in »]
4. rappela
5. personne ne répondit
6. porte-gobelet de l'appui central
7. box
8. concernant

Dear Harry Bosch, if you are the former[1] LAPD detective of the same name who sued[2] the department he served for 30-plus years[3] then I hope you get ass cancer real soon[4] and die a slow and painful death. If you are not him, then my bad[5]. Have a good day.

Bosch read the message twice and felt his blood get hot[6]. It was not because of the sentiment expressed. He didn't care about that. He hit the reply button on the e-mail and quickly typed in a response.

Detective Mattson, I am glad to know the investigators in West Valley Division carry on with[7] the level of professionalism the citizens of Los Angeles have come to expect. Choosing to insult the requestor of information rather than consider the request shows immense dedication[8] to the department's mandate[9] to Serve and Protect[10]. Thanks to you I know that the sexual predators in the West Valley live in fear.

Bosch was about to hit the send button, when he thought better of it[11] and deleted[12] the message. He tried to put his upset[13] aside. At least Mattson wasn't a detective working in either the LAPD's Mission or Foothill Division, where he felt sure the Screen Cutter must have been active.

He moved on and opened up the second e-mail. It was from a detective in Glendale. It was just an acknowledgment[14] that Bosch's request for information had been received and passed to him for action. The detective said he would ask around his department and get back to[15] Bosch as soon as possible.

1. ancien
2. a intenté un procès contre
3. pendant plus de 30 ans
4. que vous allez bientôt vous choper un cancer du fion
5. autant pour moi
6. se mit à bouillir
7. continuent de montrer
8. un dévouement
9. obligation
10. [devise du LAPD]
11. se ravisa
12. supprima
13. rage
14. la confirmation
15. reviendrait vers

Bosch had received several similar e-mails in response to his blind inquiries[1]. Luckily, only a few like Mattson's had come in. Most detectives he had contacted were professional and, while overrun with[2] cases and work, they promised to get to Bosch's request quickly.

He closed down the e-mail page and went to the department's DMV portal. It was time to find Dominick Santanello. As he logged in[3] Bosch did the math[4] on the birth date in his head. Santanello would be sixty-five years old now. Maybe newly retired, maybe living on a pension[5], with no idea that he was heir to a fortune. Bosch wondered if he had ever left his adoptive hometown of Oxnard. Did he know that he was adopted and that his mother's life had ended as his[6] began?

Bosch typed in the name and birth date from the birth certificate, and the database quickly kicked back a match[7], but it was a very short entry. It showed that Dominick Santanello had received a California driver's license on January 31, 1967, the day he turned sixteen[8] and was eligible[9] to drive. But the license had never been renewed or surrendered. The last entry in the record simply said *Deceased*.

Bosch leaned back in his seat, feeling as though he had been kicked in the gut[10]. He had been on the case less than thirty-six hours but he was invested[11]. Vibiana's story, Abigail's story, Vance's being unable to outrun the guilt of his actions[12] all these decades later. And now to come to this. According to the DMV, Vance's son died even before his first driver's license had expired.

"Harry, you all right?"

Bosch looked left and saw that Bella Lourdes had entered the bureau and was heading to her cubicle across the partition wall from his[13].

1. demandes de renseignements lancées à l'aveuglette
2. bien que surchargés d'
3. se connectait
4. calcul
5. de sa retraite
6. alors que la sienne
7. donna un résultat
8. de ses 16 ans
9. avait donc le droit
10. reçu un coup de poing dans le ventre
11. se sentait impliqué
12. surmonter sa culpabilité
13. de l'autre côté de la cloison

"I'm fine," Bosch said. "Just ... just another dead end[1]."

"I know the feeling," Lourdes said.

She sat down and dropped from his sight[2]. She was no more than five two[3] and the partition made her disappear. Bosch just stared at his computer screen. There were no details about Santanello's death, only that it occurred during the licensing period[4]. Bosch had gotten his first California license the year before Santanello, in 1966. He was pretty sure that back then the license period was four years before renewal[5]. It meant Santanello had died between the ages of sixteen and twenty.

He knew that when he reported[6] the death of his client's son, he would have to provide Vance with full and convincing details. He also knew that back in the late 1960s, most teenagers who died were killed in car accidents or in the war. He leaned back toward the computer terminal, brought up[7] the search page, and typed in *Search the Wall*. This led him to links to a number of websites associated with the Vietnam Veterans Memorial in Washington, D.C., where the names of every one of the fifty-eight-thousand-plus[8] soldiers killed during the war were etched[9] on a black granite wall.

Bosch chose the site operated[10] by the Vietnam Veterans Memorial Fund because he had been to the site before both as a donor[11] and to look up the details of men he had served with and knew hadn't made it back home[12]. He now typed in the name *Dominick Santanello* and his hunch[13] became reality as a page opened with a photo of the soldier and the details of his service.

Before reading anything, Bosch stared at the image. Until this point, there had been no photos of any of the principals[14] of the investigation. He

1. encore une impasse
2. disparut de son champ de vision
3. faisait à peine 1,60 m
4. période de validité de son permis
5. obligation de renouvellement
6. signalerait
7. revint sur
8. des plus de 58 000
9. gravés
10. géré
11. donateur
12. dont il savait qu'ils n'étaient jamais rentrés
13. intuition
14. protagonistes

had only conjured[1] images of Vibiana and Dominick. But there on the screen was the black-and-white portrait of Santanello in suit and tie and smiling at the camera. Maybe it was a high school yearbook[2] picture or a shot[3] taken during his military induction[4]. The young man had dark hair and even darker piercing eyes. Even in the black-and-white photo it was clear to Bosch that he was a mixture of Caucasian and Latino genes. Bosch studied the eyes and thought it was there that he saw the resemblance to Whitney Vance. Bosch was instinctively sure that he was looking at the old man's son.

The page dedicated to Santanello listed the panel and line number[5] where his name was etched on the Vietnam Memorial. It also carried[6] the basic details of his service and casualty[7]. Bosch wrote these down in his notebook. Santanello was listed as a Navy corpsman[8]. His date of enlistment[9] was June 1, 1969, just four months after he turned eighteen years old. His date of casualty was December 9, 1970, in the Tay Ninh Province. His assigned base at the time of his casualty was the First Medical Battalion, Da Nang. Location of final interment[10] was listed as the Los Angeles National Cemetery.

Bosch had served with the U.S. Army in Vietnam as a tunnel engineer, more commonly referred to as a tunnel rat. The specialty assignment[11] put him on callouts to[12] many of the different provinces and combat zones where enemy tunnel networks had been discovered and needed to be cleared[13]. It also put him to work with soldiers from all branches of service[14]: Air Force, Navy, Marines. It gave him a rudimentary overview[15] and knowledge[16] of the war effort that allowed him to

1. n'avait fait que se représenter
2. album de promo
3. photo
4. incorporation
5. panneau et le numéro de la ligne
6. comportait
7. de sa mort
8. infirmier de la Marine
9. engagement
10. Son lieu d'inhumation
11. Cette affectation spécialisée
12. l'avait fait se déplacer dans
13. nettoyés
14. les corps de l'armée
15. aperçu
16. connaissance

interpret the basic details supplied on the memorial site about Dominick Santanello.

Bosch knew that Navy corpsmen were the medics that backed[1] the Marines. Every Marine recon unit[2] had an attached corpsman. Though Santanello's assignment was to First Med[3], Da Nang, his death in the Tay Ninh Province, which ran along the Cambodian border, told[4] Bosch that Santanello was on a recon[5] mission when he was killed.

The memorial site[6] was set up to[7] list soldiers by date of casualty because the memorial itself listed the names of the dead on the wall in the chronological order of their deaths. This meant that Bosch could click on the right and left arrows[8] on his screen and see the names and details of the soldiers who were killed on the same day as Santanello. He did this now and determined[9] that there were a total of eight men killed in the Tay Ninh Province on December 9, 1970.

The war killed young men by the dozens[10] almost every day but Bosch thought that eight men dead in the same province on the same day was unusual. It had to have been an ambush[11] or a friendly-fire bomb drop[12]. He studied the soldiers' ranks and assignments[13] and identified them all as Marines, with two of them being pilots and one being a door gunner[14].

This was a revelation. Bosch knew that door gunners flew on slicks[15]—the transport helicopters that carried soldiers in and out of the bush. He now realized that Dominick Santanello had gone down[16] in a helicopter. He had been killed in an aircraft that his unknown father had probably helped manufacture. The cruel irony of it was stunning to Bosch[17]. He wasn't sure how he would break[18] that kind of news to Whitney Vance.

"You sure you're okay?"

1. service médical chez

2. unité de reconnaissance

3. Même si Santanello était affecté au 1er bataillon médical

4. révélait à

5. de reconnaissance

6. site Internet dédié au mémorial

7. configuré de façon à

8. flèches

9. Ce faisant, il put déterminer

10. dizaines

11. embuscade

12. bombe issue d'un tir ami

13. grades et affectations

14. mitrailleur côté porte

15. opéraient sur les « slicks » [à fuselage léger]

16. était mort

17. frappa Bosch de plein fouet

18. annoncerait

Bosch looked up and saw Lourdes looking over the separation wall into his cubicle. Her eyes were on the stack of birth certificates Bosch had put down on his desk.

"Uh, yeah, I'm fine," he said quickly. "What's up[1]?"

He tried to put his arm down casually[2] on top of the stack but the move came off as awkward[3] and he could see her register it[4].

"I got an e-mail from a friend that works sex-bats[5] at Foothill," Lourdes said. "She said she's found a case that might be related to our guy. No screen cutting but other aspects match up[6]."

Bosch felt the dread[7] rise in his chest.

"Is it a fresh[8] case?" he asked.

"No, it's old. She was backtracking in her spare time for us[9] and came up with it[10]. It could've been our guy before he started cutting screens."

"Maybe."

"You want to go with me?"

"Uh ..."

"No, it's okay, I'll go. You look like you're busy."

"I could go but if you can handle it[11] ..."

"Of course. I'll call you if it's anything to get excited about."

Lourdes left the office and Bosch went back to work. To keep his notes complete he went screen by screen and wrote down the names and details of all the men killed during the mission in Tay Ninh. In doing so he realized that only one of the men was assigned as a door gunner. Bosch knew there were always two on every slick—two sides, two doors, two door gunners. It meant that whether[12] the Tay Ninh slick had been shot down[13] or simply crashed[14], there might have been a survivor.

Before leaving the site, Bosch went back to the page dedicated to Dominick Santanello. He

1. Quoi de neuf
2. d'un air détaché
3. son geste manqua de naturel
4. vit qu'elle l'avait remarqué
5. s'occupe des agressions sexuelles
6. coïncident
7. l'appréhension
8. nouveau
9. faisait des recherches pour nous pendant son temps libre
10. elle est tombée dessus
11. t'en occuper
12. Donc, que
13. ait été abattu
14. se soit simplement écrasé au sol

clicked on a button marked *Remembrances*[1] and was taken to a page where people had left messages honoring Santanello's service and sacrifice. Bosch scrolled through these[2] without reading them and judged[3] that there were about forty messages left over a period beginning in 1999, when, Bosch presumed, the site was established. He started reading them now in the order in which they were left, beginning with a message from someone who stated that he was a classmate[4] of Dominick's at Oxnard High[5] and would always remember him for his sacrifice in a land so far away.

Some of the remembrances were from total strangers who simply wished to honor the fallen soldier and had apparently come across his entry[6] randomly[7]. But others, like the high school classmate, clearly had known him. One of these was a man named Bill Bisinger who identified himself as a former Navy corpsman. He had trained[8] with Santanello in San Diego before they were both shipped out[9] to Vietnam in late 1969 and assigned to medical duties on the hospital ship[10] *Sanctuary*, anchored on the South China Sea.

This bit of information made Bosch pause[11]. He had been on the *Sanctuary* in late 1969 after being wounded[12] in a tunnel in Cu Chi. He realized that he and Santanello had probably been on the ship at the same time.

Bisinger's remembrance gave some clarity to what had happened to Santanello. The fact that it was written as if directly to Dominick made it all the more haunting[13].

Nicky, I remember being at chow[14] *on Sanctuary when I heard about you getting shot down. The gunner that got burned up*[15] *but survived had come to us so we knew*[16] *the story. I felt so*

1. *Souvenirs*
2. les fit défiler
3. estima
4. camarade de classe
5. lycée d'Oxnard
6. tombés sur son nom
7. au hasard
8. été formé
9. envoyés par bateau
10. navire-hôpital
11. interpella Bosch
12. avoir été blessé
13. d'autant plus poignant
14. que je cassais la croûte
15. qui a brûlé
16. donc on a su

bad. For anybody to die in a place so far from home and for something that didn't seem to mean so much anymore. I remember begging you[1] *not to go out there to First Med. I begged you. I said don't get off the boat, man. But you didn't listen. You had to get that CMB*[2] *and see the war. I'm so sorry, man. I feel like I let you down*[3] *because I couldn't stop you.*

1. t'avoir supplié
2. voulais avoir ton insigne
3. J'ai l'impression de t'avoir laissé tomber

Bosch knew that *CMB* meant combat medical badge. Below Bisinger's outpouring of feelings[4] was a comment from another site visitor, named Olivia Macdonald.

4. le message plein d'émotion

Don't feel so bad, Bill. We all knew Nick and how headstrong[5] *he was and how he wanted adventure. He joined up*[6] *for adventure. He picked*[7] *medic because he thought he could be in the middle of things, but*[8] *just help people and not have to kill anybody. That was his spirit and we should celebrate that, not second-guess*[9] *our actions.*

5. têtu
6. s'était engagé
7. avait choisi
8. mais aussi
9. et non pas revenir sur

The comment showed an intimate knowledge of Santanello that made Bosch think Olivia was a family member or maybe a former girlfriend. Bisinger had written a return comment[10], thanking Olivia for her understanding.

10. réponse

Bosch continued to scroll through the messages and saw that Olivia Macdonald had posted five more times over the years, always on November 11—Veterans Day. These posts were not as intimate and always along the lines of [11] "Gone but not forgotten."

11. dans l'esprit

There was a sign-up button[12] at the top of the remembrance page that allowed users to be alerted whenever a new message was posted to the

12. bouton « s'inscrire »

Santanello page. Bosch scrolled back down to the post from Bisinger and saw that Olivia Macdonald's comment had come only a day after his original post. Bisinger's thank-you to her came on the same day as her post.

The quickness of the responses indicated to Bosch that both Macdonald and Bisinger had signed up for the post alerts. He quickly opened a comment block[1] under Bisinger's thank-you and wrote a message to both of them. He didn't want to reveal exactly what he was doing in a public forum, no matter how infrequently the Dominick Santanello remembrance page was visited. He crafted[2] a message that he hoped would draw[3] at least one of them into making contact.

Olivia and Bill, I am a Vietnam Vet[4]. I was wounded in 1969 and treated on the Sanctuary. I want to talk to you about Nick. I have information.

Bosch put both his personal e-mail and cell phone number on the message and then posted it. He hoped he would hear back[5] from one of them soon.

Bosch printed out[6] the screen that had Dominick Santanello's photo and then logged off the computer[7]. He closed his notebook and put it in his pocket. He picked up the stack of birth certificates and left the cubicle, taking the copy of the photo out of the communal printer tray[8] as he left the office.

1. champ commentaire
2. concocta
3. inciterait
4. [veteran]
5. recevoir une réponse
6. fit une impression de
7. ferma la session
8. l'imprimante commune

12

Back in his car Bosch sat still[1] for a moment and felt guilty about[2] not going to Foothill Division with Bella Lourdes to talk to the detective handling sexual batteries[3]. He was putting[4] his private investigation in front of[5] his work for the town and it was the Screen Cutter case that was more pressing. He thought about calling Lourdes and saying he was on his way[6], but the truth was, Lourdes could handle it. She was going to another police station to confer[7] with another detective. It wasn't a two-person job. Instead he pulled out of the[8] parking lot and started to cruise[9].

In the course of the investigation Bosch had been to each of the residences where the Screen Cutter had attacked women. These visits came as each case was linked to a serial rapist. None of the victims still lived in the homes, and access to them was difficult to arrange and brief[10]. In one case the victim agreed to return to the premises[11] with the detectives to walk them through the logistics of[12] the crime.

Now for the first time Bosch cruised by[13] each of the homes in the chronological order of the assaults. He wasn't really sure what he might gain from this but he knew it would help keep the investigation churning[14] in his mind. That was important. He didn't want the Vance investigation to crowd out his resolve[15] to find the Screen Cutter.

1. resta sans bouger
2. coupable de
3. agressions
4. faisait passer
5. avant
6. qu'il arrivait
7. s'entretenir
8. sortit du
9. prit la route
10. à bien organiser
11. sur les lieux
12. leur montrer comment s'était déroulé
13. passa devant
14. à maintenir l'enquête active
15. affecte sa détermination

It took him no more than fifteen minutes to make the circuit. At the last house he stopped at the curb in front, easily finding parking because it was a street-sweeping[1] day and one side of the street was clear. He reached[2] under the seat and pulled out the old Thomas Brothers map book[3]. San Fernando was small enough to fit on one page of the book. Bosch had previously charted[4] the locations of[5] the rapes on the page and now studied it once again.

There was no discernible pattern[6] to the locations[7]. Bosch and Lourdes had already exhaustively looked for commonalities[8]: repairmen, postal workers, meter readers[9], and so on[10] who might connect the victims or their addresses or neighborhoods. But the effort failed to pay off with a connection to[11] all four of the victims or their addresses.

Lourdes believed that each of the victims had somehow[12] come into visual contact with the rapist while away from her home and then was followed during the stalking phase of the crime. But Bosch was unconvinced. San Fernando was a tiny town. The idea that the rapist would lock on to[13] a potential victim in one location[14] and follow her to another stretched believability[15] when four out of four times[16] this protocol[17] led to an address in little San Fernando. Bosch believed the victims were somehow acquired[18] when the rapist saw them in or just outside their homes.

He turned and studied the front facade of the house where the Screen Cutter was last known to have attacked[19]. It was a small postwar house with a front porch and a single-car garage. The rapist had cut the screen on a rear window in an unused bedroom. Bosch could see there was perfect cover[20] from the street.

1. où la rue avait été balayée
2. mit le bras
3. guide routier
4. marqué
5. où avaient eu lieu
6. de logique visible
7. du point de vue géographique
8. cherché des points communs
9. releveurs de compteurs
10. etc.,
11. ne permit pas de faire de lien entre
12. d'une façon ou d'une autre
13. repère
14. à un endroit
15. paraissait peu crédible
16. dans les 4 cas,
17. hypothèse de travail
18. choisies
19. a pu sévir la dernière fois
20. qu'on ne pouvait rien voir

A shadow swooped by[1] his side window and Bosch turned to see a post office van coast up[2] to the curb in front of his car. The mailman[3] got out and headed toward the front door, where there was a mail slot[4]. He casually glanced[5] toward Bosch's car, recognized him behind the wheel, and held a middle finger up[6] his whole way to the door. His name was Mitchell Maron and he had briefly been a suspect in the rapes as well as the subject of a backfired[7] attempt to surreptitiously collect[8] his DNA.

It had occurred at the Starbucks on Truman[9] a month earlier. When Bosch and Lourdes found out that Maron delivered mail on a route[10] that included three of the four victims' homes, they decided the quickest way to identify or eliminate him as a suspect was to get his DNA and compare it to that from the rapist. They watched him for two days and, while he did nothing that engendered suspicion, he did stop on his morning breaks at the Starbucks, where he drank tea and ate a breakfast sandwich.

In a bit of improvising[11], Lourdes followed Maron into the coffee shop on the third day, purchased[12] an iced tea, and then sat at an outside table next to the mailman. When he was finished eating he wiped his[13] mouth with a napkin, stuffed it[14] into the empty paper bag his sandwich had come in, and tossed it[15] into a nearby trash can[16]. As he headed back to his mail van, Lourdes took a position[17] guarding the trash can from being used by other patrons[18]. When she saw Maron jump into the van, she removed the top of the trash can and looked down at the paper bag he had just discarded[19]. She put on latex gloves and pulled out a plastic evidence bag[20] to collect[21] the

1. Une ombre passa devant
2. s'avancer
3. facteur
4. la fente où glisser le courrier [passe-lettres]
5. regarda d'un œil distrait
6. lui fit un doigt d'honneur
7. ratée
8. recueillir subrepticement
9. de la rue Truman
10. selon un itinéraire
11. Improvisant
12. avait acheté
13. s'était essuyé la
14. qu'il avait fourrée
15. jetée
16. poubelle
17. se plaça de façon à
18. clients
19. jeté
20. sachet pour pièces à conviction
21. recueillir

possible DNA specimen. Bosch emerged from the follow car and pulled his phone so he could get a video of the collecting of the bag in case DNA from it was ever introduced in court[1]. The courts had upheld[2] the validity of surreptitious collection of DNA from public locations. He needed to document[3] where the specimen was collected as well.

The unforeseen[4] problem was that Maron had left his cell[5] phone on his table and realized it just as he was about to back out[6] of his parking spot. He jumped back out of his van and went to retrieve[7] the phone. Coming across Bosch and Lourdes collecting his discarded debris, he said, "What the fuck are you doing?"

At that point[8], knowing that Maron could flee[9], the detectives had to treat him as a suspect. They asked him to come to the station[10] to answer questions and he angrily agreed. During the ensuing[11] interview he denied any knowledge of the rapes. He acknowledged[12] knowing three of the victims by name but said that was because he delivered their mail.

While Bosch handled the interview, Lourdes was able to round up[13] the four known victims and get them to come in for audiovisual lineups[14]. Because the rapist had worn a mask during each assault, the detectives were hoping an identification might be made by one of the victims recognizing his voice, hands, or eyes.

Four hours after the incident at the coffee shop Maron voluntarily but sullenly[15] stood in a lineup that was viewed separately by all four women. He held his hands out and read sentences said by the rapist during the assaults. None of them identified him as their assailant.

Maron was released that day and his innocence confirmed a week later when DNA from the

1. était un jour utilisé lors d'un procès
2. confirmé
3. devait donner de quoi établir
4. imprévu
5. portable
6. ressortir
7. récupérer
8. Dès lors
9. s'enfuir
10. commissariat
11. qui s'ensuivit
12. reconnut
13. put réunir
14. séances d'identification
15. de mauvaise grâce

napkin he wiped his mouth with was deemed no match to[1] the DNA of the rapist. The chief of police sent him a letter apologizing for the incident and thanking him for his cooperation.

Now, after pushing the mail through the slot, Maron walked back toward his van and then made a sudden turn toward Bosch's car. Harry lowered[2] the window to accept the verbal confrontation.

"Hey, I want you to know, I hired a lawyer[3]," Maron said. "I'm going to sue all your asses[4] for false[5] arrest."

Bosch nodded like[6] the threat was just par for the course[7].

"I hope it's a contingency deal[8]," he said.

"What the hell are you talking about?" Maron said.

"I hope you're not paying your lawyer. Put it on contingency; that means he gets paid only if he wins. Because you aren't going to win, Mitchell. If he's telling you anything else, he's lying[9]."

"Bullshit[10]."

"You agreed to come in. There was no arrest. We even let you drive the mail van in so nothing would get stolen. You don't have a case[11] and the only one who will make book[12] are the lawyers. Think about that."

Maron leaned down and put his hand on the Jeep's windowsill[13].

"So I'm just supposed to let it go[14], then," he said. "I felt like I'm the one who got raped and it's just 'never mind'[15]."

"Not even close[16], Mitchell," Bosch said. "You say that to one of the real victims and they'd put you in your place. What you went through[17] was a shitty couple of hours[18]. There's no end to what they're going through[19]."

Maron slapped the sill and stood up straight.

1. jugé comme ne présentant aucune concordance avec
2. baissa
3. j'ai pris un avocat
4. tous vous foutre un procès aux fesses
5. arbitraire
6. comme si
7. faisait partie du jeu
8. que c'est avec convention d'honoraires [l'avocat ne touche des honoraires que si son client gagne son procès]
9. ment
10. C'est des conneries
11. d'arguments recevables
12. vont en profiter
13. appui de la vitre
14. laisser tomber
15. « c'est pas grave »
16. Absolument pas
17. Ce que vous avez subi,
18. c'est juste un sale moment
19. Elles, elles vivent un calvaire

"Fuck you!"

He stalked back[1] to his van and took off, the wheels screeching[2]. The effect was undercut[3] when sixty feet[4] later he had to hit the brakes[5] to make the delivery to the next house down.

Bosch's phone rang and he saw it was Lourdes.

"Bella."

"Harry, where are you?"

"Out and about[6]. How'd it go at Foothill?"

"A nonstarter[7]. The cases didn't match."

Bosch nodded.

"Oh, well. I just ran into[8] your boy Mitch Maron. He's still pissed at us[9]."

"At Starbucks?"

"No, I'm in front of Frida Lopez's old house. He just came by to deliver the mail and tell me what a shit I am. Says he's going to hire a lawyer."

"Yeah, good luck with that. What are you doing there?"

"Nothing. Just thinking. I guess hoping something would shake loose[10]. I think our guy—something tells me it won't be long before there's another."

"I know what you mean. That's why I was so hyped[11] about this Foothill thing. Damn it! Why are there no other cases out there?"

"That's the question."

Bosch heard the call-waiting click[12] on his phone. He checked the screen and saw that it was the number Whitney Vance had given him.

"Hey, I got a call," he said. "Let's talk tomorrow about next moves."

"You got it[13], Harry," Lourdes said.

Bosch switched over to the other call.

"Mr. Vance?"

There was no answer, only silence.

"Mr. Vance, are you there?" Silence.

1. retourna d'un pas raide
2. en faisant crisser les pneus
3. Cela eut moins d'impact
4. 20 m
5. piler
6. Je fais un tour
7. Échec
8. Je viens de croiser
9. nous en veut toujours à mort
10. J'attends le déclic, je suppose
11. excitée
12. tonalité d'appel en attente
13. Ça marche

Bosch pushed the phone hard against his ear and put the window back up[1]. He thought he might be able to hear breathing. He wondered if it was Vance and if he was unable to talk because of the health issue[2] Sloan had mentioned.

"Mr. Vance, is that you?"

Bosch waited but heard nothing and then the call was disconnected.

1. remonta sa vitre

2. problème de santé

13

Bosch made his way over to[1] the 405 freeway and headed south through the Valley and over the Sepulveda Pass[2]. It took him an hour to get down to LAX[3], where he slowly followed the loop[4] on the departures level and parked in the last garage. He grabbed a flashlight from the glove box and then got out and quickly moved around the car, crouching down[5] to point the light into the wheel wells[6] and under the bumpers[7] and the gas tank[8]. But he knew that if his car had been tagged with a GPS tracker[9], the likelihood of him finding it[10] would be very low. Advances[11] in tracking technology had made the devices smaller and easier to hide.

His plan was to go online[12] and buy a GPS jammer[13] but it would take a few days to get it. Meantime, he went into the car to return the flashlight to the glove box and gather[14] the birth certificates into a backpack[15] he kept on the floor. He then locked the car and took the pedestrian overpass[16] to the United Airlines terminal where he rode an escalator down to the arrivals level. Circling around a baggage carousel[17] that was surrounded by travelers fresh off a flight[18], he moved in and out of the crowd and went out the double doors to the pickup zone[19]. He crossed the pickup lanes[20] to the rental-car island and jumped on the first shuttle[21] he saw, a yellow bus destined for the Hertz rental counters on Airport Boulevard.

1. prit la direction de
2. col
3. l'aéroport de Los Angeles
4. bretelle
5. s'accroupissant
6. passages de roue
7. pare-chocs
8. réservoir
9. on avait collé sur sa voiture un mouchard GPS
10. probabilité qu'il le trouve
11. Les progrès
12. sur Internet
13. brouilleur
14. mettre
15. sac à dos
16. passerelle
17. tapis roulant à bagages
18. tout juste débarqués
19. voie des taxis
20. voies
21. navette

He asked the driver if they had cars available and the driver gave him the thumbs-up[1].

The Cherokee that Bosch left in the parking garage was twenty-two years old. At the Hertz counter he was offered the option of trying out a brand-new[2] Cherokee, and he took it despite the surcharge[3]. Ninety minutes after leaving San Fernando he was back on the 405, heading north in a car that could not have been tagged[4] by anyone hoping to follow him or keep GPS tabs on where he was going[5]. Just the same[6], he checked the mirrors repeatedly to be sure.

When he got up to Westwood he exited the freeway on Wilshire Boulevard and made his way into the Los Angeles National Cemetery. It was 114 acres[7] of graves containing soldiers from every war, every campaign, from the Civil War[8] to Afghanistan. Thousands of white marble stones in perfect rows standing as a testament to[9] the military precision and waste[10] of war.

Bosch had to use the *Find a Grave* screen in the Bob Hope Memorial Chapel to locate the spot where Dominick Santanello was buried on the North Campus. But soon he stood in front of it, looking down at the perfect green grass and listening to the constant hiss[11] of the nearby freeway as the sun turned the sky in the west pink[12]. Somehow[13], in little more than twenty-four hours, he had built a feeling of kinship[14] with this soldier he had never met or known. They had both been on that boat in the South China Sea. And there was the fact that Bosch alone knew the secret history and tragedy heaped upon tragedy[15] of the dead man's short life.

After a while he pulled out his phone and took a photo of the marker[16]. It would be part of the re-

1. lui fit signe que oui
2. flambant neuve
3. surcoût
4. balisée
5. surveiller ses allées et venues par GPS
6. Quand même
7. 46 ha
8. guerre de Sécession
9. témoignant de
10. du gâchis
11. chuintement
12. parait le ciel de rose au couchant
13. Curieusement
14. d'affinité
15. la succession de tragédies
16. l'inscription

port he would eventually[1] give Whitney Vance—if the old man was able to receive it.

While the phone was still in his hand it buzzed with a new call. The screen showed a number with an 805 area code and Bosch knew that was Ventura County. He took the call.

"This is Harry Bosch."

"Uh, hello. This is Olivia Macdonald. You posted a message on my brother's memorial page. You wanted to talk to me?"

Bosch nodded, noting that she had already answered one question. Dominick Santanello was her brother.

"Thank you for calling so quickly, Olivia," Bosch said. "At the moment, I'm actually standing at Nick's grave in Westwood. At the veterans' cemetery."

"Really?" she said. "I don't understand. What is going on?"

"I need to speak to you. Could we meet? I could come to you."

"Well, I guess so. I mean, wait a minute. No. Not until you tell me what this is about."

Bosch thought for a long moment before responding. He didn't want to lie to her but he couldn't reveal his true purpose[2]. Not yet. He was bound by[3] confidentiality and the sheer[4] complication of the story. She hadn't blocked her number. He knew he could find her even if she told him to pound sand[5] and hung up on him[6]. But the connection he felt with[7] Dominick Santanello extended to his sister. He didn't want to hurt or haunt this woman, who at the moment was no more than a voice on the phone.

He decided to take a shot in the dark[8].

"Nick knew he was adopted, right?" he said.

1. qu'il finirait par

2. but réel

3. lié par un accord de

4. pure et simple

5. d'aller se faire voir

6. lui raccrochait au nez

7. Son attachement envers

8. tenter sa chance

There was a long silence before she answered.

"Yes, he knew," Olivia said.

"Did he ever wonder where he came from?" Bosch asked. "Who his father was. His mother ..."

"He knew his mother's name," Olivia said. "Vibiana. She was named after a church. But that was all our adoptive parents knew. He never pursued it past that[1]."

1. n'a jamais cherché plus loin

Bosch closed his eyes for a moment. It was another piece of confirmation. It told him that since Olivia had been adopted too, she might understand the need to know.

"I know more," he said. "I'm a detective and I know the whole story."

There was another long pause before Olivia spoke.

"Okay," she said. "When do you want to meet?"

14

Bosch started Thursday morning shopping online. He studied an array[1] of GPS detectors and jammers and chose a combo device that did both[2]. It cost him two hundred dollars with two-day shipping[3].

He next went to the phone to call an NCIS[4] investigator at the National Personnel Records Center in St. Louis, Missouri. He had Gary McIntyre's name and number on a list of contacts he took with him when he left the LAPD. McIntyre was a cooperative straight shooter[5] that Bosch had worked with on at least three prior cases as a homicide investigator. He was now hoping to trade on[6] that experience and mutual trust to obtain a copy of Dominick Santanello's service package—the file[7] containing all records of his military service, ranging from his training history[8] to the location[9] of every base he was ever stationed at, medals he was awarded[10], his leave and disciplinary history[11], and the summary report on his death in combat.

The military records archive was routinely on[12] the checklist of cold case investigation because of how frequently military service played a part in people's lives. It was a good way to fill in[13] details on victims, suspects, and witnesses[14]. In this case Bosch already knew the military angle regarding Santanello but he would be able to layer it[15] with a deeper history. His investigation was

1. gamme
2. appareil double fonction
3. 2 jours pour la livraison
4. du Service d'enquêtes criminelles de la Marine
5. gars direct et coopératif
6. tirer profit de
7. dossier
8. allant de son parcours de formation
9. emplacement
10. qu'il avait reçues
11. permissions et antécédents disciplinaires
12. faisait partie de
13. d'obtenir
14. témoins
15. l'étoffer

1. presque finie
2. envisageait à présent d'établir
3. Au moins
4. se targuait d'être consciencieux et minutieux
5. accessibles
6. faire jouer sa
7. que ça lui retombe dessus,
8. au cas où
9. vérifierait que
10. joua franc-jeu
11. se procurer
12. de ne pas s'en faire
13. le croirait sur parole
14. retrouver
15. le recontacter
16. aurait le temps d'ici là de lui fournir
17. Le rendez-vous
18. Un point enthousiasmant

essentially at an end[1] and he was now looking to put[2] a full report together for Whitney Vance as well as possibly find a way to make a DNA confirmation that Dominick Santanello was his son. If nothing else[3], Bosch prided himself on being thorough and complete[4] in his work.

The files were made available[5] to family members and their representatives but Bosch was not in a position to reveal he was working for Whitney Vance. He could play the[6] law enforcement card but didn't want that blowing back on him[7] should[8] McIntyre check to see if[9] his request was part of an official investigation by the SFPD. So instead he was up front[10] with McIntyre. He said he was calling about a case he had as a private investigator where he was trying to confirm Santanello as the son of a client whose name he could not reveal. He told McIntyre that he had a meeting later with Santanello's adoptive sister and he might be able to swing[11] a permission letter from her if needed.

McIntyre told Bosch not to sweat it[12]. He appreciated the honesty and would trust him[13]. He said he needed a day or two to track down[14] the file in question and then make a digital copy of it. He promised to make return contact[15] when he was ready to send and Bosch could have until then to come up with[16] a family permission letter. Bosch thanked him and said he looked forward to his call.

Bosch's appointment[17] with Olivia Macdonald was not until 1 p.m., so he had the rest of the morning to review case notes and prepare. One thing he was already charged about[18] was that the address she had given him for her home matched the address listed for the parents of Dominick

Santanello on his birth certificate. This meant she was living in the home where her adopted brother had grown up. It might be a long shot[1] but it put the chances of finding a DNA source into the realm of possibility[2].

Bosch then made a call to defense attorney[3] Mickey Haller, his half-brother, to ask if he had a referral for[4] a private lab that would be quick, discreet, and reliable[5] in making a DNA comparison, should he come up with a source. Up until this point, Bosch had only worked[6] DNA cases as a cop and had used his department's lab and resources to get comparisons done.

"I've got a couple I use[7]—both fast and reliable," Haller said. "Let me guess, Maddie finally figured out[8] she's too smart[9] to have been your kid[10]. Now you're scrambling[11] to prove she is."

"Funny," Bosch said.

"Well, then, is it for a case[12]? A private case?"

"Something like that. I can't talk about it but I do have you to thank for it[13]. The client wanted me because of that bit of business last year in West Hollywood."

The case that[14] Whitney Vance had referenced[15] during the interview involved a Beverly Hills plastic surgeon[16] and a couple of corrupt LAPD cops[17]. It had ended badly for them in West Hollywood but it had begun with Bosch working a case for Haller.

"Then it sounds like I'm due[18] a commission on any funds you collect on this thing, Harry," Haller said.

"Doesn't sound like that to me[19]," Bosch said. "But if you hook me up[20] with a DNA lab, there might be something in it for you down the line[21]."

"I'll send you an e-mail, broheim[22]."

"Thanks, broheim."

1. Il n'y avait rien de sûr,
2. domaine du possible
3. avocat
4. pouvait l'aiguiller vers
5. fiable
6. bossé sur
7. J'en connais deux
8. a enfin compris
9. intelligente
10. pour être ta fille
11. tu te démènes
12. procès
13. c'est grâce à toi que je suis dessus
14. auquel
15. avait fait allusion
16. chirurgien esthétique
17. flics
18. je crois avoir droit à
19. Moi, je ne crois pas
20. me mets en contact
21. tu pourrais bien avoir quelque chose à glaner
22. mon pote

Bosch left the house at 11:30 so he would have time to grab something to eat on his way to Oxnard. Out on the street he checked in all directions for surveillance before hiking a block up[1] to the spot where he had parked the rented Cherokee. He ate tacos at Poquito Más at the bottom of the hill and then jumped onto the 101 and followed it west across the Valley and into Ventura County.

Oxnard was the biggest city in Ventura County. Its unattractive name was that of a sugar beet farmer[2] who built a processing plant[3] in the settlement[4] in the late nineteenth century. The city totally surrounded Port Hueneme, where there was a small U.S. Navy base. One of the questions Bosch planned to ask Olivia Macdonald was whether proximity to the base was what lured[5] her brother into enlisting[6] in the Navy.

Traffic was reasonable and Bosch got to Oxnard early. He used the time to drive around the port and then along Hollywood Beach, a strip of homes[7] on the Pacific side of the port where the streets were named La Brea and Sunset and Los Feliz after the well-known boulevards of Tinseltown[8].

He pulled up[9] in front of Olivia Macdonald's house right on time. It was in an older, middle-class neighborhood of neatly kept[10] California bungalows. She was waiting for Bosch in a chair on the front porch. He guessed that they were about the same age and he could see that, like her adoptive brother, it was likely she had both white and Latina origins. She had hair that was as white as snow and she was dressed in faded[11] jeans and a white blouse[12].

"Hello, I'm Harry Bosch," he said.

1. de remonter la rue
2. producteur de betteraves sucrières
3. usine
4. ville
5. ce qui avait incité
6. à s'engager
7. succession de résidences
8. [surnom d'] Hollywood [« ville clinquante »]
9. se gara
10. soignés
11. délavé
12. chemisier

He reached his hand down to her and she shook it.

"Olivia," she said. "Please have a seat."

Bosch sat in a wicker chair[1] across a small glass-topped table from her. There was a pitcher[2] of iced tea and two glasses on the table and he accepted her offer of a glass just to be cordial. He saw a manila[3] envelope on the table that had Do Not Bend[4] handwritten on it and assumed[5] it contained photos.

"So," she said, after pouring[6] two glasses. "You want to know about my brother. My first question is, who is it you work for?"

Bosch knew it would begin this way. He also knew that how he answered this question would determine how much cooperation and information he would get from her.

"Well, Olivia, that's the awkward[7] part," he said. "I was hired by a man who wanted to find out if he had a child back[8] in 1951. But part of the deal was that I had to agree to the strictest confidence[9] and not reveal who my employer was to anyone until he released me[10] from that promise. So I'm sort of caught in the middle here. It's a catch-22 thing[11]. I can't tell you who hired me until I can confirm that your brother was his son. You don't want to talk to me until I tell you who hired me."

"Well, how will you confirm it?" she said, waving a hand helplessly[12]. "Nicky's been dead since 1970." Bosch sensed an opening.

"There are ways. This is the house where he grew up, isn't it?"

"How do you know that?"

"The same address is on his birth certificate. The one that was filed[13] after he was adopted. There might be something here I can use. Was his bedroom left intact?"

1. fauteuil en osier
2. pichet
3. kraft
4. Ne pas plier
5. supposa
6. avoir servi
7. délicate
8. il y a longtemps,
9. confidentialité
10. me dégage
11. situation sans issue [quoi qu'on fasse]
12. levant un bras impuissant
13. L'acte de naissance inscrit

1. quelle drôle d'idée
2. Les affaires de Nick
3. ce qu'il en reste
4. au grenier
5. j'ai tout monté là-haut
6. dans un établissement
7. adultes
8. partis vivre leur vie
9. réussi à la faire parler
10. diriger
11. moi j'étais nettement basanée
12. à l'époque
13. frère ou une sœur

"What? No, that's weird[1]. Besides I raised three kids in this house after I moved back. We didn't have room to turn his bedroom into a museum. Nicky's stuff[2], what's left of it[3], is up in the attic[4]."

"What sort of stuff?"

"Oh, I don't know. His war stuff. The things he sent back and then what they sent back after he got killed. My parents kept it all and after I moved in here I shoved it all up there[5]. I wasn't interested in it but my mother made me promise not to throw it away."

Bosch nodded. He had to find a way to get up into the attic.

"Are your parents alive?" he asked.

"My father died twenty-five years ago. My mother's alive but she doesn't know what day it is or who she is anymore. She's at a facility[6] where they take good care of her. It's just me here now. Divorced, kids grown[7] and out on their own[8]."

Bosch had gotten her talking[9] without her coming back to her demand to know who his employer was. He knew he had to keep that going and drive[10] the conversation back around to the attic and what was up there.

"So you said on the phone that your brother knew he was adopted."

"Yes, he did," she said. "We both did."

"Were you also born at St. Helen's?"

She nodded.

"I came first," she said. "My adoptive parents were white and I obviously was brown[11]. It was very white out here back then[12] and they thought it would be good for me to have a sibling[13] who was the same. So they went back to St. Helen's and got Dominick."

"You said your brother knew his birth[1] mother's name. Vibiana. How did he know that? That was usually kept from everybody[2]—at least back then."

"You're right, it was. I never knew my mother's name or what the story was there. When Nicky was born he was already set to go to my parents. They were waiting for him. But he was sick and the doctors wanted him to stay with his mother for a while and have her milk. It was something like that."

"And so your parents met her."

"Exactly. For a few days they visited and spent some time with her, I guess. Later on, when we were growing up, it was pretty obvious[3] we didn't look like[4] our two Italian-American parents, so we asked questions. They told us we were adopted and the only thing they knew was that Nicky's mother was named Vibiana, because they met her before she gave him up."

It didn't appear that Dominick and Olivia were told the full story about what had happened to Vibiana, whether their adoptive parents knew it or not.

"Do you know if your brother ever tried to find his mother and father when he was growing up?"

"Not that I know of[5]. We knew what that place was, St. Helen's. It's where babies were born that were unwanted. I never tried to find my naturals[6]. I didn't care. I don't think Nicky did either."

Bosch noted a slight tone of bitterness[7] in her voice. More than sixty years later she clearly harbored[8] an animosity toward the parents who gave her up[9]. He knew it would not serve him here to tell her he didn't agree that all the babies were

1. biologique
2. tenu caché
3. clair
4. qu'on ne ressemblait pas à
5. à ma connaissance
6. parents biologiques
7. amertume
8. nourrissait
9. l'avaient abandonnée

unwanted at St. Helen's. Some mothers, maybe all of them back then, had no choice in the matter.

He decided to move the conversation in a new direction. He took a drink of iced tea, complimented her on it, and then nodded at[1] the envelope on the table.

"Are those photos?" he asked.

"I thought you might want to see him," she said. "There's also a story about him from the paper[2]."

She opened the envelope and passed Bosch a stack[3] of photos and a folded newspaper clipping[4]. They had all faded and yellowed over time.

He looked at the clipping first, carefully unfolding it so it wouldn't split along the crease[5]. It was impossible to determine what newspaper it had come from but the contents of the story made it seem very local. The headline read[6], "Oxnard Athlete Killed in Vietnam" and the story confirmed much of what Bosch had already deduced. Santanello was killed when he and four Marines were returning from a mission in the Tay Ninh Province. The helicopter they were in was hit by sniper fire and crashed in a rice paddy[7]. The story said Santanello was an all-around[8] athlete who had played varsity football, basketball, and baseball at Oxnard High[9]. The story quoted Santanello's mother as saying her son had been very proud to serve his country despite the antiwar sentiment back home[10] at the time.

Bosch refolded[11] the clipping and handed it back[12] to Olivia. He then took up the photos. They appeared to be in chronological order, showing Dominick as a boy growing into a teenager. There were shots[13] of him at the beach, playing basketball, riding a bike. There was a photo of him in a baseball uniform and another of him and a girl in formal wear[14]. A family shot included him with

1. fit un signe de tête en direction de
2. dans le journal
3. pile
4. coupure
5. pour ne pas casser le pli
6. gros titre était
7. rizière
8. polyvalent
9. dans les équipes de football, basket-ball et base-ball du lycée d'Oxnard
10. aux USA
11. replia
12. le rendit
13. des photos
14. tenue habillée

his sister and adoptive parents. He studied Olivia as a young girl. She was pretty and she and Dominick looked like real siblings. Their complexions[1], eyes, and hair color were a full match[2].

The last photo in the stack showed Dominick in his Navy dungarees[3], Dixie Cup sailor's cap tilted back[4], his hair high and tight with sidewalls[5]. He was standing with hands on hips, with a manicured green field[6] behind him. It didn't look like Vietnam to Bosch and the smile was the kind of careless, naive expression worn by someone who had not yet gotten his first taste[7] of war. Bosch guessed it was from basic training.

"I love that photo," Olivia said. "It's so Nick."

"Where did he go for basic[8]?" Bosch asked.

"San Diego area. Hospital corps school at Balboa, then combat training and the field medical school[9] at Pendleton."

"Did you ever go down there and see him?"

"Only one time, when we went down for his graduation[10] from hospital school. That was the last time I ever saw him."

Bosch glanced down at the photo. He noticed something and looked closer[11]. The shirt Santanello wore was very wrinkled from being hand-washed[12] and wrung out[13], so it was difficult to read, but the name stenciled[14] on the shirt over the pocket looked like it said[15] Lewis, not Santanello.

"The name on the shirt is—"

"Lewis. Yeah, that's why he's smiling like that. He switched shirts[16] with a friend of his[17] named Lewis who couldn't pass a swim test[18]. They all wore the same thing, they all had the same haircut. The only way to tell them apart[19] was the names stenciled on the shirts, and that's all the training people checked off[20] when they did testing[21]. So Lewis didn't know how to swim and

1. teint
2. identiques
3. salopette
4. sa casquette de marin un peu en arrière
5. rasés sur les côtés
6. pelouse bien entretenue
7. un premier aperçu
8. est-ce qu'il a fait ses classes
9. l'école militaire de médecine
10. cérémonie de remise de diplôme
11. de plus près
12. toute froissée par les lavages
13. essorages
14. écrit
15. semblait être
16. échangé sa chemise
17. un de ses amis
18. n'avait aucune chance de réussir une épreuve de natation
19. les différencier
20. vérifiaient
21. faisaient passer les épreuves

Nicky went over to the pool wearing his shirt. He got checked in[1] under his name and took[2] the test for him."

She laughed. Bosch nodded and smiled. A typical military service story, right down to[3] the guy in the Navy who didn't know how to swim.

"So what made Dominick enlist[4]?" he asked. "And why the Navy? Why did he want to be a corpsman?"

The smile left on her face from the Lewis story disappeared.

"Oh my god, he made such a mistake," Olivia said. "He was young and dumb[5] and he paid for it with his life."

She explained that her brother turned eighteen in January of his senior year of high school[6]. That made him old compared with his classmates. As was required then during the war, he presented himself to Selective Services for his predraft physical[7]. Five months later when he graduated high school[8], he got his draft[9] card and saw that he had been classified as 1A, meaning he was draft eligible[10] and likely[11] to go to Southeast Asia.

"This was before the draft lottery[12]," she said. "The way it worked was the older guys went first and he was one of the older guys coming out of high school. He knew he was going to get drafted[13]—it was just a matter of time—so he joined up so he would[14] have a choice and he went into the Navy. He'd had a summer job over by the base at Hueneme and always liked the Navy guys who came in. He thought they were cool."

"He wasn't going to go to college[15]?" he asked. "It would have been a deferment[16] and the war was winding down[17] by '69. Nixon was cutting back[18] troops."

Olivia shook her head.

1. s'est fait enregistrer
2. a passé
3. même celle avec
4. qu'est-ce qui a poussé Dominick à s'engager
5. bête
6. année de terminale
7. visite médicale d'incorporation [au service militaire]
8. a passé son bac
9. d'appel sous les drapeaux
10. admissible
11. susceptible
12. par tirage au sort
13. être appelé
14. donc il s'est engagé pour pouvoir
15. voulait pas aller à l'université
16. sursis des OM
17. était moins intense
18. réduisait

"No, no college. He was very smart but he just didn't like school. Had no patience for it. He liked movies and sports and photography. I think he also wanted to figure things out[1] a little bit. Our father sold refrigerators. There was no money for college."

Those last words —no money— echoed in Bosch's mind. If Whitney Vance had owned up to[2] his responsibility and raised and paid for his child, then there would have been money and his son wouldn't have gone anywhere near[3] Vietnam. He tried to break away from such[4] thoughts and concentrate on the interview.

"He wanted to be a corpsman—a medic[5]?" he asked.

"That's another story," Olivia said. "When he enlisted he got to choose which way he wanted to go. He was torn[6]. There was something about him; he wanted to get close but not that close[7], you know? There was a list of the different things you could do and he told them he wanted to be a journalist/photographer or a combat medic[8] because he thought it would get him to, you know, where the action was but he wouldn't have to be killing people right and left."

Bosch had known many of the same type over there. Guys who wanted to be in battle without having to be in battle. Most of the grunts[9] were only nineteen or twenty years old. It was a time to prove who you were, what you could do.

"So they made him a corpsman and trained him for battle," Olivia said. "His first assignment overseas was on the hospital ship, but that was just to get his feet wet[10]. He was there for, like, three or four months and then they put him with the Marines and he was in combat … And of course, he got shot down."

1. prendre le temps de réfléchir
2. assumé
3. n'aurait rien eu à voir avec
4. d'écarter ces
5. engagé militaire dans un service médical
6. tiraillé
7. être près de la guerre mais pas trop
8. infirmier-secouriste militaire
9. bidasses
10. se faire la main

She finished the story in a matter-of-fact[1] tone. It was almost fifty years old and she had probably told it and thought about it ten thousand times. It was family history now and the emotion had gone out of it.

"So sad," she said then. "He only had a couple weeks left[2] over there. He sent a letter saying he would be home by Christmas. But he didn't make it[3]."

Her tone had turned somber and Bosch thought maybe he had too quickly come to the conclusion that there was no longer an emotional burden[4] on her. He took another drink of iced tea before asking the next question.

"You mentioned that some of his stuff from over there was sent back. It's all up in the attic?"

She nodded.

"A couple boxes[5]. Nicky sent stuff home because he was about to get out. He was a short-timer[6] and then the Navy sent back his footlocker[7] too. My parents kept it all and I put it up there. I didn't like looking at it, to tell you the truth. It was just a bad reminder."

Despite her feelings about her brother's war things, Bosch grew nervous with the excitement of possibility.

"Olivia," he said. "Can I go up to the attic and look at his things?"

She made a face[8] like he had crossed some line[9] with the question.

"Why?"

Bosch leaned forward across the table. He knew he needed to be sincere. He needed to get up into that attic.

1. neutre
2. Il ne lui restait plus que deux semaines
3. n'a pas pu rentrer
4. charge
5. Deux cartons
6. ne devait pas rester longtemps
7. cantine
8. grimace
9. dépassé les bornes

"Because it might help me. I'm looking for something that might connect him to the man who hired me."

"You mean like DNA in stuff that[1] old?"

"It's possible. And it's because I was over there when I was your brother's age. As I said on the memorial site, I was even on the same hospital ship, maybe even at the same time he was. It will just help me to look at his things. Not just for the case. For me too."

She thought a moment before answering.

"Well, I'll tell you one thing," she said. "I'm not going up in that attic. The ladder's way too rickety[2] and I'd be scared I'd fall off. If you want to go up, you can, but it will be by yourself[3]."

"That's okay," Bosch said. "Thank you, Olivia."

He finished his iced tea and stood up.

1. des affaires aussi

2. L'échelle est bien trop branlante

3. tout seul

15

Olivia had been right about the ladder. It was a fold-down job[1] attached to the pull-down attic door[2] in the ceiling of the second-floor landing[3]. Bosch was by no means a heavy man. Wiry[4] was the description that favored him his entire life. But as he climbed the wooden ladder, it creaked under his weight and he worried the hinges on the fold[5] would give way[6] and he would fall. Olivia stood by below and nervously watched him. Four steps up he was able to reach and grab on to the framing in the ceiling[7] and safely redistribute some of his weight.

"There should be a pull string[8] for the light up there," she said.

Bosch made it to[9] the top without the ladder collapsing[10] and swung[11] his hand around in the dark until he captured the pull string. Once the light was on he looked around to get his bearings[12]. Olivia called up from below.

"I haven't been up there in years, but I think his stuff was in the back right corner."

Bosch turned that way. It was still dark in the recesses[13] of the attic. Out of his back pocket he pulled the flashlight Olivia had armed him with. He pointed the light into the back right corner, where the roof sloped sharply down[14], and immediately saw the familiar shape of a military footlocker. He had to crouch[15] to get to it and he banged his[16] head on one of the rafters[17]. At

1. machin pliable
2. trappe du grenier
3. palier du premier étage [US]
4. Sec et nerveux
5. craignit que les gonds de l'échelle
6. ne cèdent
7. s'accrocher au cadre de la trappe dans le plafond
8. cordon à tirer
9. atteignit
10. que l'échelle ne s'effondre
11. agita
12. s'orienter
13. recoins
14. s'inclinait fortement
15. s'accroupir
16. se cogna la
17. poutres

that point he lowered himself to a crawl[1] until he reached the locker.

There was a cardboard box on top of the locker. Bosch put the light on it and saw that it was the box Olivia had mentioned her brother sent home from Da Nang. Dominick Santanello was both the sender and addressee[2]. The return address was 1st Medical Battalion, Da Nang. The tape[3] was yellowed and peeling but Bosch could tell[4] the box had been opened and then later closed before being stored. He lifted it off the footlocker and put it to the side.

The footlocker was a basic plywood[5] box painted grayish green[6] and now faded to the point that the grain of the wood was readily[7] visible. There was faded black stenciling[8] across the top panel.

DOMINICK SANTANELLO HM3

Bosch easily interpreted the coding. Only in the military would HM3 stand for[9] hospital corpsman 3rd class. This meant Santanello's actual[10] rank was petty officer, 3rd class[11].

He pulled latex gloves from his pocket and put them on before handling either box. There was a single unlocked hasp[12] on the footlocker. Bosch opened it and shone[13] the light onto its contents. An earthy smell immediately caught in Bosch's nose[14] and he had a momentary flash of the tunnels he had been in over there. The wooden box smelled like Vietnam.

"Did you find it?" Olivia called from below.

Bosch collected himself[15] for a moment before answering.

"Yeah," he called out. "It's all here. I might be up here awhile."

1. s'allongea et rampa
2. l'expéditeur et le destinataire
3. Scotch
4. vit bien
5. en contreplaqué
6. en kaki
7. aisément
8. inscription
9. que HM3 signifiait
10. exact
11. caporal [dans la Marine]
12. moraillon [fermoir]
13. dirigea
14. lui assaillit les narines
15. fit effort sur lui-même

"Okay," she called back. "Let me know if you need anything. I'm going downstairs to the laundry for a minute."

The footlocker was neatly packed with folded clothes on top. Bosch carefully lifted each piece out, examined it, and put it on top of the cardboard box he had set to the side. Bosch had served in the Army but he knew that across the board of[1] military services, when the belongings[2] of a KIA[3] were shipped home to a grieving[4] family, they were sanitized[5] first, in order not to embarrass or add to the grief[6]. All magazines and books featuring nudity[7] were removed as well as any photos of Vietnamese or Filipino girls, any sort of drugs and paraphernalia[8], and any sort of personal journal that might have details of troop movements, mission tactics, or even war crimes.

What was left to return were the clothes and some of the creature comforts[9]. Bosch removed several sets of fatigues[10]—both camo[11] and green—as well as underwear and socks. At the bottom of the box were a stack of paperback novels[12] popular in the late 1960s, including a book that Bosch remembered had been in his own footlocker, *Steppenwolf* by Hermann Hesse. There was a full carton of Lucky Strikes along with a Zippo lighter[13] with a chevron on it from the Subic Bay naval base in Olongapo, Philippines.

There was a stack of letters with a rubber band[14] that broke the moment[15] Bosch tried to remove it. He looked through the envelopes. All the senders were family members and the return address was the same, the home Bosch was in at that moment. Most of the letters were from Olivia.

Bosch did not feel the need to intrude on[16] these private communications. He assumed[17] they were letters of encouragement, with his loved ones tell-

1. systématiquement au sein des
2. effets personnels
3. militaire mort au combat [killed in action]
4. en deuil
5. « nettoyés »
6. la peine
7. avec des femmes nues
8. accessoires divers
9. objets matériels
10. treillis
11. motif camouflage
12. livres de poche
13. briquet
14. élastique
15. dès que
16. s'immiscer dans
17. présuma

ing Dominick they were praying for his safe return from war.

There was a zippered leather toiletry kit[1] in the box and Bosch carefully lifted it out. More than anything else, this was what he had come for. He unzipped it and spread it open, then put the light beam[2] into it. The bag contained all the usual toiletries: razor, shaving powder, toothbrush, toothpaste, nail clippers[3], and a brush and comb[4].

Bosch took nothing out of the bag because he wanted to leave that to the DNA lab to do. The contents were so old he feared he might lose a hair follicle or some microscopic piece of skin or blood by moving it.

By holding the light at an angle, he could see hair in the bristles[5] of the brush. Each was longer than an inch[6] and he guessed that once Santanello had gotten out into the boonies[7], he had let his hair grow out like a lot of guys did.

He next put the light on an old-fashioned double-edged[8] razor which was held in the kit by a leather strap[9]. It looked clean but Bosch could only see one of its edges. He knew the DNA gold mine would be[10] if there was blood on it. One slight nick[11] with the razor could have left a microdot[12] of blood, which would be all he'd need.

Bosch had no idea whether after almost fifty years DNA could be extracted from hair or saliva dried on a toothbrush or even whiskers[13] in a double-edged razor, but he knew that blood would work. In the LAPD's Open-Unsolved Unit[14] he had worked cases where dried blood almost as old as this had given up[15] a solid DNA code. Maybe he'd get lucky with what he had in the kit. He would deliver it undisturbed[16] to one of the labs suggested by Mickey Haller. As long as he could persuade Olivia to let him borrow it.

1. trousse de toilette en cuir et à fermeture Éclair
2. faisceau lumineux
3. coupe-ongles
4. peigne
5. poils
6. faisait plus de 2,5 cm de long
7. avait débarqué dans la cambrousse
8. à double lame
9. lanière
10. ce serait le jackpot pour l'ADN
11. légère entaille
12. microgoutte
13. des poils du visage
14. service des Affaires non résolues
15. donné
16. le confierait intact

After zipping the bag closed, Bosch put it on the wood floor to his right side. There he would gather everything he intended to ask Olivia for permission to take. He went back to the seemingly empty footlocker and used the light and his fingers to check for a false bottom[1]. He knew from experience that some soldiers would take the bottom panel out of an unused footlocker and put it inside their own box, creating a secret layer under which they could hide drugs, unauthorized weapons, and *Playboy* magazines.

1. double fond

There was no removable panel. Santanello had hidden nothing in his footlocker. Bosch thought the contents were notable for their lack of photos and for having no letters from people other than family.

Bosch carefully repacked the footlocker and pulled the top over[2] to close it. When he did so, the beam from the flashlight caught something. He studied the inside top of the box closely and by holding the light at an oblique angle he could see several lines of discoloration on the wood. He realized these were marks created by adhesive that had been left on the surface after tape had been removed. Santanello must have at one time taped things—most likely photographs—to the inside of his footlocker.

2. rabattit le couvercle

It was not unusual. The inside of a footlocker was often used like the inside of a high school locker[3]. Bosch recalled[4] many soldiers who taped photos of girlfriends, wives, and children inside their boxes. Sometimes signs[5], sometimes drawings sent by their kids, and sometimes centerfolds[6].

3. casier au lycée
4. se souvenait de
5. des insignes
6. des posters

It was unknown whether Santanello had cleared these off[7] or whether the Navy's KIA unit did so while sanitizing his belongings, but it made Bosch all the more interested in what was in the box

7. les avait enlevés

Santanello had sent home. He now opened it up and put the light on its contents.

The box apparently contained the things that mattered most[1] to Santanello and that he wanted to make sure got to Oxnard as he drew close to completing[2] his tour of duty[3]. On top were two sets of folded civvies[4]—non-uniform clothing that would have been unauthorized for Santanello to have in Vietnam. These included jeans, chinos[5], collared shirts[6], and black socks. Beneath the clothes were a pair of Converse sneakers[7] and a pair of shiny black boots. Having civvies was unauthorized but commonplace[8]. It was no secret that wearing uniforms while traveling home after completing a tour of duty or while on leave[9] in foreign cities could cause confrontations with civilians because of the unpopularity of the war around the world.

But Bosch also knew that there was another purpose to having civilian clothes. In a one-year tour, a soldier was guaranteed a week's leave at six months and a standby leave at nine—where they waited on the possibility of an open seat[10] on a departing plane. There were five official leave destinations and none were in mainland USA[11] because returning to the mainland was not authorized. But a soldier who had civvies could change in a hotel room in Honolulu and then go back to the airport to hop[12] a flight to L.A. or San Francisco—as long as he avoided the MPs[13] who were on the lookout[14] in the airport for just such subterfuge. It was another reason to grow your hair out in the boonies[15], as Santanello had apparently done. A guy in civvies at the airport in Honolulu could easily be spotted[16] by the MPs if he had clean sidewalls[17] and a military cut. Long hair provided cover[18].

1. comptaient le plus
2. alors qu'il était près d'achever
3. service
4. vêtements civils
5. des pantalons de toile
6. des chemises de costume
7. baskets
8. courant
9. en permission
10. place disponible
11. continentaux [= en métropole]
12. filer prendre
13. la police militaire
14. faisait le guet
15. dans la cambrousse
16. se faire repérer
17. les oreilles très dégagées
18. permettaient de se camoufler

Bosch had done it himself twice during his time in-country[1], returning to L.A. to spend five days with a girlfriend in 1969 and then returning again six months later, even though there was no girlfriend anymore. Santanello had been killed more than eleven months into his tour of[2] Vietnam. That meant he had gotten at least one leave and probably two. Maybe he had snuck back[3] to California.

Beneath the clothing Bosch found a compact cassette tape player and a camera[4], both in original boxes, the tape player marked with a price tag[5] from the PX in Da Nang. Next to these were two neat rows[6] of cassette cases[7] lined spine out[8] on the bottom of the box. There was another carton of Lucky Strikes and another Zippo lighter, this one used and showing the Navy Corpsman chevron on the side. There was a well-worn copy[9] of *The Lord of the Rings* by J. R. R. Tolkien and he saw several beaded necklaces[10] and other souvenirs bought at different places where Santanello had been posted during his Navy service.

Bosch experienced a sense[11] of déjà vu as he looked through the contents. He had also read Tolkien in Vietnam. It was a popular book among combat veterans, a rich fantasy about another world that took them away from the reality of where they were and what they were doing. Bosch studied the names of the bands[12] and performers[13] on the plastic cassette cases and remembered hearing the same music while in Vietnam: Hendrix, Cream, the Rolling Stones, the Moody Blues, and others.

Along with that familiarity came his experience and knowledge of how things worked in Southeast Asia. The same Vietnamese girls who sold the necklaces at the White Elephant landing docks[14] at Da Nang also sold pre-rolled joints

1. sur place
2. après 11 mois de service au
3. était rentré en cachette
4. appareil photo
5. étiquette
6. rangées bien ordonnées
7. boîtiers
8. alignés la tranche en haut
9. exemplaire tout écorné
10. colliers de perles
11. eut une sensation
12. groupes
13. des musiciens
14. débarcadère

in ten packs[1] that fit[2] perfectly into cigarette packs for easy transport into the bush[3]. If you wanted fifty joints you bought a Coke can with a false top. Use of marijuana was widespread[4] and open, the popular view[5] being "What's the worst that can happen if I get caught, they send me to Vietnam?"

Bosch opened the carton of Lucky Strikes now and pulled out a pack. As he suspected, it contained ten expertly rolled joints neatly wrapped in foil[6] for freshness. He assumed each of the packs in the carton would be the same. Santanello had likely taken up a regular habit of getting high[7] while in the service and wanted to make sure he had an ample supply to bridge[8] his return home.

It was all mildly[9] interesting to Bosch because it drew on[10] his own memories of his time in Vietnam, but he didn't readily see anything in the box that might lead him further toward confirming Whitney Vance's paternity of Dominick Santanello. That was his purpose here—confirmation of paternity. If he was going to report to Vance that his bloodline[11] had ended in a helo[12] crash in the Tay Ninh Province, then he had to make every effort[13] to be sure he was telling the old man the truth.

He repacked the cigarette carton and put it to the side. He lifted out the boxes containing the camera and the cassette recorder next, and just as he was wondering where the photos were that went with the camera, he saw that the bottom of the box was spread with a cache of[14] black-and-white photos and envelopes containing strips[15] of film negatives. The photos appeared to be well preserved because they had not been exposed to light in decades.

1. par paquets de dix
2. tenaient
3. dans la brousse
4. très répandu
5. avis général
6. soigneusement enveloppés de papier alu
7. se défoncer
8. d'en avoir une provision suffisante pour assurer
9. relativement
10. cela lui évoquait
11. descendance
12. d'hélico
13. le maximum
14. recouvert d'une épaisseur bien dissimulée de
15. des bandes

He removed the two rows of cassette tapes next so he would be able to access the photos. He wondered if Santanello had purposely[1] tried to hide them from his family in case they opened the box before he arrived home. Bosch pushed them into a single stack and then brought them out of the box.

There were forty-two photos in all and they ran the gamut[2] of Vietnam experiences. There were shots from the bush, shots of Vietnamese girls at the White Elephant, shots taken on the hospital ship Bosch recognized as the *Sanctuary*, and, ironically, shots taken from helicopters flying over the bush and the seemingly endless grids of rice paddies[3].

Bosch had pushed the stack together in an order that was neither chronological nor thematic. It was a hodgepodge[4] of images that again felt all too familiar. But those misty[5] feelings crystallized into a hard memory[6] when he came across three consecutive shots of the upper deck[7] of the *Sanctuary* crowded with a couple hundred wounded servicemen[8] for a Christmas Eve show featuring Bob Hope and Connie Stevens. In the first photo the two performers stood side by side, Stevens's mouth open in song, the faces of the soldiers in the front row in rapt attention[9]. The second photo focused on the crowd at the point of the bow[10], Monkey Mountain seen in the distance across the water. The third photo showed Hope waving good-bye to a standing ovation at the end of the show.

Bosch had been there. Wounded by a bamboo spear[11] in a tunnel, he had been treated on the *Sanctuary* for four weeks in December 1969. The wound[12] itself had healed[13] quickly but the infection it had brought into his body had been more resistant. He'd lost twenty pounds off his

1. délibérément
2. montraient toute la gamme
3. quadrillages que les rizières semblaient former à l'infini
4. fatras
5. nébuleux
6. souvenir très net
7. pont supérieur
8. soldats blessés
9. captivés
10. proue
11. pointe
12. blessure
13. cicatrisé

already lean frame[1] during treatment on the hospital ship but by the last week of the month he had recovered his health enough to receive Return to Duty orders for the day after Christmas.

Hope and his troupe had been scheduled for weeks[2] and Bosch, like everybody else on board, had been looking forward to seeing the legendary entertainer and his featured guest[3], Stevens, a well-known actress and singer Bosch recognized from appearances[4] on the television shows *Hawaiian Eye* and *77 Sunset Strip*.

But on Christmas Eve[5] high winds and heavy seas swept across the South China Sea and were having their way with the ship[6]. The men on board started to gather on the upper deck, when four helicopters carrying Hope, his entertainers, and the band that would back them approached the fantail[7]. But as the choppers got close[8] it was determined that landing on the unstable ship was too risky. The *Sanctuary* had been built before helicopters had even been invented. A small landing pad[9] built on the fantail looked like a moving postage stamp[10] from the air.

The men watched as the helicopters turned and headed back toward Da Nang. A communal groan[11] moved through the crowd. The men slowly started moving off deck and back to their berths[12] when someone looked back toward Da Nang and yelled, "Wait—they're coming back!"

He was only partially right. One of the four helicopters had turned again and was coming back to the *Sanctuary*. Its pilot made landing[13] after three tense attempts and out of[14] the sliding door climbed[15] Bob Hope, along with Connie Stevens, Neil Armstrong, and a jazz saxophonist named Quentin McKinzie.

1. perdu env. 10 kg, alors qu'il était déjà maigre,
2. programmés depuis des semaines
3. invitée vedette
4. pour l'avoir vue
5. la veille de Noël,
6. malmenaient fortement le navire
7. de la poupe
8. à l'approche des hélicos,
9. plate-forme d'atterrissage
10. timbre-poste
11. grognement général
12. couchettes
13. parvint à atterrir
14. de
15. sortit

The roar[1] that went up from the crowd returning to the deck could put an electric surge down Bosch's spine[2] when he thought about it almost fifty years later. They had no backup band and no backup singers[3], but Hope and company had told the pilot to turn that slick around and land it[4]. Hell,[5] Neil Armstrong had landed on the fucking moon[6] five months earlier; how hard could it be to put a chopper down on a boat?

Armstrong offered words of encouragement to the troops and McKinzie laid down some solo licks on his axe[7]. Hope told his one-liners[8] and Stevens sang a cappella, breaking hearts with a slow rendition[9] of the Judy Collins hit "Both Sides Now." Bosch remembered it as one of his best days as a soldier.

Years later as an LAPD detective Bosch was called upon[10] to provide plainclothes security[11] at the Shubert Theatre for the West Coast premiere of a musical called *Mamma Mia!* A huge VIP turnout[12] was expected, and the LAPD was asked to supplement the theater's own security. Standing in the front lobby, his eyes moving across faces and hands, Bosch suddenly saw Connie Stevens among the VIPs. Like a stalker[13] he moved through the crowd toward her. He took his badge off his belt and palmed it[14] in case he needed it to cut through[15] and get closer. But he got to her without issue[16] and when there was a pause in her conversations he said, "Ms. Stevens?"

She looked at him and he tried to tell the story. That he was there that day on the *Sanctuary* when she and Bob Hope and the others had made the pilot turn that helicopter around. He wanted to tell her what it had meant then and now but something caught[17] in his throat and words were diffi-

1. cri immense
2. envoyait encore comme une décharge électrique dans le dos de Bosch
3. n'avaient ni musiciens ni chanteurs pour les accompagner
4. faire demi-tour et d'atterrir
5. Enfin quoi, merde,
6. atterri sur la lune
7. fit quelques solos au saxo
8. blagues
9. interprétation
10. requis
11. pour, habillé en civil, assurer la sécurité
12. public
13. Sans la quitter des yeux,
14. le plaça dans le creux de sa main
15. traverser la foule
16. problème
17. se coinça

cult. All he could manage to say was "Christmas Eve, 1969. Hospital ship."

She looked at him for a moment and understood, then just pulled him into a hug[1]. She whispered into his ear, "The *Sanctuary*. You made it home[2]."

Bosch nodded and they separated. Without thinking he put his badge into her hand. He then moved away, back into the crowd to do his job. He caught several weeks of hell[3] from the other detectives at Hollywood Division after he reported losing his badge. But he remembered seeing Connie Stevens at the Shubert as one of his best days as a cop.

"Still doin' all right[4] up there?"

Bosch came out of the memory[5], his eyes still on the photograph of the crowd on the *Sanctuary*'s upper deck.

"Yes," he called out. "Almost done[6]."

He went back to studying the photo. He knew he was in the crowd somewhere but he couldn't find his own face. He looked through all of Santanello's photos once more, knowing that Dominick was in none of them because he had been behind the camera.

Finally, Bosch held and studied one photo that was a time-lapse shot[7] showing the silhouette of Monkey Mountain lit from behind by white phosphorous flares[8] during a night battle. He remembered on the *Sanctuary* how people would line up on deck to watch the light show[9] when the communication hub[10] on top of the mountain was frequently attacked.

Bosch's conclusion was that Santanello had been a talented photographer and maybe would have had a professional career at it[11] had he[12] survived the war. Harry could have looked at the

1. le serra dans ses bras
2. avez pu rentrer
3. s'attira plusieurs semaines de réprimandes
4. Ça va toujours,
5. émergea de ses souvenirs
6. J'ai bientôt fini
7. arrêt sur image
8. lumières
9. spectacle lumineux
10. centre
11. en aurait fait son métier
12. s'il avait

photos all day but he put them aside now to finish his search of the dead soldier's belongings.

He next opened the red box containing Santanello's camera. It was a Leica M4, a compact camera that could have fit[1] in one of the thigh pockets[2] of his fatigues[3]. It had a black body[4] to make it less reflective when he was out in the bush. Bosch checked the rest of the box and there was only an instruction manual.

Bosch knew Leicas were expensive cameras, so he assumed that Santanello was serious about his photography. Yet there weren't many printed photos in the box. He checked the envelopes containing the negative strips[5] and determined that there were far more frames of developed film[6] than there were prints[7]. He figured[8] Santanello must not have had the money or access to print out all of his work while in Vietnam. He probably planned to do that when he got back home to the States.

The last thing Bosch did was open the back of the camera to see if Santanello had used the interior space to smuggle[9] more drugs. Instead he found a coil[10] of film around the take-up spool[11]. At first he thought he had opened the camera on unexposed film, but as he unfurled[12] the coil, he realized that it was a strip of developed negatives[13] that had been rolled up and then secreted[14] in the camera.

The strip was brittle[15] and it cracked and broke apart in his hands as he attempted to unfurl it and look at the images. He held one piece of three shots up to the flashlight beam. He saw that each shot was a photo of a woman with what looked like a mountain behind her.

And she was holding a baby.

1. tenir
2. poches latérales
3. son treillis
4. boîtier
5. négatifs
6. de poses
7. qu'il n'y avait de clichés
8. se dit
9. dissimuler
10. rouleau
11. enrouleur
12. en déroulant
13. pellicule
14. cachée
15. friable

16

Bosch drove out to Burbank in the morning and into a commercial industrial area near the airport and the Valhalla Memorial Park. A couple blocks from the cemetery he pulled into the lot[1] in front of Flashpoint Graphix. He had called ahead and was expected[2].

Flashpoint was a sprawling[3] business that created large-scale[4] photo-illustrations for bill-boards[5], buildings, buses, and all other advertising media[6]. On any day its fine work could be seen across a spectrum of locations in Los Angeles and beyond. There wasn't an angle anywhere on the Sunset Strip that didn't include a Flashpoint creation. And it was all run by a man named Guy Claudy, who in an earlier life had been a forensic[7] photographer for the LAPD. Bosch and Claudy had worked a number of crime scenes together in the '80s and '90s, before Claudy left to open his own photography and graphics business. The two had stayed in touch[8] over the years, usually taking in a Dodgers game[9] or two each season, and when Bosch called him that morning to ask a favor, Claudy said he should come on over[10].

Dressed casually[11] in jeans and a Tommy Bahama shirt[12], Claudy met Bosch in a nondescript[13] reception area—Flashpoint didn't rely on walk-in business[14]—and led him back to a more opulent but not over-the-top[15] office where the walls were hung with[16] framed photos from the

1. entra dans le parking
2. attendu
3. à large périmètre
4. grand format
5. panneaux d'affichage
6. supports publicitaires
7. de médecine légale
8. en contact
9. se faisant généralement un match des Dodgers [équipe de base-ball de L.A.]
10. lui dit de passer le voir
11. décontracté
12. chemise hawaiienne
13. très banale
14. ne faisait pas venir les clients sur place
15. excessivement luxueux
16. couverts de

Dodgers' glory years. Bosch knew without asking that Claudy had taken the photos during a short stint[1] as team photographer. One showed the pitcher[2] Fernando Valenzuela exulting from the mound[3]. The glasses he wore allowed Bosch to place the shot—toward the end of the storied[4] pitcher's career. He pointed at the frame.

"The no-hitter[5]," he said. "The Cardinals, 1990."

"Yep," Claudy said. "Good memory."

"I remember I was on a surveillance in Echo Park. Up on White Knoll. It was me and Frankie Sheehan—you remember the Dollmaker case?"

"Of course. You got the guy."

"Yeah, well, that night we were watching a different guy up on White Knoll and we could see the stadium from there and we listened to Vinny call the no-hitter. We could hear the broadcast[6] coming out of all the open windows of the houses. I wanted to bail out on[7] the surveillance and go over for the last inning[8]. You know, badge our way[9] into the stadium and watch. But we stayed put[10] and listened to Vinny. I remember it ended on a double-play[11]."

"Yep, and I wasn't expecting that—Guerrero hitting into a double. I almost didn't get the shot[12] because I was reloading[13]. And, man, what are we going to do now without Vinny?"

It was a reference to the retirement[14] of Vin Scully, the Dodgers' venerable announcer who had called[15] the team's games since 1950—an incredibly long record[16] going all the way back to when they were the Brooklyn Dodgers.

"I don't know," Bosch said. "He might've started in Brooklyn but he's the voice of this city. It won't be the same without him."

They somberly sat down on either side of a desk and Bosch tried to change the subject.

1. boulot
2. lanceur
3. monticule du terrain [de baseball]
4. illustre
5. match sans coup sûr [exploit réalisé par un lanceur n'accordant ni point ni coup sûr à l'adversaire]
6. retransmission du match
7. profiter de
8. manche
9. montrer nos insignes pour rentrer
10. on n'a pas bougé
11. double jeu [élimination de 2 adversaires, au base-ball]
12. J'ai failli rater la photo
13. en train de réenclencher l'appareil
14. allusion au départ à la retraite
15. commenté
16. carrière

"So this is a big place you've got here," he said, thoroughly[1] impressed by how large his friend's business was. "I had no idea."

"Forty thousand square feet[2]—that's the size of a Best Buy[3]," Claudy said. "And we need more room. But you know what? I still miss the crime stuff. Tell me you have some crime stuff for me to do."

Bosch smiled.

"Well, I've got a mystery but I don't think there's any crime involved."

"Mystery is good. I'll take[4] mystery. What've you got?"

Bosch handed him the envelope he had carried in from the car. It contained the negatives that included the shot of the woman and the baby. He had shown them to Olivia Macdonald but she had no idea who the woman or child was. Just as intrigued as Harry, she had allowed him to take the envelope along with the toiletries kit.

"I'm on a private case," Bosch said. "And I found these negatives. They're almost fifty years old and they've been in an attic without air-conditioning or heat[5]. On top of that they're damaged—they cracked and broke apart[6] in my hand when I found them. I want to know what you can do with them."

Claudy opened the envelope and poured[7] its contents out on his desk. He leaned over and looked straight down at the broken pieces of the negative strip without touching them.

"Some of them look like they show a woman in front of a mountaintop," Bosch said. "I'm interested in all of it, but in those the most[8]. The woman. I think the location is someplace in Vietnam."

"Yeah, you have some cupping[9] here. Some cracking. It's Fuji film."

1. sincèrement

2. Dans les 3 500 m^2

3. [chaîne de grands magasins vendant du matériel électronique]

4. Va pour le

5. air conditionné ni chauffage

6. se sont défaits

7. versa

8. surtout ceux-là

9. des parties gondolées

"Meaning what?"

"It usually holds up[1] pretty well. Who is she?"

"I don't know. That's why I want to see her. And the baby she's holding."

Claudy said, "Okay. I think I can do something with this. My guys in the lab can. We'll rewash and re-dry them. Then we'll print. I see some fingerprints and they might be set[2] after so long."

Bosch considered that. His assumption was that Santanello took the shots[3]. They were with his camera and other negatives taken by him. Why would someone send developed negatives to a soldier in Vietnam? But if it was ever questioned[4], the fingerprints might be useful.

"What's your time frame?[5]" Claudy asked.

"Yesterday," Bosch said.

Claudy smiled.

"Of course," he said. "You're Hurry-Up-Harry."

Bosch smiled back and nodded. Nobody had called him that since Claudy had left the department.

"So give me an hour," Claudy said. "You can go to our break room[6] and make a Nespresso."

"I hate those things," Bosch replied.

"Okay, then go take a walk in the cemetery. More your style anyway. One hour."

"One hour."

Bosch stood up.

"Give my regards[7] to Oliver Hardy[8]," Claudy said. "He's in there."

"Will do[9]," Bosch said.

Bosch left Flashpoint and walked down Valhalla Drive. It was only when he entered the cemetery by a huge memorial that he remembered that in his research of Whitney Vance he had read that Vance's father was buried here. Close to Caltech[10] and under the jet path[11] of Bob Hope Airport, the

1. résiste
2. sont peut-être fixées
3. Il avait supposé que c'était Santanello qui avait pris les photos
4. remis en cause
5. Tu les voudrais pour quand ?
6. salle de pause
7. Transmets mon bon souvenir
8. [du feuilleton « Laurel et Hardy »]
9. Entendu
10. [California Institute of Technology]
11. couloir aérien

cemetery was the final resting place for a variety of aviation pioneers, designers, pilots, and barnstormers[1]. They were interred[2] or memorialized[3] in and around a tall domed structure called the Portal of the Folded Wings Shrine[4] to Aviation. Bosch found Nelson Vance's memorial plaque on the tiled[5] floor of the shrine.

1. voltigeurs
2. enterrés
3. commémorés
4. Sanctuaire
5. dallé

NELSON VANCE
Visionary Air Pioneer
Earliest Advocate[6] of U.S. Air Power,
Whose Prophetic Vision and Leadership Was
a Primary Factor in American Supremacy
in the Air in War and Peace

6. L'un des premiers défenseurs

Bosch noticed that there was a space next to the memorial plaque for another interment and wondered if this was already on reserve as Whitney Vance's final destination.

Bosch wandered out[7] of the shrine and over to the memorial to the astronauts lost[8] in two separate space shuttle[9] disasters. He then looked across one of the green lawns[10] and saw the start of a burial service[11] near one of the big fountains. He decided not to venture further[12] into the cemetery, a tourist amid the grief[13], and headed back to Flashpoint without searching for the grave of the heavier half of the comedy team[14] of Laurel and Hardy.

Claudy was ready for him when Bosch returned. He was ushered[15] into a drying room in the lab where nine 8 x 10 black-and-white prints were clipped to a plastic board. The photos were still wet with developing fluids[16], and a lab tech[17] was just finishing using a squeegee[18] to remove the excess. The exterior framing was seen on some of the prints, and some showed the fingerprints

7. sortit d'un pas nonchalant
8. disparus
9. navette
10. pelouses
11. cérémonie d'inhumation
12. s'avancer plus
13. parmi les proches endeuillés
14. moitié la plus corpulente du duo comique
15. On le fit entrer
16. après avoir été plongées dans le révélateur
17. technicien
18. raclette

1. que Claudy avait signalés
2. effacés car surexposés
3. silhouette
4. du côté de
5. eut identifié
6. regarda de plus près
7. absolu
8. des images complètes
9. étincelantes
10. essayant de ne pas gêner Harry qui

Claudy had warned about[1]. Some of the shots were completely blown out by light exposure[2] and others exhibited varying degrees of damage to the negative. But there were three shots that were at least 90 percent intact. And one of these was a shot of the woman and child.

The first thing Bosch realized was that he had been wrong about the woman standing in front of a mountain in Vietnam. It was no mountainside and it was not Vietnam. It was the recognizable roofline[3] of the Hotel del Coronado down near[4] San Diego. Once Bosch registered[5] the location, he moved in close[6] to study the woman and the baby. The woman was Latina and Bosch could see a ribbon in the baby's hair. A girl, no more than a month or two old.

The woman's mouth was open in a smile showing unbridled[7] happiness. Bosch studied her eyes and the happy light that was in them. There was love in those eyes. For the baby. For the person behind the camera.

The other photos were full frames[8] and fragments from a series of shots taken on the beach behind the del Coronado. Shots of the woman, shots of the baby, shots of the sparkling[9] waves.

"Does it help?" Claudy asked.

He was standing behind Bosch, not getting in the way as Harry[10] studied the prints.

"I think so," Bosch said. "Yeah."

He considered the totality of the circumstances. The photos and their subjects were important enough to Dominick Santanello for him to attempt to hide them as he sent his property home from Vietnam. The question was why. Was this his child? Did he have a secret family that his family in Oxnard knew nothing about? If so, why the secrecy? He looked closely at the woman in the photo. She seemed to be in her mid to late twenties. Dominick would not yet have been twenty. Was the relationship with an older woman the reason he didn't tell his parents and sister?

Another question was about the location. The photos were taken during a trip to the beach either at or near the Hotel del Coronado. When was this? And why was a strip[1] of negatives from a photo shoot[2] that very clearly took place in the States included in property sent home from Vietnam?

Bosch scanned[3] the images again, looking for anything that would help place the shots in time. He saw nothing.

"For what it's worth[4], the guy was good," Claudy said. "Had a good eye."

Bosch agreed.

"Is he dead?" Claudy asked.

"Yes," Bosch said. "Never made it home from Vietnam."

"That's too bad[5]."

"Yeah. I saw some of his other work. From the bush. From his missions."

"I'd love to see it. Maybe there's something that could be done with it."

Bosch nodded but was concentrating on the photos in front of him.

"You can't tell[6] when these photos were taken, can you?" he asked.

"No, there was no time stamp[7] on the film," Claudy said. "Not really done back then[8]."

Bosch expected that to be the case[9].

"But what I can tell you is when the film[10] was made," Claudy added. "Down to a three-month period[11]. Fuji coded their film stock by production cycle."

Bosch turned around and looked at Claudy.

1. bande
2. séance
3. parcourut
4. En tout cas
5. Dommage
6. On ne peut pas savoir
7. horodatage
8. Ça ne se faisait pas vraiment, à l'époque
9. s'en était douté
10. pellicule
11. À trois mois près

"Show me."

Claudy came forward and went to one of the prints made from a broken negative. The negative's frame was part of the print. Claudy pointed to a series of letters and numbers in the frame.

"They marked the film by year and three-month manufacturing run[1]. You see here? This is it."

He pointed to a section of the coding: *70-AJ*.

"This film was made between April and June of 1970," he said.

Bosch considered the information.

"But it could have been used any time after that, right?" he asked.

"Right," Claudy said. "It only marks when it was made, not when it was used in a camera."

Something didn't add up about that[2]. The film was manufactured as early as April of 1970 and the photographer, Dominick Santanello, was killed in December 1970. He could have easily bought and used the film sometime in the eight intervening[3] months, then sent it home with his belongings[4].

"You know where that is, right?" Claudy asked.

"Yeah, the del Coronado," Bosch said.

"Sure hasn't changed much."

"Yeah."

Bosch stared at the photo of mother and child again and then he got it[5]. He understood.

Dominick Santanello trained[6] down in[7] the San Diego area in 1969 but he would have been shipped overseas[8] before the end of the year. Bosch was looking at photos taken in San Diego in April 1970 at the very earliest and that was well after Santanello was in Vietnam.

"He came back," Bosch said.

"What?" Claudy asked.

Bosch didn't answer. He was riding the wave[9]. Things were cascading, coming together. The

1. cycle de fabrication
2. clochait
3. intermédiaires
4. affaires
5. pigea
6. avait fait ses classes
7. dans
8. avait certainement été envoyé outre-mer
9. suivait le fil de ses pensées

civvies in the box, the long hair in the bristles of the brush, the photos removed from the inside of the footlocker, and the hidden photos of the baby on the beach. Santanello had made an unauthorized trip back to the States. He hid the photo negatives because they were proof of his crime[1]. He had risked court-martial and the stockade[2] to see his girlfriend.

And his newborn daughter.

Bosch now knew. There was an heir[3] somewhere out there[4]. Born in 1970. Whitney Vance had a granddaughter. Bosch was sure of it.

1. délit
2. prison [militaire]
3. héritier
4. dans la nature

17

Claudy put all of the photos into a stiff cardboard folder[1] to keep them from getting bent or damaged[2]. In the car, Bosch opened the folder and looked at the photo of the woman and the baby one more time. He knew there were a lot of aspects of his theory to confirm and some that could never be confirmed. The film negatives that produced the photos in the folder were found secreted[3] in Nick Santanello's camera but that did not necessarily mean he had taken the photos himself. The photos could have been taken for him and then the negatives mailed to him in Vietnam. Harry knew it was a possibility that could not be completely dismissed[4] but his gut told him[5] that it was an unlikely scenario[6]. The negatives had been found with his camera and other negatives of photos taken by him. It was clear to him Santanello had taken the shot of the woman and the baby.

The other question that hung over the[7] theory was why Santanello would keep his relationship and fatherhood[8] secret from his family, most notably[9] his sister, back in Oxnard. Bosch knew that family dynamics were almost as unique as fingerprints and it might take several more visits[10] with Olivia to get to the truth of the relationships within[11] the Santanello family. He decided that the best use of his time would be to prove or disprove[12] that Santanello was Whitney Vance's

1. chemise en carton rigide
2. éviter les pliures et autres dégâts
3. cachés
4. écartée
5. il savait au fond de lui
6. improbable
7. pesait sur sa
8. sa paternité
9. surtout à
10. entretiens
11. pour réellement comprendre les relations au sein de
12. confirmer ou infirmer

son and that he may have produced[1] an heir—the baby in the Hotel del Coronado photos. The other explanations could come later, if they still mattered at that point[2].

He closed the folder and snapped the attached elastic band back around it[3].

Before starting the car, Bosch pulled out his phone and called Gary McIntyre, the investigator at the National Personnel Records Center. The day before, Olivia Macdonald had written an e-mail to McIntyre granting[4] Bosch permission to receive and review records of her brother's military service. He now checked with McIntyre on the status of his search.

"Just finished pulling everything together," McIntyre said. "It's too big to e-mail. I'll drop it[5] on our download[6] site and e-mail you the password."

Bosch wasn't sure when he would get to a computer terminal[7] to download a dense digital file[8], or if he could even figure out how to do it[9].

"That's fine," he said. "But I'm on the road today heading to San Diego and I'm not sure I can access it. I'd love knowing what you came up with during[10] his training—since I'll be down there."

Bosch let that hang in the air[11]. He knew a guy like McIntyre would be slammed with[12] records requests from all over the country and needed to move on to the next case. But Harry hoped that the intrigue involved in the Santanello file—a soldier killed forty-six years earlier—would win the day[13] and push McIntyre toward[14] answering at least a few questions on the phone. The NCIS investigator probably spent most of his days pulling files on Gulf War vets[15] accused of drug- and alcohol-infused crimes or locked up in Baker Act wards[16].

1. engendrer
2. à ce moment-là
3. remit l'élastique autour
4. accordant à
5. Je le mettrai
6. de téléchargement
7. aurait accès à un ordinateur
8. gros fichier numérique
9. même s'il savait comment faire
10. J'aimerais bien savoir ce que tu as trouvé sur
11. laissa un blanc
12. était submergé de
13. l'emporterait
14. inciterait McIntyre à
15. des anciens combattants
16. internés en hôpital psychiatrique d'urgence [Floride]

Finally, McIntyre responded.

"If you don't mind hearing me eat the meatball sub[1] that was just delivered to my desk, I can go through the stuff[2] and answer a few questions."

Bosch pulled out his notebook.

"Perfect," he said.

"What are you looking for?" McIntyre asked.

"Just so I have it right[3], can we start with the short version of his postings[4]? You know, where and when?"

"Sure."

Bosch took notes as McIntyre, between loud bites[5] of his sandwich, read off the record of Santanello's military assignments. He had arrived at boot camp[6] at the San Diego Naval Training Center in June 1969. Upon graduation[7] he received orders moving him to the hospital corps school at Balboa Naval Hospital. His training was then continued at the Field Medical School at Camp Pendleton in Oceanside and in December he was ordered[8] to Vietnam, where he was assigned to the hospital ship *Sanctuary*. After four months on the boat, he received a TAD (Temporary Additional Duty) to First Medical Battalion in Da Nang, at which point he started[9] accompanying Marine recon units into the bush. He remained with First Med for seven months, until he was killed in action.

Bosch thought of the Zippo lighter with the Subic Bay chevron that he had found among Santanello's belongings in Olivia Macdonald's attic. It was still in its box and appeared to be a keepsake[10].

"So he was never in Olongapo?" he asked.

"No, not on here[11]," McIntyre said.

Bosch thought maybe Santanello had gotten the Zippo in a trade[12] with a medic or soldier who had previously been assigned to the base in the Phil-

1. sandwich aux boulettes de viande
2. feuilleter le dossier
3. pour être sûr d'avoir les bonnes infos
4. affectations
5. de bruyantes bouchées
6. camp d'entraînement
7. Une fois diplômé,
8. envoyé
9. et commença alors à
10. souvenir
11. d'après mes sources
12. par un troc

ippines. Possibly someone he had served with or cared for[1] on the *Sanctuary*.

"What else?" McIntyre asked.

"Okay, I'm trying to find people I can talk to," Bosch said. "People he was tight with[2]. Do you have the orders for his TAD from basic to Balboa?"

He waited. He was about to[3] ask McIntyre to go further than he probably anticipated when he agreed to answer questions while eating. From his own experience, Bosch knew that because of the random[4] nature of a soldier's training and assignments in the military, few relationships lasted. But because Santanello was on a trajectory of training as a combat medic, there might be one or two other corpsmen who made the same journey[5], and it was likely they would have bonded[6] as the familiar faces in a sea of strangers.

"Yeah, got it," McIntyre said.

"Does it list all personnel transferred on the same orders?" Bosch asked.

"Yes. Fourteen guys from his basic training class went to Balboa."

"Okay, good. Now what about the orders from Balboa to Field Medical at Pendleton? Is there anybody on that list who he went through all three steps with[7]?"

"You mean basic to Balboa to Pendleton? Shit, that could take all day, Bosch."

"I know it's a lot, but if you have the lists there, is there anybody on that list of fourteen that went with him to Pendleton?"

Bosch thought the request was less involved[8] than McIntyre was indicating but he wasn't going to suggest that[9].

"Hold on," McIntyre said gruffly[10].

Bosch was silent. He didn't want to possibly say the wrong thing and halt[11] the cooperation. Four

1. dont il s'était occupé
2. dont il était proche
3. s'apprêtait à
4. aléatoire
5. parcours
6. qu'ils se soient liés
7. avec qui il aurait effectué les trois étapes
8. compliquée
9. se garderait bien de le lui faire remarquer
10. d'un ton bourru
11. mettre fin à

minutes went by[1] before he heard any sounds, including eating, from McIntyre.

"Three guys," he finally said.

"So three guys were in all three training classes with him?" Bosch asked.

"That's right. You ready to copy?"

"Ready."

McIntyre recited and spelled[2] three names: Jorge Garcia-Lavin, Donald C. Stanley, and Halley B. Lewis. Bosch recalled the name Lewis being stenciled on the shirt that Santanello was wearing in the photo Olivia had shown him. He took it as a sign that the two were tight[3]. He now had a direction.

"By the way," McIntyre said. "Two of these guys were KIA."

The air went out of Bosch's hope[4] of finding someone who could help him identify the woman and baby in the del Coronado photograph.

"Which ones?" he asked.

"Garcia-Lavin and Stanley," McIntyre said. "And I really need to get back to my work, Harry. All of this is in the file you can download."

"I'll grab it[5] as soon as I can," Bosch said quickly. "One last quick question and I'll let you go. Halley B. Lewis. You have a hometown or DOB[6] to go with that name?"

"Says here Tallahassee, Florida. That's all I've got."

"Then that's what I'll take[7]. I can't thank you enough, Gary. Have a great day."

Bosch disconnected[8], started the car, and headed west toward the 170, which would take him up to San Fernando. His plan was to use the SFPD computer to track down[9] Halley B. Lewis and see what he could remember about his fellow corps-

1. s'écoulèrent
2. épela
3. proches
4. Bosch sentit s'effondrer ses espoirs
5. Je le récupère
6. date de naissance [date of birth]
7. Alors je m'en contenterai
8. raccrocha
9. retrouver

man Dominick Santanello. As he drove he thought about the percentages. Four men go through basic training, preliminary medical training, and then combat medical school together. They then get shipped to Vietnam together and only one out of four makes it back home alive.

Bosch knew from his own experience in Vietnam that corpsmen were high-value targets[1]. They were number three on every VC[2] sniper's list, after the lieutenant and radioman on a patrol. You take out[3] the leader, then you take out communications. After that, take out triage[4] and you have an enemy unit in complete fear and disarray[5]. Most of the corpsmen Bosch knew wore no markings indicating[6] what their role was in a recon mission.

Bosch wondered if Halley B. Lewis knew how lucky he had been.

1. des cibles très prisées
2. du Vietcong
3. On élimine
4. le triage médical
5. paniquée et désorganisée
6. ne portaient aucun insigne qui puisse indiquer

18

Bosch called Whitney Vance's private number on his way to San Fernando and got the straight-to-message beep[1] again. He once again asked Vance to call him back. After disconnecting he wondered what Vance's status was as a client. If he was no longer communicating with Bosch, was Bosch still working for him? Harry was well[2] into the case and his time was paid for. Either way[3] he wasn't stopping what he had started.

He next took a shot in the dark[4] and called directory assistance[5] for Tallahassee, Florida. He asked for a listing for Halley B. Lewis and was told there was only one listing under that name and it was for a law office[6]. Bosch asked to be connected[7], and soon the call was answered by a secretary who put Bosch on hold[8] when he identified himself and said he wanted to talk to Mr. Lewis about Dominick Santanello from the Field Medical School at Camp Pendleton. At least a minute went by and Bosch used the time to formulate what he would say to the man, should he get on the line[9], without violating his confidential agreement with Vance.

"This is Halley Lewis," a voice finally said. "What is this about?"

"Mr. Lewis, I am an investigator out in[10] Los Angeles," Bosch said. "Thank you for taking my call. I am working on an investigation involving the late[11] Dominick Santanello. I—"

1. tomba directement sur la boîte vocale
2. avait bien avancé
3. De toute façon,
4. tenta sa chance
5. les renseignements téléphoniques
6. cabinet d'avocat
7. mis en relation
8. en attente
9. s'il prenait l'appel
10. de
11. défunt

"I'll say he's late[1]. Nick died almost fifty years ago."

"Yes, sir, I know."

"What could you possibly be investigating about him?"

Bosch dropped into[2] his prepared response.

"It is a confidential investigation, but I can tell you it involves trying to determine if Dominick left behind an heir."

There was a moment of silence before Lewis responded.

"An heir? He was about nineteen when he got killed in Vietnam."

"Correct, sir. He was a month short of[3] his twentieth birthday. It doesn't mean he couldn't have fathered[4] a child."

"And that's what you are trying to find out?"

"Yes. I'm interested in the period he was in San Diego County for basic training through[5] his training at Balboa and Pendleton. I'm working with NCIS[6] on this and their investigator told me that you were in the same units with Nick until he received orders to Vietnam."

"That's true. Why is the NCIS involved in something like this?"

"I made contact to get Nick's military records archive and we were able to determine that you were one of three men who was in all three training stops[7] with Nick. You're the only one still alive."

"I know. You don't have to tell me."

Bosch had taken Victory Boulevard into North Hollywood and now turned north on the 170. The fortress of the San Gabriel Mountains crossed his entire windshield[8].

1. Ah çà, défunt, vous pouvez le dire

2. lui servit

3. Il était à un mois de

4. concevoir

5. jusqu'à

6. le Service d'enquêtes criminelles de la Marine

7. lieux de formation

8. pare-brise

"So why would you think I might know anything about whether Nick had a kid or not?" Lewis asked.

"Because you two were tight," Bosch said.

"How would you know that? Just because we were in the same training units doesn't—"

"He took[1] that swim test for you. He put on your shirt and got counted as[2] you."

1. avait passé
2. s'était fait passer pour

There was a long silence before Lewis asked Bosch how he knew that story.

"I saw the photo," Bosch said. "His sister told me the story."

"I haven't thought about that in a long time," Lewis said. "But to answer your question, I don't know if Nick had an heir. If he fathered a child he didn't tell me."

"If he fathered a child she would have been born after you all received orders at the end of Field Medical School. Nick would have been in Vietnam."

"And I in Subic Bay. You said 'she.'"

"I saw a photo he took. It showed a woman and a baby girl on the beach by the del Coronado. The mother was Latina. Do you remember him with a woman back then?"

"I remember a woman, yes. She was older and she put the hex on him[3]."

"The hex?"

"He fell under her spell[4]. That was toward the end, when we were at Pendleton. He met her in a bar in Oceanside. They came up there looking for guys like him."

3. lui avait jeté un sort
4. s'était laissé envoûter

"What do you mean, 'like him'?"

"Hispanic, Mexican. There was all this Chicano Pride stuff[5] going on down there at that time. It was like they recruited the Mexican guys off the base. Nick was brown but his parents were white.

5. ces mouvements identitaires mexicains

I knew that because I met them at the graduation. But he told me he was adopted and he knew that his real mother was Mexican. These people tapped into that[1], I guess. His true identity, you know?"

"And this woman you mentioned was part of that?"

"Yes. I remember we tried to talk sense into him[2], me and Stanley. But he said he was in love. It wasn't the Mexican thing. It was her."

"You remember her name?"

"No, not really. It was so long ago."

Bosch tried to keep his disappointment out of his voice. "What did she look like?"

"Dark hair, pretty. She was older but not too old. Twenty-five, maybe thirty. He said she was an artist." Bosch knew that if he kept Lewis thinking back to that time, more details might come to him.

"Where did they meet?"

"Must've been the Surfrider—we hung there a lot[3]. Or one of those bars near the base."

"And he'd go to see her on weekend leave?"

"Yeah. There was this place down in San Diego where he would go to see her when he got liberty. It was in the barrio[4] and under a freeway or a bridge and they called it Chicano Way or something like that. It was so long ago it's hard to remember. But he told me about it. They were trying to make it like a park and they painted graffiti on the freeway. He started calling those people his new *familia*. He used the Spanish and that was funny because he didn't even speak Spanish. He had never learned."

It was all interesting information and Bosch could see where it fit[5] with other parts of the story he already had. He was thinking of what to ask next when the true payoff to the shot-in-the-dark call to Tallahassee came[6].

1. exploitaient ce filon

2. lui faire entendre raison

3. on traînait souvent là-bas

4. quartier latino-américain

5. en quoi elles coïncidaient

6. tomba l'info qu'il avait cherchée par ce coup de fil hasardeux en Floride

"Gabriela," Lewis said. "It just came to me[1]."

"That was her name?" Bosch said.

He had failed to keep[2] the excitement out of his voice. "Yeah, I'm pretty sure now," Lewis said. "Gabriela."

"Remember a last name?" Bosch tried.

Lewis laughed.

"Man, I can't believe I pulled her first name up out of the muck[3]."

"It's very helpful."

Bosch started shutting the conversation down[4]. He gave Lewis his phone number and asked him to call if he remembered anything else about Gabriela or Santanello's time in San Diego.

"So you returned to Tallahassee after you served," Bosch said, just to move[5] the conversation toward a close[6].

"Yes, I came right back[7]," Lewis said. "Had enough of California, Vietnam, all of it. I've been here ever since."

"What kind of law[8] do you practice?"

"Oh, just about any kind of law you need. In a town like Tallahassee it pays to diversify. I like to say the one[9] thing I won't do is defend FSU football players[10]. I'm a Gator[11] and can't cross that line[12]."

Bosch guessed he was speaking to some sort of state rivalry but it was beyond him[13]. His knowledge of sports had only recently stretched past[14] the Dodgers to a cursory[15] interest in the return of the L.A. Rams.

"Can I ask you something?" Lewis said. "Who wants to know if Nick left an heir?"

"You can ask, Mr. Lewis, but that's the one question I can't answer."

1. Ça vient de me revenir
2. n'avait pu masquer
3. c'est déjà incroyable que j'aie pu me rappeler son prénom
4. à mettre fin à la conversation
5. orienter
6. son terme
7. rentré tout de suite
8. genre de droit
9. seule
10. l'équipe de football américain FSU [de Floride]
11. supporter des Gators [autre équipe de Floride]
12. je n'en démordrai pas
13. ça lui échappait
14. dépassé
15. superficiel

"Nick had nothing and his family didn't have much more. This has got to do with his adoption, right?"

Bosch was silent. Lewis had nailed it[1].

"I know, you can't answer," Lewis said. "I'm a lawyer. I guess I have to respect that."

Bosch decided to get off the line[2] before Lewis put anything else together[3] and asked another question. "Thank you, Mr. Lewis, and thank you for your help."

Bosch disconnected and decided to continue to San Fernando even though he had already found Lewis. He would check in[4] on matters relating to the Screen Cutter and do some Internet work to confirm the information Lewis had provided. But he knew without a doubt that he would eventually be heading[5] south to San Diego on the case[6].

A few minutes later he turned onto First Street in San Fernando and saw the three television trucks[7] parked in front of the police station.

1. mis le doigt dessus
2. raccrocher
3. ne fasse d'autres liens
4. jetterait un œil
5. finirait par aller vers
6. pour cette affaire
7. camions

19

Bosch entered the police station through the side door and headed down the back hall to the detective bureau. At the crossroads[1] with the main hallway he looked right[2] and saw a gathering of people outside the door to the roll-call room[3]. Among them was Bella Lourdes, who caught Bosch in her peripheral vision and signaled him over[4]. She was wearing jeans and a black golf shirt with the SFPD badge and unit designation on the left breast. Her gun and real badge were on her belt.

"What's going on?" Bosch asked.

"We got lucky," Lourdes said. "The Screen Cutter made an attempt today but the victim got away[5]. The chief said that's enough. He's going public[6]."

Bosch just nodded. He still thought it was the wrong move[7] but he understood the pressure on Valdez. Having sat on knowledge[8] of the previous cases was going to look bad enough. Lourdes was right about that. They were lucky the chief wasn't in the roll-call room telling the media about a fifth rape.

"Where's the victim?" Bosch asked.

"In the War Room," Lourdes said. "She's still pretty shaky[9]. I was giving her some time."

"How come[10] I wasn't called?"

Lourdes looked surprised.

"The captain said he couldn't reach you[11]."

1. l'intersection
2. à droite
3. de la salle de briefing
4. lui fit signe de venir
5. lui a échappé
6. Il rend l'affaire publique
7. que ce n'était pas la chose à faire
8. Le fait de ne rien avoir divulgué
9. sous le choc
10. Comment se fait-il que
11. te joindre

Bosch just shook his head and let it go[1]. It was a petty move[2] on Trevino's part, but there were more important things to worry about.

Bosch looked over the heads of Lourdes and the others in the hallway to try to get a glimpse[3] of the press conference. He could see Valdez and Trevino at the front of the room. He could not tell how many members of the media had shown up[4], because the reporters would be sitting and the camera operators would be at the back. He knew it all depended on what else was going on in Los Angeles that day. A serial rapist on the loose[5] in San Fernando, where the population largely ignored English-language[6] media, was probably not a massive draw[7]. He had seen that one of the media trucks outside was from Univision Noticias. That would get the word out[8] locally.

"So did Trevino or Valdez talk about a control?" he asked.

"A control?" Lourdes asked.

"Holding something back[9] that only we and the rapist would know. So we can kick out false confessions[10], confirm a true confession."

"Uh ... no, that didn't come up[11]."

"Maybe Trevino should have actually[12] tried to call me instead of trying to run a play on me[13]."

Bosch turned away from the group.

"You ready to go back and talk to her?" he asked. "How's her English?"

"She understands English," Lourdes said, "but likes to speak in Spanish."

Bosch nodded. They started down the hall[14] toward the detective bureau. The War Room was a large meeting room next to the bureau, with a long table and a whiteboard wall[15] where raids, cases, and deployments could be D&Ded—

1. n'insista pas
2. mesquin
3. aperçu
4. étaient venus
5. en liberté
6. anglophones
7. n'avait guère de chances d'attirer les foules
8. La nouvelle serait ainsi un peu connue
9. Taire quelque chose
10. De sorte qu'on puisse écarter les faux aveux
11. on n'en a pas parlé
12. vraiment
13. d'agir dans mon dos
14. s'engagèrent dans le couloir
15. tableau blanc

diagrammed[1] and discussed. It was usually used for operations like DUI task force sweeps and parade coverage[2].

"So what do we know?" Bosch asked.

"You probably know her or recognize her," Lourdes said. "She's a barista[3] at the Starbucks. She works part-time on the morning shift[4]. Six to eleven every day."

"What's her name?"

"Beatriz with a Z. Last name Sahagun."

Bosch couldn't connect the name with a face. There were three women who were usually working at Starbucks in the mornings when he came in. He assumed he would recognize her when he got to the War Room.

"She went right home after work?" Bosch said.

"Yes, and he's waiting for her," Lourdes said. "She lives on Seventh a block off of[5] Maclay. Fits the[6] profile: single family house, residential abutting commercial[7]. She comes in and immediately knows something's off[8]."

"She saw the screen[9]?"

"No, she didn't see anything. She smelled him."

"Smelled him?"

"She just said she came in and the house didn't smell right. And she remembered our fuckup[10] with the mailman. She was working there at the Starbucks that day we took Maron down[11]. Then the next time he came in for his coffee and breakfast sandwich, he told the girls behind the counter that the police had mistaken him[12] for a rapist that was hitting[13] in the neighborhoods. So she was immediately alarmed. She comes home, something isn't right, and she grabs a broom[14] in the kitchen."

1. schématisés
2. les opérations contre l'alcool au volant ou pour la sécurisation des défilés
3. serveuse
4. le matin
5. à un pâté de maisons de
6. Elle correspond au
7. un quartier résidentiel contigu à une zone commerciale
8. que quelque chose ne va pas
9. grillage
10. fiasco
11. où on a arrêté Maron
12. l'avait pris
13. sévissait
14. balai

"Holy shit, brave girl.[1] She should've gotten out of there."

"Fucking A[2], I know. But she sneaks up on *him*[3]. Comes into the bedroom and knows he's behind the curtain. She can tell[4]. So she takes a swing with the broom[5] like Adrian Gonzalez[6] and clocks[7] the guy. Right in the face. He falls out, brings the curtain down with him. He's dazed[8], doesn't know what the fuck happened, and then just jumps through the window and books it[9]. We're talking right through the glass[10]."

"Who's working that scene[11]?"

"The A team, and the captain put Sisto on it to babysit. But Harry, guess what? We got the knife."

"Wow."

"He dropped it when she hit him and then it got tangled up[12] in the curtain and he left it. Sisto just called me when they found it."

"Does the chief know about it?"

"No."

"That's our control. We need to tell Sisto and the A team to keep it on the down-low[13]."

"Got it."

"What mask was he wearing?"

"Didn't get to that yet with her."

"What about her menstrual cycle?"

"Didn't ask about that either."

They were now at the door to the War Room.

"Okay," Bosch said. "You ready? You take lead[14]."

"Let's do it."

Bosch opened the door and held it as Lourdes went in first. He immediately recognized the woman sitting at the big table as someone[15] who made his iced lattes[16] at the Starbucks around the corner. She was always smiling and friendly and

1. Nom de Dieu, quel courage !
2. 20/20 ouais
3. le prend par surprise
4. en est sûre
5. lui envoie un coup de balai
6. [joueur de baseball]
7. assomme
8. tout étourdi
9. fiche le camp
10. Carrément à travers la vitre
11. sur place
12. est resté pris
13. de ne pas en parler
14. C'est toi qui mènes l'entretien
15. comme la personne
16. cafés au lait glacés

was usually making his drink before he had even ordered it[1].

Beatriz Sahagun was texting someone[2] on her phone as they entered. She looked up solemnly and recognized Bosch. A small smile played on[3] her face.

"Iced latte," she said.

Bosch nodded and smiled back. He offered his hand and she shook it.

"Beatriz, I'm Harry Bosch. I'm glad you're okay."

Bosch and Lourdes took seats across the table from her[4] and began asking her questions. With the general story already known, Lourdes was able to take a deeper dive[5], and new details emerged. On occasion Bosch would ask a question and Lourdes would repeat it in Spanish to make sure there was no misunderstanding[6]. Beatriz answered the questions slowly and thoughtfully[7] and that allowed Bosch to understand most of what was said without needing Lourdes to translate back to him.

Beatriz was twenty-four years old and fit the[8] physical profile of the Screen Cutter's prior[9] victims. She had long brown hair, dark eyes, and a slight build[10]. She had worked at Starbucks for two years and primarily as a barista because her English-language skills were not up to the level required for taking orders[11] and payments. She reported to Bosch and Lourdes that she had had no troubling encounters[12] with customers or fellow employees[13]. She had no stalkers or issues with former[14] boyfriends. She shared her house with another Starbucks barista who usually worked the day shift[15] and was gone at the time of the intrusion.

In the course of the interview Beatriz revealed that the intruder in her house was wearing a

1. qu'il ait même passé commande
2. était en train d'envoyer un SMS
3. éclaira
4. en face d'elle, de l'autre côté de la table
5. put aller plus en profondeur
6. de malentendu
7. soigneusement
8. correspondait au
9. précédentes
10. silhouette fine
11. les commandes
12. n'avait pas eu d'expérience désagréable
13. des collègues
14. ne se faisait pas suivre et n'avait pas de problèmes avec d'anciens
15. dans la journée

Lucha Libre wrestling mask[1] and she offered the same description of it as the previous Screen Cutter victim—black, green, and red.

She also revealed that she tracked[2] her menstrual cycle on a calendar she kept on her bedside table. She explained that she was raised as a strict Catholic and had practiced the rhythm method of birth control[3] with her former boyfriend.

The detectives paid particular attention to what had alerted Beatriz to the possibility that there was an intruder in her house. The smell. Under careful questioning she revealed that she believed it was not the smell of cigarettes but the smell exuded[4] by someone who smokes. Bosch understood the distinction and thought it was a good get[5]. The Screen Cutter was a smoker. He didn't smoke while he was in her house but he had a scent trail that she picked up on[6].

Beatriz hugged her body[7] during most of the interview. She had acted instinctively to find the intruder rather than to flee[8] and now in the aftermath[9] was realizing how risky a decision it had been. When they were finished with the interview the detectives suggested that they take her out the side door to avoid any reporters still in the vicinity[10]. They also offered to take her home to gather clothes and belongings[11] she would need for at least the next few days. It was recommended that she and her roommate not stay in the home for a while, both[12] because crime scene techs and investigators would want access and for security reasons. The detectives did not specifically suggest[13] that the Screen Cutter might come back but it wasn't far from their minds[14].

1. masque de lutte mexicaine
2. suivait
3. méthode contraceptive Ogino
4. dégagée
5. info intéressante
6. il émanait de lui une odeur particulière qu'elle avait perçue
7. resta à se tenir le corps des bras
8. s'enfuir
9. qu'elle subissait le contrecoup, elle
10. parages
11. les affaires
12. à la fois
13. n'allèrent pas jusqu'à dire
14. ils y pensaient très fort

Lourdes called Sisto to give him the heads-up[1] that they were coming and then they drove in Lourdes's city car over to the victim's house.

Sisto was waiting in front of the house. He was born and raised local[2] and the SFPD was the only department he had ever worked for. Lourdes had outside experience with the L.A. County Sheriff's Department before coming over to San Fernando. Sisto was dressed similarly to Lourdes in jeans and black golf shirt. It seemed to be the casual detective uniform[3] employed most often by the pair[4]. Since coming to work at SFPD Bosch had been impressed with Lourdes's skill and dedication[5] and less so with Sisto's[6]. He appeared to Bosch to be marking time[7]. He was always on his phone texting[8] and was more likely to discuss the morning surf report[9] when making small talk[10] than to bring up[11] cases or police matters. Some detectives put photos and other reminders[12] of cases on their desks and bulletin boards[13], some put reminders of their interests outside the job[14]. Sisto was one of the latter. His desk was festooned with[15] surfing and Dodgers paraphernalia[16]. Looking at it the first time, Bosch could not even tell[17] it was a detective's desk.

Lourdes stuck close to Beatriz as she went into the house and gathered clothes and toiletries into a suitcase and duffel bag[18]. After she was packed[19] Lourdes asked if she could tell her story once more and walk the investigators through it[20]. Beatriz obliged[21] and once again Bosch marveled at her choice to go through the house looking for the intruder rather than to run as fast as she could from the premises[22].

Lourdes volunteered to drive Beatriz to her mother's home, also in San Fernando, and Bosch

1. l'informer
2. avait grandi dans la région
3. l'uniforme naturel
4. que l'un comme l'autre mettaient le plus souvent
5. les compétences et la motivation
6. un peu moins par celles de Sisto
7. Bosch avait l'impression qu'il meublait ses heures
8. à faire des SMS,
9. bulletin météo des plages
10. il papotait
11. d'aborder
12. mémentos
13. panneaux d'affichage
14. activités non professionnelles
15. orné de
16. bibelots
17. n'avait rien vu montrant que
18. un sac en toile
19. Une fois ses bagages terminés,
20. refaire son parcours avec les enquêteurs
21. accepta
22. des lieux

stayed behind with Sisto and the forensic team[1]. He first inspected the rear window where the screen had been cut out and the initial entry made into the house. It was very similar to the other cases.

Bosch next asked Sisto to show him the knife that was recovered from the tangle[2] of the fallen curtain. Sisto pulled a plastic evidence bag[3] from a brown paper bag holding several collected items.

"Forensics already checked it," Sisto said. "It's clean. No prints. Guy[4] wore gloves and a mask."

Bosch nodded as he studied the knife through the plastic. It was a black folding knife[5] and the blade[6] was open. He could see the manufacturer's logo stamped on the blade along with[7] some code numbers too small and difficult to read through the plastic. He would make sure he looked at it back in the controlled environment[8] of the detective bureau.

"Nice knife, though," Sisto added. "I looked it up[9] on my phone. It's made by a company called TitaniumEdge. It's called Socom Black. The powdered black blade is so it doesn't reflect light[10]—you know, when you're out at night and have to shank[11] somebody."

He said it with sarcasm that didn't amuse Bosch.

"Yeah, I know," Bosch said.

"I looked at a couple knife blogs while I was waiting here—yes, they have knife blogs[12]. A lot of them say the Socom Black is one of the best out there."

"Best for what?" Bosch asked.

"Scary shit[13], I guess. Wet work[14]. Socom probably stands for[15] some kind of special forces black ops stuff[16]."

1. police scientifique

2. récupéré dans l'enchevêtrement

3. sortit un sachet pour [recueil des] éléments de preuves

4. Le type

5. canif

6. la lame

7. ainsi que

8. ambiance calme

9. J'ai cherché

10. lame thermolaquée noire ne reflète pas la lumière

11. trucider

12. les blogs sur les couteaux, ça existe

13. Les trucs louches

14. Les meurtres

15. correspond à

16. opérations occultes

"Special Operations Command. Delta Force."

Sisto looked surprised.

"Whoa. I guess you know your military shit[1]."

"I know a few things."

Bosch carefully handed him back the knife.

Bosch wasn't sure what Sisto thought of him. They'd had little interaction even though their desks in the bureau were only a privacy wall apart[2]. Sisto handled[3] property crimes and Bosch wasn't spending his time on[4] unsolved property crimes, so there had been little reason for conversation beyond the routine salutations each day. Bosch assumed that Sisto, who was half Harry's age, viewed the older detective as some kind of relic from the past. The fact that Bosch most often wore a jacket and tie when he came in to work for free[5] was probably confounding to him[6] as well.

"So the blade was not folded when you found it?" Bosch asked. "The guy was behind the curtain with the blade out?"

"Yes, out and ready," Sisto said. "Think we ought to fold it closed[7] so nobody gets cut?"

"No. Book it[8] the way you found it. And just be careful with it. Warn[9] people it's open. Maybe see about getting[10] a box when you take it back to Evidence Control[11]."

Sisto nodded as he carefully placed the knife back in the larger evidence bag. Bosch stepped over to[12] the window and looked down at the broken glass in the backyard[13]. The Screen Cutter had hurled himself into[14] the window and broken through the framing[15] as well as the glass. Bosch's first thought was that he had to have been hurt. The whack[16] with the broomstick must have been so stunning[17] that he chose to flee instead of fight—the opposite reaction of his intended victim. But going through the window and taking

1. T'as l'air d'en connaître un rayon sur les trucs militaires
2. n'étaient séparés que d'une demi-cloison
3. s'occupait des
4. n'allait sûrement pas se consacrer à
5. gratis
6. déconcertant
7. Tu penses qu'on devrait le replier
8. Enregistre-le
9. Préviens
10. essaie de trouver
11. Contrôle des indices
12. marcha jusqu'à
13. jardin de derrière
14. s'était jeté contre
15. le chambranle
16. coup
17. surprenant

out the frame as well as the glass took[1] a lot of force.

"Any blood or anything in the glass?" he asked.

"Not that we found so far[2]," Sisto said.

"You got the word on[3] the knife, right? We don't talk about it with anybody—especially the brand[4] and model."

"Roger that.[5] You think people are really going to come in and confess to this?"

"I've seen stranger things. You never know."

Bosch pulled his phone and started moving away from Sisto so he could make a call in private. He stepped into the hallway and then into the kitchen, where he called his daughter's number. As usual, she didn't answer. Her primary use of the cell phone was for texting and checking her social media. But Bosch also knew that while she might not answer[6] his calls or even know about them—her phone's ringer[7] was perpetually silenced—she did listen to the messages he left.

As expected, the call rang through to message[8].

"Hey, it's your dad. Just wanted to check on you[9]. Hope everything is good and you're safe. I might be traveling through the OC[10] sometime this week on my way to San Diego on a case. Let me know if you want to grab coffee or something to eat. Maybe dinner. Okay, that's it[11]. Love you and hope to see you soon—oh, and put water in that dog bowl."

After disconnecting he stepped out the front door of the house, where there was a patrol officer on post. His name was Hernandez.

"Who's boss[12] tonight?" Bosch asked.

"Sergeant Rosenberg," Hernandez said.

"Can you hit him up[13] and see if he'll swing by and grab me[14]? I need to get back to the station[15]."

1. avait demandé
2. Non, rien pour l'instant
3. On t'a dit, pour
4. marque
5. Bien reçu !
6. même si elle ne répondait pas à
7. sonnerie
8. tomba sur sa boîte vocale
9. prendre des nouvelles
10. [Orange County]
11. c'est tout
12. Qui supervise
13. le joindre
14. s'il peut passer me prendre
15. commissariat

"Yes, sir."

Bosch walked out to the curb to wait for the patrol car with Irwin Rosenberg to come along. He needed a ride but he also needed to tell Rosenberg, who was watch commander[1] for the night, to have patrol keep an eye on Beatriz Sahagun's house.

He checked his phone and saw that he had just gotten a text back from Maddie saying she was up[2] for dinner if he was passing through and that there was a restaurant she had been wanting to try. Bosch replied that they would set it up[3] as soon as his schedule[4] became clear. He knew that his daughter, the San Diego trip, and the Vance case were all going to be put on hold[5] for at least a couple days. He would have to stay with the Screen Cutter case, if only to[6] be ready to respond to what the media spotlight would invariably bring in.

1. chef de veille
2. d'accord
3. organiseraient cela
4. emploi du temps
5. en attente
6. ne serait-ce que pour

20

Bosch was the first one into the detective bureau Saturday morning, and the only thing that would have made him prouder[1] was if he had stayed all night working the case. But his status as volunteer allowed him to choose his hours and he chose a solid night's sleep[2] over chasing a case till dawn[3]. He was too old for that. That he would reserve for homicides.

On his way through the police station he had stopped by the communications room and picked up the stack of messages that had come in since the news about the serial rapist hit the[4] media the evening before. He also dropped by[5] the evidence control unit and checked out[6] the knife recovered[7] at the crime scene.

Now at his desk he sipped[8] the iced latte he had picked up at Starbucks and started wading through[9] the messages. As he did an initial run-through[10] he created a second pile for messages in which it was noted that the caller spoke Spanish only. These he would give to Lourdes to review and follow up on[11]. She was expected to work the Screen Cutter case through[12] the weekend. Sisto was on call[13] for all other cases needing a detective, and Captain Trevino was due in[14] because it was his rotation weekend to be in charge of the department.

Among the Spanish-only messages was an anonymous call from a woman who reported that

1. encore plus fier

2. bonne nuit de sommeil

3. plutôt que suivre une affaire jusqu'au petit matin

4. avaient été connues des

5. était aussi passé par

6. pour reprendre

7. retrouvé

8. sirota

9. à éplucher

10. Après une première lecture rapide,

11. Il les ferait relire et suivre par Lourdes

12. pendant tout

13. d'astreinte

14. de garde au poste

she had also been attacked by a rapist who wore a mask like those worn by Mexican wrestlers[1]. She refused to reveal her name because she admitted she was illegally in the country[2] and the police operator could not convince her that no action would be taken against her on her immigration status if she fully reported the crime[3].

Bosch had always expected that there were other cases he didn't know about[4] but it was still a heartbreaking[5] message to read because the woman told the operator that the attack had occurred almost three years earlier. Bosch realized that the victim had lived with the psychological and perhaps even physical consequences of the horrible assault for all that time without even being able to hold on[6] to the hope that justice would someday prevail[7] and her attacker would be held to answer for[8] his crime. She had given all of that up[9] when she chose[10] not to report the crime for fear it would lead to her deportation[11].

There were people who would have no sympathy[12] for her, Bosch knew. People who would argue that her remaining silent about the attack[13] allowed the rapist to move on to the next victim without concern about police attention. Bosch could find some validity in that but he was more sympathetic to the plight of[14] the silent victim. Without even knowing the details of how she had gotten to this country, Bosch knew her path here had not been easy and her desire to stay no matter what[15] the consequences—even to be silent about a rape—was what touched him. Politicians could talk about building walls and changing laws[16] to keep people out, but in the end they were just symbols. Neither[17] would stop the tide[18] any more than the rock jetties at the mouth[19] of the port did. Nothing could stop the tide of hope and desire.

1. lutteurs
2. en situation irrégulière
3. signalait officiellement
4. dont il n'avait pas eu connaissance
5. déchirant
6. s'accrocher
7. justice serait rendue
8. devrait répondre de
9. renoncé à tout ça
10. en choisissant
11. expulsion
12. compassion
13. soutiendraient que son silence
14. avait tendance à compatir avec
15. quelles que soient
16. les lois
17. Aucune des deux solutions
18. marée
19. plus que les jetées à l'entrée

Bosch walked around the cubicle and put the stack of Spanish-only messages down on Lourdes's desk. It was the first time he had ever come around and seen her work space from this angle. There was the usual array[1] of police bulletins and Wanted flyers[2]. There was a flyer depicting[3] a missing[4] woman that had haunted the department for ten years because she had never been found and foul play was feared[5]. Pinned[6] at center to the half wall separating their desks were several photos of a child, a boy. Some of the photos showed him being held by Lourdes or another woman, and some depicted all three in group hugs[7]. He paused for a moment to lean down and look at the happiness in the photos and just then the door to the bureau opened and Lourdes entered.

"What are you doing?" she asked as she picked up a marker and wrote her start time[8] on the squad attendance board.

"Uh, I was just putting these phone messages down for you," he said as he backed up to give her room to enter her space. "The Spanish-language calls from last night."

Lourdes swung around him and[9] into her cubicle.

"Oh, okay. Thank you."

"Hey, is that your kid?"

"Yes. Rodrigo."

"I didn't know you had a kid."

"It happens."

There was an awkward[10] silence while she waited for Bosch to ask if the other woman was part of the relationship and which one actually bore[11] the child or if he was adopted. Bosch chose not to pursue it.

"That top message there is from another victim," he said, as he started moving back around the

1. étalage
2. d'avis de recherche
3. prospectus représentant
4. portée disparue
5. l'on craignait un meurtre
6. Épinglées
7. enlacés
8. heure d'arrivée
9. le contourna pour rentrer
10. gêné
11. avait porté

cubicles to his own desk. “Wouldn’t give a name but said she was an illegal. The com center[1] said she called on a pay phone[2] by the courthouse[3].”

“Well, we knew there were probably more out there,” Lourdes said.

“I’ve got a stack over here to go through[4] as well. And I pulled[5] the knife from evidence control.”

“The knife? Why?”

“These high-end[6] military knives are collectors’ items[7]. It might be traceable.”

He returned to his desk and dropped out of Lourdes’s sight[8].

Bosch looked first at the stack of messages that he knew would probably exhaust[9] a good part of his day with little or no return, and then at the knife.

He chose the knife. He first put on a pair of latex gloves and then removed the weapon from the plastic evidence bag. The noise made during the removal from the bag drew Lourdes up on her feet and looking over the partition.

“I never saw it last night,” she said.

Bosch held it up so she could see it close.

“That looks completely fucking savage,” she said.

“Definitely for use on a silent kill squad[10],” he said.

He drew the knife back and held it horizontally with the edge[11] of the blade out[12]. He pantomimed[13] attacking someone from behind, covering the mouth with his right hand and then sticking the point of the blade into a target’s neck[14] with his left. He then sliced outward[15] with the knife.

“You go in the side[16] and slice out through all of the bleeders[17] and the throat,” he said. “No sound, the target bleeds out in under[18] twenty seconds. Done.”

1. centre de communication
2. d’une cabine téléphonique
3. près du tribunal
4. à étudier
5. j’ai retiré
6. haut de gamme
7. des objets de collection
8. disparut du champ de vision de Lourdes
9. qui, il le savait, lui prendrait
10. Le genre qu’on utilise pour poignarder en douce
11. bord
12. vers l’extérieur
13. fit mine d’
14. cou imaginaire
15. Puis il fit mine de trancher une gorge
16. plantes sur le côté
17. veines
18. cible se vide de son sang en moins de

"The target?" Lourdes said. "Were you one of those guys, Harry? In a war, I mean."

"I was in a war long before you were born. But we didn't have anything like this. We used to put boot polish[1] on our blades."

She looked confused.

"So they wouldn't catch a reflection[2] in the dark," he said.

"Of course," she said.

He put the knife down on his desk, embarrassed by his demonstration.

"You think our guy is ex-military?" Lourdes asked.

"No, I don't," Bosch said.

"Why?"

"Because he ran[3] yesterday. I think if he had any training, he would have regrouped, recovered[4], and advanced[5]. He would have gone right back at[6] Beatriz. Maybe killed her."

Lourdes stared at him for a moment and then nodded toward the iced latte putting a water mark[7] on the blotter[8].

"Was she there today when you went in?"

"No, not there. Not surprising. But she might just be off[9] on Saturdays."

"Okay, well, I'm going to start calling some of these people back. Hope it doesn't bother you."

"No, no bother."

She disappeared from sight again and Bosch put on his reading glasses to examine the knife, but as he looked down at the weapon on his blotter he saw something else. He saw the face of a man he had killed in a tunnel more than forty years before. Bosch had pushed himself back[10] into a crevasse in the tunnel and the man had come right past him in the darkness. Hadn't seen him, hadn't smelled him. Bosch grabbed him from behind,

1. du cirage

2. ne brillent pas

3. a fui

4. aurait pris le temps de se remettre

5. de repasser à l'attaque

6. réattaqué

7. qui laissait une trace humide

8. sous-main

9. en congé

10. s'était retranché

put one hand over his face and mouth and tore through[1] the man's throat with his knife. It was over[2] so quickly and efficiently that not a drop of the arterial spray got on[3] Bosch. He always remembered the man's last breath[4] exhaling against the palm of the hand he had clamped over[5] his mouth. He remembered closing the man's eyes with his hand as he laid him down in his blood.

"Harry?"

Bosch came out of the memory. Captain Trevino was standing behind him in the cubicle.

"Sorry, I was just thinking," Bosch sputtered[6]. "What's up, Cap?"

"Sign the board," Trevino said. "I don't want to have to keep telling you[7]."

Bosch swiveled[8] in his chair to see Trevino pointing toward the door where the board was located[9].

"Right, right. I'll do it now."

He stood up and Trevino stepped back[10] so he could leave the cubicle. The captain spoke to his back.

"That's the knife?" Trevino asked.

"That's the knife," Bosch said.

Bosch grabbed a marker off the board's sill[11] and put down that he had arrived at 6:15 that morning. He hadn't exactly checked the time but he knew he had been at the Starbucks at 6:00.

Trevino went into his office and shut the door. Bosch returned to the knife on his desk. This time he put the time travel aside[12] and leaned down so he could read the numbers stamped[13] on the black blade. On one side of the TitaniumEdge logo was the date of manufacture—09/08—and on the other side was a number Bosch assumed was the weapon's unique serial number[14]. He wrote both

1. avait sectionné
2. Ça s'était fait
3. pas une seule goutte de sang [de la carotide] n'avait aspergé
4. souffle
5. qu'il maintenait serrée sur
6. bredouilla
7. vous le répéter sans cesse
8. pivota
9. situé
10. recula
11. rebord
12. ses souvenirs de côté
13. inscrits
14. numéro de série

of these down and then went online to see if TitaniumEdge had a website.

As he did so he heard Lourdes start one of the callbacks[1] in Spanish. Bosch understood enough to know she was calling someone who had fingered[2] a person she knew as the rapist. Bosch knew it would be a quick call. The investigators were 95 percent sure they were looking for a white man. Any caller accusing a Latino would be wrong and most likely engaged in[3] trying to make a personal enemy's life difficult.

Bosch found the TitaniumEdge site and quickly learned that owners of their knives could register them at purchase or thereafter[4]. It was not required and Bosch guessed that in most cases purchasers had not bothered[5]. The knife manufacturer was located in Pennsylvania—close to the steel mills[6] that produced the raw materials[7] of their weapons. The website showed that the company made several different folding knives. Not knowing if the business would be open on a Saturday, Bosch took a shot[8] and called the number listed on the website. His call was answered by an operator and he asked for the supervisor on duty[9].

"We have Johnny and George here today. They're the guys in charge[10]."

"Is one of them available[11]?" he asked. "Doesn't matter which[12]."

She put Bosch on hold and two minutes later a gruff[13] male voice came on the line. If there was a voice to match a black blade knife maker, it was this one.

"This is Johnny."

"Johnny, this is Detective Bosch with the SFPD out in[14] California. I was wondering if I could have a few minutes of your time to help with an investigation we have going out here."

1. rappels
2. balancé
3. vraisemblablement déterminé à
4. à l'achat ou ultérieurement
5. ne s'en étaient pas donné la peine
6. aciéries
7. matière première
8. tenta sa chance
9. chef de service
10. Ce sont eux les responsables
11. disponible
12. lequel
13. bourrue
14. depuis la

1. pris l'habitude
2. soit plus disposé
3. la petite ville de

There was a pause. Bosch had taken[1] to using the abbreviation SFPD when making calls outside the city because the chances were good that the receiver of the call would jump to the conclusion that Bosch was calling from the San Francisco Police Department and be more willing[2] to help than if they knew he was calling from tiny[3] San Fernando.

"SFPD?" Johnny finally said. "I've never even been to California."

"Well, it's not about you, sir," Bosch said. "It's about a knife that we recovered from a crime scene."

"Was someone hurt with it?"

4. Pas que nous sachions
5. cambrioleur
6. dans laquelle il était entré [par effraction]

"Not that we're aware of[4]. A burglar[5] dropped it when he was chased from a house where he had broken in[6]."

"Sounds like he was going to use it to hurt somebody."

7. trouver où il a été acheté

"We'll never know. He dropped it and I'm trying to trace it[7]. I see from your website that purchasers can register them. I was wondering if I could find out if this one is registered."

"Which one is it?"

8. d'une dizaine de centimètres

"It's a Socom Black. Four-inch[8] black powdered blade. On the blade it says it was made in September '08."

"Yeah, we don't make that one anymore."

9. très prisé

"But it is still highly regarded[9] and a collector's item, from what I've been told."

"Well, let me look it up here on the computer and see what we got."

10. se sentit encouragé
11. directement sur

Bosch was buoyed[10] by the cooperation. Johnny asked for the serial number and Bosch read it to him off[11] the blade. Harry could hear him tap it into a computer.

"Well, it's registered," Johnny said. "But unfortunately, that's a stolen[1] knife."

"Really?" Bosch said.

But this was not surprising to him. He thought it unlikely[2] that a serial rapist would use a weapon that could be traced directly to him, even if he narcissistically assumed that he would never lose the knife or be identified as a suspect.

"Yeah, stolen a couple years after the original purchaser bought it," Johnny said. "At least that's when he notified us[3]."

"Well, it's been recovered," Bosch said. "And that owner will be getting it back[4] after we're finished with the case. Can you give me that information?"

Here was where Bosch hoped that Johnny wouldn't ask for a warrant[5]. That would slow pursuit of this lead down to a crawl[6]. Rousing[7] a judge on a weekend to sign a warrant for a small part of an investigation was not something he relished[8] doing.

"We are always happy to help out the military and law enforcement[9]," Johnny said patriotically.

Bosch then wrote down the name and address as of[10] 2010 of the original buyer of the knife. He was Jonathan Danbury and his address, at least back then[11], was in Santa Clarita, no more than a thirty-minute drive up[12] the 5 freeway from San Fernando.

Bosch thanked Johnny the knife maker for his cooperation and ended the phone call. He immediately went to the DMV database to see if he could locate Jonathan Danbury. He quickly learned that Danbury still lived in the same house as when he reported the knife stolen in 2010. Bosch also learned that Danbury was now thirty-six years old and had no criminal record[13].

1. volé
2. trouvait peu crédible
3. nous l'a signalé
4. son propriétaire le récupérera
5. mandat
6. Ce serait un terrible contretemps pour suivre la piste
7. Sonner
8. qu'il aimait
9. la police
10. en
11. à l'époque
12. en prenant par
13. casier judiciaire

Bosch waited while he heard Lourdes finish a call in Spanish. The moment she hung up[1] he got her attention.

"Bella."

"What?"

"Ready to take a ride[2]? I've got a line on[3] the knife. A guy up in Santa Clarita who reported it stolen[4] six years ago." She popped her head up over the privacy wall.

"I'm ready to shoot myself is what I am[5]," she said. "These people, they're just ratting out[6] their old boyfriends, anybody they want to have the cops hassle[7]. And a lot of date rapes[8], sad to say. Women who think the guy who forced himself on them[9] is our guy."

"We're going to keep getting those calls until we find the real guy," Bosch said.

"I know. I was just hoping to spend tomorrow with my son. But I'll be stuck here if these calls keep coming."

"I'll take tomorrow[10]. You take off[11]. I'll leave all the Spanish-only calls for Monday."

"Really?"

"Really."

"Thank you. Do we know how the knife was stolen back then?"

"Not yet. You ready to go?"

"Could this be our guy? Report the knife stolen as a cover[12]?"

Bosch shrugged[13] and pointed at his computer.

"His record's clean[14]," he said. "The profiler said look for priors[15]. Little stuff that builds up to the big stuff."

"Profilers don't always get it right," she said. "I'll drive[16]."

That last sentence was a joke between them. As a reserve officer Bosch was given no city vehicle.

1. Dès qu'elle raccrocha,
2. aller faire un tour
3. piste pour
4. a signalé son vol
5. Je suis plutôt prête à me tirer une balle dans la tête
6. tout ce qu'elles font, c'est balancer
7. faire embêter par les flics
8. viols commis par une connaissance
9. les a violées
10. Je me charge de demain
11. Prends ta journée
12. pour se couvrir
13. haussa les épaules
14. Il n'a pas de casier
15. de chercher ceux avec des antécédents
16. C'est moi qui conduis

Lourdes had to drive if they were conducting official police business.

On the way out of the bureau Lourdes stopped to note the time and their destination—SCV[1]—on the board by the squad room door.

Bosch didn't.

1. Santa Clarita Valley

21

1. immense ville-dortoir
2. vallée
3. protégée de son influence et de ses maux
4. critères
5. ce qui attirait
6. policiers
7. au fil du temps,
8. quasiment à chaque coin de rue
9. aspect dissuasif
10. cols de montagne
11. en témoigner
12. en plein dans l'allée
13. Et comble d'ironie
14. pile en face de chez
15. adjoint
16. fossé d'écoulement
17. était venu ouvrir

The Santa Clarita Valley was a sprawling bedroom community[1] built into the cleft[2] of the San Gabriel and Santa Susana Mountains. It was north of the city of Los Angeles and buffered from it and its ills[3] by those same mountain chains. It was a place that from its beginning drew families north from the city, families looking for cheaper homes, newer schools, greener parks, and less crime. Those same features[4] were also the draw for[5] hundreds of law officers[6] who wanted to get away from the places they protected and served. It was said that over time[7] Santa Clarita became the safest place in the county to live because there was a cop residing on almost every block[8].

But even with that deterrent[9] and the mountains as a wall, the ills of the city were inescapable and they eventually started to migrate through the mountain passes[10] and into the neighborhoods and parks. Jonathan Danbury could attest to that[11]. He told Bosch and Lourdes that his $300 TitaniumEdge knife had been stolen from the glove compartment of his car parked right in the driveway[12] of his house on Featherstar Avenue. To add insult to injury[13], the theft occurred right across the street from the home of[14] a Sheriff's deputy[15].

It was a nice neighborhood of middle- to upper-middle-class homes, with a natural drainage swale[16] called the Haskell Canyon Wash running behind it. Danbury had answered the door[17] in a T-shirt, board shorts[1], and flip-flops[2]. He explained that he was an Internet-based travel agent who worked from home[3], while his wife sold real estate[4] in the Saugus area of the Valley. He said he had forgotten all about his stolen knife until Bosch presented it in its evidence bag.

"Never thought I'd see that again," he said. "Wow."

"You reported it stolen to TitaniumEdge six years ago," Bosch said. "Was there a report made with the[5] Sheriff's Department too?"

Santa Clarita had no police department and had contracted[6] since its inception[7] with the Los Angeles County Sheriff's Department.

"I called them," Danbury said. "In fact, Tillman, the deputy who lived across the street back then, came over and took the report. But nothing ever came of it[8]."

"You get a follow-up[9] from a detective?" Bosch asked.

"I think I remember getting a call but they weren't too enthused about it[10]. The detective thought it was probably just kids in the neighborhood. I thought that was pretty bold[11]."

He pointed across the street to illustrate the story. "There was a sheriff's car parked right there and my car is right here, twenty feet away[12], and these kids have the cojones to break into[13] the car to steal my knife."

"They break the window, set off the car's alarm?"

"Nope. The detective concluded I left the car unlocked[14], made it sound like I was at fault. But I didn't leave it unlocked. I never do. I think those kids had a Slim Jim[15] or something and they got in without breaking the window."

1. short de bain
2. en tongs
3. faisait du télétravail
4. des biens immobiliers
5. une plainte auprès du
6. passé un contrat
7. débuts
8. ça n'a jamais rien donné
9. Vous avez eu un suivi
10. ça n'avait pas l'air de les passionner
11. plutôt audacieux
12. à 6 mètres
13. les couilles de forcer
14. que je n'avais pas verrouillé ma voiture
15. un « rossignol » [pour forcer la portière]

1. n'a eu lieu
2. S'il y en a eu, y me l'ont pas dit, je vous le garantis
3. que je ne vous fais pas entrer
4. poignardé ou je ne sais quoi
5. il nous est interdit d'en dire plus
6. fit comme s'il
7. tapota
8. cigarette
9. Ça vaut probablement
10. C'est ce qu'on dit

"So no arrests came about[1] as far as you know?"

"If there were, they sure as shit didn't tell me[2]."

"Did you keep a copy of the report, sir?" Lourdes asked.

"I did but that was a long time ago," Danbury said. "I got three kids and run a business out of here. That's why I'm not asking you in[3]. The place is a perpetual mess and I would need some time to look for the report in all the debris that we call a house."

He laughed. Bosch didn't. Lourdes just nodded. Danbury pointed at the evidence bag.

"So I don't see any blood on it," Danbury said. "Please don't tell me someone was stabbed or something[4]."

"Nobody was stabbed," Bosch said.

"Seems like it would be something serious for you to come all the way up here."

"It was serious but we're not at liberty to discuss it[5]."

Bosch reached into the inside pocket of his jacket and acted like he[6] didn't find what he was looking for. He then patted[7] his other pockets.

"You don't have a smoke[8] I could borrow, do you, Mr. Danbury?" he asked.

"No, don't smoke," Danbury said. "Sorry."

He pointed to the knife.

"Well, will I get it back?" he asked. "It's probably worth[9] more than what I paid for it. People collect those."

"So I've heard[10]," Bosch said. "Detective Lourdes will give you her card. You can check with her in a few weeks about getting it back. Can I ask you something? Why'd you have the knife?"

"Well, to be honest, I've got a brother-in-law who's ex-military and he collects this sort of stuff. I thought maybe it would be good to have some protection but I think I mostly got it to impress him. I ordered it and at first I kept it in my night table. But then I realized that was stupid. It might end up hurting one of the kids. So I put it in the glove box. I actually forgot about it until I got in the car one day and saw the box was open. I checked and the knife was gone."

"Anything else taken?" Lourdes asked.

"No, just the knife," Danbury said. "That was the only thing of value in the whole car."

Bosch nodded, then turned and glanced back[1] to the house across the street.

"Where did the deputy move?" he asked.

"I don't know," Danbury said. "We weren't really friends. I think it might've been Simi Valley."

Bosch nodded. They had gleaned[2] what they could about the knife from Danbury and he had seemingly passed the smoke test[3]. He decided to ask a door slammer[4]—a question that could result in the angry end of a[5] voluntary conversation.

"Do you mind telling us where you were yesterday around lunchtime?" he asked.

Danbury looked at them uncomfortably for a moment and then broke into an awkward smile[6].

"Hey, come on[7], what is this?" he asked. "Am I a suspect in something?"

"It's a routine question," Bosch said. "The knife was recovered in a burglary yesterday about noon. It would just save us[8] some time if you could tell us where you were. That way our boss doesn't see it's not in the report and send us back to bother you."

Danbury reached back[9] and put his hand on the doorknob. He was close to ending things and slamming the door on them[10].

"I was here all day long," he said curtly[11]. "Except when I took two of my kids home

1. jeta un coup d'œil

2. glané

3. n'était apparemment pas fumeur

4. poser la question qui fâche

5. la question qui pouvait énerver et mettre fin à toute

6. eut un sourire gêné

7. dites donc

8. Ça nous ferait juste gagner

9. se retourna à demi

10. près de couper court et de leur fermer la porte au nez

11. sèchement

sick from school[1] to the doctor around eleven. All that can be easily checked. Anything else?"

"No, sir," Bosch said. "Thanks for your time."

Lourdes handed[2] Danbury a business card and followed Bosch off the front stoop[3]. They heard the door close sharply behind them.

They drove back toward the freeway and stopped at the drive-thru at a fast-food franchise[4] so Bosch could eat something while they headed south. Lourdes said she had eaten earlier and passed[5]. They did not speak about the interview at first. Bosch wanted to think about the conversation with Danbury before discussing it. Once they were on the 5 and Lourdes had opened the windows to blow out the smell[6] of fast food, he brought it up[7].

"So what do you think about Danbury?" he asked.

Lourdes closed the windows.

"I don't know," she said. "I was hoping he'd know who took the knife. We need to pull[8] the Sheriff's report, just to see if they did look at anybody."

"So you're not thinking he reported it stolen as a cover?"

"Reported it stolen and then two years later started raping people in San Fernando? I don't think it hunts[9]," Lourdes said.

"The *reported* rapes started two years later. As we know from last night's callers, there are probably other rapes. They could have started earlier."

"True. But I don't see Danbury. His record's clean. He doesn't fit the profile. Doesn't smoke. Is married, has kids."

"You said profilers aren't always right," Bosch reminded her. "He has his lunchtimes free working from home and with the kids in school."

1. pour passer prendre à l'école deux de mes enfants malades et les emmener
2. tendit à
3. pour quitter le perron
4. au drive-in d'une chaîne de fast-food
5. ne voulait rien prendre
6. dissiper l'odeur
7. aborda le sujet
8. Il faut qu'on trouve
9. Ça me paraît douteux

"But not yesterday. He gave us an alibi we could easily check with the doctor and the school. It's not him, Harry."

Bosch nodded. He agreed but felt it was good to play devil's advocate to avoid tunnel thinking[1].

"It's still weird[2] when you think about it," Lourdes said.

"Think about what?" Bosch asked.

"How a knife stolen up here in blue-eyed[3] Santa Clarita ends up with[4] a white guy wearing masks and going after[5] Latinas in San Fernando."

"Yeah. We've talked about the racial side of this. Maybe we have to hit that harder[6] now."

"Yeah, how?"

"Go back to the LAPD. They probably keep files at Foothill and Mission on racist threats, arrests, that sort of thing. Maybe we come up with[7] some names."

"Okay, I can do that."

"Monday. Take tomorrow off."

"Planning on it[8]."

But he knew she had volunteered to make the contact with the LAPD divisions because of the animosity toward Bosch in some quarters of the department. She wanted to make sure she got access to LAPD files and didn't get stiffed[9] because somebody had a grudge against[10] Bosch.

"Where do you live, Bella?" he asked.

"Chatsworth," she said. "We have a house off Winnetka[11]."

"Nice."

"We like it. But it's the same everywhere. It's all about the schools. We've got good schools."

Bosch guessed from the photos he saw pinned to the separation wall that Rodrigo was no more than three years old. Lourdes was already worried about his future.

1. d'avoir l'esprit borné
2. Quand même, c'est bizarre,
3. la blanche
4. arrive entre les mains d'
5. qui s'en prend aux
6. le creuser un peu plus
7. va pêcher
8. J'y compte bien
9. de ne pas se faire rembarrer
10. par quelqu'un ayant une dent contre
11. près de l'avenue Winnetka

"I've got a nineteen-year-old," he said. "A girl. She had some hard knocks[1] in her life. Lost her mother young. But she made it through[2]. Kids are amazing, as long as they have the push in the right direction at home."

Lourdes just nodded and Bosch felt like a fool for dispensing unwanted and obvious advice.

"Rodrigo a Dodgers fan?" he asked.

"He's a little young but he will be," she said.

"Then it's you. You said Beatriz swung the broomstick like Adrian Gonzales."

Gonzalez was a fan favorite, especially among the Latino fan base.

"Yeah, we love going to Chavez Ravine[3] and watching Gonzo."

Bosch nodded and changed the subject back to work.

"So, nothing of value in the calls this morning?"

"Nothing. You were right. I don't think anything is going to pan out[4] and now this guy knows we've connected the dots[5]. Why stick around[6]?"

"I haven't even gotten to my stack[7]. Maybe we'll get lucky."

Once back at the station Bosch finally dug[8] into his stack of tips and phone messages. He spent the next six hours working his way through it[9], making calls and asking questions. As with Lourdes, he ended up with nothing to show for it[10] except a reinforcement of his belief that humans will sink to the lowest depths[11] if the right opportunity presents itself. They were trying to catch a serial rapist who was evolving, according to the profile, into a murderer, and people were out there using[12] the situation to settle scores[13] and fuck over[14] their enemies.

1. coups durs
2. s'en est sortie
3. [stade de baseball situé au nord du centre de L.A.]
4. en sortir
5. qu'on a fait le rapprochement
6. insister
7. n'ai pas encore regardé ma pile
8. se plongea
9. à travailler dessus
10. n'obtint rien d'intéressant
11. peuvent tomber bien bas
12. profitaient de
13. régler des comptes
14. pourrir la vie de

22

Sunday was no different. He was greeted upon his arrival with a fresh batch of call-in tips[1]. These he went through quickly in his cubicle, first separating out the Spanish-only calls and putting them on Lourdes's desk for her to handle the following day. He then responded to the remaining tips with calls when necessary and the trash can[2] when warranted[3]. By noon he had completed the task and had only one potentially viable lead to show for the effort[4].

The lead came from an anonymous female caller[5] who reported seeing a man wearing a mask running down Seventh Street toward Maclay shortly after 12 p.m. Friday. She refused to give her name and had called in on a cell phone with a blocked[6] number. She told the operator that she had been driving west on Seventh when she saw the man in the mask. He was running east on the opposite side of the street and stopped at one point to try the door handles on[7] three cars parked along Seventh. When he was unable to open these cars he continued running toward Maclay. The caller said she lost sight of the man[8] after she passed by him.

Bosch was intrigued by the tip[9] because the timing[10] of the sighting[11] coincided with the attempted assault on Beatriz Sahagun just a few blocks away. What pushed the tip even further toward legitimacy[12] was that the caller described the mask worn by the runner as black with a green-

1. nouveau lot de signalements par téléphone

2. corbeille à papier

3. c'était justifié

4. n'en avait tiré qu'une piste possible

5. interlocutrice

6. sur liste rouge

7. poignées de

8. avait perdu l'homme de vue

9. cette information

10. l'heure

11. où elle l'avait vu

12. Ce qui rendait le signalement encore plus valable

1. celui qui avait voulu la violer
2. cette description

and-red design. This matched Sahagun's description of the mask worn by her would-be rapist[1], and these descriptors[2] had not been released publicly through the media.

What troubled Bosch about the tip was why the suspect would have kept the mask on while fleeing from Sahagun's house. A man running while wearing a mask would draw far more attention than just a man running. Harry thought that maybe the man was still disoriented after being struck by Sahagun with the broomstick. Another reason could be that he was known to people in that neighborhood and wanted to shield[3] his identity.

3. protéger

The caller said nothing about whether the man was wearing gloves but Bosch assumed that if he kept the mask on, he had also kept his gloves on.

Bosch got up from his desk chair and started pacing[4] in the tiny detective bureau as he considered the tip and what it could mean. The scenario as reported by the anonymous caller suggested that the Screen Cutter was trying to find an unlocked car that he could steal in order to make his getaway[5]. This suggested that he did not have a getaway vehicle or the one he did have had for some unknown reason become unavailable to him. This idea intrigued Bosch the most. The previous assaults credited[6] to the Screen Cutter appeared to be carefully planned and choreographed[7]. Escape is always a critical part of any plan. What happened to the getaway car? Was there an accomplice who panicked and took off[8]? Or was there another reason for the escape on foot[9]?

4. à faire les cent pas
5. pour s'enfuir
6. attribuées
7. organisés
8. avait décampé
9. qu'il se soit enfui à pied

The second issue[10] was the mask. The caller said the suspect was running toward Maclay, a commercial street lined with[11] small shops and

10. problème
11. bordée de

mom-and-pop-style[1] restaurants. At noon on Friday motorists and pedestrians[2] would be on Maclay and the appearance of a man wearing a Mexican wrestling mask would be noticed by many. And yet this was the only tip so far that mentioned the running man. This told Bosch that the Screen Cutter pulled the mask off just as he got to the corner and either turned onto Maclay or crossed it.

Bosch knew the answers to his questions wouldn't be found while pacing in the detective bureau. He went back to his desk and grabbed his keys and sunglasses off the desk.

As he exited the bureau, he almost ran into Captain Trevino, who was in the hallway.

"Hey, Cap."

"Harry, where are you going?"

"Going to grab lunch[3]."

Bosch kept going. It might have been his intention to get lunch while he was out but he wasn't interested in sharing his real destination with Trevino. If it went from anonymous tip to legitimate lead[4] he would inform the boss. He picked up speed[5] so he would be to the side door of the station before Trevino checked the attendance board in the bureau and saw that Bosch had once again failed to sign in or out[6].

It took him three minutes to drive to the corner of Maclay and Seventh. Bosch parked his rented[7] Cherokee and got out. He stood on the corner and looked around. It was an intersection of commercial and residential zones. Maclay was lined with small businesses, shops, and restaurants. Seventh was lined with small, gated properties[8] that were supposed to be single-family homes. But Bosch knew that many of those homes were shared by

1. familiaux
2. des automobilistes et des piétons
3. me chercher un casse-croûte
4. le signalement anonyme devenait une piste valable,
5. accéléra le pas
6. omis d'inscrire son heure d'arrivée ou de sortie
7. de location
8. propriétés sécurisées

multiple families, and even more people lived in illegally converted[1] garages.

He spotted a trash can[2] near the corner and got an idea. If the Screen Cutter pulled off his mask and gloves when he got to Maclay, would he keep them? Would he carry them in his hands or stuff them into his pockets? Or would he dump them[3]? It was known that he had access to and had used other masks in his crimes. Dumping the wrestling mask and gloves would have been the smart move[4] once he was on the busy commercial street.

Bosch went to the trash can and lifted the top off. It had been little more than forty-eight hours since the attempted assault on Beatriz Sahagun. Bosch doubted the city had emptied the can in that time and he was right. It had been a busy weekend on Maclay and the trash can was nearly full. Bosch took a pair of latex gloves out of his jacket pocket and then removed the jacket and hung it over the back of a nearby bus bench[5]. He then put on the gloves, rolled up his sleeves[6], and went to work[7].

It was a disgusting process with the can[8] largely filled with rotting food and the occasional disposable baby diaper[9]. It also appeared that at some point during the weekend someone had vomited directly into the receptacle. It took him a solid ten[10] minutes to thoroughly dig through it to the bottom[11]. He found no mask and no gloves.

Undaunted[12], Bosch went to the next trash can twenty yards[13] further down Maclay and started the same process. Without his jacket on, his badge was visible on his belt, and that probably stopped shop owners and passersby[14] from asking what he was doing. At the second can he drew the attention of a family eating at the front window of a taqueria[15] ten feet away[16]. Bosch tried to

1. aménagés
2. repéra une poubelle
3. les aurait-il jetés
4. était la meilleure chose à faire
5. banc
6. remonta ses manches
7. se mit au boulot
8. poubelle
9. de quelques couches jetables
10. dix bonnes
11. la fouiller de fond en comble
12. Sans se laisser décourager
13. mètres
14. les passants
15. restaurant mexicain [spécialisé dans les tacos]
16. à 10 mètres à peine

conduct[1] his search while positioning his body as a visual blind to them[2]. It was more of the same detritus in the second can but he hit pay dirt[3] halfway through the excavation. There in the debris was a black leather wrestling mask with a green-and-red design.

Bosch straightened up out of the can[4] and stripped off[5] his gloves, dropping them to the ground next to the trash can. He then pulled his cell phone and took several photos of the mask in place in the can. After documenting the find[6] he called the SFPD com room[7] and told the officer in charge he needed to call in an evidence team[8] from the Sheriff's Department to collect[9] the mask from the trash receptacle.

"You can't bag it and tag it[10] yourself?" the officer asked.

"No, I can't bag it and tag it," Bosch said. "There is going to be genetic evidence inside and possibly outside the mask. I want to go four by four on it[11] so some lawyer down the line doesn't get to[12] tell a jury I did it all wrong and tainted the case[13]. Okay?"

"Okay, okay, I was just asking. I need to get Captain Trevino to sign off on this and then I'll call the Sheriff's. It might be a while[14]."

"I'll be here waiting."

A while turned out to be[15] three hours. Bosch waited patiently, spending part of the time talking to Lourdes when she called him after he had texted her a photo of the mask. It was a good find and would help bring a new dimension to their understanding of the Screen Cutter. They also agreed there would undoubtedly be genetic material inside the mask that could be linked to the rapist. In that regard[16] it would be like the semen[17]

1. poursuivre
2. en se plaçant de façon à leur cacher la poubelle
3. gagna le gros lot
4. se redressa
5. retira
6. avoir donné de quoi situer sa trouvaille,
7. salle de communication
8. faire venir une équipe de la police scientifique
9. récupérer
10. l'étiqueter
11. être très réglo sur ce dossier
12. pour éviter qu'un avocat puisse plus tard
13. rendu la preuve irrecevable
14. Ça peut durer un moment
15. Le moment dura
16. À cet égard,
17. sperme

1. lien fiable
2. gardait l'
3. avait été enfilé
4. n'avait peut-être jamais laissé d'empreintes génétiques
5. ses empreintes digitales avaient peut-être déjà été relevées
6. empreinte du pouce
7. le tour serait joué
8. avaient été trouvées sur
9. irréaliste
10. permette de résoudre l'affaire
11. as fait du bon boulot
12. Que ce soit toi ou moi, c'est la même chose
13. cherchons tous
14. chasser
15. qui voulaient
16. La seule fois
17. y était arrivé quand même
18. le chercher
19. poussette

collected in three of the other assaults: a definitive link[1], but only if the suspect was identified. Bosch said he was holding out[2] hope that they would do better and that the treated leather of the mask would hold a fingerprint left when the mask was pulled on[3] and adjusted. A fingerprint would be a whole new angle. The Screen Cutter may never have been DNA-typed[4], but he could have been fingerprinted[5]. A driver's license in California required a thumbprint[6]. If there was a thumbprint on the mask, they might be in business[7]. Bosch had worked cases with the LAPD where prints were pulled off of[8] leather coats and boots. It wasn't a reach[9] to hope the mask could be the case breaker[10].

"You done good[11], Harry," Lourdes said. "Now I wish I was working today."

"It's okay," Bosch said. "We're both on the case now. My get is your get and vice versa[12]."

"Well, that attitude will make Captain Trevino happy."

"Which is what we are all striving for[13]."

She was laughing as they disconnected.

Bosch went back to waiting. Repeatedly through the afternoon he had to shoo away[14] pedestrians aiming to[15] use the trash can for its public purpose. The one instance[16] where someone got by him[17] was when he remembered he had left his sports coat on the bus bench up at the corner and walked back to retrieve it[18]. When he turned back around he saw a woman who was pushing a baby carriage[19] throw something into the receptacle containing the mask. She had come out of nowhere and Bosch was too late to stop her. He expected to find another disposable diaper when he returned but instead found a half-eaten ice-cream cone splatted[1] directly on the mask.

Cursing to himself[2], Bosch put on latex again, reached in[3], and flipped the melting chocolate mess off the mask[4]. When he did so he saw a single glove much like the one he was wearing underneath the mask. It reduced his frustration level but not by much[5].

The two-man forensic team[6] from the Sheriff's Department didn't arrive until almost 4 p.m. and they didn't seem too pleased about the Sunday afternoon callout[7] or the fact that they would be working in a trash can. Bosch was unapologetic[8] and asked them to photograph, chart[9], and collect the evidence. That process, which included emptying the entire contents of the can onto plastic sheets[10] and then examining each piece before transferring it to a second sheet took nearly two hours.

In the end, the mask and two gloves were recovered and taken to the Sheriff's lab for analysis along all lines of evidence[11]. Bosch asked for a rush[12] but the lead forensic tech[13] just nodded and smiled as though he was dealing with a naive child who thought he was first in line in life[14].

Bosch got back to the detective bureau at seven and saw no sign of Captain Trevino. The door to his office was closed and the transom window dark[15]. Bosch sat down in his cubicle and typed up an evidence report on the recovery of the mask and gloves and the anonymous tip that led to them. He then printed two copies[16], one for his file and one for the captain.

He went back to the computer and filled out[17] a supplemental lab request form that would be sent to the Sheriff's lab at Cal State L.A. and serve as

1. écrasé

2. Étouffant un juron

3. plongea le bras

4. écarta du masque la masse de chocolat fondu

5. de peu

6. deux techniciens de la police scientifique

7. cette convocation dominicale

8. resta sans remords

9. faire les relevés

10. bâches

11. y subir toute la batterie de tests appliqués aux indices

12. que ce soit fait en urgence

13. technicien en chef

14. croyait que tout lui était dû

15. l'imposte n'était pas éclairée

16. exemplaires

17. remplit

a means of doubling-down on the request for a rush[1]. The timing was good. A courier[2] from the lab made a weekly stop at the SFPD on Mondays to drop off and pick up evidence. Bosch's request for a rush would get to the lab by the next afternoon, even if the forensic tech who collected the evidence didn't pass along[3] his verbal request. In the request Bosch asked for a complete examination of the mask inside and out for fingerprints, hair, and all other genetic material. Additionally, he asked the lab to check the inside of the latex gloves for similar evidence. He cited[4] the fact that the investigation was a serial offender case as the reason for fast-tracking[5] the analysis. He wrote: "This offender will not stop his terror and violence against women until we stop him. Please speed this along[6]."

This time he printed out three copies of his work—one for his own case file, one for Trevino, and the third for the lab courier. After dropping off[7] the third copy at the evidence control room, Bosch was clear to head home[8]. He had put in a solid day[9] and had broken out a good lead[10] with the mask and gloves. But instead he headed back to his cubicle to shift cases[11] and spend some time on the Vance investigation. Thanks to the attendance board, he knew that Trevino had long ago signed out for the day and that he need not worry about being discovered.

Bosch was intrigued by the story Halley Lewis had told him about Dominick Santanello being drawn into the Chicano Pride movement while in training down[12] in San Diego. His description of the park beneath a freeway overpass[13] was particularly worth checking into[14]. Bosch came at it from several angles on Google and soon enough[15] was looking at photos and a map of a place called

1. servirait à étayer sa demande d'analyse express
2. coursier
3. ne transmettait pas
4. signala
5. accélérer
6. Merci de faire vite
7. avoir déposé
8. pouvait enfin rentrer chez lui
9. fait une grosse journée de travail
10. trouvé une bonne piste
11. passer à une autre affaire
12. alors qu'il faisait ses classes
13. pont autoroutier
14. méritait d'être vérifiée
15. assez vite

Chicano Park, which was located beneath the 5 freeway and the exit to the bridge crossing San Diego Bay to Coronado Island.

The photos of the park showed dozens of murals[1] painted on every concrete pillar and stanchion[2] supporting the overhead[3] freeway and bridge. The murals depicted[4] religious allegories, cultural heritage, and individuals of note[5] in the Chicano Pride movement. One pillar was painted with a mural that marked the founding of the park in April 1970. Bosch realized that Santanello was in Vietnam by then, which meant that his association with the woman Lewis identified as Gabriela began before the park was formally approved by the city and dedicated[6].

The mural he was looking at listed the park's founding artists at the bottom. The list was long and the paint faded[7]. The names disappeared behind a bed[8] of zinnias that circled the bottom of the pillar like a wreath[9]. Bosch did not see the name Gabriela but realized that there were names on the pillar he could not make out[10].

He closed the photo and spent the next twenty minutes searching the Internet for a better angle on the pillar or an early shot[11] taken before the flower wreath grew to obscure[12] the names. He found nothing and was frustrated. There was no guarantee that Gabriela would even be listed on the mural, but he knew he would need to stop at the park and check when he went down to San Diego to look for 1970 birth records of a girl with a father named Dominick Santanello.

After a stop for a combined lunch and dinner at Art's Deli in Studio City, Bosch got[13] to Woodrow Wilson Drive late in the evening. He parked as usual around the bend[14] and then walked back to his house. He pulled a week's

1. peintures murales
2. étai et pilier en béton
3. aérien
4. représentaient
5. éminents
6. inauguré
7. passée
8. parterre
9. couronne
10. déchiffrer
11. cliché plus ancien
12. ait poussé jusqu'à cacher
13. arriva
14. après le virage

worth of deliveries[1] out of the mailbox, including a small box that had been stuffed in as well[2].

He went into the house and dumped[3] the envelopes onto the dining room table to be dealt with[4] later. But he opened the box and found the GPS detector/jammer he had ordered.

He grabbed a beer out of the fridge and stripped off[5] his jacket before taking the device over[6] to the reclining chair[7] in front of the living room TV. Normally, he would have put on a disc but he wanted to check the news and see if they were still pumping the Screen Cutter story[8].

He turned on channel 5 because it was a local independent channel that paid attention to news stories[9] outside of Hollywood. Bosch had seen a news van[10] with a 5 on the side at the police station on Friday when the press conference took place.

The news was already under way[11] when he turned the television on. He started reading through the instruction manual[12] that came with[13] the GPS device and kept one ear on the TV.

He was halfway through learning how to identify a GPS tracker and jam[14] its signal when the drone[15] of the news anchor[16] caught his attention.

"... Vance was instrumental[17] in the development of stealth[18] technologies."

He looked up and saw a photo of a much younger Whitney Vance on the screen and then it was gone and the anchor was on to the next story[19].

Bosch leaned forward in his chair, fully alert. He grabbed the remote[20] and switched over to channel 9 but there was nothing on Vance. Bosch got up and went to the laptop[21] on the dining

1. l'équivalent d'une semaine de courrier
2. colis qui y avait été également déposé
3. jeta
4. dans l'intention de s'en occuper
5. se débarrassa de
6. d'emporter l'appareil
7. fauteuil inclinable
8. on parlait encore du Coupeur de portes
9. informations
10. fourgonnette de reportage
11. avaient déjà commencé
12. mode d'emploi
13. accompagnait
14. brouiller
15. débit monotone
16. présentateur
17. a joué un rôle clé
18. furtives
19. passa à l'info suivante
20. télécommande
21. l'ordinateur portable

room table. He went to the home[1] page of the *Los Angeles Times*. The top headline read[2]:

Report: Billionaire[3] Whitney Vance Dies
Steel Tycoon[4] Also Left Mark on Aviation

The story was short because information was short. It simply said that *Aviation Week* was reporting on its website that Whitney Vance had died after a brief illness. The report cited unnamed[5] sources and gave no details other than to say Vance had died peacefully at his home in Pasadena.

Bosch slammed the laptop closed[6].

"Goddamn it[7]," he said.

The report in the *Times* didn't even confirm the report in *Aviation Week*. Bosch got up and paced the living room, not sure what he could do but feeling guilty[8] in some way and not trusting the report that Vance died peacefully in his home.

As he came back toward the dining room table he saw the business card Vance had given him. He pulled his phone and called the number. This time it was answered.

"Hello?"

Bosch knew the voice did not belong to Whitney Vance. He didn't say anything.

"Is this Mr. Bosch?"

Bosch hesitated but then answered.

"Who is this?"

"It's Sloan."

"Is he really dead?"

"Yes, Mr. Vance has passed on[9]. And that means your services are no longer needed. Good-bye, Mr. Bosch."

"Did you kill him, you bastards?"

1. d'accueil
2. gros titre annonçait
3. Le milliardaire
4. Le magnat de l'acier
5. anonymes
6. ferma son ordinateur d'un clac
7. Nom de Dieu !
8. coupable
9. est décédé

Sloan hung up halfway through the question. Bosch almost hit the redial button[1] but knew that Sloan would not take the call. The number would soon be dead and so too would Bosch's connection to the Vance empire.

"Goddamn it," he said again.

His words echoed through the empty house.

1. faillit appuyer sur la touche de rappel

23

Bosch stayed up half the night jumping from CNN to Fox News and then online to the *Times* website, hoping for an update[1] on the death of Whitney Vance. But he came away disappointed in[2] the supposed twenty-four-hour news cycle. There were no updates on the cause of or details about the death. All each entity did was add backstory[3], digging out old clips[4] and adding them to the tail[5] of the very thinly reported breaking news of the death. At about 2 a.m. CNN reran[6] the 1996 interview Larry King did with Vance on his book publication. Bosch watched this with interest because it showed a much more spry[7] and engaging version of Vance.

Sometime after that Bosch fell asleep in the leather chair in front of the television, four empty bottles on the table next to him. The TV was still on when he awoke and the first image he saw was the Coroner's van exiting through the gate of the Vance estate on San Rafael and driving past the camera. The camera then held on the black steel gate rolling closed[8].

In the video, it was dark on the street but there was no time stamp[9]. Because Vance would get the VIP treatment from the Coroner's Office, Bosch guessed that the body was not removed until the middle of the night after a thorough investigation[10] that would have included detectives from the Pasadena Police Department.

1. de nouvelles informations
2. fut déçu par
3. Site ou chaînes se contentaient d'en rajouter sur sa vie
4. ressortant de vieux reportages
5. suite
6. repassa
7. alerte
8. resta fixée sur le portail métallique noir qui se refermait en coulissant
9. horodatage
10. examen approfondi

1. chaîne de la côte Est
2. avait déjà bien progressé sur
3. présentateur
4. passa l'antenne à
5. les parts majoritaires
6. d'héritier connu
7. testament
8. fortune
9. laissa entendre
10. conseiller juridique spécialisé en droit des successions
11. [quartier de Los Angeles]
12. s'extirpa
13. le revigora
14. mourait de faim
15. se prépara
16. perdu l'habitude de
17. placards
18. remplis
19. gaufres
20. spécimens desséchés par la congélation
21. en espérant que ça irait
22. s'avaler ses gaufres sans rien dessus

It was 7 a.m. in Los Angeles and that meant the eastern media[1] was already well into[2] the Vance story. The CNN anchor[3] flipped the story to[4] a financial reporter who talked about Vance's majority holdings[5] in the company his father had founded and what could happen now that he had died. The reporter said that Vance had no "known heirs[6]" and so it remained to be seen what instructions he left in his will[7] for the distribution of his wealth[8] and holdings. The reporter intimated[9] that there could be surprises in the will. He added that Vance's probate attorney[10], a Century City[11] lawyer named Cecil Dobbs, could not be reached for comment because of the early hour in Los Angeles.

Bosch knew he had to get up to San Fernando to continue working through the latest call-in tips and leads on the Screen Cutter case. He slowly climbed out[12] of the leather chair, felt his back protest in a half dozen places, and made his way to his bedroom to shower and prepare for the day.

The shower made him feel crisp[13]—at least temporarily. As he dressed he realized he was famished[14].

In the kitchen he brewed[15] a half pot of coffee and then began searching for something to eat. Without his daughter living in the house anymore, Bosch had fallen off on[16] keeping the cabinets[17] and refrigerator stocked[18]. All he found was a box of Eggo waffles[19] in the freezer containing two last soldiers exhibiting freezer burn[20]. Bosch put them both in the toaster and hoped for the best[21]. He checked the cabinets and refrigerator a second time and found no syrup, butter, or even peanut butter anywhere. He was going to have to go dry with the waffles[22].

He took the coffee in a mug left over[1] from his LAPD homicide days. Printed around its circumference was *Our Day Begins When Your Day Ends.* And he learned that eating waffles without syrup or other additives made them portable[2]. He sat down at the dining room table and ate them by hand while sorting through[3] the mail[4] that had accumulated on the table. It was an easy process because four out of every five pieces[5] were junk[6] mail that he could easily identify without opening them. He put these in a pile to the left and the mail he would have to open and deal with[7] to the right. This included pieces of correspondence addressed to his neighbors but mistakenly stuffed[8] into his box.

He was halfway through the pile when he came to an 8 × 5 padded manila envelope[9] with a heavy object in it. There was no return address and his own address was scrawled[10] in an unsteady hand[11]. The envelope had a South Pasadena postmark. He opened it and slid out the object, a gold pen he immediately recognized. It now had a cap[12] but he knew it was Whitney Vance's. There were also two separately folded pieces of stationery of a high-grade pale yellow stock[13]. Bosch unfolded the first one and found himself looking at a handwritten letter to him from Whitney Vance. The stationery had Vance's name and the San Rafael Avenue address printed across the bottom.

The letter had the previous Wednesday's date on it. The day after Bosch had gone to Pasadena to meet Vance.

Detective Bosch,
If you are reading this then my most loyal and trusted[14] Ida has been successful in getting this envelope to you. I am placing my trust in you as I have done with her for many decades.

1. datant
2. faciles à transporter
3. tout en triant
4. courrier
5. quatre enveloppes sur cinq
6. publicitaire
7. traiter,
8. fourrées
9. enveloppe kraft matelassée de 20 × 12 cm
10. griffonnée
11. écriture mal assurée
12. bouchon
13. papier à lettres de luxe jaune pâle
14. digne de confiance

It was a pleasure to meet you yesterday and I can sense that you are an honorable man who will do what is right in any circumstance. I am counting on your integrity. No matter what happens to me I want you to continue your search. If there is an heir to what I have on this earth then I want that person to have what is mine. I want you to find that person and I trust that you will. It gives an old man a sense of redemption to know he has done the right thing at last[1].

Be safe[2]. Be vigilant and determined.

Whitney P. Vance
October 5, 2016

Bosch reread the letter before unfolding the second document. It was handwritten in the same shaky but legible[3] scrawl as the first.

Whitney Vance
Last Will and Testament[4]
October 5, 2016

I, Whitney Vance, of Pasadena, Los Angeles County, California, write this Will by hand to declare my desires for the disposition of my estate[5] after my death. As of[6] the date of this Will, I am of sound mind[7] and am entirely capable of determining my own affairs. I am not married. By this Will I expressly revoke[8] any and all previous, antecedent Wills and Codicils, declaring any and all to be null, void[9], and invalid.

I have currently employed the[10] investigative services of Hieronymus Bosch to ascertain and locate my issue[11] and the heir of my body conceived[12] in spring 1950 by Vibiana Duarte and born of her in due course[13]. I charged Mr. Bosch to

1. enfin
2. Soyez prudent
3. lisible
4. volontés
5. succession
6. À
7. sain d'esprit
8. j'annule
9. non avenus
10. J'ai recours actuellement aux
11. établir l'existence et le lieu de ma descendance
12. de mon héritier biologique
13. qu'elle a mis au monde

bring forward[1] the heir of my body, with reasonably sufficient genealogical and scientific proof of heredity and genetic descent, so that the heir of my body may receive my estate[2].

I appoint[3] Hieronymus Bosch sole executor of this, my Will[4]. No bond or other security[5] shall be required of Mr. Bosch as executor of my Will. He shall pay my just debts and obligations, which shall include a reasonably generous fee[6] for his service. To Ida Townes Forsythe, my secretary, friend and confidante of 35 years, I give, devise, and bequeath[7] $10,000,000.00 (ten million US Dollars), together with my thanks and gratitude for her loyal service, counsel, and friendship.

To the heir of my body, my issue, my genetic descendant, and the last of my bloodline[8], I give, devise, and bequeath all of the remainder[9] of my estate, in its entirety, of any, all, and whatever kind and character[10], which shall include all my bank accounts, all my stocks[11], bonds[12], and business interests, my homes and all my real property[13] in fee simple[14], and all my personal property, possessions, and chattels[15]. In particular, to the heir of my body I bequeath[16] the pen with which this Will is written. It is made of gold mined by our progenitors and passed down through generations to have and hold until it is passed to succeeding generations of our blood.

Done by and in my own hand

Whitney P. Vance
October 5, 2016, at 11:30 A.M. Pacific Standard Time

Bosch was stunned[17] by what he had in his hands. He reread the will and it didn't lessen his wonder[18]. He held a document that was essentially worth[19] billions of dollars, a document that

1. faire connaître
2. hériter de mon patrimoine
3. nomme
4. mon unique exécuteur testamentaire
5. Aucune caution
6. rémunération
7. et lègue
8. lignée
9. le reste
10. toute nature
11. actions
12. titres
13. biens immobiliers
14. nue-propriété
15. biens meubles
16. lègue
17. abasourdi
18. n'atténua pas sa stupéfaction
19. valait

could change the course of a giant corporation and industry, not to mention the life and family of an unsuspecting woman born forty-six years ago of a father she never knew.

That is[1], if she was still alive and Bosch could find her.

Bosch read the first letter for the third time and took Whitney Vance's charge[2] to heart. He would be vigilant and determined.

He refolded the two documents and returned them to the envelope. He hefted[3] the heavy pen in his hand for a moment and then placed it back in the envelope as well. He realized that at some point, there would be an authentication process[4] and he might have already damaged it by his handling of the stationery[5]. He took the envelope into the kitchen and found a large resealable[6] plastic bag to preserve it in.

Bosch also knew he had to safeguard[7] the package. He suspected that there would be many forces out there bent on[8] destroying it. The thought reminded him of when Howard Hughes died and various wills came to the surface. He didn't remember how that probate was decided[9] but he recalled the multiple claims[10] to the fortune. The same could be the case with Vance. Bosch knew he needed to make copies of the documents in the envelope and then secure the originals in his safe deposit box[11].

Bosch went back into the living room and turned off the TV so he could make a call. He hit the speed dial for[12] Mickey Haller's cell phone and his half-brother picked up the call after one ring.

"What's up, broheim?"

"Are you my lawyer?"

"What? Of course I am. What did you do now[13]?"

1. Enfin
2. les recommandations
3. soupesa
4. procédure d'authentification
5. en manipulant le papier à lettres
6. refermable
7. placer en lieu sûr
8. de nombreux intérêts déterminés à
9. lequel des testaments avait obtenu l'homologation
10. prétendants
11. coffre-fort
12. numéro préenregistré de
13. Qu'est-ce que tu as encore fait

"Funny. But you're not going to believe this. Are you sitting down?"

"I'm sitting in the back of the Lincoln, heading in to see my girl Clara Foltz."

The translation[1] was that Haller was heading to court[2]. The downtown[3] courthouse was formally known as[4] the Clara Shortridge Foltz Criminal Justice Center.

"You heard about Whitney Vance dying?" Bosch asked.

"I heard something about it on the radio, yeah," Haller said. "But what do I care about some billionaire kicking the bucket[5]?"

"Well, I'm holding his last will and testament. He sent it to me. It names me executor and I don't know the first thing about[6] what to do with it."

"Are you pulling my dick[7], broheim?"

"No, broheim. I'm not pulling your dick."

"Where are you?"

"Home."

"Hold on[8]."

Bosch then heard Haller redirect his driver from the downtown destination to the Cahuenga Pass, where Bosch lived. Then he got back on the line.

"How the fuck did you end up[9] with his will?"

Bosch gave him a short summary of the Vance case. He also revealed that this was the case he had called Haller about to get the referral to[10] a private DNA lab.

"Okay, who else knows you have this will?" Haller asked.

"No one," Bosch said. "Actually, somebody might[11]. It came in the mail and Vance's letter says he gave the task to his longtime secretary. But I don't know if she knew what was in the package she mailed. She's in the will to the tune[12] of ten million."

1. sens réel

2. se rendait au tribunal

3. du centre-ville

4. s'appelait officiellement

5. qui casse sa pipe

6. n'ai pas la moindre idée de

7. Tu te fous de ma gueule

8. Attends

9. Putain, comment t'as fait pour te retrouver

10. pour qu'il lui recommande

11. Enfin, si, peut-être

12. à hauteur

1. C'était une bonne raison pour qu'elle te fasse parvenir le testament
2. en recommandé
3. en douce
4. Le faire sortir en passant par
5. paraître pour moi à l'audience
6. toi, ne bouge pas
7. J'arrive
8. photocopieuse
9. en homologation de testaments
10. Prendre le client, et avancer
11. gérer
12. pour ce que je ne sais pas
13. faire appel à quelqu'un
14. dans moins de 30 mn
15. grave
16. manque
17. compensé
18. débrouillardise
19. sa rouerie en matière juridique
20. qu'on n'apprenait pas à l'école
21. grand creux
22. qu'il remplissait en jouant
23. qu'il s'agisse de la grande puissance
24. qu'Haller protégerait ses arrières

"That's a big reason to make sure she got the will to you[1]. You said it came in the mail? Was it certified[2]—did you have to sign for it?"

"No, it was stuffed into the box with all the junk mail."

"That was risky but maybe it was the best way to get it to you under the radar[3]. Slip it out with[4] the secretary, have her drop it in a mail box. Okay, listen, I need to get off the line so I can get somebody to take my appearance in arraignment court[5]. But you sit tight[6]. I'm heading your way[7]."

"Do you still have that copier[8] in the car?"

"Sure do."

"Good. We need to make copies."

"Definitely."

"Do you even know anything about wills and probate[9], Mick?"

"Hey, bro, you know me. Have case, will travel[10]. Doesn't matter what kind of case it is, I can handle it[11]. And what I don't know[12], I can bring somebody in on[13] to help. I'll be there inside of thirty[14]."

As Bosch put the phone down he wondered if he had made a critical[15] mistake bringing the Lincoln Lawyer into the case. His instincts were that Haller's lack[16] of experience in probate and inheritance law would be more than balanced[17] by his street smarts[18] and legal cunning[19]. Bosch had seen him work and knew he had something that didn't come with training[20], no matter what the school or specialty. He had a deep hollow[21] that he somehow filled by standing as a[22] David against the Goliaths of the world, whether in the form of the power and might[23] of the state or a billion-dollar corporation. Bosch also had no doubts about Haller guarding his back[24]. He could trust him. And he had a growing feeling that this might be the most important support to have in the days ahead.

He checked his watch and saw it was near nine now and Bella Lourdes would be at the station. He called but she didn't answer. He assumed that was because she was already working the phones[1] responding to the batch of call-in tips he had left on her desk. He was leaving her a message telling her to call him back when his call-waiting[2] indicated she was already doing so.

"Good morning," he said.

"Good morning," she said. "Where are you?"

"I'm still at home. You're going to have to handle things on your own[3] today."

She groaned and asked why.

"Something's come up on a private case I'm working," he said. "It can't wait."

"The one with all the birth certificates?" she asked.

"How did you—"

He remembered her eying[4] the stack of copies he had placed on his desk in the cubicle.

"Never mind," he said. "Just don't mention that to anybody. I should be back in a couple days."

"A couple days?" Lourdes exclaimed. "Harry, the proverbial iron is hot right now[5]. This guy just tried to strike[6] for the first time we know about in eight months. We now have the mask. Things are happening and we really need you in here."

"I know, I know. But this other thing can't wait and it looks like I have to go to San Diego."

"You're killing me, Harry. What's the case?"

"I can't tell you right now. When I can, I will."

"That's nice of you. And it's more important than a guy running around up here raping Mexican girls."

1. au téléphone

2. signal d'appel

3. toute seule

4. qu'elle avait vu

5. il faut battre le fer, là

6. vient d'essayer de frapper

"It's not more important. But we both know that the Screen Cutter is lying low[1] right now with all of this attention. Unless he's already split[2]. And if he has, then we're spinning our wheels[3], anyway."

"Okay, fine, I'll let the cap know[4] and I'm sure he'll be happy not to have you around. Last thing he wants is for you to crack this thing anyway."

"There you go[5]."

"No, there *you* go[6]. Running out on the case[7]."

"Look, I'm not running out. This other thing will clear soon[8]. And I'm only a phone call away[9]. In fact, there's something I was going to do today but you need to do it now instead."

"And what's that?"

"The caller who led me to the mask said the guy was checking car doors while he was running."

"So?"

"So something happened that messed up his getaway[10]."

"Yeah, Beatriz clocked him[11] with the broomstick."

"Something more. He lost his ride[12]."

"You mean you think he had a getaway driver[13]? Maybe we're looking for more than one suspect. Different masks, different rapists, but working together—is that it?"

"No, the DNA is from one offender."

"Right, forgot[14]. So you think he's a rapist with a getaway driver?"

"I thought about that but it's a long shot[15]. Most serial offenders are loners[16]. There are exceptions but it's rare. Most of the time you go with the percentages[17] and you come out ahead[18]."

"Okay, then what?"

"I think you should go out and search Beatriz's house again. Do you guys have a metal detector?"

"A metal detector? For what?"

1. fait profil bas
2. qu'il ait déjà fichu le camp
3. on perd notre temps
4. je vais mettre le capitaine au courant
5. Ben tu vois : ça va
6. Non, c'est toi qui *t'en* vas
7. Tu te défiles
8. sera bientôt résolue
9. je suis joignable d'un coup de fil
10. qui a chamboulé ses plans de fuite
11. l'a assommé
12. sa voiture avec chauffeur
13. complice au volant d'une voiture
14. j'avais oublié
15. peu probable
16. solitaires
17. on se fie aux statistiques
18. on a raison

"The backyard by the window the Screen Cutter jumped through. I think maybe he lost the keys to his getaway car when he went through the window and hit the ground. There's a bed of vines[1] and ground cover[2] there."

"Right, I saw."

"It was a panic move. He's disoriented by the blow from the broomstick, he drops the knife, jumps through the window, and falls on the ground. His keys could have gone flying[3]. So what's he do? He can't sit there looking through the bushes and vines. He's gotta get out of there. He just starts running."

"That to me sounds like the long shot[4]."

"Maybe. But this guy is a planner[5] and there he was, running down the street, trying to find an unlocked car to boost[6]."

"True."

"Anyway, what else are you going to do, chase call-in tips and look-alikes[7] all day?"

"There you go again against the tip line[8]. But you do have a point[9]. And they do have a metal detector over at Public Works for finding underground pipes and cables and stuff. We used it once to find a gun a banger[10] wrapped in plastic and buried in his backyard. Tied him to an assault with a deadly[11]. If Dockweiler's over there, he'll let us use it. If he's in a good mood."

"Grab that[12] and run it[13] through the bushes and the ground cover under that window."

"You don't grab it. It's like a lawnmower[14]. It's got wheels."

"Then take Sisto with you. Give him a chance to redeem himself[15]."

"Redeem himself for what?"

"I don't really think his heart was in it the other day. He was babysitting[16] the scene for us, playing

1. plantes rampantes
2. des buissons
3. ont pu être projetées
4. Pour moi, c'est plutôt ça qui a l'air peu probable
5. organisé
6. qu'il aurait pu faucher
7. les sosies
8. Voilà que tu recommences ton cirque contre les signalements téléphoniques
9. tu n'as pas tort
10. qu'un voyou
11. On l'a inculpé pour agression à main armée
12. Prends-le
13. passe-le
14. tondeuse à gazon
15. se racheter
16. surveillait

on his phone the whole time, not paying attention. Not his case, not invested[1]. Between you and me, his search was lazy[2]. We're lucky he found the knife without cutting himself on it."

"But we're not judgmental, are we[3]?"

"Back in the day[4], we'd say a guy like that couldn't find shit in his mustache with a comb."

"We are just brutal[5]!"

"I know what I saw. I'm glad I'm working with you and not him."

She paused and Bosch knew it was to smile.

"I think there's a compliment in there somewhere," she said then. "From the great Harry Bosch, no less. Anyway, sounds like a plan[6]. I'll let you know."

"Remember, you find something, you owe me a beer. You also should ask Sisto about auto thefts[7] Friday from Area Two—the other side of Maclay. Maybe the Screen Cutter grabbed a car over there."

"Aren't you just full of ideas today."

"Yeah, that's why I get the big bucks[8]."

"And all because of one of the tip line calls that you swore up and down were going to be[9] a complete waste of time."

"When you're wrong, you're wrong, and I admit I was wrong."

"You heard it here first, folks[10]."

"I gotta go, Bella. Be careful out there."

"You too—with whatever your super-secret case is."

"Roger that[11]."

They disconnected.

1. impliqué
2. il ne s'est pas trop foulé pour la fouille de la maison
3. on ne se permettrait pas de juger, si
4. De mon temps
5. Tu y vas fort
6. c'est une idée
7. des vols de voiture commis
8. pour ça qu'on me paye si bien
9. que tu as appelé haut et fort
10. Vous êtes témoins, les gars
11. Entendu

24

While Haller studied the letter and will that Bosch had unpackaged and spread with gloved hands on the dining room table, Harry worked[1] his computer, seeing if he could get access to 1970 birth records in San Diego County. Whitney Vance's death was a game changer[2]. He felt a more urgent need to nail down[3] the heir question. He needed to get this to the DNA level. He needed to find Dominick Santanello's daughter.

Unfortunately he found that the Bureau of Vital Records and Statistics had digital records[4] going back only twenty-four years. As he had in his search for Santanello's birth certificate, Bosch would need to look through physical records[5] and microfilm by hand to find a San Diego County birth in 1970. He was writing down the address for the Bureau on Rosecrans Street when Haller completed his first assessment[6] of the two documents.

"This is off the charts[7]," he said.

Bosch looked at him.

"What is?" he asked.

"Every damn thing about this," Haller said. "What you have here is a holographic will[8], okay? That means it was handwritten. And I checked on the way over[9]. Holographic wills are accepted as legal instruments upon verification[10] in California."

"Vance probably knew that."

1. était sur

2. changeait la donne

3. régler

4. des archives numériques

5. parcourir des registres papier

6. acheva sa première estimation

7. du jamais-vu

8. testament olographe [en entier de sa main, et non écrit devant notaire]

9. en venant

10. une fois authentifiés

"Oh, he knew a lot. That's why he sent you the pen. Not for the bullshit[1] reason in the will. He sent it because he knew verification is the key. You say that when you met with him last week at the mansion[2], he was of sound mind and body—like he says here?"

"That's right."

"And exhibiting no sign of illness or health threat?"

"Other than being old and fragile, none."

"I wonder then what the coroner[3] will find."

"I wonder if the coroner will even look. An eighty-five-year-old man comes through[4], they're not going to look too long and hard at him. Eighty-five-year-olds die. It's no mystery."

"You mean there won't be an autopsy?"

"There should be but that doesn't mean there will be. If the Pasadena Police signed off on it at the scene as a natural[5], there might not be a full autopsy unless there's visible evidence to the contrary upon medical examiner's inspection."

"I guess we'll see. You have a connection inside Pasadena PD[6]?"

"Nope. You?"

"Nope."

Upon his arrival, Haller's driver had carried in the photocopier/printer from the Lincoln, then returned to wait behind the wheel[7]. Haller now pulled gloves from the cardboard dispenser[8] Bosch had placed on the table. He stretched a pair on and started making copies of the documents.

"Why don't you have a copier here?" he asked while he worked.

"I did," Bosch said. "Had a printer-copier combo but Maddie took it to school with her. Haven't gotten around[9] to getting another."

"How's she doing down there?"

1. naze
2. dans sa villa
3. médecin légiste
4. qui trépasse
5. a déclaré sur place qu'il s'agissait d'une mort naturelle
6. la police [Police Department]
7. au volant
8. boîte en carton
9. J'ai pas pris le temps

"Good. How about Hayley?"

"She's good too. Totally into it[1]."

"That's good."

An awkward[2] silence followed. Both their daughters—the same age and each the other's only cousin[3]—had gone to Chapman University, but because of different majors[4] and interests, they had not formed the tight bond their fathers had hoped for and expected. They had shared a dorm room in the first year but gone separate ways the second. Hayley had stayed in the dorms and Maddie had rented the house with girls from the Psychology Department.

After making at least a dozen copies of the will, Haller moved on to the letter Vance wrote to Bosch and started making an equal number of copies.

"Why so many?" Bosch asked.

"'Cause[5] you never know," Haller said.

That was a non-answer, Bosch thought.

"So what do we do from here[6]?" he asked.

"Nothing," Haller said.

"What?"

"Nothing. For now. Nothing public, nothing in the courts. We just lie low[7] and wait."

"Why?"

"You keep working the case. Confirm that Vance has an heir. Once we have that, we see who makes a move, see what the corporation does. When they make their move we make ours. But we make our move from a position of knowing what they're up to[8]."

"We don't even know who 'they' are."

"Sure we do. It's all of them. It's the corporation, the board of directors, the security people, it's all of them."

"Well, 'they' may be watching us right now."

1. À fond dedans

2. gêné

3. unique cousine

4. spécialités

5. [Because]

6. maintenant

7. On se tient à carreau

8. ce sera en sachant ce qu'ils mijotent

1. le présupposer
2. ne serait pas resté
3. c'est-à-dire
4. Tu trouveras bien un endroit
5. Au cas où je recevrais
6. le fournir
7. Astucieux
8. l'a déposé en douce
9. consigner
10. sa déclaration
11. devrons pouvoir prouver
12. être pris en défaut

"We have to assume they are[1]. But they don't know what we have here. Otherwise this package wouldn't have sat[2] in your mailbox for four days."

Bosch nodded. It was a good point. Haller gestured to the documents on the table, meaning[3] the two originals.

"We have to safeguard these," he said. "At all costs."

"I have a safe deposit box," Bosch said. "Studio City."

"You can bet they already know that. They probably know everything about you. So we make copies and you put copies in your bank box. If they're watching you they'll think that's where the will is."

"And where will it really be?"

"You'll figure something out[4]. But don't tell me."

"Why not?"

"In case I get hit with[5] an order from a judge to produce the will. If I don't have it and don't know where it is, I can't produce it[6]."

"Smart[7]."

"We need to get to Ida Forsythe too. If you're right about her being the one who smuggled this stuff[8] to the post office, then we need to lock[9] her story down in a statement[10]. It will be part of the chain of authenticity. We'll need verification of[11] every step we take. When I finally go into court with this, I don't want my ass hanging out in the wind[12]."

"I can get her address. If she has a driver's license."

Still wearing gloves, Haller picked up the gold pen.

"And this," he said. "You're sure it's the one he had last week?"

"Pretty sure. I saw it in photos, too, on a wall in the mansion. A photo of him signing a book to Larry King."

"Cool. Maybe we'll bring Larry into court to verify[1]—that'll get a headline or two[2]. We'll also need Ida to confirm it as well. Remember, verification on all levels. His pen, his signature in the pen's ink. We'll match it[3]. I have a lab that will do that—when the time is right[4]."

Finished with the copying, Haller started collating[5] the documents, creating a dozen sets of both.

"You have paper clips[6]?" he asked.

"No," Bosch said.

"I have some in the car. You take half of these and I'll take half. Put a set[7] under the mattress, in the safe deposit box. Doesn't hurt to have them in many places. I'll do the same."

"Where do you go from here?"

"I go to court and act like I don't know shit about any of this while you find and confirm that heir."

"When I get to her, do I tell her or confirm on the sly[8]?"

"That's gotta be your call[9] when you reach that point. But whatever you decide, remember that secrecy is our edge[10]—for now."

"Got it."

Haller went to the front door and whistled[11] to get his driver's attention. He signaled him to come in to get the printer/copier. He then stepped out onto the front stoop[12] and looked both ways up the street before coming back in.

The driver entered, unplugged[13] the machine, and wrapped the cord around it so he could carry it back out without tripping on it[14]. Haller walked over to the sliding glass doors in the living room to look out at the view of the Cahuenga Pass.

1. reconnaître formellement
2. ça fera les gros titres
3. On comparera
4. en temps voulu
5. à rassembler
6. des trombones
7. un lot
8. j'obtiens ma confirmation en douce
9. Ce sera à toi de voir
10. avantage
11. siffla
12. porche
13. débrancha
14. se prendre les pieds dedans

"Your view is quieter," he said. "Lots of trees."

Haller lived on the other side of the hill with an unfettered[1] view across the Sunset Strip and the vast expanse[2] of the city. Bosch stepped over and slid the door open a few feet so Haller could hear the never-ending hiss of the freeway at the bottom of the pass[3].

"Not so quiet," Bosch said.

"Sounds like the ocean," Haller said.

"A lot of people up here tell themselves that. Sounds like a freeway to me."

"You know, you've seen a lot with all the murders you worked for all those years. All the human depravity. The cruelty."

Haller kept his eyes focused out into[4] the pass. There was a red-tailed hawk[5] floating on spread wings[6] above the ridgeline[7] on the other side of the freeway.

"But you haven't seen anything like this," he continued. "There are billions of dollars on the line[8] here. And people will do anything—I mean anything—to maintain control of it. Be ready for that."

"You too," Bosch said.

1. imprenable
2. l'immensité
3. col
4. le regard fixé sur
5. buse à queue rousse
6. qui planait
7. crête
8. en jeu

25

Twenty minutes later Bosch left the house. When he got to the rented Cherokee he used the GPS detector for the first time, walking completely around the SUV[1], holding the device down low[2] with its antenna pointed toward the undercarriage[3] and wheel wells[4]. He got no response. He popped[5] the front hood[6] and went through a similar process as instructed in the manual. Again, nothing. He then switched[7] the device to its jamming frequency[8] as a precaution and got behind the wheel[9].

He took Wrightwood down to Ventura in Studio City and then jogged[10] west to his bank, which was located in a shopping plaza off[11] of Laurel Canyon Boulevard. He had not been to the safe deposit box in at least two years. It contained primarily his own documents—birth and marriage and divorce certificates and military service documentation[12]. He kept his two Purple Hearts[13] in a box in there along with a commendation[14] he had received from the chief of police for pulling a pregnant woman out of a fiery wreck[15] when he was a boot[16]. He put one copy of the Vance documents in the box and then returned it to the handler[17] from the bank.

Bosch checked his surroundings when he got back to the rental car and initially saw no sign of surveillance. But when he pulled out of the bank's parking lot onto Laurel Canyon he saw in his rearview[18] a car with dark tinted windows pull out of

1. 4×4
2. en tenant l'appareil bien bas,
3. dessous du châssis
4. les passages de roues
5. ouvrit
6. capot
7. régla
8. fréquence de brouillage
9. se mit au volant
10. partit tranquillement
11. centre commercial à proximité
12. ses papiers
13. [médaille militaire]
14. citation
15. voiture en feu
16. n'était encore qu'un bleu
17. manutentionnaire
18. rétroviseur

1. parking
2. le suivre à une centaine de mètres

the same lot[1] but at a different exit point and fall in behind him a hundred yards back[2].

Bosch knew it was a busy shopping plaza so he didn't immediately jump to the conclusion that he was being followed. But he decided to avoid the freeway and stay on Laurel Canyon so he could keep a better eye on[3] the traffic behind him. Continuing north, he checked the mirror[4] every block or so. By its distinctive grille work[5], he identified the dark green car trailing him[6] as a BMW sedan[7].

3. de manière à mieux voir
4. son rétro
5. calandre [grille protégeant le radiateur]
6. qui le suivait
7. berline

After two miles he was still on Laurel Canyon, and the BMW was still in traffic behind him. Even though Bosch had slowed at times and sped up at others and the Beemer[8] had occasionally changed lanes[9] on the four-lane boulevard, it had never changed the distance between them.

8. BMW
9. de file

Bosch became increasingly convinced he was being tailed[10]. He decided to try to confirm it by doing a basic square-knot maneuver[11]. He took the next right, pinned[12] the accelerator, and drove down to the stop sign at the end of the block. He took another right and then turned right again at the next stop sign. He then drove at the speed limit back to Laurel Canyon Boulevard. He checked the mirrors. The Beemer had not followed him through the maneuver.

10. filé
11. bête tête-à-queue
12. pila sur

He turned back onto Laurel Canyon and continued north. He saw no sign of the Beemer. It was either well north of him because the driver was not tailing him, or it was gone because Bosch's maneuver had revealed to the driver that he had spotted the tail[13].

13. repéré la filature

Ten minutes later Bosch pulled into the employee lot at the San Fernando police station. He entered through the side door and found the detective bureau empty. He wondered if Sisto had gone with Lourdes to re-search[1] the Sahagun house. Maybe Bella had told Sisto about Bosch's poor review[2] of Friday's search and Sisto had insisted on going as a result[3].

At his desk, Bosch picked up the phone and called Lourdes to inquire about the search but the call rang through to voice mail[4] and he left word for her to call back when she was free.

With no sign of Trevino around, he next ran a DMV search on Ida Townes Forsythe and picked up[5] an address on Arroyo Drive in South Pasadena. He thought of the envelope from Vance having a South Pasadena postmark as he jumped over to Google Maps and plugged in[6] the address. He pulled up a visual[7] and saw that Forsythe had a very nice home on a street overlooking the Arroyo Seco Wash[8]. It appeared that Vance had taken good care of his most trusted and long-term employee.

His last move in the detective bureau was to pull out the file on one of the unsolved murders he was working and fill out an evidence recovery form[9]. He listed the evidence as "victim's property," then put the two original Vance documents and the gold pen, contained in the original mailing envelope, into a plastic evidence bag. He sealed the bag and put it into a cardboard evidence storage box. He sealed this as well with red breakaway tape[10], which would show any sign of tampering[11].

Bosch walked the box back[12] to the evidence control room and checked it into the locker[13] where other evidence accumulated during the investigation was already being stored. Bosch believed the original of the Vance will was now properly hidden and secured. The evidence con-

1. refouiller
2. maigres résultats
3. pour y retourner
4. tomba sur sa boîte vocale
5. trouva
6. entrait
7. obtint une photo
8. rivière
9. formulaire de collecte de preuves matérielles
10. ruban adhésif pour scellés
11. rendrait visible toute tentative d'ouverture
12. rapporta le carton
13. le déposa dans le casier

trol officer printed a receipt for him and he took it back to the bureau to put it in the case file. He was just locking his file drawer when his phone buzzed with a call on the intercom[1]. It was the front desk officer[2].

"Detective Bosch, you have a visitor up front[3]."

Bosch guessed that it was somebody coming in with what they believed was a tip on the Screen Cutter. He knew that he couldn't get bogged down with[4] that case today. He hit the intercom button.

"Is it a tip about the Screen Cutter? Can you ask whoever it is to come back this afternoon and ask for Detective Lourdes?"

There was no immediate response and Bosch assumed the desk officer was asking the visitor to state his or her business[5]. He knew that if it was another Screen Cutter victim, he would need to drop everything and handle it. He could not let a potential sixth victim walk out of the police station without being interviewed.

He went to his screen, clicked back to the DMV page on Ida Forsythe, and printed it out so he would have her address handy[6] when he went to her home to talk to her. He was about to go retrieve it[7] from the communal printer[8], when the desk man's voice came back over the intercom.

"He's asked for you specifically, Detective Bosch. He says it's about the Vance case."

Bosch stared at his desk phone for a long moment before responding.

"Tell him I'm coming out. One minute."

Bosch signed off[9] his computer and left the bureau. But he went out the side door rather than taking the main hallway to the front lobby of the station. He then walked around the outside of the station to the front, where he stood at the corner

1. à l'Interphone
2. l'agent de l'accueil
3. à l'accueil
4. s'empêtrer dans
5. dire ce qui l'amenait
6. à portée de main
7. s'apprêtait à la récupérer
8. à l'imprimante partagée
9. éteignit

of the building and checked the street to try to determine if his visitor had come alone.

He noticed no one who looked suspicious but he did see a dark green BMW with near-black[1] tinted windows parked at the curb in front of the Department of Public Works across from the police station. The car was as long as Haller's Town Car and Bosch could see a driver waiting behind the wheel.

He quickly doubled back[2] to the side entrance of the station and went back through to the front lobby. He was expecting the visitor to be Sloan, but when he got there he realized he had shot low[3]. It was Creighton, the man who had sent him down the path to Vance in the first place.

"Having trouble[4] following me?" Bosch said by way of a[5] greeting. "You come in to get my itinerary?"

Creighton nodded his confirmation that he had been tailing Bosch.

"Yes, I should have known better[6]," he said. "You probably had us[7] since the bank."

"What do you want, Creighton?"

Creighton frowned. Bosch's dispensing with[8] first names and titles signaled that the old LAPD bonds were of no use to him here.

"I want you to stand down[9]," Creighton said.

"I don't know what you're talking about," Bosch said. "Stand down from what?"

"Your employer has died. Your employment is now terminated. Speaking for the corporation, which is all there is now, stop what you're doing."

"What makes you think I'm doing anything?"

"We know what you're doing and we know why. We even know what your low-rent attorney[10] is doing. We've been watching you."

1. presque noires

2. rebroussa chemin

3. s'était quelque peu trompé

4. Vous avez du mal à

5. en guise de

6. n'ai pas été très malin

7. nous avez probablement repérés

8. Le fait que Bosch ait omis d'utiliser les

9. que vous laissiez tomber

10. petit avocat minable

Bosch had thoroughly scoured[1] the street before leaving his house. He now knew that rather than looking for people and cars, he should have looked for cameras. He now wondered if they had been inside his home as well. And making the jump[2] to Haller, Bosch assumed that the lawyer had made a call about the case that had put him on their radar[3] as well.

He looked at Creighton without showing any indication of being intimidated.

"Well, I'll take all of this under advisement[4]," he said. "You know your way out.[5]"

He stepped away[6] from Creighton but then the former[7] deputy chief spoke again.

"I don't think you really understand the position you're in."

Bosch turned and came back to him. He got up in his face.

"What position is that?"

"You are on very dangerous ground. You need to make careful decisions. I represent people who reward[8] those who make careful decisions."

"I don't know if that is a threat or a bribe[9] or maybe both."

"Take it any way you want."

"Okay, then, I will take it as a threat and a bribe and you are under arrest[10]."

Bosch grabbed him by the elbow and in one swift move[11] directed him face-first to the tiled wall[12] of the lobby[13]. With one hand pressing against Creighton's back, he snaked[14] his other hand under his jacket and behind his own back to his handcuffs[15]. Creighton tried to turn his head to face him.

"What the hell are you doing?" Creighton barked[16].

1. minutieusement inspecté
2. repensant aussitôt à
3. l'avait fait repérer
4. je prendrai tout cela en considération
5. Au revoir
6. s'écarta
7. l'ancien
8. savent remercier
9. proposition malhonnête
10. je vous arrête
11. d'un geste prompt,
12. face contre le mur carrelé
13. l'entrée
14. glissa
15. pour prendre ses menottes
16. aboya

"You are under arrest for threatening a police officer and attempted bribery[1]," Bosch said. "Spread[2] your legs and keep your face against that wall."

Creighton seemed too stunned[3] to react. Bosch kicked one of his heels[4] and the man's foot slipped across the tile. Bosch finished cuffing him[5] and then did a hand search, coming up with[6] a holstered[7] pistol on Creighton's right hip[8].

"You're making a big mistake," Creighton said.

"Maybe," Bosch said. "But it feels right because you're such a pompous ass[9], Cretin."

"I'll be out in fifteen minutes."

"You know they always called you that, right? Cretin? Let's go."

Bosch nodded to the desk officer behind the plexiglass window and he buzzed the door open. Bosch walked Creighton back to the holding section[10] of the station[11], where he turned him over to[12] the jail officer.

Bosch filled out an arrest report and booked[13] the gun into a property locker, then took the jail officer aside and told him to take his time getting around to letting[14] Creighton make his lawyer call[15].

The last he saw of Creighton was him being locked behind a solid steel door in a single-bed[16] cell. He knew he wouldn't be in there long but it would give Bosch enough time to head south[17] without being followed.

Bosch decided to leave the interview with Ida Townes Forsythe for another day. He jumped on the 5 freeway, which would take him all the way to San Diego, with a possible stop in Orange.

He checked his watch and did some math[18], then called his daughter. As usual the call went straight to message. He told her he would be pass-

1. tentative de corruption
2. Écartez
3. abasourdi
4. talons
5. de le menotter
6. qui lui fit découvrir
7. dans un étui
8. la hanche droite
9. tu es si arrogant que ça paraît une bonne chose
10. service de détention
11. commissariat
12. remit au
13. rangea
14. avant d'autoriser
15. appeler l'avocat auquel il avait droit
16. individuelle
17. prendre la direction du sud
18. quelques calculs

ing through her area between 12:30 and 1 p.m., and made the offer to take her to lunch or to grab a cup of coffee if she had the time and was up for it[1]. He told her he had something to talk to her about.

A half hour later he was just moving past downtown L.A. when he got the call back from Maddie.

"Are you coming down the Five[2]?" she asked.

"Hello to you too," he said. "Yes, I'm on the Five. It's moving pretty good so I think I'll be down your way closer to twelve-fifteen[3]."

"Well, I can do lunch[4]. What did you want to tell me?"

"Well, let's talk at lunch. You want to meet or should I come in and pick you up?"

It would be about a fifteen-minute ride from the freeway to campus.

"I've got such a good parking spot, any chance you can come get me?"

"Yeah, I just offered to. What do you feel like eating?"

"There's a place I wanted to try over on Bolsa."

Bosch knew that Bolsa was in the heart of an area known as Little Saigon, and far from campus.

"Uh," he said. "That's kind of far out[5] from the school. To come in to get you, then go out there and then back in to drop you is probably going to take too much time. I need to get down to—"

"Okay, I'll drive. I'll meet you there."

"Can we just go someplace near the school, Mads? If it's Vietnamese, you know that I don't …"

"Dad, it's been, like,[6] fifty years. Why can't you just eat the food? It's really being racist."

Bosch was quiet for a long moment while he composed an answer. He tried to speak calmly as he delivered it, but things were boiling up in-

1. l'envie
2. par l'autoroute 5
3. plutôt vers midi quinze
4. veux bien déjeuner
5. plutôt loin
6. ça fait quelque chose comme

side him. Not just what his daughter had said. But Creighton, the Screen Cutter, all of it.

"Maddie, racism has nothing to do with it and you should be very careful about throwing an accusation like that around," he said. "When I was your age I was *in* Vietnam, fighting to protect the people over there. And I had volunteered to be there. Was that racist?"

"It wasn't that[1] simple, Dad. You were supposedly[2] fighting communism. Anyway, it just seems weird[3] that you put up this big stand against the food[4]."

Bosch was silent. There were things about himself and his life that he never wanted to share with her. The whole four years of his military service was one of them. She knew he had served but he had never spoken to her about details of his time in Southeast Asia.

"Look, for two years when I was over there I ate that food," he said. "Every day, every meal."

"Why? Didn't they have regular[5] American food on the base or something?"

"Yes, but I couldn't eat it. If I did they would smell me in the tunnels. I had to smell like them."

Now it was her turn to be silent.

"I don't—what does that mean?" she finally said.

"You smell like what you eat. In enclosed spaces. It comes out of your pores. My job—I had to go into tunnels, and I didn't want the enemy to know I was there. So I ate *their* food every day, every meal, and I can't do it anymore. It brings it all back to me. Okay?"

There was only silence from her. Bosch held the top of the wheel[6] and drummed his fingers[7] against the dashboard[8] beyond it. He immediately regretted telling her what he just had.

1. aussi
2. soi-disant
3. bizarre
4. fasses une telle histoire pour de la cuisine vietnamienne
5. normale
6. volant
7. tapota des doigts
8. tableau de bord

"Look, maybe we skip[1] lunch today," he said. "I'll get to San Diego earlier and take care of my business, then maybe tomorrow on my way back up we get together for lunch or dinner. If I'm lucky down there and get everything done we might be able to do breakfast tomorrow."

Breakfast was her favorite meal and the Old Towne near the college was full of good places to get it.

"I have morning classes," Maddie said. "But let's try it tomorrow for lunch or dinner."

"You sure that's okay?" he asked.

"Yes, sure. But what were you going to tell me?"

He decided he didn't want to scare her by warning her to be extra careful[2] because the case he was working might overlap into her world[3]. He'd save that for the next day and an in-person[4] conversation.

"It can wait," he said. "I'll call you in the morning to figure out what will work[5]."

They ended the conversation and Bosch brooded on it[6] for the next hour as he made his way down through Orange County. He hated the idea of burdening[7] his daughter with anything from his past or his present. He didn't think it was fair[8].

1. laissons tomber
2. de faire spécialement attention
3. s'inviter dans sa vie
4. en chair et en os
5. pour voir comment on s'organise
6. la rumina
7. d'accabler
8. trouvait ça injuste

26

Bosch was making slow but steady progress[1] toward San Diego when he caught the call from Chief Valdez he knew would come[2].

"You busted[3] Deputy Chief Creighton?"

It was said equally as both a question and a statement of shock.

"He's not a deputy chief anymore," Bosch said. "He's not even a cop."

"It doesn't matter," Valdez said. "You have any idea what this is going to do for relations between the two departments?"

"Yeah, it's going to improve them. Nobody liked the guy at LAPD. You were there. You know that."

"No, I don't and it doesn't matter. I just kicked the guy loose[4]."

Bosch was not surprised.

"Why?" he asked anyway.

"Because you've got no case," Valdez said. "You had an argument[5]. That's all Lopez heard. You say you were threatened. He can turn around and say you threatened him. It's a pissing match[6]. You've got no corroborating witness[7] and no one at the D.A.'s Office will go anywhere near this."

Bosch assumed Lopez was the desk officer. It was good to know that Valdez had at least investigated the complaint[8] Bosch had written before he released Creighton.

"When did you kick him loose?" he asked.

1. avançait lentement mais sûrement
2. qu'il attendait
3. avez arrêté
4. viens de le relâcher
5. vous êtes pris le bec
6. C'est à qui gueulera le plus fort
7. témoin
8. plainte

"He just walked out the door," Valdez said. "And he wasn't happy. Where the hell are you and why'd you leave?"

"I'm working a case, Chief, and it doesn't involve San Fernando. I had to keep moving."

"It involves us now. Cretin says he going to sue[1] you and us."

It was good to hear Valdez use the name the rank and file had christened Creighton with[2]. It told Bosch that the chief was ultimately in his corner[3]. Bosch thought of Mitchell Maron, the mailman, who was threatening a lawsuit as well[4].

"Yeah, well, tell him to get in line[5]," he said. "Chief, I gotta go."

"I don't know what you are doing, but watch yourself out there," Valdez said. "Guys like Cretin, they're no good."

"I hear you," Bosch said.

The freeway opened wide[6] when he finally crossed into San Diego County. By 2:30 he had parked underneath the section of the 5 that was elevated over Logan Barrio and was standing in Chicano Park.

The Internet photos didn't do the murals justice[7]. In person[8] the colors were vibrant and the images startling[9]. The sheer number of them was staggering[10]. Pillar after pillar, wall after wall of paintings greeted the eye from every angle. It took him fifteen minutes of wandering[11] through to find the mural that listed the names of the original artists. The wreath[12] of zinnias was now hiding even more of the lower mural—and the names of the artists. Bosch squatted down[13] and used his hands to part[14] the flowers and read the names.

While many of the murals in the park looked like they had been repainted over the years to keep the colors and messages vibrant, the names

1. poursuivre en justice

2. dont les flics de base avaient baptisé Creighton

3. de son côté

4. menaçait lui aussi d'un procès

5. se mettre dans la file d'attente

6. était parfaitement dégagée

7. ne rendaient pas justice aux peintures murales

8. En vrai,

9. saisissantes

10. Rien que leur nombre était époustouflant

11. promenade

12. couronne

13. s'accroupit

14. écarter

behind the flowers had faded and were almost unreadable. Bosch took out his notebook. He was thinking that he might need to write down the names he could read and then hope those artists could be contacted and lead him to Gabriela. But then he saw the tops of letters from names that were below the soil line[1]. He put down the notebook, reached in[2] and started pulling back the dirt[3] and uprooting[4] the zinnias.

The first name he uncovered was Lukas Ortiz. He moved right and continued his trenching[5], his hands getting dirty with the dark, moist soil. Soon he uncovered the name Gabriela. He excitedly picked up the pace[6] and was just clearing the dirt from the last name[7] Lida when a booming[8] voice struck him from behind.

"Cabrón[9]!"

Bosch startled[10], then turned and looked over his shoulder to see a man behind him with his arms stretched wide in the universal stance that says[11], What the fuck are you doing! He was wearing a green work uniform.

Bosch jumped up.

"Hey, sorry," he said. *"Lo siento[12]."*

He started wiping the dirt off his hands but both were caked with wet soil[13] and it wasn't going anywhere[14]. The man in front of him was mid fifties with graying hair and a thick, wide mustache to go with a thick, wide body. An oval patch over the pocket of his shirt said *Javier*. He wore sunglasses but they didn't hide his angry stare[15] at Bosch.

"I wanted to see …" Bosch began.

He turned and pointed down toward the bottom of the pillar.

"Uh, *los nombres[16]?*" he said. "Under—uh, *debajo la tierra?*"

1. les lettres d'autres noms dépasser du terreau des plantations

2. plongea les mains

3. écarter la terre

4. à déraciner

5. à creuser

6. accéléra la cadence

7. nom de famille

8. tonitruante

9. *salaud* [espagnol]

10. sursauta

11. ouverts dans ce geste universel qui signifie

12. Je suis désolé [esp.]

13. pleines de glaise

14. qui ne partait pas

15. regard

16. les noms

1. êtes en train de foutre en l'air

2. toujours là

3. carrelée

4. portefeuille

5. billets de 20

6. balles

"I can speak English, fool. You're fucking up[1] my garden. What's wrong with you?"

"Sorry, I was looking for a name. An artist who was one of the originals here."

"There was a lot of them."

Javier walked past Bosch and squatted down where Bosch had been. He started using his own hands to carefully put the uprooted flowers back into place, handling each one far more gently than Bosch had.

"Lukas Ortiz?" he asked.

"No, the other," Bosch said. "Gabriela Lida. Is she still around[2]?"

"Who wants to know?"

"I'm a private invest—"

"No, who wants to know?" Bosch understood.

"If you can help me, I'd like to pay for the damage I did there."

"How much you pay?"

It was time for Bosch to reach into his pocket for his money but his hands were dirty. He looked around and saw a tiled[3] fountain that was part of the centerpiece of the park.

"Hold on," he said.

He walked over and dipped his hands into the fountain's pool and rubbed the dirt off. He then shook them and reached into his pocket. He checked his money fold[4] and chose three of the four twenties[5] he had. He went back to Javier. He hoped he wasn't about to spend sixty bucks[6] to be told Gabriela Lida was dead and in the ground like her name on the pillar.

Javier shook his head when Bosch got back to him.

"Now you fucked up my fountain," he said. "The dirt gets in the filter and I gotta clean it."

"I've got sixty bucks," Bosch said. "It covers everything. Where can I find Gabriela Lida?"

He held the money out and Javier took it with a dirty hand.

"She use to work here and was in charge of the collective[1]," he said. "But now she's retired[2]. Last I heard, she still lived in the Mercado."

"She lives in a market?" Bosch asked.

"No, *cabrón*, the Mercado. It's a housing complex[3], man. Over there on Newton."

"Her last name is still Lida?"

"That's right."

That's all Bosch needed. He headed back to his car. Ten minutes later he parked in front of the main entrance of a sprawling[4] complex of nicely kept low-income apartments[5] in a neo-adobe style[6]. He checked a residents' listing in the entryway and soon afterward knocked on a freshly painted green door.

Bosch was holding the cardboard folder[7] from Flashpoint Graphix down by his side. He raised his other hand to knock again just as the door was pulled open by a statuesque woman who, by Bosch's calculations, had to be at least seventy but looked younger. She had sharply defined cheekbones[8] and startling dark eyes set against still-smooth brown skin. Her hair was long and silver. Polished turquoise hung from her ears.

Bosch slowly lowered his hand. He had no doubt that this was the woman from the photo, all these years later.

"Yes?" she said. "Are you lost?"

"I don't think so," Bosch said. "Are you Gabriela Lida?"

"Yes, I am. What is it you want?"

Haller had told Bosch it would be his call to make[9] when the moment arose. That moment was

1. coopérative
2. à la retraite
3. résidence
4. vaste
5. HLM bien entretenus
6. de style imitation mexicain classique
7. chemise en carton
8. des pommettes anguleuses
9. que ce serait à lui de décider

now and Bosch felt there was no need and no time to run a game[1] with this woman.

"My name's Harry Bosch," he said. "I'm an investigator down from[2] L.A. and I'm looking for Dominick Santanello's daughter."

The mention of the name seemed to sharpen her eyes. Bosch saw equal parts curiosity and concern[3]. "My daughter doesn't live here. How do you know she is Dominick's daughter?"

"Because I started with him and it brought me to you. Let me show you something."

He brought up the folder, took the elastic band off it, and opened it in front of her, holding it like a music stand[4] so she could see the photos and page through them[5]. He heard her breath catch in her throat[6] as she reached forward and lifted the 8 × 10 of her holding the baby. Bosch saw tears start to show in her eyes.

"Nick took these," she whispered. "I never saw them."

Bosch nodded.

"They were in his camera in an attic for many years," he said. "What is your daughter's name?"

"We called her Vibiana," Gabriela said. "It was the name he wanted."

"After his mother."

Her eyes came up off the photo to his.

"Who are you?" she asked.

"If I could come in, there is a lot I need to tell you," Bosch said.

She hesitated for a moment, then stepped back and allowed him in[7].

Bosch initially explained his presence by telling Gabriela that he had been hired by someone in Dominick Santanello's family to see if he had fathered a child before he passed[8]. She accepted that, and over the course of the next hour they sat

1. tourner autour du pot
2. qui vient de
3. qu'elle était partagée entre l'inquiétude et la curiosité
4. pupitre
5. les feuilleter
6. son souffle se couper
7. le laissa entrer
8. son décès

in her small living room and Bosch heard the story of the short-lived[1] love affair between Gabriela and Dominick.

It was a different angle on the story that Halley Lewis from Tallahassee had told Bosch. Gabriela had met Dominick in a bar in Oceanside with the express purpose[2] of awakening him[3] to his cultural roots and pride. But those motives soon took a backseat to the passion that bloomed[4] between them and they became a couple.

"We made plans for after he came back and was discharged[5]," Gabriela said. "He wanted to be a photographer. We were going to do a project together, on the border[6]. He was going to shoot it[7]; I was going to paint it."

She said that she found out she was pregnant when he was near the end of his training at Pendleton and was waiting to receive orders to Vietnam. It was a heart-wrenching time[8] and he repeatedly offered to desert the Navy to stay with her. Each time she talked him out of it[9], an effort that later brought a crushing guilt down on her[10] after she learned he was killed overseas.

She confirmed that Dominick had snuck back[11] into the country twice while on leaves[12] from Vietnam. The first time he attended the dedication[13] of Chicano Park and the second time it was to see his newborn daughter. The family spent the only four days they'd ever have together at the del Coronado. She said the photograph that Bosch showed her was taken after an impromptu "marriage" on the beach officiated by an artist friend who was ordained[14] in a cult-like Mexican religion called *brujeria*.

"It was in fun," she said. "We thought we would get the chance to get married for real[15] when he came back at the end of the year."

1. brève
2. dans le but
3. le sensibiliser
4. passèrent au second plan lorsque la passion éclata
5. serait rendu à la vie civile
6. frontière
7. le photographier
8. période déchirante
9. l'en avait dissuadé
10. l'avait écrasée de culpabilité
11. était rentré en cachette
12. ses permissions
13. avait assisté à l'inauguration
14. avait été ordonné prêtre
15. pour de vrai

Bosch asked why Gabriela never reached out to[1] Dominick's family after his death and she explained that she had feared his parents might try to take the baby from her.

"I lived in a barrio[2]," she said. "I had no money. I was worried that they could win in court and take Vibiana from me. That would have killed me."

Bosch did not mention how closely Gabriela's feelings mirrored[3] the plight[4] of her daughter's grandmother and namesake[5]. But her answer served as a segue to[6] questions about Vibiana and where she was. Gabriela revealed that she lived in Los Angeles and was an artist as well. She was a sculptress living and working in the Arts District downtown[7]. She had been married once but now was not. The kicker[8] was that she was raising a nine-year-old boy from that marriage. His name was Gilberto Veracruz.

Bosch realized he had found another heir. Whitney Vance had a great-grandson he never knew about.

1. n'avait jamais essayé de contacter
2. quartier pauvre [latino]
3. rappelaient
4. sort tragique
5. homonyme
6. transition pour lui poser
7. du centre-ville
8. problème

27

The San Diego County Bureau of Vital Records[1] and Statistics was open until 5 p.m. Bosch walked hurriedly through the door at 4:35 and luckily found no one in line[2] at the window[3] marked *Birth Certificates, Death Certificates, Changes of Name.* He had only a single document to request and getting it now would save him from having to stay in San Diego overnight[4].

Bosch left the Mercado Apartments convinced that Vibiana and Gilberto Veracruz were direct descendants of Whitney Vance. If that could be proved, they were in line[5] to inherit the Vance fortune. Genetic analysis would of course be the key but Bosch also wanted to gather legal documentation that would go hand in hand[6] with the science and be part of a judge-convincing package[7]. Gabriela had told him that she put Dominick's name down on her daughter's birth certificate. Details like that would make the package complete.

At the window Bosch provided the name Vibiana Santanello and the date she was born, and requested a certified copy of her birth certificate. While he waited for the clerk to find and print it, he considered[8] some of the other revelations and confirmations that came out of his conversation with Gabriela.

Bosch had asked her how she had learned of Santanello's death in Vietnam and she said she knew in her heart that he had been killed when a

1. l'état civil
2. faisant la queue
3. au guichet
4. lui éviterait de passer la nuit à San Diego
5. sur les rangs
6. de pair
7. dossier juridiquement irréprochable
8. réfléchit à

week went by and she did not receive a letter from him. He had never gone that long[1] without writing her. Her intuition was sadly confirmed when later she saw a story[2] in the newspaper about how the shooting down of a single helicopter in Vietnam had hit Southern California particularly hard. All the Marines on the chopper[3] had California hometowns[4] and had previously been stationed at El Toro Marine Air Base in Orange County. The lone corpsman who was killed had trained at Camp Pendleton in San Diego after being raised in Oxnard.

Gabriela also told Bosch that Dominick's face was on one of the murals at the park. She had put it there many years before. It was on the mural called the Face of Heroes—several depictions[5] of men and women forming one face. Bosch remembered seeing the mural as he had walked through the park earlier that day.

"Here you are[6], sir," the clerk said to Bosch. "You pay at the window to your left."

Bosch took the document from the clerk and proceeded to the cash window. He studied it as he walked and saw the name Dominick Santanello listed as father. He realized how close he was to finishing the journey Whitney Vance had sent him on. He was disappointed that the old man would not be on hand at the finish line[7].

He was soon back on the 5 and heading north. He had told Gabriela that it was in her best interests to reveal nothing about her conversation with Bosch to anyone else. They had not immediately reached out to[8] Vibiana because Gabriela said her daughter led a life devoid of the trappings[9] of digital technology. She had no cell phone and rarely answered the phone in the studio-loft where she lived and worked.

1. n'était jamais resté si longtemps
2. article
3. de l'hélico
4. venaient de Californie
5. représentations
6. Voilà
7. ne puisse être là à la ligne d'arrivée
8. contacté
9. dépourvue des accessoires

Bosch planned to be at Vibiana's studio the next morning. Meanwhile, on the brutal rush-hour drive back up to[1] L.A. he spoke at length[2] on his cell[3] to Mickey Haller, who said he had made some subtle inquiries of his own[4].

"Pasadena did sign off on it as a natural[5] but there will be an autopsy," he said. "I think Kapoor wants the headlines[6] so he's going to milk cause of death for all it's worth[7]."

Bhavin Kapoor was the embattled[8] chief medical examiner[9] of Los Angeles County. In recent months he had come under fire[10] for mismanagement[11] and delays in processing autopsies at the office that handled more than eight thousand of them a year. Law enforcement agencies and loved ones[12] of murder and accident victims complained that some autopsies were taking months to complete, delaying investigations, funerals, and closure[13]. The media piled on further[14] when it was revealed that some bodies got mixed up[15] in the Big Crypt, a giant refrigerated storage center that held over a hundred cadavers. Toe tags[16] blown off by the giant turbine fans[17] that kept things cold had been reattached to the wrong toes.

Looking for headlines that didn't involve scandal, Kapoor had evidently decided to proceed with an autopsy on Whitney Vance's body so that he could hold a press conference that was about something other[18] than his handling of[19] his duties and department.

"You watch, though[20]," Haller said. "Some smart reporter[21] will turn this against him by pointing out[22] that the billionaire didn't have to wait in line[23] for an autopsy while every other body does. Even in death the rich get treated special—that'll be the headline."

1. de retour en pleine heure de pointe sur la route de
2. longuement
3. portable
4. de son côté
5. l'a bien déclarée comme mort naturelle
6. faire la une
7. chercher à fond la cause du décès
8. en difficulté
9. médecin légiste
10. essuyé des critiques
11. mauvaise gestion
12. les proches
13. empêchant les familles de faire leur deuil
14. en avaient rajouté une couche
15. avaient été mélangés
16. Les étiquettes d'identification [que l'on fixe aux orteils]
17. ventilateurs
18. qui parle d'autre chose
19. sa façon de gérer
20. Mais tu vas voir
21. Un petit futé de journaliste
22. en faisant remarquer
23. son tour

Bosch knew the observation was dead-on accurate[1] and was surprised that Kapoor's advisers, if he had any, had not warned him[2].

Haller asked what Bosch had found in San Diego and Harry reported that there might be two blood descendants in play. He recounted his conversation with Gabriela and told Haller that it might soon be time for DNA analysis. He outlined[3] what he had: A sealed sample[4] from Vance, though he did not witness the old man being swabbed[5]. Several items[6] that belonged to Dominick Santanello, including a razor that might have his blood on it. A swab sample he had taken from Gabriela Lida in case it was needed. And he planned to swab Vibiana when he met her the following day. For the moment he planned to leave Vibiana's son—Vance's presumed great-grandson—out of it.

"The only thing that's going to matter is Vibiana's DNA," Haller said. "We will need to show the hereditary chain, which I think you have in hand. But it's going to come down to[7] her DNA and whether they match it[8] to Vance's as direct descendant."

"We need to do it as a blind[9], right?" Bosch said. "Not tell them the swab is from Vance. Just give them the swab from Vibiana. Then see what they say."

"Agreed. Last thing we want is for them to know whose DNA they have. I will work on that and set something up[10] in one of the labs I gave you. Whichever one will do it the fastest[11]. Then when you get the blood from Vibiana, we go in."

"I'm hoping that will be tomorrow."

"That'll be good. What did you do with the swab from Vance?"

"My refrigerator."

1. tout à fait pertinente
2. ne l'aient pas mis en garde
3. lista
4. échantillon
5. bien qu'il n'ait pas vu le vieil homme se le faire prélever
6. objets
7. ce qui compte, c'est surtout
8. de voir s'il correspond
9. à l'aveugle
10. organiser ça
11. Celui des deux qui le fera le plus vite

"Not sure that's the safest place. And I don't think refrigeration is required."

"It's not. I just hid it in there."

"I like the idea of keeping it separate from the will and the pen. Don't want everything in the same place. I'm just concerned with it being in your house. It's probably the first place they'll look."

"There you go with that 'they' thing again[1]."

"I know. But it is what it is. Maybe you should think of another place."

Bosch told Haller about his run-in[2] with Creighton and Harry's suspicion that there might be camera surveillance on his house.

"I'll check it out tomorrow morning first thing[3]," he said. "It will be dark by the time I get there tonight. The point is, there was nobody out there this morning when I left. I checked my car for a GPS tag and yet somehow Creighton's following me up Laurel Canyon Boulevard."

"Maybe it was a fucking drone," Haller said. "They're being used all over the place[4] now."

"I'll have to remember to start looking up. You too. Creighton said they knew you were on the case, too."

"Not a surprise."

Bosch could see the lights of downtown now through the windshield[5]. He was finally getting close to home[6] and he could feel the exhaustion[7] from the day on the road settling on his body[8]. He was bone tired[9] and wanted to rest. He decided that he would skip dinner[10] in favor of extra sleep time[11].

His mind wandered[12] from the conversation when the thought of food reminded him that he needed to call or text[13] his daughter to tell her he had driven home and wouldn't be passing by cam-

1. Et voilà que tu recommences avec tes « ils »
2. confrontation
3. à la première heure
4. partout
5. pare-brise
6. près de chez lui
7. épuisement
8. l'envahir
9. moulu
10. sauterait le dîner
11. pour dormir plus longtemps
12. se détachait
13. faire un SMS à

pus the next day. Their getting together would have to wait.

Maybe that was a good thing, Bosch thought. After their last phone call it might be better to have some time and distance between them.

"Harry, you still there?" Haller said.

Bosch came out of the unrelated thoughts[1].

"Here," he said. "You just cut out[2] for a second. I'm going through a bad cell area[3]. Go ahead."

Haller said he wanted to discuss a strategy involving where and when they should make a move in court[4]. It was a subtle form of judge shopping[5] but he explained that deciding in what courthouse to file the will[6] could give them an advantage. He said he assumed that probate on[7] Vance would be opened in Pasadena, near where he lived and died, but that did not require a claimant to file[8] there as well. If Vibiana Veracruz was determined to establish herself as Vance's heir, then she could file her claim at a courthouse convenient to her[9].

To Bosch these were decisions that were above his pay grade[10] and he told Haller so. His job here, and his responsibility and promise to Vance, was simply to find the heir, if one existed, and gather the evidence[11] to prove the bloodline. Legal strategies involving the subsequent claim to[12] the Vance fortune were for Haller to decide.

Bosch added something that he had been thinking about since his conversation with Gabriela.

"What if they don't want it?" he asked.

"What if who doesn't want what?" Haller replied.

"The money," Bosch said. "What if Vibiana doesn't want it? These people are artists. What if they don't want to be involved in running a corporation, sitting on a board of directors[13], being in that world? When I told Gabriela that her daughter and grandson might be in line for a lot of mon-

1. émergea de ses pensées

2. Ça a coupé

3. une zone où le réseau passe mal

4. porter l'affaire devant un tribunal

5. recherche du juge accommodant

6. présenter le testament

7. l'homologation du testament de

8. qu'on dépose une requête

9. au tribunal de son choix

10. le dépassaient

11. de rassembler les preuves

12. entreprises pour prétendre à

13. faire partie du conseil d'administration

ey, she just shrugged it off[1]. She said she hadn't had any money for seventy years and didn't want any now."

"Not going to happen[2]," Haller said. "This is change-the-world money. She'll take it. What artist doesn't want to change the world?"

"Most want to change it with their art, not their money."

Bosch got a call-waiting signal and saw that it was from one of the SFPD exchanges[3]. He thought maybe it was Bella Lourdes calling with the results of the second search of the Sahagun house. He told Haller he needed to go and would check in with him[4] the next day after he found Vibiana and spoke to her.

He switched over[5] but it wasn't Lourdes calling.

"Bosch, Chief Valdez. Where are you?"

"Uh, heading north, just passing by downtown. What's up[6]?"

"Are you with Bella?"

"Bella? No, why would I be with Bella?"

Valdez ignored Bosch's question and asked another. The serious tone in his voice had[7] Bosch's attention. "Have you heard from her today?"

"Not since this morning when we talked on the phone. Why? What's going on, Chief?"

"We can't find her and we're not getting any answers on her cell[8] or the radio. She signed in this morning on the board in the D bureau but never signed out. It's not like her[9]. Trevino was working on budgets with me today, so he was never in the D bureau. He never saw her."

"Her car in the lot[10]?"

"Both her personal car and her plain wrap[11] are still in the lot and her partner[12] called and said she hasn't come home."

1. a haussé les épaules

2. Aucun risque

3. standards

4. le recontacterait

5. prit l'autre appel

6. Que se passe-t-il

7. retint

8. portable

9. Ça ne lui ressemble pas

10. est dans le parking

11. véhicule banalisé

12. compagne

1. grand vide
2. sur le terrain
3. pris par

A hollow[1] opened up in the middle of his chest. "Did you talk to Sisto?" he asked.

"Yeah, he hasn't seen her either," Valdez said. "He said she called him this morning to see if he was available to go with her into the field[2] but he was tied up on[3] a commercial burglary."

Bosch pushed his foot further down on the gas pedal.

"Chief, send a car right now up to the Sahagun house. That was where she was going."

"Why, what was—"

"Just send the car, Chief. Now. Tell them to search inside and outside the house. The backyard in particular. We can talk after. I'm on my way and will be there in thirty minutes or less. Send that car."

"Right away."

Bosch disconnected and called Bella's number, though he knew it was unlikely she would answer for him if she wasn't answering for the police chief.

It rang through to voice mail and Bosch disconnected. He felt the hollow in his chest growing wider and deeper.

28

Bosch broke away from the crushing evening traffic after passing by downtown. With speed and illegal use of the carpool lane[1], he covered the remaining distance to San Fernando in twenty minutes. He felt lucky to be in the rental[2], because he knew his old Cherokee wouldn't have reached the speeds he maintained on his way.

In the station he moved quickly through the back hallway to the chief's office but found it empty, the hanging toy helicopter[3] moving in a circular pattern[4], propelled[5] by a breeze from the overhead air-conditioning vent[6].

He then moved on to the detective bureau and found Valdez standing at Lourdes's cubicle along with Trevino, Sisto, and Sergeant Rosenberg, the evening watch commander. He could tell by the concerned looks on their faces[7] that they still hadn't located[8] the missing detective.

"You checked the Sahagun house?" he asked.

"We sent a car over[9]," Valdez said. "She's not there, doesn't look like she ever was."

"Damn," Bosch said. "Where else are you looking?"

"Never mind that[10]," Trevino said. "Where were you today?"

He said it in an accusatory tone, as if Bosch had some knowledge of the missing detective's whereabouts[11].

1. voie réservée au covoiturage

2. voiture de location

3. petit hélicoptère suspendu

4. tournant en rond

5. mû

6. conduit de climatisation du plafond

7. leur air inquiet

8. retrouvé

9. sur place

10. Peu importe

11. savait où se trouvait l'enquêtrice disparue

"I had to go to San Diego," Bosch said. "One of my private cases. Went there and back[1]."

"Then who the hell is Ida Townes Forsythe?"

Bosch looked at Trevino.

"What?"

"You heard me. Who is Ida Townes Forsythe?"

He held up a printout[2] of Forsythe's DMV[3] information and Bosch suddenly realized he had left it in the printer tray[4] that morning when he was distracted by the call to the lobby to see Creighton.

"Right, I forgot, I was here this morning for about twenty minutes," he said. "I printed that out, but what's that got to do with Bella?"

"We don't know," Trevino said. "We're trying to figure out what the fuck is going on here. I find this in the printer and then check our DMV account to see if it was Bella who pulled it up and instead I see that you ran this[5]. Who is she?"

"Look, Ida Forsythe has nothing to do with this, okay? She's part of the private case I'm working."

Bosch knew it was an admission[6] he should not have made but he wasn't in the mood for sparring[7] with Trevino and he wanted to get the focus quickly back[8] on Bella.

For a moment Trevino's face betrayed him[9]. Bosch could see his barely masked delight[10] in knowing he had just outed[11] Bosch in front of the man who had brought him into the department.

"No, not okay," Trevino said. "That's a firing offense[12]. And it could mean charges[13] as well."

Trevino looked at Valdez as he said it, as if to say, I told you this guy was just using us for access.

"Tell you what, Cap," Bosch said. "You can fire me and charge me as soon as we find Bella."

Bosch turned and directed the next question to Valdez.

"What else are we doing?" he asked.

1. J'ai fait l'aller et retour
2. sortie papier
3. de carte grise [Department of Motor Vehicles]
4. sur l'imprimante
5. c'est vous qui avez fait la recherche
6. aveu
7. d'humeur à se bagarrer
8. recentrer rapidement l'attention
9. le trahit
10. sa joie mal dissimulée
11. démasqué
12. motif de renvoi
13. entraîner des poursuites

"We've brought everybody in and they're out looking," the chief said. "We've put it out[1] to the LAPD and Sheriff's Department as well[2]. Why did you tell us to check the Sahagun house?"

"Because she told me this morning that she would go search it again," Bosch said.

"Why?"

Bosch quickly explained the conversation he'd had with Lourdes that morning, including his theory that the Screen Cutter might have lost the key to his getaway car, which would explain his running from the scene of the crime and trying to find an unlocked car to boost[3].

"There was no key," Sisto said. "I would've found it."

"Never hurts to double-check with fresh eyes[4]," Bosch said. "When she called to see if you could go into the field, did she ask about GTAs[5] in Area Two on Friday?"

Sisto realized that was a detail he had not mentioned to the chief and the captain earlier.

"Yeah, that's right, she did," he said. "I told her I hadn't had time to look at auto thefts from Friday yet."

Trevino moved quickly to the row of clipboards[6] hung on the wall behind Sisto's desk. This was where the property crime reports[7] were kept on different clipboards depending on the crime. Trevino grabbed the clipboard marked AUTOS and looked at the top sheet. He then flipped back through[8] several of the reports.

"We've got one Friday in Area Three," he said. "Another on Saturday."

Valdez turned to Rosenberg.

"Irwin, take those reports," he said. "Send a car to each location, have them find out if Lourdes was out there doing follow-up[9]."

1. On en a référé

2. aux flics de la ville et du comté

3. à mettre en route

4. Ça ne fait pas de mal de faire revérifier par quelqu'un d'autre

5. s'il y avait eu des vols de voiture

6. écritoires à pinces

7. atteintes aux biens

8. feuilleta

9. y est passée dans le cadre de l'enquête

1. Entendu
2. dépôt
3. C'est là qu'on fait le plein
4. portefeuille
5. se séparèrent
6. se dirigea
7. atelier
8. divers établis
9. tendue
10. interrupteur
11. des râteliers
12. fixées
13. des coupe-tubes
14. des meuleuses

"Roger that[1]," Rosenberg said. "I'll take one myself."

He took the whole clipboard from Trevino and quickly headed out of the bureau.

"Is there anybody still over in Public Works?" Bosch asked.

"This time of night, they're closed," Valdez said. "Why?"

"Can we get in? This morning Bella said she was going over there to borrow a metal detector for the search up at the Sahagun house."

"I know we can at least get into the yard[2]," Trevino said. "We gas up the cars in there[3]."

"Let's go," Valdez said.

The four men left the station through the front door and quickly crossed the street to the Public Works complex. They walked down the left side of the structure to the vehicle and storage yard's entrance gate, which Valdez opened with a key card pulled from his wallet[4].

As they entered the yard the men split up[5] and started looking for Lourdes in and among the various work trucks and vans. Bosch headed[6] toward the back wall, where there were a covered workshop[7] and assorted tool benches[8]. Behind him he heard the vehicle doors being opened and closed and the chief's strained[9] voice calling out Bella's name.

But there was no response.

Bosch used the light from his phone to find a switch[10] that turned on the fluorescent lights in the workshop. There were three separate benches positioned perpendicular to the back wall. These benches had racks[11] of tools and materials as well as anchored[12] machines and devices like pipe cutters[13], grinders[14], and woodworking drills and saws[1]. It looked like projects were left in mid-course[2] on each of the benches.

Above the third bench, there was an overhead[3] rack holding several eight-foot lengths of stainless-steel pipe[4]. Bosch remembered Lourdes saying they used a metal detector to find underground pipes. He assumed the third bench was for plumbing and drainage-related projects[5] and that if there was a metal detector, it would be there.

Lourdes had described the metal detector as something with wheels[6] like a lawnmower and not the kind of handheld[7] detector he had seen used by treasure hunters on the beach.

Bosch didn't see anything and turned in a circle with his eyes scanning all of the equipment[8] on and surrounding the workbenches. He finally spotted[9] a crossbar handle[10] extending out from under one of the benches. He walked over and pulled out a bright orange device on wheels that was about half the size of a push mower[11].

He had to study it to know what it was. There was a control panel attached to the crossbar. He pushed the on/off button, and an LED screen lit with a triangular radar display and other controls[12] for scope[13] and depth.

"It's here," he said.

His words drew the other three men over from their own fruitless[14] searches.

"Well, if she used it, she brought it back," Valdez said.

The chief kicked one of his boots against the concrete[15] floor, showing his frustration with another lead that didn't pan out[16].

Bosch put both hands on the metal detector's handle and lifted. He got the two back wheels off the ground but even that was a struggle[17].

1. des perceuses et scies à bois
2. en plan
3. suspendu
4. tuyaux en Inox de 2,5 m
5. les chantiers de plomberie et de tuyauterie
6. sur roues
7. portatif
8. balaya tout l'atelier du regard,
9. discerna
10. poignée en forme de guidon
11. tondeuse manuelle
12. Voyants
13. portée
14. vaines
15. de béton
16. pour cette piste qui, encore une fois, n'avait rien donné
17. tout juste

"This thing is heavy," he said. "If she used it, then she had help getting it out there to the Sahagun house. It wouldn't have fit in a plain wrap[1]."

"Should we check inside for her?" Sisto asked.

The chief turned and looked at the door that led to the Public Works offices. Three of them walked over and Bosch followed after parking the metal detector back in its place. Valdez tried the door but it was locked with a dead bolt[2]. Valdez turned to Sisto, the youngest among them.

"Kick it[3]," he said.

"It's a metal door, Chief," Sisto said.

"Try," Valdez said. "You're a young stud[4]."

Sisto took three shots at the door with his heel. Each one was stronger than the one before it but the door didn't give[5]. His brown face turned a deep maroon[6] with the effort. He took a deep breath and was about to try a fourth, when the police chief raised an arm and stopped him.

"Okay, hold on, hold on," Valdez said. "It's not going to give. We'll have to see if we can get somebody out here with a key."

Trevino looked at Bosch.

"You got your picks[7] on you, Big Time[8]?" he asked.

It was the first time Trevino had ever called him that to his face[9], an obvious reference to Bosch's LAPD pedigree.

"Nope[10]," Bosch said.

Harry stepped away from them and over to the nearest work truck. He reached over the hood[11], pulled the windshield wiper back[12] on its hinge[13] and twisted it right and then left. He pulled it sharply[14] and ripped it off the[15] truck.

"Harry, what are you doing?" Valdez said.

"Just give me a minute," Bosch said.

1. Ça n'aurait pas pu rentrer dans sa voiture
2. verrouillée
3. Enfonce-la
4. jeune et costaud
5. ne céda pas
6. vira au rouge foncé
7. crochets
8. Super Flic
9. en face
10. Nan
11. se pencha sur le capot
12. leva l'essuie-glace
13. charnière
14. d'un coup sec
15. le détacha du

He took the wiper over to one of the benches and used a pair of pliers[1] to pull the rubber blade[2] off the flat thin metal strip that backed it[3]. He then took a pair of metal snips[4] to cut off two three-inch lengths of the strip[5]. He picked up the pliers again and fashioned[6] the two metal strips into a pick and a flat hook[7]. He had what he needed in less than two minutes.

Bosch went back to the door, squatted[8] in front of the dead bolt[9], and went to work.

"You've done that before," Valdez said.

"A few times," Bosch said. "Somebody[10] put a phone light on this."

All three of the other men turned on cell lights and put the beams over Bosch's shoulder and onto the dead bolt. It took Bosch three more minutes to turn the lock and open the door.

"Bella?" Valdez called out as they entered.

No answer. Sisto hit the light switches and they went down a hallway[11] as the fluorescents[12] blasted[13] the darkness, peeling off one at a time[14] into the offices they passed. Valdez kept calling out his missing detective's name but the offices were as quiet as a church on a Monday night. Bosch was the last to peel off, entering the code enforcement bullpen[15] whose three cubicles were just as cramped[16] as the detective bureau across the street[17]. He made his way around the room looking down into each cubicle but seeing no sign of Lourdes.

Soon Sisto came in.

"Anything?"

"No."

"Shit."

Bosch saw the nameplate[18] on one of the desks. It reminded him of something else from his morning conversation with Lourdes.

1. pinces

2. détacher la languette de caoutchouc

3. de sa fine plaque métallique

4. cisailles à métaux

5. bandelettes d'environ 8 cm

6. transforma

7. en un jeu de crochets

8. s'accroupit

9. serrure

10. Est-ce que quelqu'un peut

11. marchèrent dans un couloir

12. tubes au néon

13. perçaient

14. chacun se détachant du groupe et entrant

15. grand bureau de l'inspection de la voirie

16. exigus

17. d'en face

18. plaque nominative

"Sisto, did Bella have a problem with Dockweiler?"

"What do you mean?"

"This morning when she said she was going to come over here to borrow the metal detector, she said she could ask Dockweiler for help. Then she said something about hoping he was in a good mood[1]. Was there a problem between them?"

"Maybe because she kept her job and he got transferred to Public Works?"

"Sounded like something else."

Sisto had to consider the question further[2] before coming up with another answer.

"Uh, I don't think it was that big of a deal[3] but back when[4] he was in the bureau with us I remember there was sometimes friction between them. I don't think at first Dock picked up on the fact[5] that she played for the other team[6]. He made a comment[7] about a lesbian—I forget who she was, but he called her a carpet muncher[8] or something like that. But Bella jumped all over his shit[9] and things were kind of tense[10] for a while there."

Bosch studied Sisto, expecting more.

"That was it[11]?" he prompted.

"I guess so," Sisto said. "I mean, I don't know."

"What about you? You have a problem with him?"

"Me? No, we were fine."

"You talk to him? Shoot the shit[12]?"

"Yeah, some. Not a lot."

"Does he not like lesbians, or is it women he doesn't like?"

"No, he isn't gay, if that's what you mean."

"That's not what I mean. Come on, Sisto, what kind of guy is he?"

1. de bonne humeur
2. réexaminer la question
3. grave
4. à l'époque où
5. ait capté
6. était homo
7. une réflexion
8. l'a traitée de brouteuse
9. l'a très mal pris
10. un peu tendues
11. C'est tout
12. Vous discutez le coup

"Look, man, I don't know. He told me once that when he worked for the Sheriff's up at[1] Wayside, they did things to the gays."

That struck a chord with[2] Bosch. Wayside Honor Rancho was a county jail[3] located in the Santa Clarita Valley. All new deputies were assigned to jail duty[4] right out of the academy[5]. Bosch remembered Lourdes telling him that when it appeared that it would be several years before she got a chance to transfer out of the jail division, she started applying to other departments and ended up at San Fernando.

"What things did they do?"

"He said they'd put them in situations, you know. Put them in modules where they knew they would get fucked with[6], beat up[7]. They took bets and stuff[8] on how long they'd last before they got jumped[9]."

"Did he know Bella when she was there?"

"I don't know. I never asked."

"Who came to San Fernando first?"

"Pretty sure it was Dock."

Bosch nodded. Dockweiler had seniority on[10] Bella, yet she was retained instead of him when the budget crisis hit. That had to have built animosity.

"What happened when he got moved out of the department?" he asked. "Was he angry?"

"Well, yeah, wouldn't you be?" Sisto answered. "But he was cool about it. They found him the spot[11] over here. So it was kind of lateral[12]—he didn't even lose salary."

"Except no badge and no gun."

"I think code enforcement has a badge."

"Not the same, Sisto. You ever heard the phrase 'If you're not cop, you're little people[13]'?"

"Uh, no."

1. à
2. rappela quelque chose à
3. prison locale
4. affectés au service carcéral
5. à leur sortie de l'école de police
6. se feraient emmerder
7. tabasser
8. faisaient des paris et tout
9. de se faire passer à tabac
10. plus d'ancienneté que
11. lui ont trouvé ce poste
12. un peu à la marge
13. Si t'es pas flic, t'es pas grand-chose

Bosch grew quiet as he studied the top of Dockweiler's desk. Nothing he saw seemed suspicious. He heard the dinging of a text[1] on Sisto's phone.

Pinned[2] to the privacy wall[3] between Dockweiler's and another desk was a map of the city, partitioned[4] into four code enforcement zones that mirrored the police department's patrol areas. There was also a list of tips[5] for spotting illegal garage conversions[6] with photo examples of each giveaway[7]:

Extension cords[8], cables, and hoses[9] running from house to garage
Tape[10] over the seams[11] of the garage door
Air-conditioning units on garage walls
Barbecue grills closer to the garage than the house
Boats, bikes, and other garaged property stored outside

Studying the list, Bosch pictured[12] the houses where the Screen Cutter rapes had occurred. Just three days ago, he had driven the circuit[13] that included all four places. He saw now what he didn't see then. Each had a garage, each was in a neighborhood where illegal garage conversions were a problem and would draw the attention of code inspectors[14]. Beatriz Sahagun's house had a garage too.

"It was him," Bosch said quietly.

Sisto didn't hear him. Bosch kept grinding it down[15], putting things together. Dockweiler could roam[16] the city as a code inspector. He could have knocked on doors to perform inspections and selected his victims when he saw them in the course[17] of his work. It was the reason to wear the mask each time.

1. sonnerie d'un SMS
2. Épinglé
3. la cloison
4. divisé
5. trucs
6. savoir repérer les aménagements illégaux de garages
7. élément suspect
8. rallonges
9. tuyaux d'arrosage
10. Scotch
11. jointures
12. se représenta
13. suivi un itinéraire
14. inspecteurs municipaux
15. continua à cogiter
16. sillonner
17. l'exercice

He realized also that it was Dockweiler who had the extra[1] key to Bosch's desk. He'd kept it when he left the department but snuck back[2] to read the file on the investigation once Bosch had connected the cases. He knew what Bosch knew and what he was doing at every step[3] of the investigation. And the horror of it all, Bosch knew, was that he had sent Lourdes right to him. The fear and guilt of that realization boiled up in him. He turned away from the desk and saw Sisto typing a text on his phone.

"Is that Dockweiler?" he demanded. "Are you texting Dockweiler?"

"No, man, it's my girlfriend," Sisto said. "She wants to know where I am. Why would I text—"

Bosch snatched[4] the phone out of Sisto's hand and looked at the screen.

"Hey, what the fuck!" Sisto exclaimed.

Bosch read the text and confirmed it was an innocuous *Home soon* missive[5]. He then flipped the phone back[6] at the young detective but the toss[7] was too hard for such a close distance[8]. It went right through Sisto's hands, hit him square in the chest[9], and then clattered[10] to the floor.

"You asshole[11]!" Sisto yelled as he quickly dropped down to grab the phone off the floor. "It better not be[12]—"

As he straightened up Bosch moved in, grabbed him by the front of his shirt, and drove him back into the room's door, banging his back and head hard against it. He then moved right up into his face.

"You lazy fuck[13], you should've gone with her today. Now she's out there somewhere and we have to find her. Do you understand?"

Bosch racked him hard against[14] the door again.

"Where does Dockweiler live?"

1. supplémentaire
2. était revenu en cachette
3. étape
4. saisit brusquement
5. inoffensif « Je rentre bientôt »
6. renvoya
7. geste
8. trop violent pour une si courte distance
9. en plein dans la poitrine
10. tomba bruyamment
11. Connard
12. T'as intérêt à ce qu'il soit pas
13. Sale flemmard
14. l'envoya cogner

"I don't know! Get the fuck off me[1]!"

Sisto shoved Bosch off[2] with such force that he was nearly driven into the opposite wall. He hit a counter[3] with his hip and an empty glass coffeepot[4] fell off its hot plate[5] and shattered[6] on the floor.

Drawn by the harsh voices and crashing glass, Valdez and Trevino came charging through the door[7]. It swung right into Sisto, hitting him from behind and knocking him out of the way.

"What the hell's going on?" Valdez demanded.

One hand holding the back of his head, Sisto pointed a finger at Bosch with the other.

"He's crazy! Keep him the fuck away from me."

Bosch pointed right back at him.

"You should've gone with her. But you gave her a bullshit line[8] and she went up there on her own[9]."

"What about you, old man? It wasn't my case. It was yours. *You* shoulda been there, not me."

Bosch turned away from him and looked at Valdez.

"Dockweiler," he said. "Where does he live?"

"Up in Santa Clarita, I think," Valdez said. "At least he did when he worked for me. Why? What's going on here?"

He put a hand on Bosch's shoulder to keep Bosch from moving toward Sisto. Bosch shrugged it off[10] and pointed at Dockweiler's desk like it was incontrovertible evidence[11] of something only he could see.

"It's him," Bosch said. "Dockweiler's the Screen Cutter. And he's got Bella."

1. Lâchez-moi, putain
2. repoussa Bosch
3. placard bas
4. cafetière
5. plaque chauffante
6. se brisa
7. déboulèrent, enfonçant la porte
8. excuse bidon
9. toute seule
10. s'en défit d'un mouvement d'épaule
11. la preuve irréfutable

29

They took two cars and headed code 3[1] up the 5 freeway. Valdez and Bosch were in the lead car[2] with Valdez behind the wheel. The police chief had wisely[3] separated Bosch from Sisto, who drove the second car with Trevino riding shotgun[4] and probably miffed[5] that the tensions between Bosch and Sisto had resulted in his being separated from the chief.

Valdez was on the phone barking[6] an order to someone in the communications center.

"I don't care," he said. "Call whoever you have to call. Just get me the goddamn[7] address. I don't care if you need to send cars to their houses to get a response."

He disconnected and cursed[8]. So far[9] the com center had not been able to make contact with the director of Public Works or the city manager[10] to get access to city payroll records[11] and Dockweiler's address. They had checked DMV records before leaving the station and found that Dockweiler had somehow managed[12] himself or benefited from a bureaucratic glitch[13] to keep a law enforcement officer block on his address[14] nearly five years after leaving the police department.

So they were heading to the Santa Clarita Valley based solely[15] on Valdez's memory that Dockweiler lived somewhere up there five years ago.

"We might get up there and have no place to go," Valdez said.

1. avec gyrophares et sirène [en vertu du Code pénal californien]

2. véhicule de tête

3. avec sagesse

4. assis à sa droite

5. mécontent

6. aboyant

7. cette foutue

8. jura

9. Pour l'instant,

10. gestionnaire municipal

11. au registre des fonctionnaires municipaux

12. s'était débrouillé pour

13. dysfonctionnement

14. rester sur liste rouge en tant que policier

15. en se fondant uniquement

1. frappa le volant

He banged the steering wheel[1] with an open palm and changed the subject.

"What was that all about back there with Sisto, Harry?" he asked. "I've never seen you act like that."

2. J'ai pété les plombs

3. m'en suis pris à

4. À propos de quoi

"I'm sorry, Chief," Bosch said. "I lost it[2]. If I could have thrown myself against the door, I would have. But I took it out on[3] Sisto."

"Took what out[4]?"

"I should've been with Bella today. My case, I should've been there. Instead, I told her to take Sisto and I should've known she'd go alone if he wasn't around."

5. véridique

6. arrêtez de culpabiliser

7. que vous restiez concentré

"Look, we don't even know if this Dockweiler thing is legit[5]. So hold off on beating yourself up[6]. I need you focused here[7]."

Valdez pointed north through the windshield.

8. auraient du mal

9. surveillants de prison

10. assez peu probable

Bosch tried to think of another source for Dockweiler's address. If he was still employing law enforcement protection measures they would be hard-pressed[8] to find him. He thought about calling Wayside and seeing if any of the jail deputies[9] remembered him and might know his address. It seemed like a long shot[10] since Dockweiler had left the Sheriff's Department so long ago. "When did he first come to work for San Fernando?" Bosch asked.

11. en 2005

12. venait de célébrer ses 5 ans de service et avait acquis ses points de retraite

13. le virer

"It was '05[11] or '06, I think," Valdez said. "He was already here when I got here. Yeah, it would have been '06. Because I remember he was just past five years and vested[12] when I had to chop him[13]."

14. influençait des gardes à vue

15. organisait des bagarres

"Sisto told me about him saying he was part of a group of deputies at Wayside that manipulated custodies[14] and staged fights[15]."

"I remember they weeded out a bunch of[1] jail deputies back around then. The Wayside Whities[2], remember?"

It was coming back to Bosch. It was hard to remember specific groups or incidents because it seemed to him that the Sheriff's Department had suffered one jail scandal after another[3] in the last decade. The previous sheriff had resigned in disgrace[4] during an FBI investigation of jail issues[5]. He faced a corruption trial[6] and several of his deputies[7] had already gone to prison. These were some of the reasons Bella Lourdes had told Bosch she'd needed to get out, even if it meant moving to a much smaller department like San Fernando's.

"So why did you chop him instead of Bella?" Bosch asked. "He had seniority[8], right?"

"He did but I had to do what was best for the department," Valdez said.

"Nice political answer."

"It's the truth. You know Bella. She's a go-getter[9]. Loves the job, wants to give back[10]. Dockweiler … he was a bit of a bully[11]. So when Marvin told me I could offer one of my people the job in code enforcement, I kept Lourdes and transferred Dockweiler. I thought it suited him. You know, telling people to cut their lawns[12] and trim their hedges[13]."

Marvin was Marvin Hodge, the city manager[14]. Bosch shook his head as the chief's answer reminded him of his failings[15] on the Screen Cutter case.

"What?" Valdez asked. "I think I made the right choice."

"No, it's not that," Bosch said. "You did make the right choice. But you probably didn't with me.

1. avaient expulsé plusieurs
2. Blancs
3. n'avait cessé d'être embourbé dans les scandales carcéraux
4. avait été contraint de démissionner
5. sur les prisons
6. risquait un jugement pour corruption
7. adjoints
8. plus d'ancienneté
9. battante
10. elle se donne à fond
11. brute
12. tondre leur pelouse
13. tailler leurs haies
14. DRH municipal
15. manquements

I missed a lot on this one. I guess the time off made me rusty[1]."

"What did you miss?"

"Well, last Friday I took a drive past[2] the first four crime scenes—the ones we knew about. You know, all in one trip and in the order of occurrence. I'd never done that before and I was trying to see if anything would spark[3], if I would finally figure out[4] what the link was[5]. And I didn't see it. It was right there[6] and I didn't see it. All of the houses had garages."

"Yeah, but that's so common. Practically every house built since World War Two has a garage. In this town, that's just about[7] everybody."

"Doesn't matter. I should have put it together[8]. I'll bet you my next paycheck[9] that we're going to find that Dockweiler inspected those houses and those garages for unpermitted[10] conversion and habitation—he has the damn tip sheet[11] pinned to the wall of his cubicle. That's how he picked his victims. That's why he wore the masks. Because the victims might remember him from the inspection."

"You don't get a paycheck[12], Harry."

"And after this I don't deserve one[13]."

"Look, as far as Dockweiler goes, this is all just theory right now. We don't have a shred of evidence[14] he's the Screen Cutter. The theory looks good but theories don't get convictions[15]."

"It's him."

"Just because you keep saying it doesn't make it so."

"Well, you better hope it is[16]. Otherwise we're looking for Bella in the wrong place."

That was a thought that brought silence to the car for the next few miles. But after a while Bosch

1. m'a rouillé
2. suis passé devant
3. ferait tilt
4. comprendre
5. quel était le lien
6. sous mon nez
7. quasiment
8. J'aurais dû faire le rapprochement
9. salaire
10. illégale
11. foutue feuille d'indices
12. On ne vous verse aucun salaire
13. n'en mérite plus
14. la moindre preuve
15. ne font condamner personne
16. espérons que ce soit le cas

started asking questions so he didn't have to dwell on thoughts[1] about Bella.

"How did Dockweiler take getting shit-canned[2]?" he asked.

"Well, when you put it like that it sounds pretty bad," Valdez said. "But every time we had to make a cutback[3] we did our best to place people or come up with a plan for them. So, like I said, Marvin gave me the slot[4] at Public Works to use and I came to Dockweiler with that[5]. He took it but he wasn't too happy about it. He wanted us to move the position[6] from Public Works to the Police Department, but it doesn't work that way."

"Did he resent that Lourdes and Sisto weren't cut[7] first?"

"Well, I don't know if you know this but Sisto is the son of a longtime city council member. So he wasn't going anywhere and Dockweiler knew that. So, yes, he mostly focused his upset[8] on Bella, said she was staying and he was going because she was a twofer[9]. Then he asked me if her being a lesbian made her a three-fer[10]."

The chief's phone rang and he immediately took it.

"Go," he said.

He listened and then repeated an address on Stonington Drive, Saugus, for Bosch to memorize. Bosch recognized the address and immediately felt a charge[11] as one more confirmation on Dockweiler clicked[12].

"Interesting," Valdez said into the phone. "Shoot[13] me a map link on a text[14] for that second place. And you better start the callouts on[15] SRT[16]. Depending on what we get up here, I'll make the call on that[17]. Send me another text when you've got everybody ready to roll[18]."

1. s'appesantir
2. le fait de s'être fait virer
3. réduire les effectifs,
4. créneau
5. l'ai proposé à Dockweiler
6. transférer le poste
7. éjectés
8. frustration
9. avait deux points en sa faveur
10. lui donnait un 3e point
11. comme une décharge
12. lui apparut
13. Envoyez
14. par SMS
15. à prévenir
16. l'équipe d'intervention [Special Response Team]
17. je déciderai
18. agir

Bosch knew that the Special Response Team was the SFPD's version of SWAT[1]. The officers on the team came from all over the Department and all had critical incident and high-level weapons training[2].

Valdez disconnected.

"Did you plot[3] that address on GPS?" he asked.

"No," Bosch said. "I already know how to get there. It's up in Haskell Canyon, and Bella and I were up in that neighborhood Saturday tracing the Screen Cutter's knife."

"You're kidding me.[4]"

"Nope[5]. Dockweiler's gotta be the guy. The original owner of the knife reported it stolen out of his car in his driveway. He told us a Sheriff's deputy was living across the street from him at the time. Dockweiler probably knew that deputy, had been in that part of the neighborhood. Maybe he saw the original owner with the knife. I don't know how exactly but I do know it's too close to be a coincidence. There are no coincidences. Dockweiler stole the knife."

Valdez nodded. He was becoming a believer[6].

"It's coming together[7], Harry," he said.

"Let's just hope it's not too late for Bella," Bosch said.

1. équivalent local du GIGN [Special Weapons And Tactics]

2. avaient été formés dans les gestions de crise et armes de haute technologie

3. entré

4. Vous plaisantez ?

5. Oh non

6. se convertissait à la théorie

7. Ça commence à prendre forme

30

Bosch directed Valdez into Saugus and into a neighborhood on the other side of the Haskell Canyon Wash[1] from where the Screen Cutter's knife had been stolen from its original owner.

Along the way the police chief filled Bosch in[2] on the second part of the phone call he had received from the com center. He explained that the city had a policy[3] that required all employees to seek approval[4] if they worked[5] second jobs. This allowed the city to guard against[6] employees getting involved in conflicts of interest or second jobs that might be embarrassing. The policy was enacted[7] a decade earlier when the *Los Angeles Times* reported that an assistant city manager was also producing and performing[8] in porno videos under the name Torrid Tori.

"So two years ago Dockweiler applied for and got clearance[9] to work a part-time night security job at the Harris Movie Ranch over in Canyon Country," Valdez said. "Gives us a secondary location. You ever been up there?"

"Never have," Bosch said.

"Pretty cool place[10]. I went up there a couple times with my brother-in-law who's a screenwriter[11]. It's huge, like a couple hundred acres[12] where they film all kinds of things. Westerns, detective shit, even sci-fi[13]. There's all kinds of structures in the woods that they use for shoot-outs[14] and that kind of stuff. If Dockweiler has access,

1. rivière
2. renseigna Bosch
3. politique
4. obtenir l'approbation des autorités
5. exerçaient
6. d'empêcher les
7. avait été promulguée
8. jouait
9. a demandé et obtenu le droit
10. Très chouette, comme endroit
11. scénariste
12. [env. 80 ha]
13. de la science-fiction
14. des tournages

then I hate[1] to say it but we could be searching up there for Bella till dawn[2]. So I put SRT on standby. We'll know if we need them after we get to Dockweiler's house and see what's there."

Bosch nodded. It was a good plan.

"How do you want to do his house?" he asked. "Go straight at it or skee it first?"

"Or do *what* first?" Valdez asked.

"Skee it. You don't remember that from LAPD? Short for[3] *schematic*. You know, check the place out on the sly[4], then draw up a plan. As opposed to just knocking on the door."

"Okay, then, I think we should skee it. You?"

"Agreed."

Valdez called Trevino and filled him in on[5] everything, including the movie ranch angle that might come into play later. He gave them the confirmed address of Dockweiler's house and they worked out[6] a plan in which the cars would enter the block from opposite ends[7], park[8], and then the four men would proceed on foot, checking out the house and meeting in the backyard if it was accessible.

"Remember," Valdez said. "This guy was a cop. We need to count on him having[9] weapons."

By the time the call was finished they were in the neighborhood and it was time to split off. Valdez killed the lights[10]. He entered the block from the north side and parked three houses short of[11] the Dockweiler address. Before getting out of the car both Bosch and Valdez drew their weapons and pulled back the slides[12] to make sure there was a round[13] in the chamber. They then reholstered[14].

Bosch assumed that he had more tactical experience than the police chief so he took the

1. ça m'embête
2. jusqu'à l'aube
3. L'abréviation de
4. en douce
5. le mit au courant de
6. élaborèrent
7. par les deux extrémités de la rue
8. se gareraient
9. On doit s'attendre à ce qu'il ait
10. éteignit ses phares
11. avant
12. tirèrent la glissière
13. cartouche
14. rengainèrent

lead[1] without talking about it first. Valdez fell in behind[2] as they moved up the street. It was not an urban environment. There were no cars parked on the street and very few in driveways. It afforded little cover and[3] Bosch easily zeroed in on[4] Sisto and Trevino working their way down the opposite end of the block.

Bosch cut in toward the front of the house that was next door to Dockweiler's. He held by the[5] corner of the garage. Valdez came up next to him and they studied Dockweiler's home. It was a ranch-style house of modest size. There were no fences[6] preventing access to the rear yard[7]. That most likely meant no dogs. The light over the front door was on[8] but there appeared to be no lights on inside the house.

Bosch nodded to Valdez and they moved across the side yard and then toward the rear of Dockweiler's house. Bosch tried to get a view inside through every window they passed but curtains were pulled or it was too dark in the house to see inside.

When Bosch and Valdez got to the backyard Trevino and Sisto were already there, standing by an outdoor barbecue. There was also a light on over the back door but the wattage was low and it didn't reach very far.

The four men convened[9] by the barbecue. Bosch looked around. The backyard sloped down into the wash[10], where it was pitch-black[11]. He checked the back of the house once more and noticed a build-out[12] from the right side, a small room with mostly glass walls. It looked like a mismatched addition[13] to the house and he wondered if Dockweiler, a code enforcement officer, had added on the room without permit.

1. direction des opérations
2. se rangea derrière lui
3. Bénéficiant d'une vue dégagée,
4. repéra
5. resta près du
6. clôture
7. l'arrière de la maison
8. allumée,
9. se rassemblèrent
10. descendait jusqu'à la rivière
11. faisait noir comme dans un four
12. construction
13. extension disparate

"Looks like nobody's home," Sisto said.

"We need to be sure," Bosch said. "How about you two stay on the back door and the chief and I go knock on the door up front?"

"Sounds like a plan[1]," Valdez said before either of the other two could object to their backup duties.

Bosch headed back down the side of the house and Valdez followed, after instructing the backyard team to stay alert. They were almost to the front corner when headlights swept across the lawn as[2] a vehicle turned into the driveway.

Bosch ducked in[3] against the house and Valdez posted up[4] behind him. There was a rumbling sound and Bosch knew it was the sound of the garage opening. But it wasn't followed by the sound of the vehicle pulling in. Instead, Bosch heard the engine die[5], followed by the vehicle's door opening and closing. A few seconds later, there was another heavy metal banging sound that Bosch could not identify.

Bosch looked back at Valdez and nodded. He then edged up to the[6] corner and looked into the front yard. The vehicle was a white pickup truck with a camper shell[7]. Bosch could see a man standing at the tailgate[8] he had just dropped. He was leaning into the back of the truck but Bosch could not see what he was doing. He saw no one else in or around the truck. He turned back to Valdez and whispered.

"Switch places with me and tell me if that's him," he said.

They traded positions[9] and Valdez looked around the edge of the house. He had to wait to see him until the man ducked out of[10] the rear of the truck. He then held out a thumbs-up[11]. It was Dockweiler.

1. Bonne idée
2. des phares balayèrent la pelouse :
3. se colla
4. se posta
5. s'éteindre
6. se faufila jusqu'au
7. toit de camping-car
8. devant le panneau arrière
9. échangèrent leurs places
10. émerge de
11. leva son pouce en signe d'affirmation

"Can you see what he's doing?" Bosch asked. "Is Bella in the truck?"

Valdez shook his head. Bosch didn't know if that was no to both questions or just the first.

Suddenly there was a loud chirping sound[1] coming from the chief and he quickly grabbed the phone off his belt and killed the sound.

Of course, it was too late.

"Hold it right there[2]!"

The voice boomed from the front yard. It was Dockweiler.

"Don't fucking move!"

Bosch was behind Valdez and could not see Dockweiler. He stayed tight[3] against the side of the house, knowing that if Dockweiler thought there was only one prowler[4] then Bosch might be able to do something here.

"I've got a gun and I'm a qualified marksman[5]," Dockweiler yelled. "Step out[6] and let me see your hands."

Now the beam of a flashlight hit the corner of the house and Valdez was lit up like a target[7]. Valdez saw what Bosch couldn't see but knew was most likely the gun Dockweiler was threatening to use. Valdez raised his hands and stepped out into the light. It was a brave move and Bosch knew it was to draw Dockweiler's attention away from the corner.

"Hey Dock, take it easy[8]," Valdez said. "It's Chief Valdez. You can put the gun down."

Dockweiler's voice carried genuine surprise[9].

"Chief? What are you doing here?"

Valdez kept walking straight out from the corner toward the street. Bosch quietly slipped his weapon out of its holster and held it at the ready with two hands[10]. If he so much as heard[11]

1. forte sonnerie
2. Restez où vous êtes
3. collé
4. rôdeur
5. bon tireur
6. Sortez de là
7. une cible
8. ne t'énerve pas
9. trahit une surprise non feinte
10. se tint prêt, la tenant à deux mains
11. entendait seulement

Dockweiler cock[1] his weapon he would step out and take the man down[2].

"I was looking for Bella," Valdez said.

"Bella?" Dockweiler said. "You mean Lourdes? Why would she be up here? I think she lives in the city."

"Come on, Dock. Put the weapon down. You know me. There is no threat here. I'm standing out in the open. Put it down."

Bosch wondered if Sisto and Trevino had heard any of the confrontation and what action they might be taking. He looked down the side of the house in the direction of the backyard and saw no one. If they were coming, they were doing so on the other side of the house. It was a good move, giving them two angles on the man with the gun.

He turned back around and edged closer to the[3] corner. Valdez was now almost twenty feet out[4] from the house and halfway to the street. He still had his hands held up, and in the flashlight beam Bosch was reminded by[5] the smooth fit[6] of his black polo shirt that the chief was not wearing a ballistic vest[7] underneath. It was a detail that would factor[8] into the decisions Harry was about to make. He knew he might have to engage first[9] to prevent Dockweiler from taking a shot at Valdez.

"Why are you here, Chief?" Dockweiler demanded.

"I told you," Valdez said calmly. "Looking for Bella."

"Who sent you here? Was it that guy Bosch?"

"What makes you bring him up[10]?"

Before Dockweiler could respond, there was a chorus of shouts[11] from the front yard and Bosch recognized the voices of Trevino and Sisto.

1. armer
2. le descendrait
3. se rapprocha tout doucement du
4. à 6 m
5. se rappela en voyant
6. coupe ajustée
7. gilet pare-balles
8. entrerait en compte
9. tirer en premier
10. Pourquoi tu me parles de lui
11. clameur

"Put the gun down!"

"Dockweiler, put the gun down!"

Bosch moved forward and out from the side of the house. Dockweiler had swung[1] the flashlight and the aim of his gun to the other side, where Trevino and Sisto were side by side in combat firing stances[2].

Bosch realized he had the drop[3] on Dockweiler, who was so preoccupied by the other three men in the yard that he was not expecting a fourth. Bosch covered the ground[4] to the back of the pickup truck in less than three seconds.

Valdez saw Bosch and knew he needed to move the aim of Dockweiler's weapon off the[5] other two men before the impact from Bosch.

"Kurt, right here!" he yelled.

Dockweiler started to swing the light back toward the police chief, the muzzle[6] of his handgun moving with it. Bosch hit him with his body, smashing his chest into Dockweiler's left arm and upper torso. Dockweiler made an *oof* sound as the air blasted out of his lungs[7] and he fell heavily to the ground. Bosch bounced off the bigger man[8] and went the opposite way to the ground.

No shot was fired. Sisto moved in and jumped on Dockweiler before he could recover from the impact. He grabbed his gun hand with two hands and wrested it free[9], then threw it onto the lawn a safe distance away. Valdez soon followed on the pile and Dockweiler, a larger man than any of the other four, was controlled. Bosch crawled over[10] and put his weight[11] on the back of the man's legs while Trevino moved in and pulled his arms behind his back for cuffing[12].

"What the fuck is this?" Dockweiler yelled.

"Where is she?" Valdez yelled right back. "Where is Bella?"

1. braqué

2. position de tir

3. l'avantage

4. franchit la distance

5. devait lui enlever du viseur

6. canon

7. fusait de ses poumons

8. rebondit sur le corps massif de son adversaire

9. lui arracha son arme

10. rampa jusqu'à eux

11. pesa de tout son poids

12. le menotter

"I don't know what you're talking about," Dockweiler managed to say, despite Sisto pushing his face into the grass of his front lawn. "I haven't seen or talked to that bitch in two years."

Valdez backed off the pile and stood up.

"Get him up," he ordered. "We'll get him inside. See if he's got the keys on him."

The flashlight had fallen to the grass and was pointing away from the men. Bosch reached over and grabbed it and started sweeping it over the grass, looking for the gun. When he spotted it he got up and went to claim it[1].

1. le récupérer

Dockweiler took the opportunity to attempt one last effort at standing up. Trevino drove[2] a knee into the side of his torso and the impact ended the move. Dockweiler stopped resisting.

2. lui enfonça

"Okay, okay," he said. "I give up[3]. You assholes, what is it? Four against one? Fuck you."

3. J'abandonne

Trevino and Sisto started checking his pockets for keys.

"No, fuck you, Dockweiler," Sisto said. "Tell us where Bella is. We know you grabbed her."

"You are out of your fucking minds[4]," Dockweiler responded.

4. complètement ravagés

Bosch put the light on the truck's open tailgate. He moved so that he could angle the light into the camper shell, fearful of what he might see.

But there was only an assortment of tools in the back of the truck and it was not readily[5] apparent to him what Dockweiler had been doing at the tailgate when they watched him from the corner of the house.

5. facilement

Bosch noticed a key ring[6] sitting on the tailgate and grabbed it.

6. porte-clés

"I have the keys," he reported to the others.

While Sisto and Trevino stood Dockweiler up, Valdez came over to get a look at the back of the pickup.

"This didn't exactly go down textbook[1]," Bosch said. "How do you want to handle it from here[2]? No warrant[3] and he's not going to be inviting us in."

"No PC but plenty of EC[4], if you ask me[5]," Valdez said. "We need to get into the house. Let's open it."

Bosch agreed but it was always better when the police chief himself made the call[6]. Probable cause[7] and a judge's signature were needed for a search warrant[8], but exigent circumstances[9] trumped all[10]. There was no definitive[11] legal definition that perfectly outlined the bounds of[12] which emergencies allowed for the relaxing of[13] constitutional protections. But Bosch felt that a missing police officer and a gun-wielding former colleague[14] would qualify in any court in the land[15].

He checked the open garage as he walked to the front door. It was stacked full[16] with boxes and pallets[17]. There was no room to park the truck in there, so he wondered why Dockweiler had opened the door.

When he got to the front door he put the light on[18] the key ring. There were several keys, including one Bosch recognized as the universal key that started[19] all police and city vehicles, as well as a small bronze key that would open a smaller lock. He reached into his pocket and brought out his own keys. He compared the small bronze key to the filing cabinet in his cubicle at the detective bureau to the one on Dockweiler's ring. The teeth lined up[20] exactly.

1. On n'a pas joué très réglo, là
2. maintenant
3. Aucun mandat
4. Pas de « motif raisonnable», mais des « circonstances sacrément impérieuses »
5. voulez mon avis
6. prenait la décision
7. Un motif dit raisonnable
8. nécessaires pour un mandat de perquisition
9. « circonstances impérieuses »
10. l'emportaient
11. absolue
12. cernant parfaitement
13. d'assouplir
14. ancien collègue muni d'une arme
15. seraient des arguments recevables dans n'importe quel tribunal du pays
16. rempli
17. de palettes
18. éclaira
19. démarrait
20. correspondaient

Bosch had no doubt now. Dockweiler had kept a key to his desk in the detective bureau after transferring[1] to Public Works and was the one who had clandestinely been checking the Screen Cutter file.

Bosch opened the front door with the second key he tried and then held the door as Dockweiler was walked in[2] by Sisto and Trevino.

Valdez was the last to enter. Bosch was holding up Dockweiler's key ring by the file key.

"What's that?" Valdez asked.

"The key to my file drawer on his ring," Bosch said. "I figured out last week that somebody was reviewing[3] my files— especially on the Screen Cutter. I, uh, thought it was someone in the bureau. But it was him."

Valdez nodded. It was another detail falling into place[4].

"Where do we put him?" Sisto asked.

"In the kitchen, if there's a table and chairs," Trevino said. "Lock him to a chair."

Bosch followed the chief down the entrance hall and to the left into the kitchen and watched as Sisto and Trevino used two pairs of cuffs to secure[5] Dockweiler to a chair in front of a cluttered[6] table in a small dining nook[7] that was the glass add-on[8] Bosch had noticed from the backyard. It had floor-to-ceiling windows on three sides with venetian blinds[9] to help control the heat[10] the sun generated on the glass. Bosch wondered if Dockweiler had considered that when he added the atrium room to his house.

"This is bullshit[11]," the former detective said as soon as he was secured to the chair. "You got no warrant, you got no case, you come busting in[12] here. This won't stand[13]. This will go down in

1. avoir été muté
2. conduit
3. fouillait dans
4. qui complétait le tableau
5. attacher
6. encombrée
7. coin repas
8. l'extension vitrée que
9. stores
10. pour atténuer la chaleur que
11. n'importe quoi
12. débarquez
13. Ça tiendra pas

flames and then I'll own all of you assholes. And the city of San Fernando."

Dockweiler's face was dirty from the struggle on the front lawn. But in the harsh fluorescent light from the kitchen ceiling fixture[1] Bosch could see slight discoloration in the corners of his eyes and an unnatural thickness in the upper nose. Residual bruising and swelling[2] from a significant impact. He could also see that Dockweiler had tried to hide the purplish-yellow bruising with makeup[3].

The kitchen table had been set up as a bill-paying station[4]. There were credit-card invoices[5] and two checkbooks stacked sloppily[6] on the left. On the right were pay stubs[7], financial records, and unopened mail in piles. At center was a coffee mug filled with pens and pencils and an ashtray overflowing with cigarette butts[8]. The house had the distinct smell of a smoker's home. Bosch picked it up with[9] every breath.

Bosch went to the window over the kitchen sink[10] and unlocked and opened it to let some fresh air in. He then went to the table. He moved the mug to the left side of the table because he wanted nothing between himself and Dockweiler when they talked. He started to pull out the chair directly across the table from him. He knew that there were two things at stake[11] in the interrogation that was about to begin: Bella Lourdes and the Screen Cutter case.

Bosch was about to sit down, when Trevino stopped him.

"Hold on, hold on."

He pointed toward the hallway.

"Chief, let's step out and talk for a minute," Trevino said. "Bosch, you too. Sisto, you stay with him."

1. plafonnier
2. des vestiges de bleus et d'œdèmes
3. du maquillage
4. en bureau de comptabilité
5. reçus
6. maladroitement empilés
7. bulletins de paie
8. débordant de mégots
9. le sentait à
10. au-dessus de l'évier
11. en jeu

"Yeah, you guys go out and talk about it," Dockweiler mocked[1]. "Try to figure out how you fucked this whole thing up and how you're going to unfuck it."

Bosch turned at the archway[2] that led from the kitchen into the hallway. He looked at Dockweiler, then at Sisto. He nodded. Whatever their differences, Sisto and Trevino had played it right[3] when they had come up the side of the house. The chief might be a dead man if they hadn't.

Sisto nodded back.

Trevino led the way down the hallway to the front door. Bosch and Valdez followed. They spoke in low voices and Trevino got right to the point.

"I'm going to handle the interview," Trevino said.

Bosch looked from Trevino to Valdez and waited a moment for the chief to speak against that idea. But Valdez said nothing. Bosch looked back at Trevino.

"Wait a minute," he said. "It's my case. I know it better than anybody. I should do the interview."

"The priority here is Bella," Trevino said. "Not the case. And I know her better than you."

Bosch shook his head like he didn't get it[4].

"That makes no sense[5]," he said. "It doesn't matter how well you know her. It's how well you know the case. He's the Screen Cutter. He grabbed Bella because she got too close on the case or figured it out when she was with him. Let me talk to him."

"We don't know he's the Screen Cutter for sure yet," Trevino said. "We need to first—"

"Did you see his eyes?" Bosch said, interrupting. "Swollen and purple from where Beatriz Sahagun hit him with the stick. He tried to cover it

1. ricana
2. voûte
3. bien joué
4. s'il ne comprenait pas
5. C'est absurde

with makeup. There's no doubt. He's the Screen Cutter. You may not know it but I do."

Bosch again turned to Valdez on appeal[1].

"Chief, I've got to do this," he said.

"Harry," the chief said. "The captain and I talked about this before any of this with Bella even came up. It's about what could happen down the line[2], you know, in court with your history[3]."

"My history?" Bosch asked. "Really? You mean the hundred-plus murders I've cleared[4]? That history?"

"You know what he means," Trevino said. "Your controversies. They make you a target in court. They undercut you[5]."

"We also have the reserve issue," Valdez added. "You're not full-time and that's something that a lawyer will pick apart[6] in court. It won't look good in front of a jury."

"I probably put in[7] as many hours a week as Sisto does," Bosch said.

"Doesn't matter," Trevino said. "You're a reserve. It is what it is. I'm going to do this interview and I want you to go through the house and look for any sign of Bella, any evidence at all that he had her here. And when you're finished with that, go search[8] the truck."

For a third time Bosch looked at Valdez, and it was clear he was siding with[9] Trevino on this.

"Just do it, Harry," he said. "Do it for Bella, okay?"

"Yeah, sure thing[10]," Bosch said. "For Bella. Call me when you need me."

Trevino turned and started back toward the kitchen.

Valdez lingered[11] a bit and just nodded to Bosch before following his captain. Bosch was supremely frustrated at being pulled away[12] from his own

1. pour tenter d'obtenir son soutien
2. en aval
3. antécédents
4. élucidés
5. t'écrasent
6. démontera
7. fais
8. fouiller
9. du côté de
10. bien sûr
11. s'attarda
12. de se voir évincer

case but not interested in putting his professional pride and emotions above the ultimate goal, especially with Bella Lourdes unaccounted for[1]. He had no doubt he should be handling the interview and had the better skills for[2] drawing information from Dockweiler. But he also believed that he would eventually get the chance to use them[3].

1. qui manquait toujours à l'appel
2. était le mieux à même de
3. finirait par en avoir l'occasion

"Captain?" he said.

Trevino turned around to look back at him.

"Don't forget to read him his rights," Bosch said.

"Of course," Trevino said.

He then went through the archway into the kitchen.

31

Bosch moved into the living room and then down a hallway leading to bedrooms. He knew he had to be very careful and put emotions aside here. He believed that the exigent[1] circumstances of having an officer missing allowed him to search Dockweiler's house without legal[2] risk. But searching for evidence in the Screen Cutter case was different. He would need a warrant for that. The contradiction put him in a legal predicament[3]. He had to search the house for Lourdes and any indication or evidence of her location, but he couldn't dig deeper for evidence[4] that Dockweiler committed the rapes.

He had to be realistic too. His newfound knowledge of[5] Dockweiler and the fact that he had kept a key and had been secretly entering the police station to read the investigative file was convincing evidence[6] that he was Screen Cutter. With that conclusion in mind it seemed unlikely to Bosch that they were going to find Bella alive, and possibly unlikely they would find her at all. He needed to put the Screen Cutter case first here[7] and preserve it against any future legal challenge.

He put on a pair of latex gloves and began the search by starting at the end of the bedroom hallway and working his way back[8] toward the kitchen. There were three bedrooms but only one was used as such[9]. He searched Dockweiler's room first and found it to be a mess[10], with clothes

1. impérieuses

2. judiciaire

3. situation judiciaire difficile

4. continuer à chercher la preuve

5. récentes découvertes sur

6. prouvait

7. devait donner la priorité à l'affaire du Coupeur de portes

8. en remontant

9. en tant que telle

10. la trouva dans un désordre indescriptible

1. éparpillés
2. sans doute à l'endroit même où il les laissait en se déshabillant
3. repoussante couleur grisâtre
4. sentait l'odeur aigre de la sueur
5. salle de bains contiguë
6. tout aussi mal entretenue
7. dégoûtantes
8. ramassa un cintre
9. farfouilla
10. avoir été salis différemment de ceux
11. couverts d'une
12. de la poussière de béton
13. cabine de douche
14. grisâtres
15. bonde
16. dressing
17. bien rangé
18. des espaces de rangement
19. encombrée de râteliers vitrés
20. carabines et fusils de chasse exposés
21. des étiquettes
22. sous-gardes
23. sans doute dans le chargeur
24. chambre d'amis, plus grande,
25. provisions de survie

and shoes strewn[1] on the floor everywhere around the bed, most likely in the spots where they were shed[2]. The bed was unmade and the sheets had a dingy gray cast to them[3]. The walls were yellowed but not with paint. The room smelled sour with perspiration[4] and cigarette smoke. Bosch kept a rubber-gloved hand over his mouth as he moved through it.

The attached bath[5] was just as unkempt[6], with more clothing thrown in the bathtub and a horribly stained[7] toilet. Bosch picked a hanger up[8] off the floor and fished around[9] in the bathtub to make sure there wasn't anything or anyone hidden beneath the clothes. The clothes in the tub seemed dirty in a way separate from the clothes[10] left on the floor of the bedroom. They were caked with a[11] granular gray dust that Bosch believed might be concrete dust[12]. He wondered if it was debris from an inspection or a Public Works project.

The phone booth shower[13] was empty, its white tiles as dingy[14] as the bedroom sheets, and the drain[15] had trapped more of the concrete powder and granules. He next moved into a small walk-in closet[16] in the bathroom and found it to be surprisingly neat[17], primarily because most of the items of clothing it would normally hold were on the bedroom floor and in the bathtub.

The two other bedrooms were used for storage[18]. The small room was lined with glass-door gun cabinets[19] with several rifles and shotguns on display[20]. Most had tags[21] attached to the trigger guards[22] that identified the ammunition they were presumably loaded with[23]. The larger guest bedroom[24] was used for storage of life-sustaining supplies[25]. There were stacked pallets of bottled water and energy drinks and boxes of canned and powdered goods[1] that would presumably have distant[2] expiration dates.

The closets[3] of both rooms were similarly stacked, and there was no sign of Bella in that side of the house. As Bosch worked his way through the bedroom wing[4] he could hear muffled voices from the kitchen. He could not make out[5] words but he could detect tones and individual voices. It was Trevino doing almost all of the talking. He wasn't getting anywhere with[6] Dockweiler.

In the hallway near the bedrooms Bosch noticed an attic access door[7] in the ceiling. There were fingerprint smears[8] on the frame around it but these offered no hint as to[9] how long it had been since Dockweiler was up there.

Bosch looked around and saw a four-foot-long wooden dowel[10] with a hook on the end of it leaning against the wall in the corner. Grabbing it and threading[11] the hook through the metal eyelet[12] on the attic door, he pulled it open and found it very similar to the attic entrance at Olivia Macdonald's house. He folded the hinged ladder down[13] and started the climb.

Bosch found the pull string[14] for an overhead light and soon was scanning the attic. The space was small and more boxes of survivalist supplies were stacked to the roof rafters[15]. He climbed all the way up so he could see around boxes and into every angle of the attic to make sure Bella Lourdes was not there. He then climbed back down but left the attic open and the ladder unfolded so it could be accessed for a more thorough[16] search with a warrant.

When Bosch moved into the living room and dining area he could clearly hear what was being said in the kitchen. Dockweiler was not co-

1. d'aliments déshydratés
2. lointaines
3. placards
4. parcourait l'aile des chambres,
5. distinguait pas
6. n'obtenait rien de
7. trappe d'accès à un grenier
8. traces de doigts
9. ne permettaient pas de savoir
10. perche en bois de 1,20 m
11. passant
12. œillet
13. déplia l'échelle escamotable
14. cordon
15. sous les combles
16. approfondie

operating and Trevino had moved to a threatening form of interrogation that Bosch knew was rarely successful.

"You're cooked[1], my friend," Trevino said. "It's a DNA case. As soon as we match yours to the evidence collected from the[2] victims, it's over. You're over. You'll get consecutive sentences[3] and never breathe free air again. The only way you can help yourself is to give us back Bella. Tell us where she is and we'll go to bat for you[4]. With the DA[5], with the judge, you name it[6]."

Trevino's plea was met with silence[7]. Everything the captain said was true but delivering it as threat[8] would rarely get a suspect with the Screen Cutter's profile to cooperate and talk. Bosch knew that a proper interview would appeal to[9] his narcissism, his genius. Harry would've attempted to make Dockweiler think he was controlling the interview and bleed[10] information out of him bit by bit.

Bosch crossed through the living room and into the entrance hallway. He saw Valdez leaning against the wall next to the archway to the kitchen, watching the interview with Dockweiler go nowhere[11]. He looked back at Bosch and raised his chin, asking if Harry had found anything. Bosch just shook his head.

Just before the kitchen entrance, there was a door that led into the garage. Bosch entered, flicked on the overhead lights[12], and closed the door behind him. The space was also used for storage of survival supplies. More pallets of canned goods, water, and powdered mixes. Somehow Dockweiler had gotten hold of[13] a supply of U.S. Army-produced MREs—Meals Ready to Eat. There were also nonedible supplies[14] here. Boxes of batteries, lanterns, first-aid kits[15], tool kits,

1. foutu
2. Dès qu'on comparera le tien à celui des
3. des peines cumulatives
4. on interviendra en ta faveur
5. procureur [District Attorney]
6. ou qui tu voudras
7. La requête de Trevino eut le silence pour toute réponse
8. l'exprimer sous la forme d'une menace
9. flatterait
10. aurait soutiré
11. n'arriver à rien
12. alluma les plafonniers
13. Dockwiler avait réussi à se procurer
14. des non-comestibles
15. trousses de premiers secours

CO2 scrubbers[1], water filters, and enzyme additives for water filtration and use in chemical toilets. There were boxes of light sticks[2] and medical supplies such as Betadine and potassium iodide. Bosch remembered those from his military training, when the threat of nuclear holocaust from the Soviet Union seemed real. Both chemicals[3] acted as thyroid protection against cancer-causing radioactive iodine. It looked like Dockweiler was prepped for[4] all possibilities, from terrorist attack to nuclear detonation.

Bosch returned to the door and stuck his head back into the entrance hallway. He drew Valdez's attention and signaled him[5] into the garage.

As the police chief entered, his eyes held on the stacks of supplies in the center of the garage.

"What is all of this?" he asked.

"Dockweiler's a survivalist[6]," Bosch said. "Looks like he must put all his money into this stuff. The attic and two of the bedrooms are full of D-day supplies and weapons. He's got an arsenal in one bedroom. And it looks like he could go three or four months with this stuff as long as he doesn't mind eating Army beef stew[7] out of a can[8]."

"Well, I hope he packed a can opener."

"It might explain some of his motivation. When the world is coming to an end, people act out[9], take what they want. Is Trevino getting anywhere?"

"No, nowhere. Dockweiler's just playing games, denying everything, then hinting[10] he might know something."

Bosch nodded. He assumed that he would get his shot[11] as soon as he was finished with the search.

1. épurateurs d'air
2. bâtons lumineux
3. produits chimiques
4. s'était préparé à
5. lui fit signe de venir
6. [écologiste extrême vivant en autarcie pour pouvoir survivre à une éventuelle catastrophe planétaire]
7. ragoût
8. en boîte
9. vivent leurs fantasmes
10. insinuant
11. aurait son tour

"I'm going to take a quick look at the truck and then call a judge. I want a legit warrant[1] to really do a down-and-dirty search[2] of this place."

Valdez was smart enough to read Bosch's thinking.

"So you think Bella's gone[3], huh?"

Bosch hesitated but then nodded somberly.

"I mean, why would he keep her alive?" he said. "Our profiler said this guy was going to graduate to murder[4]. Bella could ID him[5]. Why let her live?"

Valdez dropped his chin to his chest.

"Sorry, Chief," Bosch said. "Just being realistic about things."

"I know," Valdez said. "But we're not going to stop until we find her. One way or the other."

"I wouldn't want to[6]."

Valdez clapped him on the arm and went back through the door into the house.

Bosch moved down a narrow passageway through the stacks to the driveway and Dockweiler's truck. The front cab[7] was unlocked and he opened it on the passenger side since it was most likely that side would show an indication if Bella Lourdes had been in the truck. On the passenger seat sat[8] a large closed bag from a McDonald's restaurant. Bosch stripped off[9] a glove and placed the back of his fingers against the bag. It was slightly warm to the touch and Bosch assumed that Dockweiler's arrival at the house had come after he went out to pick up dinner.

Bosch put the glove back on and opened the bag. He still had the flashlight he'd collected off[10] the front lawn. He pulled it from his back pocket and pointed the beam down into the bag. He counted two cardboard sandwich cartons[11] and two large sleeves[12] of French fries.

1. mandat en bonne et due forme
2. fouille costaud
3. morte
4. passer au niveau meurtrier
5. l'identifier
6. Absolument
7. cabine avant
8. il y avait
9. enleva
10. qu'il avait ramassée sur
11. boîtes
12. cornets

Bosch knew that the contents[1] of the bag could easily constitute dinner for one big man like Dockweiler, but he also knew it was more likely dinner for two. For the first time since they had entered Dockweiler's house, he was hit with[2] the hope that Bella was alive. He pondered[3] whether[4] Dockweiler was stopping by his house before taking the food to his captive someplace else, or whether she was here somewhere and he just hadn't found her. He thought of the drainage wash[5] down the slope behind Dockweiler's house. Maybe she was down there.

He left the food bag in place and used the flashlight beam to comb[6] the dark carpet and sides of the passenger seat. He saw nothing that held his attention or indicated Bella had been in the truck.

He kept the flashlight on and moved to the back of the pickup. He pointed the beam into the far corners of the truck's bed and camper shell[7]. Again he saw nothing that connected to Lourdes or to the Screen Cutter. Still[8], Dockweiler had been doing something at the tailgate when the chief's phone sounded the alarm. He had also opened the garage with a purpose other than parking his truck. Bosch still couldn't figure out what he had been up to[9].

Stored in the back of the pickup was an upside-down wheelbarrow[10], a two-wheeled hand truck[11], and several long tools—three shovels[12], a hoe[13], a push broom[14], and a pick[15]—as well as several drop cloths[16] for keeping work spaces clean. The shovels were not duplicates[17]. One had a pointed spade[18] for digging[19] and the other two had straight edges of different widths, and Bosch knew these would be used for scooping up[20] debris. Each of them was dirty—the pointed

1. contenu
2. gagné par
3. se demanda
4. si
5. rivière
6. ratisser
7. la partie habitable
8. Et pourtant
9. ce qu'il avait eu l'intention de faire
10. brouette
11. diable [petit chariot manuel]
12. pelles
13. binette
14. balai-brosse
15. pioche
16. bâches en toile
17. identiques
18. était pointue
19. creuser
20. ramasser

spade with a dark red soil[1] and the straight-edge blades[2] with the same gray concrete dust as in the bathtub.

He put the light on the wheelbarrow's rubber wheel and saw larger chunks[3] of concrete caught in the tread[4]. Dockweiler had no doubt been involved in a recent project involving concrete but Bosch held off concerns[5] that he had buried Bella Lourdes. The clothes in the bathtub with the same debris as the tools accounted for[6] several changes of clothes. The indications were that this was a longtime project, not something taken on[7] in the last eight hours, when Bella had gone missing.

The orange soil on the digging spade gave him pause[8], however. That could have been used and dirtied anytime.

Bosch pulled the hand truck out to the tailgate so he could look at it more closely. He assumed that Dockweiler used it to move the stacks of boxes he kept in his home and garage. He then noticed a label taped to the axle[9] between the two rubber wheels. It said:

Property of City of San Fernando
Department of Public Works

Dockweiler had stolen or borrowed the hand truck for his own purposes[10]. Bosch assumed that if he looked closely enough[11], many of the tools in the truck and garage would be seen to have come from the workbenches[12] in the Public Works yard[13]. But he wasn't sure how the hand truck fit[14] with what Dockweiler was doing that night at the tailgate.

Bosch felt he had worked the exigent circumstances to the maximum allowed[15]. He backed away from the truck and pulled his phone. He

1. terre
2. les pelles à bords droits
3. morceaux
4. bande de roulement
5. écarta l'idée
6. indiquaient
7. entrepris
8. lui donna à réfléchir
9. axe
10. usage personnel
11. d'assez près
12. établis
13. dépôt
14. en quoi le chariot avait à voir
15. se dit qu'il avait fait le maximum autorisé en situation d'urgence

scrolled through[1] his contact list to the letter *J*, where he kept the contact information of judges that he'd had good enough experiences with to ask for and receive their cell numbers.

He first called Judge Robert O'Neill, who had presided over a four-month murder trial on which Bosch had been lead detective[2]. Bosch checked his watch after sending the call and saw it was not yet 11 p.m., which always seemed to be the witching[3] hour with judges. They got upset when you called them later, even in an emergency.

O'Neill answered promptly with no sign of sleep or intoxicants in his voice. This was something to note. Bosch had once had a case where the defense lawyer challenged[4] the validity of a search warrant because it had been signed by a judge at 3 a.m. after Bosch had woken him from sleep.

"Judge O'Neill, it's Harry Bosch. I hope I'm not waking you."

"Harry, how are you? And, no, you didn't wake me. These days I stay up late[5] and sleep even later." Bosch wasn't sure what he'd meant by the last part.

"Are you on vacation[6], sir? Could you still approve a telephonic affidavit[7]? We've got a missing—"

"Let me stop you right there, Harry. You apparently didn't hear the news. I'm off the bench[8]. I pulled the plug[9] three months ago."

Bosch was stunned[10] and embarrassed. Since his own retirement from the LAPD he had not kept track[11] of who held sway[12] in the courtrooms in the Foltz building.

"You retired?" he asked.

"I did," O'Neill said. "And last I heard, you did too. Is this some kind of a prank[13]?"

1. fit défiler
2. enquêteur principal
3. fatale
4. avait cherché à récuser
5. me couche tard
6. en vacances
7. valider par téléphone une déclaration sous serment
8. Je n'exerce plus
9. J'ai raccroché
10. consterné
11. ne s'était pas tenu au courant
12. régnait
13. farce

"Uh, no, sir. No prank. I'm doing some work for the San Fernando Police Department now. And I need to go. We have an emergency situation here and I'm sorry to have bothered you."

Bosch disconnected before O'Neill could ask anything else and waste Harry's time. He quickly went back to his contact list, deleted[1] O'Neill, and then called Judge John Houghton, who was next in line[2] on the list of judges friendly to Bosch. He was known as[3] Shootin' Houghton among local cops and lawyers because he had a concealed-carry permit[4] and once fired a shot into the ceiling of his courtroom to restore order during a brawl[5] between defendants[6] in a Mexican mafia prosecution. He was subsequently censured[7] by the county judicial committee and the California Bar[8], and was also charged[9] by the City Attorney with illegal use of a firearm, a misdemeanor[10]. Despite all of that he routinely won landslide re-election each term[11] as a law and order judge.

He, too, answered with a clear voice.

"Harry Bosch? I thought you retired."

"Retired and hired[12], Judge. I'm working for San Fernando PD now. Part-time, on their backlog of cold cases[13]. But I'm calling because we have an all-hands emergency going[14]—a missing officer—and I'm outside a suspect's house and need to conduct a search. We're hoping to find her still alive."

"A female officer[15]?"

"Yes, sir. A detective. We think the suspect in a serial rape case grabbed her[16] about seven or eight hours ago. We did a quick run-through[17] of the property under exigent circumstance. Now we would like to go back in for a deep look for the officer and anything relating to the underlying rape case[18]."

"I understand."

1. supprima
2. le suivant
3. On le surnommait
4. permis de port d'armes dissimulées
5. bagarre
6. les parties au procès
7. réprimandé
8. barreau
9. poursuivi
10. qui était un délit
11. remportait une victoire écrasante à chaque réélection
12. mais réembauché
13. arriérés d'affaires non résolues
14. cas d'urgence extrême
15. policière
16. s'est emparé d'elle
17. fouille
18. crime initial de viol

"This is all moving very quickly and I don't have time to go back to the station to print up an affidavit. Can I run down the probable cause for you[1] and follow up with the paperwork tomorrow?"

"Go ahead. Give it to me."

The first hurdle jumped[2], Bosch spent the next five minutes going through the steps and the evidence that led them to Dockweiler as the Screen Cutter suspect. He threw in[3] many other bits of information that he could not connect to either the Screen Cutter case or the abduction[4] of Bella Lourdes but that he knew would help paint the picture for the judge and lead to his approval to search. Things like the digging tools in the truck, the warm bag of food for two, the terrible condition of the home. All of it, combined with Dockweiler's pedigree[5] as a former police officer, won the day[6], and Houghton gave Bosch permission to search Dockweiler's house and vehicle.

Bosch thanked the judge profusely and promised to turn in[7] a written search warrant affidavit the next day.

"I'll hold you to that[8]," Houghton said.

1. vous exposer le motif raisonnable

2. Une fois le premier obstacle franchi

3. ajouta

4. enlèvement

5. le statut

6. remporta l'adhésion du juge

7. lui fournir

8. J'y veillerai

32

After disconnecting he went back into the house and signaled down the hallway to Valdez, who was back in the same spot under the archway entrance to the kitchen.

The police chief hurried down the hallway to where Bosch waited by the front door. Bosch heard voices from the kitchen but this time it wasn't Trevino talking. It was Dockweiler.

Valdez spoke before Bosch could tell him about the telephonic warrant he had just procured.

"Trevino broke him[1]," he whispered excitedly. "He's going to tell us where she is. Says she's still alive."

The news took Bosch by surprise.

"Trevino broke him?"

Valdez nodded.

"It was deny, deny, deny, then 'okay, you got me'."

Bosch had to see this. He started down the hallway toward the kitchen, questioning whether[2] it was his own vanity and wounded pride[3] that made him doubt Trevino's success, or something else.

He entered the kitchen and Dockweiler was still at the table, hands double-cuffed behind his back and to the chair. When he glanced up and saw it was Bosch and not Valdez, a momentary look[4] passed over his face. Bosch wasn't sure if it was disappointment or some other reaction. He

1. lui a fait cracher le morceau
2. se demandant si
3. son orgueil blessé
4. expression fugace

had never seen Dockweiler before the events of this night and had no precursors for facial reads of him[1]. But soon enough he got a translation. Dockweiler pointed at him with his chin.

"I don't want him in here," he said. "I'm not talking if he's here."

Trevino turned around and saw it was Bosch, not Valdez, who had upset the[2] suspect.

"Detective Bosch," he said. "Why don't you—"

"Why not?" Bosch said over the captain's voice. "Afraid I'll know that you're spinning a line of bullshit[3]?"

"Bosch!" Trevino barked. "Leave the room. Now. We are getting this man's full cooperation, and if he wants you out, then you're out."

Bosch didn't move. This was ridiculous.

"She's only got so much air[4]," Dockweiler said. "If you want to play games, what happens is on you[5], Bosch."

Bosch felt Valdez grab his upper arm from behind. He was about to be pulled out of the room. He looked over at Sisto, who was leaning against the counter behind Trevino. He smirked[6] and shook his head like[7] Bosch had become some sort of pitiful nuisance that had to be put up with[8].

"Harry, let's walk out," Valdez said.

Bosch looked at Dockweiler one last time and tried to get a read on him[9]. But his eyes were dead. A psychopath's eyes. Unreadable. In that moment he knew there was a play here[10]. He just didn't know what it was.

Now Bosch felt a tug on his arm from Valdez[11] and he finally turned toward the archway. He stepped out of the kitchen and started down the hallway to the front door. Valdez followed him to make sure he didn't double back[12].

"Let's go out," Valdez said.

1. ne savait comment interpréter ses mimiques

2. déplu au

3. nous racontez des bobards

4. n'a qu'une quantité d'air limitée

5. c'est vous qui serez responsable

6. eut un petit sourire narquois

7. comme si

8. qu'il fallait bien supporter

9. déchiffrer son expression

10. qu'il jouait une comédie

11. que Valdez lui tirait le bras

12. qu'il ne ferait pas demi-tour

They stepped through the front door and Valdez closed it behind them.

"Harry, we have to play it this way," Valdez said. "The guy's talking and says he'll take us to her. We have no choice."

"That's a ploy[1]," Bosch said. "He'll just be looking for a chance to make a move."

"We know that. We're not stupid. We're not taking him on a field trip[2] in the middle of the night. If he really wants to cooperate and show us where Bella is, then he can draw us a map. But he's staying in that chair, no question."

"Look, Chief … there's something not right here[3]. Things don't add up[4] with what I'm seeing in his truck and the house and everything. We need—"

"What doesn't add up?"

"I don't know yet. If I had been in there and heard what he was saying or if I was asking the questions, then I'd have a handle on it[5]. But—"

"Look, I have to go back in there and watch over this. Just sit tight[6] and when we get what we need from him, I'll relay it right to you. You can lead the charge[7] and go get Bella."

"I don't need to be the hero—that's not what this is about. I still think it's bullshit[8]. He's not going to do this. You read the Screen Cutter profile. It's all in there. Guys like this don't ever admit to anything. They have no guilt[9], so there's nothing to admit to. They're manipulators to the end[10]."

"I can't keep debating it, Harry. I have to go in. You stay out of the house."

Valdez turned and went back in through the front door. Bosch stood there for a long moment, thinking and trying to get a read on the look he had seen on Dockweiler's face.

1. ruse
2. en excursion
3. qui ne va pas
4. Ça ne colle pas
5. je pourrais me faire une idée
6. Ne bougez pas d'ici
7. pourrez prendre les devants
8. suis persuadé qu'il nous mène en bateau
9. n'éprouvent aucune culpabilité
10. jusqu'au bout

After a few moments he decided to move around to the back of the house to try to see what was going on in the kitchen. Valdez had instructed him to stay outside the house. He didn't say where outside.

Bosch quickly moved down the side and into the backyard. The kitchen was at the opposite corner and the table where Dockweiler and Trevino sat facing each other was in an eating nook located in the glass sunroom. The blinds[1] were three-quarters open and the room glowed with the interior lights. Bosch knew that the men inside would only see their own reflections[2] in the glass and not him standing outside.

He could hear what was being said in the room because of the open window over the sink. And almost all of it was coming from Dockweiler. One of his hands had now been uncuffed so that he could use a pencil to draw a map on a large piece of paper spread on the table.

"They call this section the John Ford Forty," he said. "I think he filmed part of one of his John Wayne epics[3] there and it's mostly used for westerns and horror stuff—the cabin-in-the-woods screamers[4] they make all the time and go straight to[5] streaming. There's like[6] sixteen different cabins back in there that can be used for filming."

"So where is Bella?" Trevino pressed.

"She's in this one here," Dockweiler said.

He used the pencil to draw something on the map but his upper torso blocked Bosch's view from behind him. Dockweiler then put the pencil down on the table and did some tracing on the map with his finger.

"You go in here, tell whoever's at the gate[7] that you need to get to the Bonney house. They'll take you up there and that's where you'll find her.

1. stores

2. reflets

3. films à grand spectacle

4. ces histoires de cabanes dans les bois

5. qui passent directement en

6. quelque chose comme

7. au type de l'entrée

Everything's breakaway[1] in these houses. Walls, windows, floors. You know, for filming. Your girl's in a camera trench[2] under the flooring[3]. It lifts up in one piece."

"This better not be bullshit, Dockweiler," Valdez said.

"No bullshit," Dockweiler said. "I can lead you there if you want."

Dockweiler gestured as if to say, Why not give me a chance? And when he did so, his elbow hit the pencil and it rolled off the table, bouncing off his thigh[4] to the floor.

"Oops," he said.

He leaned down and reached to the floor[5] to retrieve[6] the pencil, a maneuver made difficult because his left wrist[7] was still handcuffed behind his back to one of the rungs[8] of the chair.

Through the window behind Dockweiler, Bosch had a unique vantage point[9] on what happened next. It seemed to unfold before him in slow motion[10]. Dockweiler took a swipe at[11] the fallen pencil on the floor, but couldn't quite reach it[12] because he was bound[13] to the chair in which he sat. However, the momentum of the swing[14] carried his arm up and under the table. He gripped[15] something attached to the underside[16] of the table, then swung his arm out and above it[17].

He was now pointing a semiautomatic pistol directly across the table at Trevino. "Nobody fucking move!"

The three men facing Dockweiler froze[18].

Bosch slowly and quietly pulled his weapon from its holster and put a two-handed aim on[19] Dockweiler's back. He knew in a legal sense he was clear[20] to shoot and it would be a righteous[21]

1. en kit
2. fosse à caméras
3. plancher
4. rebondissant sur sa cuisse avant de tomber
5. tendit la main par terre
6. pour ramasser
7. poignet
8. barreaux
9. point de vue privilégié
10. au ralenti
11. essaya d'attraper
12. l'atteindre
13. attaché
14. vitesse de son geste
15. saisit
16. dessous
17. ramena le bras au-dessus
18. s'immobilisèrent
19. visa des deux mains
20. autorisé
21. justifié

kill, but he didn't have a clean shot[1], with Trevino sitting on the other side of the target.

Dockweiler used the barrel[2] of his gun to point Valdez farther[3] into the kitchen. The police chief complied[4], holding his hands up in front of his chest.

In front of Dockweiler the kitchen counters created a *U* where he corralled[5] the three cops. He told Trevino to stand up and back into the *U* with Valdez and Sisto.

"Easy now[6]," Trevino said as he backed up. "I thought we were talking and that we were going to figure this thing out."

"You were talking," Dockweiler said. "And now it's time to shut the fuck up[7]."

"Okay, okay, no problem."

Dockweiler then ordered them one at a time to unholster[8] their weapons, put them on the floor, and kick them across the floor toward him. Dockweiler rose from the chair and brought his left arm around, the chair dangling by the[9] handcuffs. He brought his hand down on the table and ordered Sisto to come over and remove the cuffs from his wrist. Sisto complied and then moved back into the confines of the kitchen counters.

With Dockweiler now standing, Bosch had a bigger target but he still didn't have a safe shot. He didn't know enough about the science of ballistics to guess how much a shot through glass would deviate from aim. He just knew that if he fired multiple shots, those that followed the first should be clean[10].

Additionally, there was the risk that Dockweiler might be able to squeeze off[11] a shot if the first bullet through the glass did not hit its mark[12].

1. sa ligne de mire n'était pas assez sûre
2. canon
3. pour faire signe à Valdez de reculer
4. obtempéra
5. rassembla
6. Du calme
7. fermer vot' gueule
8. dégainer
9. se balançant au bout des
10. devraient faire mouche
11. esquiver
12. cible

Bosch looked down to be sure of his footing[1] on the concrete patio and took a step closer to the glass. Dockweiler was less than eight feet away[2] with a plate of glass[3] of unknown thickness between them. Bosch was resigned to hold off[4] until he had to fire.

"Where's Bosch?" Dockweiler asked.

"He's out front going through[5] your truck," Valdez said.

"I want him in here."

"I can get him."

Valdez made a move toward the archway, which immediately drew Dockweiler's aim[6].

"Don't be stupid," Dockweiler said. "Call him and tell him to get in here. Don't tell him why, just tell him to get in here."

Valdez slowly reached to his belt and pulled off his phone. Bosch realized that his own phone was about to ring and it would give away his position. He was about to reach into his pocket to silence it, when he realized that he wanted exactly that to happen.

Bosch shifted one step to his right[7] so that he was on an angle that put Dockweiler directly between his aim and Valdez. Trevino and Sisto were in the clear[8] and Bosch was counting on LAPD training still being ingrained[9] in Valdez and his knowing[10] when the shot would come.

He maintained the two-handed grip and waited for the call. His phone buzzed at first, giving him a split-second warning[11]. Then came the chirping sound—a piercing ringtone[12] chosen long ago by his daughter. Bosch had his aim on center mass[13]—Dockweiler's back—but his attention was focused[14] on the back of his head.

1. d'avoir les pieds bien calés
2. à moins de 2,50 m
3. vitre
4. attendre
5. devant la maison, à fouiller
6. et Dockweiler se tourna pour le garder dans le viseur
7. se décala d'un pas à droite,
8. hors d'atteinte
9. bien ancrée
10. qu'il saurait deviner
11. une fraction de seconde pour anticiper
12. sonnerie
13. visait le centre de sa cible
14. rivée

He saw Dockweiler react. He had heard the phone. He raised his head a few centimeters and then turned it slightly left as he attempted to locate the origin of[1] the sound. Bosch waited another split second for Valdez to react and then opened fire.

Bosch put six bullets through the window in less than three seconds. The sound reverberated off the glass and the roof overhang[2], creating a tremendous blowback[3] of sound. Glass crashed and the blinds kicked up and splintered[4] as bullets tore through them. Bosch was careful to keep his aim on a horizontal plane. He wanted no shots to angle down toward the floor, where he hoped Valdez was.

Dockweiler dropped[5] forward onto the table and then rolled left and fell off onto the floor. Bosch raised his aim and watched while Trevino and Sisto, who were still standing, moved toward the man.

"Hold fire!" Trevino yelled. "He's down, he's down!"

The glass in the window frame was gone and the blinds hung in tatters[6]. The smell of burnt gunpowder seared[7] Bosch's nose. He grabbed the blinds and tore them down[8] so he could enter through the door-size window.

He first checked Valdez, who was sitting on the floor, his legs spread in front of him, his back to the lower cabinets. His phone was still in his hand but his call to Bosch had now gone to message. He was staring at Dockweiler on the floor five feet[9] from him. His eyes came up to Bosch's.

"Everybody okay?" Bosch asked.

Valdez nodded and Bosch noticed the bullet hole in the drawer two feet[10] to the left of his head.

1. savoir d'où venait
2. avant-toit
3. retour
4. remontèrent et se fendirent en éclats
5. tomba
6. étaient tout déchiquetés
7. piqua
8. les arracha
9. à 1,50 m
10. 50 cm

Bosch next looked down on Dockweiler. The big man was chest-down[1] on the floor, his face turned to the left. He was not moving but his eyes were open and he was breathing, a labored whistling sound[2] to each of his intakes[3]. Bosch saw three bullet impacts. One was center left about halfway down his back, one was on his left buttock[4], and one was on his left elbow.

Bosch got down on the floor next to the suspect and looked across his torso at Trevino.

"Good shooting," Trevino said.

Bosch nodded. He then leaned further down and looked up under the table. He saw the holster attached to the underside of the tabletop. Trevino followed his eye line[5] and did the same.

"Son of a bitch," he said.

"A good survivalist is ready for anything," Bosch said. "I think we're going to find weapons hidden all over the place[6] in here."

Bosch pulled a set of latex gloves out of his pocket. As he was putting them on, he leaned down close to Dockweiler's face.

"Dockweiler, can you hear me?" he asked. "Can you talk?"

Dockweiler swallowed hard before trying to respond.

"Get me … hosp … hospital." Bosch nodded.

"Yeah, we're going to get to that," he said. "But first, we need to know where Bella is. You tell us that and we call in the RA[7]."

"Harry," Valdez said.

Bosch leaned back on his haunches[8].

"You guys might want to step out," he said. "I'll handle this."

"Harry," Valdez said again. "We can't do it this way."

"You want Bella alive?" Bosch asked.

1. à plat ventre
2. émettant un sifflement laborieux
3. inspirations
4. fesse gauche
5. regard
6. partout
7. ambulance [Rescue Ambulance]
8. se remit en position accroupie

"You said before you doubted she was alive."

"That was before I found hot food for her in the truck. She's alive and he's going to tell us where."

Sisto stepped over to the table and grabbed the map that Dockweiler had drawn.

"We have this," he said.

"Yeah, that's a treasure map," Bosch said. "If you think that's where she is, you better run over there and be the hero."

Sisto looked over at Valdez and then down at Trevino, not quite comprehending that Dockweiler had been playing them the whole time[1] in order to get a hand free to grab his hidden gun.

Valdez raised his phone and clicked off the call to Bosch. He then hit a speed-dial button.

"We need a rescue ambulance to this address," he said. "Suspect is down, multiple gunshot wounds[2]. We'll need the Sheriff's Department to roll[3]. Tell them we need an OIS team[4]."

Valdez looked at Bosch as he disconnected, the silent message being that they would do this by the book[5].

Bosch leaned down and tried one more time with Dockweiler.

"Where is she, Dockweiler?" he said. "Tell us now or you won't make it[6] to the hospital alive."

"Harry," Valdez said. "Get up and go outside."

Bosch ignored him. He leaned further down to[7] Dockweiler's ear.

"Where is she?" he demanded.

"Fuck … you," Dockweiler said between gulps of air. "I tell you, nothing changes for me. Better you know … that you failed her[8]."

He managed to curl his lip back, in what Bosch assumed was a smile. Bosch started to reach a gloved hand toward the bullet wound on his back.

1. s'était joué d'eux tout du long

2. blessures par balles

3. que la police du comté prenne le relais

4. d'une équipe de la police des polices [Officer-Involved Shooting ; en cas de fusillade]

5. dans les règles

6. n'arriveras pas

7. se baissa encore plus près de

8. l'as laissée tomber

"Bosch!" Valdez yelled. "Outside now! That's an order!"

The chief climbed to his feet[1] and moved in to yank Bosch away[2] from Dockweiler if necessary. Harry looked up at him and then stood. They stared at each other until finally Bosch spoke.

"I know she's here," he said.

1. se releva tant bien que mal
2. éloigner Bosch *manu militari*

33

Bosch knew he had little time to stay on the case before the Sheriff's Department Officer-Involved Shooting team arrived on scene and sequestered him and the other San Fernando officers. While paramedics[1] worked to stabilize Dockweiler and then lift him onto an ambulance gurney[2], Bosch took a high-powered flashlight out of one of the boxes in the garage and headed down the sloping backyard[3] toward the Haskell Canyon Wash.

He was forty yards from the house when he heard his name called from behind. He turned to find Sisto running to catch up.

"What are you doing?" he said.

"Going to search the wash," Bosch said.

"For Bella? Then I'll help."

"What about Dockweiler? Who's going to the hospital with him?"

"I think the captain. But it doesn't matter. Dockweiler's not going anywhere. I heard the EMTs[4] talking. They said a bullet mighta cut his spinal cord[5]."

Bosch thought about that for a moment. The idea that Dockweiler might survive and finish his life in a wheelchair[6] invoked no sympathy in him[7]. What Dockweiler had done to his victims—including Bella, though Bosch didn't yet know exactly what Bella had suffered at Dockweiler's hands—disqualified him from ever earning anything like compassion[8].

1. les ambulanciers

2. chariot-brancard

3. jardin en pente

4. ambulanciers [Emergency Medical Technicians]

5. pourrait lui avoir sectionné la moelle épinière

6. chaise roulante

7. ne lui inspirait aucune pitié

8. empêcherait Bosch de sentir une quelconque compassion pour lui

"Okay, but we've gotta move quickly," Bosch said. "Once the shooting team gets here, I'm out. We all are."

"So what do you want me to do?"

Bosch reached into his pocket. He still had the flashlight he had grabbed off the front lawn as backup[1]. He turned it on and tossed it to Sisto.

"You go one way and I'll go the other."

"You think she's tied up to a tree or something?"

"Maybe. Who knows? I just hope she's alive. When we get down there, we split up and look[2]."

"Roger that[3]."

The men continued down the slope. The wash was little more than an overgrown ravine[4] that was left undeveloped because of the potential for flooding[5]. Bosch guessed that most days it was a creek[6] but during storms it could become a river. They passed signs[7] warning of flash flooding[8] during rainstorms, signs meant to keep[9] kids from playing in the wash.

As the slope started to level off[10], the ground was softer and Bosch noticed what looked like a track worn[11] into the pathway. It was no more than six inches wide[12] and three inches deep and he followed it all the way to the water's edge. Before splitting from Sisto he crouched down[13] and put his light into the mini-trench. He saw what looked like a tire tread[14].

Bosch raised the beam of his light and followed the track to the shallow waters of the wash. The water was clear and he could see to the bottom. He saw what looked like gray sand in places[15], large chunks of gray rock in others. Some of the flat polished edges were the giveaway[16]. It was concrete that had been formed and hardened and then broken. It was construction debris.

1. en guise de dépannage
2. on se sépare et on cherche
3. Compris
4. lit de la rivière n'était qu'un fossé envahi par la végétation
5. en friche en raison des risques d'inondation
6. ruisseau
7. devant des panneaux
8. prévenant du risque de crues subites
9. destinés à empêcher
10. s'aplanir
11. sillon creusé
12. ne faisait pas plus de 15 cm de large
13. s'accroupit
14. trace de pneu
15. par endroits
16. caractéristiques

"Harry, come on, are we going to look for her?" Sisto asked.

"Just hold on a second," Bosch said. "Be still[1]."

Bosch turned off his light and stayed at the water's edge. He thought about what he had seen and what he knew. The concrete rubble[2]. The guns and supplies. The wheelbarrow and the hand truck stolen from Public Works. The hot food on the front seat of the truck. He realized what Dockweiler had been up to[3] and what he was doing at the tailgate of his truck earlier that night when the chief's phone interrupted him.

"Dockweiler's been building something," he said. "He was taking wheelbarrows of concrete and dirt down here and dumping it[4] in the wash."

"Okay," Sisto said. "What does that mean?"

"It means we're looking in the wrong place," Bosch said.

He abruptly stood up and turned his light back on. He turned and looked back up the slope toward the kitchen lights of Dockweiler's house.

"I had it wrong[5]," he said. "We have to go back."

"What?" Sisto asked. "I thought we were going to—"

Bosch was already running back up the slope. Sisto stopped talking and started following him.

The climb back up winded[6] Bosch and he was moving at a modest trot[7] by the time he was passing by the house. Through the windows of the sunroom[8] he could see men in suits[9] and knew that Sheriff's investigators were now on the scene. He didn't know if they were members of the Officer-Involved Shooting team and didn't stop to find out[10]. He saw Chief Valdez with them. He was gesturing and pointing, most likely giving them the initial rundown[11] of what had happened.

1. Ne bouge pas
2. gravats
3. comprit ce que Dockweiler avait manigancé
4. pour les déverser
5. me suis trompé
6. essouffla
7. ne courait plus que par petites foulées
8. véranda
9. en costume
10. vérifier
11. leur faisant un premier résumé

Bosch continued down the side of the house and into the front yard.

There were now two Sheriff's patrol cars and one plain wrap[1] parked out front[2], but everybody was apparently inside. Bosch went straight to the back of Dockweiler's pickup and started pulling out the two-wheeled hand truck. Sisto caught up with him[3] at the back of the truck and helped him lower the heavy cart to the ground.

"What are we doing, Harry?" he asked.

"We have to move those boxes in the garage," Bosch said.

"Why? What's in them?"

"Not what's in them. What's under them."

He pushed the cart toward the garage.

"Dockweiler was about to take this out of his truck and start moving these boxes," he said.

"How come[4]?" Sisto asked.

"Because he had hot food in the truck and wanted to deliver it."

"Harry, I'm not following."

"That's okay, Sisto. Just start moving boxes."

Bosch attacked the first row of boxes with the hand truck, sliding its blade[5] under the bottom box and then tilting the cart[6] and the column of boxes back. He quickly backed out of the garage and to the front of the pickup. He placed the column down, yanked the hand truck back[7], and quickly went back for more. Sisto worked with only his own muscles. He moved two and three boxes at a clip[8], stacking them[9] out on the driveway near the pickup.

In five minutes they had made a large inroad[10] into the stacks, and Bosch came upon a rubber mat[11] that covered the floor and was designed to be used to catch oil[12] from the vehicle parked in the garage. He used the hand truck to move a few

1. véhicule banalisé
2. devant la maison
3. le rattrapa
4. Comment ça
5. glissant la partie horizontale
6. inclinant le chariot
7. recula le chariot
8. à toute vitesse
9. les empilant
10. travée
11. trouva bientôt un tapis en caoutchouc
12. les fuites d'huile

more stacks of boxes and then reached down and rolled back the mat.

There was a round metal manhole cover[1] flush with the[2] concrete floor. It had the seal of the city of San Fernando embossed[3] on it. Bosch crouched down and put two fingers into what looked like air holes[4] and tried to pull up the heavy metal plate. He couldn't do it. He looked around for Sisto.

"Help me with this," he said.

"Hold on, Harry," Sisto said.

He disappeared from Bosch's view and was gone for a few seconds. When he came back he had a long iron bar bent into a handle[5] on one end and a hook on the other.

"How the hell did you find that?" Bosch asked as he got out of the way.

"I saw it on the workbench and wondered what it was for," Sisto said. "Then I figured it out. I'd seen the guys from Public Works using them in the street."

He fit the hook into one of the holes in the iron plate and started pulling it up.

"That's where he probably stole it from," Bosch said. "You need help?"

"I got it," Sisto said.

He hoisted the manhole out[6] and it clattered[7] onto the concrete floor. Bosch leaned over the hole and looked down. The overhead light in the garage revealed a ladder[8] leading into darkness. Bosch went over to the stack of boxes where he had seen the light sticks[9] earlier. He yanked open the box[10] and took out several. Behind him he heard Sisto yell into the hole he had opened.

"Bella?"

There was no response.

Bosch returned and started opening the sticks, snapping them on[11] and dropping them down the

1. plaque d'égout
2. au ras du
3. gravé
4. des trous d'aération
5. courbée en forme de poignée
6. souleva la plaque
7. retomba bruyamment
8. échelle
9. bâtons chimioluminescents
10. ouvrit le carton d'un geste brusque
11. les pliant pour les allumer

hole. He then started down the ladder. The descent was no more than ten feet[1] but there was no last rung[2] on the ladder and he almost fell as he placed his foot where the rung should have been. He lowered himself the rest of the way and then reached into his back pocket for the flashlight. He turned it on and played it against[3] the concrete walls of a chamber that was still clearly under construction. There were iron supports and plywood molds[4] for concrete. Plastic sheeting[5] hung from makeshift scaffolding[6]. There was air but not enough of it. Bosch found himself on the verge of hyperventilating as he gulped for oxygen[7]. He guessed that an air-cleaning and -filtration system was not in place or not operating. The only fresh air entering the chamber was from the opening above.

He realized that this was Dockweiler's dream. He had been building an underground bunker where he would be able to retreat and hide when the big quake[8] hit or the bomb was dropped or the terrorists came.

"Anything?" Sisto called down.

"Still looking," Bosch said.

"I'm coming down."

"Just watch the[9] last rung. It isn't there."

Bosch started making his way around the construction debris and down the length of the chamber. When he pushed through a plastic curtain he had to step up[10] to a section that was nearly complete, its walls smooth and floor level[11] and carpeted in black rubber matting[12]. He swept his flashlight across all surfaces and saw nothing. Bella was not here.

Bosch turned in a complete circle. He had been wrong.

Sisto pushed through the plastic curtain.

1. 3 m
2. échelon
3. balaya
4. des moules en contreplaqué
5. Des bâches
6. échafaudages de fortune
7. à deux doigts de suffoquer par manque d'oxygène
8. séisme
9. Fais attention au
10. dut monter une marche
11. nivelé
12. revêtu d'une carpette de plastique noir

"She's not here?"

"No."

"Shit."

"We've got to look in the house."

"Maybe he was telling the truth about the movie ranch."

Bosch pushed back through the plastic and made the step down[1] into the first chamber. When he got to the ladder, he realized that there wasn't a missing rung. The ladder simply extended down to the level the floor would be at when the chamber was completed.

He turned around and almost banged[2] into Sisto. He pushed past him and then again through the plastic curtain to the finished room. He trained his light over the floor[3], looking for a seam[4].

"I thought we were going back up," Sisto said.

"Help me," Bosch said. "I think she's here. Pull up this matting[5]."

They each went to a side of the room and started pulling the rubber matting back. It was one piece cut to fit[6] the space. As it was rolled back Bosch could see wooden planking[7] beneath. He started looking for a hinge[8] or a seam or some indication of a hidden compartment but he saw nothing.

Bosch banged his fist down[9] on the wood and determined there was a definite hollow[10] below it. Sisto started pounding the floor as well.

"Bella? Bella?"

Still no response. Bosch scuttled across the floor to the[11] plastic curtain, grabbed it, and jerked it down[12], bringing a metal frame crashing down with it.

"Watch it[13]!" Sisto yelled.

1. descendit la marche
2. faillit rentrer
3. balaya le sol avec sa lampe
4. jointure
5. Enlève le tapis
6. aux dimensions de
7. les lattes d'un plancher
8. charnière
9. donna un coup de poing
10. déduisit qu'il y avait une cavité
11. courut jusqu'au
12. l'arracha complètement
13. Attention

One arm[1] of the frame hit Bosch on the shoulder but he wasn't fazed[2]. He was flying on[3] adrenaline.

He dropped down to the front chamber again and put the light on the facing of the eight-inch step riser[4]. He saw a seam running completely around the facing that curved with the contour of the concrete floor. On his knees, he moved in and tried to open it but he couldn't figure it out[5]. "Help me get this open," he called to Sisto.

The young detective got down next to Bosch and tried to get his fingernails into the seam. He could not get a grip[6].

"Look out[7]," Bosch said.

He grabbed a piece of the curtain's fallen frame and drove[8] its edge into the seam. Once it was jammed in tightly[9] he levered the frame upward[10] and the seam opened an inch[11]. Sisto put his fingers in and pulled the board free[12].

Bosch dropped the frame with a metal clatter[13] and put his light into the shallow space[14] under the second room's floor.

He saw bare feet heels-down[15] on a blanket and tied together. The space under the floor was recessed and[16] deeper than the dimensions of the floor and step indicated[17] from the outside.

"She's here!"

He reached in and gripped either side of the blanket and pulled it out. Bella Lourdes came sliding out of the shallow black space on a blanket spread over a plywood pallet[18]. She barely cleared[19] the opening created by the step's riser[20]. She was bound and gagged[21] and bloodied[22]. Her clothes were gone and she was either dead or unconscious.

"Bella!" Sisto yelled.

1. côté
2. ne s'en soucia pas
3. était mû par l'
4. la contremarche de 20 cm de haut
5. ne trouva pas comment
6. trouver une prise
7. Attention
8. inséra
9. bien enfoncé,
10. souleva
11. s'ouvrit de quelques centimètres
12. retira la planche
13. dans un cliquetis métallique
14. le creux
15. des pieds nus, talons au sol,
16. formait une cavité
17. ne le laissaient supposer
18. planche de contreplaqué
19. passa tout juste par
20. contremarche
21. bâillonnée
22. ensanglantée

"Call for another RA[1]," Bosch ordered. "They'll need a portable stretcher[2] to get her through[3] the manhole."

As Sisto pulled his phone, Bosch turned back to Bella's side. He bent down and put his ear to her mouth. He felt the faint wind of breath[4]. She was alive.

"I got no signal[5]!" Sisto said in frustration.

"Go up," Bosch yelled back. "Go back up!"

Sisto ran to the ladder and started climbing. Bosch pulled his jacket off and put it over Bella's body. He pulled the pallet closer to the ladder and the air from the manhole.

Bella started to regain consciousness as she got more air. Her eyes opened and they were startled[6], confused. She started shaking.

"Bella?" Bosch said. "It's me, Harry. You're safe and we're going to get you out of here."

1. Demande une autre ambulance

2. brancard avec sangle

3. pour la faire passer par

4. un souffle ténu

5. réseau

6. apeurés

34

Bosch spent the entire night with the Sheriff's investigators, first talking them through the steps[1] that led to the arrival of the San Fernando officers at Dockweiler's home and then walking them through a play-by-play accounting of[2] the moves that led to the shooting. Bosch had just been through the process[3] the year before after a shooting in West Hollywood. He knew what to expect and knew it was routine, and yet he could not take it as such[4]. He knew he needed to carefully make the case[5] that his decision to fire through the window at Dockweiler's back was warranted[6] and unavoidable[7]. Essentially, Dockweiler's pointing a weapon at the three officers in the kitchen made the use of deadly force acceptable.

The investigative report would take weeks to put together[8] as investigators waited on ballistic and forensic reports and collated it all[9] with the interviews of the officers involved and schematic drawings of the shooting scene. It would then be presented to the district attorney's police shooting unit for another review, which would also take several weeks. A final declaration of the shooting as justified and within the scope[10] of police authority would then be issued[11].

Bosch wasn't worried about his actions and he also knew that Bella Lourdes would be a significant factor in the investigation. The fact that she was rescued from Dockweiler's underground

1. en leur détaillant les différentes étapes
2. en leur rejouant séquence par séquence
3. avait déjà vécu cela
4. pourtant, il ne parvenait pas à le considérer comme tel
5. établir
6. justifiée
7. inévitable
8. rapport d'enquête prendrait des semaines,
9. comparerait
10. du ressort
11. établie

shelter[1] would blow away any possible media backlash[2] that could put pressure on the D.A.'s Office. It would be hard to question[3] the tactics resulting in the shooting of a man who had abducted[4] a police officer, sexually assaulted her, and then held her in an underground chamber with the obvious intention of keeping her alive—the food he had brought home—for repeated assaults before eventually killing her.

It was dawn by the time the investigators said they were finished with Bosch. They told him to go home and get some rest and that they might have further questions over the next couple of days before they moved into the collating and writing phase[5] of the investigation. Bosch said he would be available.

Harry had learned during the course of his interview that Lourdes had been transported to the trauma center at Holy Cross. On his way home he stopped by the hospital to see if he could get an update on her condition[6]. He found Valdez in the waiting room of the trauma center and he could tell he had been there all night since being released[7] by the Sheriff's investigators. He was sitting on a couch next to a woman Bosch recognized as Bella's partner[8] from the photos on her cubicle's wall.

"You finished with the Sheriff's investigators?" Valdez said.

"For now[9]," Bosch said. "They sent me home. How is Bella?"

"She's sleeping. Taryn here has been allowed to go back and see her a couple of times."

Bosch introduced himself to Taryn and she thanked him for his part[10] in the rescue. Bosch just nodded, feeling more guilty for his part in

1. abri
2. anéantirait tout éventuel contrecoup médiatique
3. mettre en cause
4. enlevé
5. ne passent à la phase de synthèse et de rédaction
6. essayer d'avoir de ses nouvelles
7. depuis qu'il avait été relâché
8. la compagne
9. Pour l'instant
10. rôle

sending Lourdes to Dockweiler than good about rescuing her from him.

Bosch looked at Valdez and made a slight head nod[1] toward the hallway. He wanted to talk but not within earshot[2] of Taryn. Valdez got up and excused himself and then walked with Bosch into the hallway.

"So did you get a chance to talk to Bella and find out what happened?" Bosch asked.

"Briefly," Valdez said. "She's in bad shape emotionally and I just didn't want to put her through it[3]. I mean, there's no hurry, is there?"

"No."

"Anyway, she said she went over to the yard[4] about noon and nobody was around because it was lunchtime. She went into the offices and found Dockweiler eating at his desk. When she asked about the metal detector, he volunteered to put it in a truck and take it up there to the house."

"And she said yes because I wasn't there to help."

"Don't beat yourself up[5]. You told her to take Sisto, and besides, Dockweiler, no matter what kind of an asshole he is[6], is a former cop. She had no reason to feel unsafe."

"So when did he grab her?"

"They went to the house and searched. The metal detector was heavy and he volunteered to drive it up in a city truck and operate it. You were right. There were keys in the bushes. She just didn't know they were his. He had parked the truck in the back by the garage so it was pretty secluded[7]. The victim from the attempted assault Friday had not come back yet and there was nobody around. He asked her to help him get the metal detector back in the truck and that's when he grabbed her from behind and choked her out[8].

1. léger signe de tête
2. à portée de voix
3. lui faire revivre tout ça
4. dépôt
5. Arrêtez de vous en vouloir
6. a beau être une ordure
7. assez isolé
8. lui a fait perdre connaissance par suffocation

He must've drugged her[1] then, because she was out a long time[2]. When she woke up she was already down in that dungeon[3] and he was on top of her. He was rough[4] … she's pretty banged up[5]."

Bosch shook his head. It was impossible to imagine what Lourdes had experienced.

"The sick fuck[6]," Valdez said. "He told her he was going to keep her alive down there. He said she would never see sunlight again …"

Bosch was rescued from the grim[7] details by Taryn, who entered the hallway looking for him.

"I just went back to tell her you were here," she said to Bosch. "She's awake and wants to see you."

"She doesn't have to see me," Bosch said. "I don't want to intrude[8]."

"No, she wants to. Really."

"Okay, then."

Taryn led Bosch back through the waiting room and into another hallway. As they walked she shook her head in anguish.

"She's tough," Bosch said. "She'll get through this[9]."

"No, that's not it," Taryn said.

"Then what?"

"I just can't believe that he's here, too."

Bosch was confused[10].

"The chief?"

"No, Dockweiler! They have him in this hospital." Now Bosch got it.

"Does Bella know?"

"I don't think so."

"Well, don't tell her."

"I wouldn't[11]. It would freak her the fuck out[12]."

"As soon as he's stabilized they'll move him. They have a jail hospital down at County-USC. He'll go there."

1. a dû la droguer
2. est restée longtemps sans connaissance
3. cachot
4. a été brutal
5. pas mal amochée
6. Quel salopard
7. terribles
8. la déranger
9. surmontera ça
10. ne comprit pas
11. Bien sûr que non
12. Ça la ferait complètement flipper

"Good."

They came to an open door and entered a private room, where Lourdes lay in a bed with side guards up[1]. She was turned away from the door, gazing at[2] the room's window. Her hands lay limply[3] at her sides. Without looking at her visitors she asked Taryn to give them privacy[4].

Taryn left and Bosch stood there. He could only see Bella's left eye but could tell it was swollen and bruised[5]. She also had swelling and a bite mark[6] on her lower lip.

"Hey, Bella," he finally said.

"I guess I owe you[7] that beer you were talking about," she said.

Bosch remembered telling her she would owe him if she found something with the metal detector.

"Bella, I should've been there with you," he said. "I am so sorry. I messed up[8] and you paid an awful price."

"Don't be silly," she said. "You didn't mess up. I did. I should never have turned my back on him."

She finally looked at him. There was hemorrhaging around both eyes from when Dockweiler had choked her. She turned a hand up on the bed, an invitation to hold it. Bosch moved closer and squeezed her hand, trying somehow to communicate what he couldn't find the words to say.

"Thanks for coming," she said. "And for saving me. The chief told me. You, I would have guessed. Sisto, that was a surprise."

She tried to smile. Bosch shrugged.

"You solved the case," he said. "And that saved a lot of other women from him. Remember that."

She nodded and closed her eyes. Bosch could see tears.

"Harry, I have to tell you something," she said.

1. des protections latérales
2. fixant
3. mollement
4. les laisser seuls
5. enflé et contusionné
6. trace de morsure
7. Je crois que je te dois
8. J'ai merdé

"What is it?" he asked.

She looked up at him again.

"He made me tell him about you. He ... hurt me and I tried but I couldn't take it[1]. He wanted to know how we knew about the keys. And about you. He wanted to know if you had a wife or kids. I tried to hold out[2], Harry."

Bosch squeezed her hand.

"Don't say any more, Bella," he said. "You did great. We got the guy and it's over now. That's all that matters."

She closed her eyes again.

"I'm going to go back to sleep now," she said.

"Sure," he said. "I'll be back soon, Bella. You hang in there[3]."

Bosch headed down the hall, thinking about Dockweiler torturing Bella to get information about him. He wondered where that would have led if things hadn't ended that night.

In the waiting room Bosch found Valdez but no Taryn. The chief explained that she went home to get clothes for Bella for when she was released[4], whenever that would be. They spoke about the Screen Cutter case and what needed to be completed on their end[5] for both the Sheriff's shooting investigation and the prosecution of[6] Dockweiler. They had forty-eight hours to present their case[7] against the suspected rapist to the D.A.'s Office and ask for charges[8]. Because Lourdes was out of commission[9] in the hospital, Bosch was going to have to be point[10].

"I want this case to be airtight[11], Harry," Valdez said. "And I want to hit him with everything we can. Every charge possible. I don't want him ever breathing free air again."

1. n'ai pas pu supporter
2. tenir bon
3. Tiens le coup
4. sortirait
5. de leur côté
6. poursuites judiciaires contre
7. avant d'exposer leur affaire
8. demander la mise en examen
9. hors circuit
10. le principal interlocuteur
11. un dossier en béton

"Got it," Bosch said. "That's not going to be a problem. I'm going to go home, sleep till about noon, and then I'll get back on it."

Valdez clapped him on the upper arm in encouragement.

"Let me know what you need," he said.

"You're staying here?" Bosch asked.

"Yeah, for a while. Sisto texted and said he wanted to come by. I think I'll wait for him. When this thing levels out[1], we need to all get together for some beers, make sure everybody's okay."

"That'll be good."

Bosch left the hospital then and ran into Sisto in the parking garage. He was in fresh clothes and looked like he might even have gotten some sleep[2].

"How's Bella?" he asked.

"I don't really know," Bosch said. "She's been through a kind of hell[3] that's hard to imagine."

"Did you see her?"

"For a few minutes. The chief's up there in the waiting room. He'll get you in if he can."

"Cool. See you back at the bureau."

"I'm going to go home and sleep first."

Sisto nodded and walked off. Bosch thought of something and then called after him. "Hey, Sisto."

The young detective walked back.

"Yeah, listen, I'm sorry for losing my cool[4] and pushing you," Bosch said. "And throwing your phone. It was just a tense situation, you know?"

"No, man, it was cool," Sisto said. "You were right. I don't want to be a fuckup[5], Harry. I want to be a good detective like you."

Bosch nodded his thanks[6] for the compliment.

"Don't worry," he said. "You'll get there[7]. And you did good work last night."

"Thanks."

1. tout ça sera terminé
2. avait même l'air d'avoir pu dormir un peu
3. a vécu un enfer
4. d'avoir perdu mon sang-froid
5. raté
6. le remercia d'un hochement de tête
7. Tu y arriveras

"You want to do something after you see Bella?"

"What do you mean?"

"Go over to Public Works and tape off[1] Dockweiler's desk. We'll need to go through it[2]. Then get the supervisor over there to pull records on[3] all code inspections he did over the last four years. You're looking for unpermitted dwellings[4]."

"You think that's how he picked the victims?"

"I guarantee it. Pull all of those[5] and put 'em on my desk. I'll go through them when I get in and put him on[6] the streets where our victims lived."

"Cool. We need a warrant?"

"I don't think so. Public records[7]."

"Okay, Harry, I'm on it[8]. They'll be on your desk." Bosch gave him a fist bump[9], then headed off to his car.

1. mets sous scellés

2. le fouiller

3. sortir la liste de

4. résidences illégales

5. Sors-les toutes

6. vérifierai qu'il a inspecté

7. C'est des archives en accès libre

8. je m'y mets

9. le salua avec le poing

35

Bosch went home, took a long shower, and then crawled[1] into his bed for what he intended to be a four-hour nap[2]. He even tied a bandanna around his head and over his eyes to keep out the light of the day. But less than two hours into a deep trench of sleep[3] he was awakened by a blaring[4] guitar riff[5]. He yanked the bandanna off[6] and tried to do the same with the vestiges of sleep. Then clarity came and he realized it was the ringtone his daughter had programmed into his phone so he would know when she was calling: "Black Sun" by Death Cab for Cutie. She had programmed it into her own phone for his calls to her as well.

He grabbed at the phone, knocking it off the bed table to the floor, before finally picking it up and answering.

"Maddie? What's wrong?"

"Uh, nothing. What's wrong with you? You sound weird[7]."

"I was sleeping. What's going on?"

"Well I thought we were maybe going to have lunch today. Are you still at your hotel?"

"Shoot[8], I'm sorry, Maddie. I forgot to call you. I'm back home. I got called back last night on an emergency. An officer got abducted and we worked all night on it."

"Holy shit[9]! Abducted? Did you get him back?"

"It was a she, and yes, we got her back. But it was a long night and I'm just catching up[10]. I think

1. se glissa
2. sieste
3. après s'être profondément endormi
4. assourdissant
5. air de guitare
6. enleva le foulard d'un coup sec
7. T'as une drôle de voix
8. Zut
9. Oh, la vache
10. j'essaie de dormir un peu

I'm going to be kind of busy for a few days. Can we do lunch or dinner this weekend or early next week?"

"Yeah, no worries. But how was she abducted?"

"Uh, it's kind of a long story but he was a wanted guy[1] and he sort of grabbed her before she grabbed him[2]. But we got her back, he's under arrest, and everything's okay."

He left the explanation short because he didn't want her to know the details of what had happened to Bella Lourdes or that he had shot her abductor. That would make for a long conversation.

"Well, good. I guess, then, I'll let you go back to sleep."

"Did you have classes this morning?"

"Psychology and Spanish. I'm finished for the day."

"That's nice."

"Uh, Dad?"

"Yeah."

"I kind of also wanted to say I was sorry about what I said yesterday about the restaurant and everything. I didn't know your reasons and it kind of sucked that I jumped on you[3]. I'm really sorry."

"Don't worry about it, baby. You didn't know and it's all right."

"So we're cool[4]?"

"We're cool."

"Love you, Dad. Now go to sleep."

She laughed.

"What?"

"That's what you used to say to me when I was little. 'Love you, now go to sleep.'"

"I remember that."

After disconnecting, Bosch pulled the bandanna back over his eyes and tried to go back to sleep.

1. c'est un type qu'on recherchait

2. d'une certaine façon, il l'a chopée avant qu'elle ne le chope

3. ça me fait chier que je te sois rentrée dedans

4. Tout va bien, alors

And failed.

Twenty minutes into the effort, with the Death Cab guitar hook[1] an earworm playing in his head[2], he gave up on finding the sleep trench again[3] and got out of bed. He took another quick shower to refresh himself and headed back north to San Fernando.

The number of media trucks outside the police station had doubled since the week before when the Screen Cutter was just a wanted man. Now that he had been identified, had abducted one cop, and had been shot by another, the case was big news[4]. Bosch went in the side door as usual and was able to escape notice[5] from the reporters gathered in the front lobby. The department's media officer was usually the captain, as part of his catchall duties[6], but Bosch assumed[7] Trevino would not be the point man[8] on a story he had played a significant part in. He suspected the media management on this story would fall to[9] Sergeant Rosenberg, who was affable and telegenic in a cop sort of way. He looked like a cop and talked like a cop and that's what the media wanted.

The detective bureau was deserted and that was the way Bosch needed it. After an event like that of the night before, people tended to want to talk. They'd gather around the desk and tell it from their point of view, listen to it from somebody else's point of view. It was therapeutic. But Bosch didn't want to talk. He wanted to work. He had to write what he knew would be a lengthy[10] and detailed charging document[11] that would be first scrutinized[12] by his superiors in the department, then by multiple prosecutors[13] with the District Attorney's Office[14] and then a defense lawyer and, eventually[15],

1. refrain
2. qu'il n'arrivait pas à se sortir de la tête
3. renonça à retrouver le sommeil
4. l'affaire faisait la une
5. à l'attention
6. rôle multitâche
7. présumait
8. principal interlocuteur
9. incomberait au
10. très long
11. document d'inculpation
12. examiné
13. procureurs
14. rattachés au procureur général
15. enfin

even the media. He wanted focus[1], and the quiet detective bureau would be perfect.

Sisto wasn't in the bureau but his presence was immediately felt[2]. When Bosch got to his desk and dropped his car keys, he found four neat stacks[3] of code inspection reports waiting for him. The young detective had come through[4].

Bosch sat down to work and almost immediately felt the weight of exhaustion settle onto him. He had not gotten enough rest after the events of the night before. His shoulder was aching from[5] the impact of the curtain frame in Dockweiler's fallout shelter[6], but where he was feeling it most was in his legs. That run back up the slope of the wash[7] was the first time he had fired the pistons[8] in a long time and he was sore[9] and fatigued. He signed in to[10] the computer, opened a blank[11] document, and left it ready while he went down the hallway to the station's kitchen.

On the way he passed the open door of the chief's office and saw Valdez seated at his desk, the telephone to his ear. The snippet[12] of conversation he heard was enough for Bosch to know the chief was talking to a reporter, saying that the department was not going to identify[13] the officer who had been abducted, because she was the victim of a sexual assault. Bosch thought that in a department as small as San Fernando's it would not take a good reporter more than a few calls to figure out who was being protected. That would result in reporters camped[14] on the front lawn of Bella Lourdes's house, unless her address was protected by being deeded in[15] Taryn's name.

There was a fresh pot of coffee already brewed[16] and Bosch poured two cups, leaving both black. On the way back to the bureau he stopped by the

1. se concentrer
2. passage était palpable
3. piles bien rangées
4. assurait enfin
5. lui faisait mal après
6. abri antiatomique
7. Cette course pour remonter la berge pentue
8. qu'il s'était autant remué
9. courbatu
10. ouvrit une session sur
11. vierge
12. bribes
13. révéler l'identité de
14. installés
15. en ayant été acquise au
16. préparé

open door of the chief's office and held one up as an offer[1]. Valdez nodded and covered the phone to respond.

"Harry, you're the man[2]."

Bosch stepped into the office and put the cup down on the desk.

"Knock 'em dead[3], Chief."

Five minutes later Bosch was back in his cubicle and going through the inspection reports. It only took him an hour because once he became familiar with the form[4], he was able to quickly go through it and identify the street where each inspection took place. He was looking for the five streets where the known victims, including Beatriz Sahagun, lived. At the end of the hour he had placed Dockweiler on each victim's street in the months before her assault or attempted assault. In two of the cases he had actually inspected the victim's home as long as nine months earlier.

The information garnered[5] from the reports helped draw a solid picture of Dockweiler's MO[6]. Bosch believed that he first saw the victims while conducting[7] inspections, then stalked them[8] and carefully planned the assaults for weeks and sometimes months. As a code inspector and former police officer he had skills that aided this process. Bosch had no doubt that Dockweiler entered and prowled[9] the homes of the victims, possibly even while they were at home and asleep.

Finished with the code inspection piece of the puzzle, Bosch began writing the charging document. He was a two-finger typist[10] but he was fast just the same[11], especially when he knew and was confident in the story he wanted to tell.

He worked another two hours without a break or even a look up from the computer screen. When he was finished he took a gulp[12] of cold black cof-

1. lui en proposa une d'un geste
2. l'homme de la situation
3. Flanquez-leur une raclée
4. formulaire
5. recueillies
6. mode opératoire
7. lors de ses
8. les suivait de près
9. rôdait dans
10. tapait avec seulement deux doigts
11. quand même rapide
12. gorgée

fee and hit the print button. The universal printer on the other side of the room spit out[1] six single-spaced[2] pages of a chronology that began with the first Screen Cutter rape four years earlier and ended with Kurt Dockweiler lying facedown on his kitchen floor with a bullet lodged in his spine[3]. Bosch proofed it[4] with a red pen, made the corrections on the computer, and printed it again. He then took it to the chief's office, where he found him talking on the phone to yet another reporter. He covered the receiver again.

"*USA Today*[5]," he said. "This story is going coast to coast."

"Make sure they spell your name right," Bosch said. "I'm going to need you to read and approve this. I want to file on[6] Dockweiler first thing[7] tomorrow morning. I'm going for five counts of forcible rape[8], one count attempted rape[9], then kidnapping, assault with a deadly weapon[10], and multiple counts of theft of government property."

"The kitchen-sink approach[11]. I like it."

"Let me know. I have to go write up the evidence report and the search warrant that we got approved last night."

Bosch was about to leave the office, when Valdez held up a finger, then returned to his phone call.

"Donna, I need to go," he said. "You have the details in the press release[12], and like I said, we're not putting out either officer's name[13] at this time[14]. We took a really bad character[15] out of circulation and we're all very proud of that. Thank you."

Valdez hung up the phone, even as he and Bosch could hear the reporter's voice asking another question.

1. recracha
2. à simple interligne
3. colonne vertébrale
4. le corrigea
5. [quotidien national américain]
6. engager une procédure contre
7. à la première heure
8. Je retiens cinq chefs d'accusation : viol caractérisé
9. une tentative de viol
10. attaque à main armée
11. La totale, quoi
12. communiqué de presse
13. nous ne divulguons le nom d'aucun des deux agents
14. pour l'instant
15. individu

"All day long," Valdez said. "They're calling from all over the place. Everybody wants to get photos of the dungeon[1]. Everybody wants to talk to Bella and you."

"I heard you on the phone earlier when you used that word *dungeon*," Bosch said. "That's how things take on a whole new life[2] in the media. It's a fallout shelter[3], not a dungeon."

"Well, as soon as Dockweiler has a lawyer he can sue me[4]. These reporters ... One of them told me the average[5] cost of incarcerating an inmate[6] is thirty K[7] a year but with Dockweiler likely being a paraplegic now, it will double for him. I said, so what are you saying, we should have just executed him on the spot[8] to save the money?"

"We did have our chance."

"I'll forget you said that, Harry. I don't even want to think about what you were going to do to him last night."

"Just what was necessary to find Bella."

"Well, we did anyway."

"We got lucky."

"That wasn't luck. That was good detective work. Anyway, you should be ready. They're trying to find out who the shooter was and when they learn it was you, they'll connect it to West Hollywood last year and everything else before. Be prepared."

"I'll take a vacation[9] and disappear."

"Good idea. So this is good to go?"

He had picked up the document Bosch had delivered.

"You tell me," Bosch said.

"Okay, give me fifteen minutes," Valdez said.

"By the way, where's the captain been all day? Sleeping?"

1. cachot
2. comme ça que les choses se retrouvent déformées
3. abri antiatomique
4. pourra me poursuivre en justice
5. moyen
6. d'un détenu
7. mille dollars
8. sur place
9. des vacances

"No, he's staying at the hospital with Bella. I wanted someone there to keep the media away and in case she needed anything."

Bosch nodded. It was a good move[1]. He told Valdez he would be in the bureau and to call or e-mail if he wanted any changes to the charging document.

He returned to his computer in the detective bureau. He was just putting the finishing touches on a report summarizing the physical evidence[2] they had amassed in the case when his cell phone buzzed. It was Mickey Haller calling.

"Yo, Bro[3], haven't heard from you," the lawyer said. "You talk to the granddaughter yet?"

The Vance case had been so thoroughly crowded out of Bosch's mind[4] with the events of the past eighteen hours that it seemed like his trip to San Diego had been a month ago.

"No, not yet," Bosch said.

"What about Ida Parks Whatever-Her-Name-Is[5]?" Haller asked.

"Ida *Townes* Forsythe. No, haven't gotten to her yet either[6]. Things have sort of been crazy with my other job."

"Holy shit. You're on that thing with the guy and the dungeon up there in Santa Clorox[7]?"

It was an old nickname[8] for Santa Clarita, reflecting its early incarnation as[9] a destination for white flight from[10] Los Angeles. It seemed somehow inappropriate coming from a guy Bosch knew grew up in Beverly Hills, the county's first bastion of white isolationism and privilege.

"Yes, I'm on the case," Bosch said.

"Tell me, is the guy hooked up with a lawyer yet[11]?" Haller asked. Bosch hesitated before answering.

"You don't want to go there[12]," he said.

1. idée
2. preuves matérielles
3. Salut, frangin
4. lui était tellement sortie de la tête
5. Machinchose
6. je ne l'ai pas contactée non plus
7. [marque d'eau de Javel]
8. surnom
9. le temps où c'était
10. privilégiée par les Blancs fuyant
11. le type a-t-il déjà un avocat
12. Ce n'est pas une bonne idée

"Hey, I'll go anywhere," Haller said. "Have case, will travel. But you're right, this probate stuff[1] may keep me occupied for a while."

"They file probate on Vance yet?"

"Nope. Waiting."

"Well, I should be back on that sometime tomorrow. When I find the granddaughter I'll let you know."

"Bring her in[2], Harry. I'd like to meet her."

Bosch didn't answer. His attention was drawn to his screen, where he had just received an e-mail from Valdez approving his case summary and charging affidavit[3]. He now had to finish the evidence report and the search warrant and he would be good to go[4].

1. histoire d'homologation de testament

2. Amène-la-moi

3. ses motifs de mise en examen

4. pourrait y aller

36

On Wednesday morning Bosch was at the District Attorney's Office as soon as the doors opened. Because it was a high profile case[1] he had arranged to come in for an appointment[2] to file charges against Dockweiler. Rather than going to an intake prosecutor who would file the case and then pass it on, never to see it again[3], the Dockweiler prosecution was assigned from the start to a veteran trial attorney[4] named Dante Corvalis. Bosch had never worked with Corvalis previously but knew of him by reputation—his nickname in the courthouse was "The Undefeated[5]" because he had never lost a case.

The process of filing[6] went smoothly, with Corvalis only rejecting Bosch's request for charges relating to the property crimes Dockweiler had committed. The prosecutor explained that it would already be a complicated case with the testimony of multiple victims and DNA analysis to explain to the jury. There was no need to spend prep[7] time or court time on Dockweiler's theft of tools, concrete[8], and a manhole cover[9] from the Department of Public Works. That, simply, was small-time stuff[10] that might create jury backlash[11].

"It's the effect of TV," Corvalis said. "Every trial you see on the box[12] lasts an hour. Juries on real cases get impatient. So you can't overprosecute a case[13]. And the bottom line is[14], we don't need it. We've got enough here to put him away forever[15].

1. affaire très médiatisée,

2. pris rendez-vous

3. Au lieu d'atterrir chez un procureur qui se bornerait à l'enregistrer pour ensuite ne plus jamais mettre le nez dedans

4. procureur d'assises chevronné

5. L'Invincible

6. enregistrement des motifs de mise en examen

7. [preparation]

8. vol d'outils, de béton

9. d'une plaque d'égout

10. des vétilles

11. faire mal réagir le jury

12. à la télé

13. multiplier les chefs d'accusation

14. surtout

15. pour lui en faire prendre pour perpète

And we will. So let's forget about the manhole cover—except for when you testify about finding Bella. It will be a nice detail to draw out in your testimony."

Bosch couldn't argue the point[1]. He was happy just to have one of the office's major players on the case from the start[2]. Bosch and Corvalis agreed to set a schedule of meeting[3] every Tuesday to discuss preparations for the case.

Bosch was out of the Foltz Building by ten[4]. Rather than go to his car, he walked down Temple and then crossed over the 101 freeway at Main Street. He walked through Paseo de la Plaza Park and then down Olvera Street through the Mexican bazaar, assuring himself that he could not be followed by car.

At the end of the long passage through the souvenir stalls[5] he turned and looked back to see if he had a tail on foot[6]. Satisfied[7] after several minutes that he was alone, he continued anti-surveillance measures by crossing Alameda and entering Union Station. He passed through the giant waiting room and then took a circuitous path to the roof[8], where he pulled a TAP card[9] out of his wallet and got on the Metro's Gold Line.

He studied every person on the train as it left Union Station and headed into Little Tokyo. At the first stop, he exited the train but then paused next to the sliding door. He checked every other commuter[10] who got off, and none seemed suspicious. He stepped back onto the train to see if any of them did the same, waited until the bell warned that the doors were closing[11], and jumped off at the last moment.

No one followed.

He walked two blocks down Alameda and then cut in toward the river. The address he had for Vi-

1. y trouver à redire

2. des pointures du parquet soient dans la procédure dès le début

3. convinrent de se voir

4. à dix heures

5. étals

6. s'il était filé par quelqu'un à pied

7. S'étant assuré

8. alla tout en haut par des voies détournées

9. sortit sa carte de transports en commun [Transit Access Pass]

10. un passager sur deux

11. prévienne de la fermeture des portes

biana Veracruz put her studio on Hewitt near Traction in the heart of the Arts District. Circling back to Hewitt, he repeatedly stopped and checked his surroundings[1]. Along the way he passed several old commercial structures that were restored or in the process of being restored for use as loft homes[2].

The Arts District was more than a neighborhood[3]. It was a movement. Beginning almost forty years earlier, artists of all disciplines started to take over[4] millions of square feet of empty space in the abandoned factories and fruit-shipping warehouses[5] that had thrived[6] in the area before World War II. Paying pennies per foot[7] for massive live-work spaces, some of the city's most notable artists thrived here. It seemed appropriate that the movement was anchored in an area where in the early 1900s artists had vied[8] to design the colorful images that graced the crates and boxes[9] of fruit shipped across the country, popularizing a recognizable California style that said life was good on the West Coast. It was one of the small things that helped inspire the wave of westward movement[10] that now made California the most populous state in the union[11].

The Arts District now faced many of the issues[12] that came with success, namely the swift spread of gentrification[13]. In the past decade the area started drawing big developers interested in big profits. The cost of a square foot of space was no longer measured in pennies but in dollars. Many of the new tenants[14] were upscale professionals[15] who worked in downtown[16] or Hollywood and wouldn't know the difference between a stippling and a stencil brush[17]. Many of the restaurants went upscale[18] and had celebrity chefs and valet parking[19] that cost more than a whole

1. autour de lui
2. en lofts
3. quartier
4. investir
5. entrepôts de fruits
6. prospéré
7. trois sous
8. rivalisé
9. ornaient les cageots et les caisses
10. avaient contribué à la vague vers l'ouest
11. USA
12. devait aujourd'hui affronter bon nombre des problèmes
13. notamment la rapide inclusion dans la zone chic
14. locataires
15. des cadres supérieurs
16. le centre-ville
17. brosse à lisser ou à pocher
18. avaient monté en gamme
19. des services de voituriers

meal in the old corner cafés where artists once congregated[1]. The idea of the district being a haven[2] for the starving artist[3] was becoming more and more unfounded.

As a young patrol officer in the early '70s Bosch had been assigned to Newton Division, which included what was then called the Warehouse[4] District. He remembered the area as a barren wasteland[5] of empty buildings, homeless encampments, and street crime. He had transferred[6] to Hollywood Division before the arts renaissance had begun. Now as he walked through, he marveled at the[7] changes. There was a difference between a mural and a piece of graffiti. Both were arguably works[8] of art, but the murals in the Arts District were beautiful and showed care[9] and vision similar to those he had seen a few days earlier down in Chicano Park.

He passed by The American, a building more than a hundred years old that originally served as a hotel for black entertainers[10] during segregation and later was ground zero for[11] both the arts movement and the burgeoning punk rock scene in the 1970s.

Vibiana Veracruz lived and worked across the street in a building that had once been a cardboard plant[12]. It was where many of the waxed[13] fruit boxes with labels[14] that served as California's calling cards[15] were produced. It was four stories tall[16] with brick cladding[17] and steel-framed[18] warehouse windows still intact. There was a brass[19] plaque next to the entrance that stated[20] its history and the year of its construction: 1908.

There was no security or lock on the entrance. Bosch entered a small tiled lobby[21] and checked a board that listed artists and their loft numbers. Bosch found the name Veracruz next to 4-D. He

1. se retrouvaient jadis
2. refuge
3. les artistes sans le sou
4. des entrepôts
5. comme d'un vaste terrain vague
6. été muté
7. s'émerveillait des
8. peuvent être considérés comme des œuvres
9. dénotaient une attention
10. comédiens
11. le berceau
12. usine de carton
13. paraffinés
14. leurs étiquettes
15. cartes de visite
16. avait trois étages [USA]
17. un parement de brique
18. à cadre métallique
19. en cuivre
20. retraçait
21. entrée carrelée

also saw on a community bulletin board[1] several notices about tenant and neighborhood meetings regarding issues[2] like rent stabilization and protesting[3] building-permit applications[4] at city hall. There were sign-up lists[5] and he saw the name Vib scrawled[6] on all of these. There was also a flyer for a showing[7] of a documentary film called *Young Turks* on Friday evening in loft 4-D. The flyer said the film was about the founding of the Arts District in the 1970s. "See this place before the greed[8]!" the flyer trumpeted. It appeared to Bosch that Vibiana Veracruz had inherited some of the community activism that had charged[9] her mother's life.

With his legs still feeling the pain of his run up the slope two nights before, Bosch didn't want to walk up three flights of stairs[10]. He found a freight elevator[11] with a pull-down door and rode[12] to the fourth floor at a turtle's pace[13]. The elevator was the size of his living room and he felt self-conscious[14] about riding up alone and wasting what must have been an enormous amount of energy to move the platform. It was obviously a design element left over[15] from the building's early incarnation as a cardboard factory.

The top floor was quartered[16] into four live-work lofts accessible off an industrial gray lobby. The lower half of the door to 4-D was plastered with cartoon stickers[17] obviously placed haphazardly[18] by a small person—Vibiana's son, Harry assumed. Above this was a card with posted[19] hours when Vibiana Veracruz would receive patrons[20] and viewers of her art. On Wednesdays those hours were from 11 a.m. to 2 p.m. and that put Bosch fifteen minutes early. He considered just knocking on the door, since he was not there

1. panneau d'information de la résidence
2. concernant des questions
3. les manifestations contre
4. les demandes de permis de construire
5. des pétitions
6. griffonné
7. la projection
8. l'appât du gain
9. empli
10. étages
11. monte-charge
12. monta
13. vitesse d'escargot
14. un peu coupable
15. datant
16. divisé
17. couverte d'autocollants de héros de dessins animés
18. n'importe comment
19. affichant les
20. les acheteurs

with the purpose of seeing her art. But he was also hopeful that he could somehow take a measure of the woman[1] before he decided how to tell her she might be heir to a fortune with more zeroes attached to it than she could imagine.

While he was deciding what to do he heard someone coming up the stairs next to the elevator shaft[2]. A woman soon appeared, carrying a frozen coffee drink in one hand and a key in the other. She wore overalls[3] and had a breathing mask down around her neck. She looked surprised to see a man waiting at her door.

"Hi," she said.

"Hi," Bosch said.

"Can I help you?"

"Uh, are you Vibiana Veracruz?"

He knew it was her. There was a clear resemblance to Gabriela in the Coronado Beach photos. But he pointed at the door to 4-D as if he had to back up[4] his presence with the posted hours[5].

"I am," she said.

"Well, I'm early," he said. "I didn't know your hours. I was hoping to look at some of your work."

"That's okay. You're close enough[6]. I can show you around[7]. What's your name?"

"Harry Bosch."

She looked like she recognized the name and Bosch wondered if her mother had found a way to contact her after promising she wouldn't attempt to.

"That's a famous artist's name," she said. "Hieronymus Bosch[8]."

Bosch suddenly realized his mistake.

"I know," he said. "Fifteenth century. It's actually[9] my full name."

She used a key to unlock her door. She looked back at him over her shoulder.

1. évaluer la jeune femme
2. cage d'ascenseur
3. une salopette
4. expliquer
5. par les heures affichées
6. C'est presque l'heure
7. vous faire visiter l'atelier
8. Jérôme Bosch [peintre mort en 1516]
9. en réalité

"You're kidding[1], right?"

"No."

"You had some strange parents."

She opened the door.

"Come on in," she said. "I only have a few pieces here at the moment. There's a gallery over on Violet[2] that has a couple more and then there are a couple out[3] at Bergamot Station. How did you hear about me?"

Bosch hadn't prepared a story, but he knew Bergamot Station was a conglomeration of galleries housed in an old rail station in Santa Monica. He had never been there but quickly adopted it as a cover.

"Uh, I saw your pieces at Bergamot," he said. "I had some business downtown this morning and thought I would see what else you have."

"Cool," Veracruz said. "Well, I'm Vib."

She reached out a hand and they shook. Her hand was rough and callused[4].

The loft was quiet as they entered and Bosch assumed[5] her son was in school. There was a sharp smell of chemicals that reminded Bosch of the fingerprint lab, where they used cyanoacrylate to fume objects and raise prints[6].

She gestured to her right and behind Bosch. He turned and saw that the front space of the loft was used as her studio[7] and gallery. Her sculptures were large and Bosch could see how the freight elevator and the twenty-foot ceilings[8] here gave her freedom to go big[9]. Three finished pieces sat on wheeled pallets so they could easily be moved. Movie night[10] on Friday would probably be in this space after the sculptures were moved out of the way.

1. Vous plaisantez

2. rue Violet

3. une ou deux qui sont

4. calleuse

5. présuma que

6. faire apparaître des empreintes

7. atelier

8. grande hauteur sous plafond

9. faire du grand format

10. La soirée projection

1. établis

2. de la mousse de caoutchouc

3. les arêtes du nez et des sourcils

4. eut l'impression d'avoir gaffé

5. va avec

There was also a work area with two benches[1] and racks of tools. A large block of what looked like foam rubber[2] was on a pallet and it appeared that an image of a man was emerging from a sculpting process.

The finished pieces were multi-figure dioramas made of pure white acrylic. All were variations on the nuclear family: mother, father, and daughter. The interaction of the three was different in each sculpture but in each the daughter was looking away from her parents and had no clearly defined face. There were nose and brow ridges[3] but no eyes or mouth.

One of the dioramas showed the father as a soldier with several equipment packs but no weapon. His eyes were closed. Bosch could see a resemblance to the photos he had seen of Dominick Santanello.

Bosch pointed to the diorama with the father as soldier figure.

"What is this one about?" he asked.

"What is it about?" Veracruz repeated. "It's about war and the destruction of families. But I don't really think my work needs explanation. You absorb it and you feel something or you don't. Art shouldn't be explained."

Bosch just nodded. He felt he had blundered[4] with his question.

"You probably notice that this one is the companion piece to[5] the two you saw at Bergamot," Veracruz said.

Bosch nodded again but in a more vigorous manner as if to communicate that he knew what she was talking about. Her saying so, however, made him want to go to Bergamot and see the other two.

He kept his eyes on the sculptures and walked further[1] into the room to see them from different angles. Bosch could tell[2] that it was the same girl in all three pieces, but her ages were different.

"What are the ages of the girl?" he asked.

"Eleven, thirteen, and fifteen," Veracruz said. "Very observant[3]."

He guessed that the incomplete face on each had to do with abandonment, not knowing one's origin, being one of the faceless and nameless. He knew what that was like.

"Very beautiful," he said.

He meant it sincerely.

"Thank you," she said.

"I didn't know my father," he said.

It startled him when it came out[4]. It wasn't part of his cover. The power of the sculptures made him say it.

"I'm sorry," she said.

"I only met him one time," he said. "I was twenty-one and I had just come back from Vietnam."

He gestured toward the war sculpture;

"I tracked him down[5]," he said. "Knocked on his door. I was glad I did it. He died soon after."

"I supposedly met my father one time when I was a baby. I don't remember it. He died soon after, too. He was lost in the same war."

"I'm sorry."

"Don't be. I'm happy. I have a child and I have my art. If I can keep this place from falling into greedy[6] hands, then all will be perfect."

"You mean the building? It's for sale[7]?"

"It's sold, pending[8] the city's approval to change it into residential. The buyer wants to cut every loft into two, get rid of the[9] artists, and, get this[10], call it the River Arts Residences."

1. avança
2. voyait bien
3. Bien observé
4. Il fut surpris de se l'entendre dire
5. J'avais fini par le retrouver
6. avides
7. à vendre
8. et dans l'attente
9. se débarrasser des
10. tenez-vous bien

Bosch thought for a long moment before responding. She had given him the opening.

"What if I told you there was a way to do that?" he asked. "Keep things perfect."

When she didn't answer, he turned and looked at her. Then she did speak.

"Who are you?" she asked.

37

Vibiana Veracruz was stunned to silence[1] when Bosch told her who he was and what he was doing. He showed her his credentials[2] as a state-licensed private investigator. He didn't mention Whitney Vance by name but told her that he had tracked her through her father's lineage and believed she and her son were the only two heirs by blood to an industrial fortune. It was she who brought up[3] Vance, having seen media stories in the past few days about the passing[4] of the billionaire industrialist.

"Is that who we're talking about here?" she asked. "Whitney Vance?"

"What I want to do is confirm the link genetically[5] before we get into names," Bosch said. "If you are open to it I would take a sample of your DNA[6] through a saliva swab[7] and turn it in[8] to the lab. It should only take a few days, and if we get confirmation, you would have the opportunity[9] to use the attorney I have working with me on this or to seek your own representation[10]. That would be your choice."

She shook her head as if still not comprehending and sat down on a stool she had pulled away from one of the workbenches.

"It's just so hard to believe this," she said.

Bosch remembered a television show from when he was a kid in which a man traveled the country and gave checks for one million dollars

1. resta coite, sidérée,
2. papiers
3. mentionna
4. décès
5. avoir une confirmation génétique de la filiation
6. j'aimerais vous faire un prélèvement d'ADN
7. en prenant un peu de salive sur Coton-Tige
8. le confier
9. possibilité
10. de vous en chercher un

from an unknown benefactor to unsuspecting recipients[1]. He realized he felt like that man. Only[2] Bosch was handing out billions[3], not millions.

"It is Vance, isn't it?" Vibiana said. "You haven't denied it."

Bosch looked at her for a long moment.

"Does it make a difference who it is?" he asked.

She stood up and came toward him. She gestured at the sculpture with the soldier.

"I read about him this week," she said. "He helped build the helicopters. His company was part of the war machine that killed his own son. My father, who I never got to know. How could I take that money?"

Bosch nodded.

"I guess it would depend on what you did with it," he said. "My lawyer called it change-the-world money."

She looked at him but he could tell she was seeing something else. Maybe an idea that was planted by his words[4].

"All right," she said. "Swab me[5]."

"Okay, but you have to understand something," Bosch said. "There will be people with power involved in the corporations that currently[6] hold this fortune. They will not be happy to part with it[7] and may go to great lengths[8] to stop it. Not only will your life be changed by the money, but you and your son will have to take measures to protect yourselves until the case runs its course[9]. You will not be able to trust anyone[10]."

His words clearly gave her pause[11], as he wanted them to.

"Gilberto," she said, thinking out loud[12]. Then her eyes flashed toward Bosch. "Do they know you're here?"

1. à des bénéficiaires qui ne s'y attendaient pas
2. Sauf que
3. proposait des milliards
4. que ses mots avaient fait germer dans son esprit
5. Faites le prélèvement
6. actuellement
7. s'en séparer
8. sont prêts à aller très loin
9. aboutisse
10. faire confiance à quiconque
11. la firent réfléchir
12. tout haut

"I've taken precautions," he said. "And I'll give you a card. If you see anything unusual or feel any kind of threat, you can call me at any time."

"It's so surreal," she said. "When I was coming up the steps today with my coffee, I was thinking about how I didn't have enough money for resin. I haven't sold any of my art in seven weeks and I have an arts grant[1] but it just covers living for me and my son. So I'm sculpting my next piece but can't get the material I need to wrap it and finish it[2]. And then you were just standing there. And you had this crazy story about money and inheritance."

Bosch nodded.

"So should we do the swab now?" he asked.

"Yes," she said. "What do I do?"

"You just have to open your mouth."

"I can do that."

Bosch took a tube out of his inside coat pocket and unscrewed the cap[3]. He removed the swab stick[4] and stepped closer to[5] Vibiana. Holding the stick with two fingers he wiped the swab end up and down the inside of her cheek, turning it to get a good sample. He then sealed the stick back in its tube.

"You usually do two—just in case," he said. "Do you mind?"

"Go ahead[6]," she said.

Bosch repeated the process. It seemed so intrusive[7] to him, his hand so close to her mouth. But Vibiana seemed unfazed by it[8]. He put the second swab back in its tube and sealed it.

"I took a swab from your mother on Monday," he said. "It will be part of the analysis. They will want to identify her chromosomes and separate them from your father's and grandfather's."

"You went down to San Diego?" she asked.

1. touche une subvention
2. dont j'ai besoin pour les finitions
3. dévissa le bouchon
4. Coton-Tige
5. s'approcha de
6. Allez-y
7. importun
8. ne semblait pas s'en offusquer

"Yes. I went by Chicano Park and then over to her apartment. Is that where you grew up?"

"Yes. She's still in the same place."

"I showed her a photo. It was of you on that day you met your father. He's not in it[1] because he was the one who took it."

"I'd like to see that."

"I don't have it with me but I'll get it to you."

"So she knows about this. The inheritance. What did she say?"

"She doesn't know the details. But she told me where to find you and said it was your choice."

Vibiana didn't respond. She seemed to be thinking about her mother.

"I'm going to go now," Bosch said. "I'll be in touch[2] as soon as I know something."

He handed her one of the cheap business cards he'd had printed with his name and number, then turned toward the door.

Bosch made his way back to his car, which he had left parked in a lot[3] near the courthouse before his appointment at the D.A.'s Office. As he walked he repeatedly checked his perimeter for surveillance. He saw nothing and soon he was back to the rented Cherokee. He opened the rear hatch[4] of the SUV and flipped up the rug liner[5] in the back. He lifted the lid[6] of the spare tire and tools compartment[7] and removed the padded envelope he had put there that morning.

Closing up the back, he got in behind the wheel[8] and opened the padded envelope. It contained the swab tube provided by Whitney Vance and marked *W-V.* It also contained two tubes collected from Gabriela Lida marked *G-L.* With a Sharpie marker[9] he wrote *V-V* on the side of the two tubes containing the swabs he had just collected[10] from Vibiana.

1. sur la photo
2. Je vous recontacte
3. sur un parking
4. coffre
5. souleva le tapis
6. couvercle
7. compartiment du pneu de rechange et de ses outils
8. s'assit au volant
9. marqueur,
10. les échantillons qu'il venait de recueillir

He put the extra tubes from Vibiana and her mother into his coat pocket and repackaged the envelope so it contained one swab from each of the principals[1]. He put the envelope down on the seat next to him and called Mickey Haller.

"I have the granddaughter's sample," he said. "Where are you?"

"In the car," Haller said. "The Starbucks in Chinatown, parked under the dragons."

"I'll be there in five. I have hers, her mother's, and Vance's with me. You can take the package to the lab."

"Perfect. They opened probate today in Pasadena. So I want to get this going. Need confirmation before we make a move."

"On my way."

The Starbucks was at[2] Broadway and Cesar Chavez. It took Bosch less than five minutes to shoot over[3] and then spot[4] the Lincoln at a red curb[5] under the twin-dragon gateway to Chinatown. Bosch parked behind Haller's car, put on the flashers[6], and got out. He walked up and got in through the door behind the driver. Haller was in the opposite seat with his laptop computer[7] open on a fold-down desk[8]. Bosch knew he was stealing Wi-Fi from the Starbucks.

"There he is," the lawyer said. "Boyd, why don't you go in and get us a couple lattes[9]. You want anything, Harry?"

"I'm good[10]," Bosch said.

Haller handed a twenty-dollar bill over the seat and the driver got out of the car without a word and closed the door. Bosch and Haller were alone now. Bosch handed the package across the seat to him.

"Guard it with your life[11]," Bosch said.

1. protagonistes
2. à l'angle des avenues
3. s'y rendre
4. repérer
5. en stationnement interdit
6. ses warnings
7. ordinateur portable
8. tablette rabattable
9. deux cafés au lait
10. Non, ça va
11. précieusement

"Oh, I will," Haller said. "I'm going to take it in[1] straight from here[2]. Going with[3] CellRight if that's okay with you. They are close[4], reliable[5], and AABB accredited[6]."

"If you're okay with them, I'm okay with them. How will this work now?"

"I get this in today, and we will probably hear yea or nay[7] by Friday. Comparing grandparent to grandchild, we're talking[8] about a twenty-five percent passage of chromosomes. That's a lot for them to work with."

"What about the stuff from Dominick?"

"We wait on that. Let's see what the swabs get us first."

"Okay. And have you looked at the probate filing yet?"

"Not yet, but I'll get it by the end of the day. I did hear that they're saying the decedent[9] had no blood heirs."

"So what do we do?"

"Well, we wait for confirmation from CellRight, and if we get that, then we put our package together[10] and seek an injunction[11]."

"Which does what?"

"We ask the court to stop the distribution of the estate[12]. We say, 'Hold on[13] a minute, we have a valid heir and a holographic will[14] and the means of proving authenticity.' Then we brace ourselves for the onslaught[15]."

Bosch nodded.

"They'll come after us," Haller said. "You, me, the heir, everybody. Make no mistake, we're all fair game[16]. They'll try to make us out as[17] charlatans. You can count on that."

"I warned Vibiana," Bosch said. "But I don't think she understood how relentless[18] they might be."

1. la déposer
2. directement
3. Je vais la confier à
4. proches
5. fiables
6. accrédités auprès de l'Association [américaine] des banques du sang
7. on aura probablement un oui ou un non
8. ça signifie
9. défunt
10. on boucle notre dossier
11. on demande un arrêté du juge
12. la répartition de l'héritage
13. Attendez
14. testament
15. on se tient prêts à parer les déferlements
16. des proies idéales
17. nous faire passer pour des
18. déterminés

"Let's see how the DNA comes back[1]. If it's what we think and she's the heir, then we'll circle the wagons[2] and get her ready. We'll probably have to move her and hide her."

"She's got a kid."

"The kid too, then."

"She needs a big space for her work."

"Her work might need to be put on hold[3]."

"Okay."

Bosch didn't think that would go over well[4].

"I told her what you said about it being change-the-world money," he said. "I think that's what pulled her in[5]."

"Does every time[6]."

Haller bent down to look through the windows and see if his driver was waiting to get back behind the wheel. There was no sign of him.

"I heard in the CCB[7] that you filed on the dungeon master," Haller said.

"Don't call him that," Bosch said. "Makes it sound like a joke, and I know the woman he had down there in that place. She's going to be dealing with the aftermath[8] for a long time."

"Sorry, I'm just a callous defense attorney[9]. Did he lawyer up[10] yet?"

"I don't know. But I told you, you don't want that case[11]. Guy's[12] a soulless[13] psychopath. You don't want to get near that."

"True."

"This guy, he should get the death penalty, you ask me[14]. But he didn't kill anyone—that we know about yet[15]."

Out his window Bosch saw the driver standing in front of the coffee shop. He was holding two coffee cups and waiting to be called back to the Lincoln. He appeared to Bosch to be looking

1. Attendons le retour sur l'ADN

2. on resserre les rangs

3. devra peut-être attendre

4. qu'elle apprécierait

5. ce qui l'a convaincue

6. Ça marche à tous les coups

7. au tribunal [Criminal Court Building]

8. en subir les conséquences

9. avocat sans cœur

10. s'est trouvé un avocat

11. ne devrais pas prendre cette affaire

12. Ce type est

13. acharné

14. si tu veux mon avis

15. à notre connaissance pour l'instant

across the street at something. He then made a slight nod.

"Did he just ..."

Bosch turned and peered out[1] the back window of the Lincoln to try to see what the driver was looking at.

"What?" Haller said.

"Your driver," Bosch said. "How long have you had him?"

"Who, Boyd? About two months now."

"He one of your reformation projects[2]?"

Bosch now leaned forward to look past Haller and out his window. Haller had a history of taking on his clients as drivers[3] in order to help them pay off their legal fees[4]—to him.

"I've helped him through a couple of scrapes[5]," Haller said. "What's going on?"

"Did you mention CellRight in his presence?" Bosch asked in response. "Does he know where you're taking the samples?"

Bosch had put two and two together[6]. He had forgotten that morning to check his house and the street out front for cameras, but he remembered Creighton mentioning Haller during the confrontation in the lobby of the police station. If they knew about Haller, then they might also have him under surveillance. There could be a plan to intercept the DNA samples either before they reached CellRight or once they had been turned in.

"Uh, no, I haven't told him where we're going," Haller said. "I haven't spoken about it in the car. What's going on?"

"You are probably under surveillance," Bosch said. "And he might be in on it[7]. I just saw him nod to somebody."

"Fucking A[8]. Then his ass is grass[9]. I'll—"

1. regarda par

2. Il fait partie de tes tentatives de réinsertion

3. l'habitude de prendre ses clients comme chauffeurs

4. frais judiciaires

5. à sortir d'un ou deux mauvais pas

6. fait la relation

7. est peut-être dans le coup

8. Nom de Dieu

9. c'est un homme mort

"Hold on a second. Let's think about this. Do you—"

"Wait."

Haller put his hand up to stop Bosch from speaking. He then moved his laptop and folded up the desk. He got up and leaned over the seat toward the steering wheel. Bosch heard the air compression thump[1] of the car's trunk opening[2].

Haller got out of the car and went to the trunk. Soon Bosch heard it slammed shut[3] and Haller got back into the car with a briefcase[4]. He opened the case and then opened a secret compartment inside it. There was an electronic device[5] secreted in the space[6] and he turned on a switch, then put the case down on the seat between them.

"It's an RF jammer[7]," he said. "I take this baby[8] in with me to every client meeting I have in the jail—you never know who's listening. If anybody's listening to us now, they're getting an earful[9] of white noise."

Bosch was impressed.

"I just bought one of those," he said. "But it wasn't in a fancy[10] briefcase."

"Took it as a partial fee[11] payment from a former client. A cartel courier[12]. He wasn't going to need it where he was going. So what's your plan?"

"Do you know of another place to take the swabs?"

Haller nodded.

"California Coding up in[13] Burbank," he said. "It was down to them or[14] CellRight and CellRight agreed to the push[15]."

"Give me back the package," Bosch said. "I'll take the tubes to CellRight. You take a phony[16] package to California Coding. Make them think[17] that's where we're doing the analysis."

1. bruit sourd
2. du coffre qui s'ouvrait
3. qui se refermait
4. attaché-case
5. appareil électronique
6. caché dedans
7. brouilleur radio
8. truc
9. ils se prennent une bonne dose
10. sophistiqué
11. de mes honoraires
12. passeur de drogue
13. à
14. Le choix était soit eux, soit
15. était d'accord pour le faire en priorité
16. bidon
17. On leur fait croire

Bosch took the extra tubes containing swabs from Vibiana and Gabriela out of his coat pocket. He didn't have an extra[1] from Whitney Vance, so, to sell the misdirection[2] in case the tubes fell into the wrong hands, he used the Sharpie to change the initials marked on the tubes. He turned[3] *V-V* into[4] *W-V* and *G-L* to the randomly chosen[5] *G-E*. He then signaled for[6] the padded envelope. He removed the tubes containing swabs from Vance, Lida, and Veracruz and put them into his coat pocket. He then put the two altered[7] tubes into the envelope and handed it back.

"You take that to California Coding and ask for a blind[8] comparison," he said. "Don't let on to[9] your driver or anybody else you think you're being followed. I'll go to CellRight."

"Got it[10]. I still want to kick his ass[11]. Look at him over there."

Bosch checked the driver again. He was no longer looking across the street. "There will be time for that later. And I'll help."

Haller was writing something on a legal pad[12]. He finished, tore the page off the pad, and handed it to Bosch.

"That's CellRight and my contact there," Haller said. "He's expecting the package."

Bosch recognized the address. CellRight was out near Cal State L.A.[13], where the LAPD lab was located[14]. He could get there in ten minutes but would take thirty to make sure he wasn't followed.

He opened his door and turned to look back at Haller.

"Keep that cartel briefcase close[15]," he said.

"Don't worry," Haller said. "I will."

Bosch nodded.

"After I drop this I'm going up to see Ida Townes Forsythe," he said.

1. d'échantillon supplémentaire
2. pour faire passer l'erreur d'acheminement
3. changea
4. en
5. choisi au hasard
6. fit signe à Haller de lui passer
7. modifiés
8. à l'aveugle
9. Ne montre pas à
10. Compris
11. J'ai quand même envie de le virer
12. bloc-notes
13. près du campus de l'université de Californie
14. situé
15. près de toi

"Good," Haller said. "We want her on our side."

Bosch got out just as Boyd came around to the driver's door. Bosch said nothing to him. He went back to his own car and sat behind the wheel and watched the intersection[1] as Haller's Lincoln pulled onto[2] Cesar Chavez and headed west. There was a lot of traffic moving through the intersection, but Bosch saw no vehicle that he thought was suspicious or that might be tailing the Lincoln.

1. carrefour
2. prenait

38

1. dépôt des prélèvements
2. se passa
3. avoir remis en mains propres
4. bifurqua
5. à suivre des chemins détournés
6. se prendre un gros sandwich
7. l'emballage
8. sonna
9. La nouvelle s'était vite ébruitée
10. petit groupe
11. composé
12. policières d'origine latino-américaine
13. des liens étroits
14. que je la renseignais sur ton compte
15. a dégusté
16. c'est une dure à cuire

The drop-off[1] at CellRight went down[2] without incident after Bosch took anti-surveillance measures that included driving completely around Dodger Stadium in Chavez Ravine. After hand delivering[3] the three tubes to Haller's contact, Bosch made his way over to the 5 freeway and headed north. Along the way he diverted[4] at the Magnolia exit in Burbank to continue his circuitous driving patterns[5] and to grab a submarine sandwich[6] at Giamela's. He ate in the car and kept his eyes on the comings and goings in the parking lot.

He was putting the empty sandwich wrap[7] back in the bag when his phone chirped[8] and he took a call from Lucia Soto, his former partner at LAPD.

"How is Bella Lourdes?" she asked.

Word had spread fast[9] for a name not released publicly.

"You know Bella?" he asked.

"A little. From *Las Hermanas*."

Bosch remembered that Soto was part of an informal group[10] made up[11] of Latina police detectives[12] from all of the departments in the county. There weren't many, so the group forged some tight bonds[13].

"She never told me she knew you," he said.

"She didn't want you to know she was checking you out with me[14]," Soto said.

"Well, she went through a lot[15]. But she's tough[16]. I think she'll be okay."

"I hope so. It's an awful story."

She waited a beat[1] for him to start telling her the details but Bosch kept quiet. She finally got the picture[2].

"I heard you filed on the guy[3] today," she said. "I hope you've got him dead to rights[4]."

"He's not going anywhere," Bosch said.

"Good to hear. So, Harry, when are we going to have lunch and catch up[5]? I miss you."

"Damn[6], I just ate. But we'll do it soon—next time I'm downtown. I miss you too."

"I'll see you[7], Harry."

Bosch pulled out of the lot and followed a roundabout[8] route west toward South Pasadena. He drove by Ida Townes Forsythe's home on Arroyo Drive four times over a spread[9] of thirty minutes, each time noting the cars parked on the street and anything else that might indicate that Whitney Vance's longtime secretary and assistant was being watched. He saw no indicators of surveillance and after a couple passes[10] in the alley behind the house he decided it was safe to knock on the door.

He parked on a side street and walked around to Arroyo and up to the house. Forsythe's home was much nicer in person[11] than on his viewing on Google street view. It was a classic California Craftsman[12] that had been meticulously cared for[13]. He stepped up[14] onto a wide, long front porch and knocked on a coffered[15] wood door. He had no idea whether Forsythe was home or still had duties to perform inside the Vance home. If that was the case, he was prepared to wait until she returned.

But he didn't have to knock a second time. The woman he had come to see swung the door open

1. quelques secondes
2. finit par capter
3. que tu avais fait mettre le type en examen
4. que tu as pu le coincer
5. se donner des nouvelles
6. Mince
7. À bientôt
8. prit un rond-point pour suivre une
9. en l'espace
10. être passé deux fois
11. en vrai
12. une maison californienne typique du début du XXe siècle
13. entretenue
14. monta
15. à panneaux

and looked at him with eyes that did not register any[1] familiarity. "Mrs. Forsythe?"

"It's Ms.[2]"

"I'm sorry, Ms. Forsythe. Do you remember me? Harry Bosch? I came to see Mr. Vance last week?"

The recognition was there now.

"Of course. Why are you here?"

"Uh, well, first I wanted to express my sympathies[3]. I know you and Mr. Vance worked together a long time."

"Yes, we did. It's been quite a shock. I know he was old and ill, but you don't expect a man of such power and presence to suddenly be gone. What can I do for you, Mr. Bosch? I guess whatever it is Mr. Vance had you investigating[4] doesn't really matter anymore."

Bosch decided that the best move would be the head-on[5] approach.

"I'm here because I want to talk to you about the package Mr. Vance had you mail to me[6] last week."

The woman in the doorway stood frozen for almost ten seconds before answering. She looked fearful.

"You know that I am being watched, right?" she said.

"No, I don't know that," Bosch said. "Before knocking I looked and didn't see anyone. But if that's the case you should invite me in. I parked around the corner. Right now, standing out front is the only giveaway[7] that I'm here."

Forsythe frowned[8] but then stepped back and opened the door wider.

"Come in," she said.

"Thank you," Bosch said.

1. n'exprimaient aucune
2. [titre permettant d'ignorer si elle est mariée ou non]
3. vous présenter mes condoléances
4. suppose que ce sur quoi Mr Vance vous avait demandé d'enquêter
5. directe
6. vous a fait m'envoyer par la poste
7. seul signe
8. fronça les sourcils

The entry room was broad and deep. She led Bosch down the length of it and then into a rear sitting room off the kitchen where there were no windows facing the street. She pointed to a chair.

"What is it you want, Mr. Bosch?"

Bosch sat down, hoping it would persuade her to do the same but she remained standing. He did not want this to be an adversarial conversation[1].

"Well, first, I need to confirm what I said at the door," he said. "You did send that package to me, didn't you?"

Her arms were folded now.

"I did," she said. "Because Mr. Vance asked me to."

"Did you know what was in it?" Bosch asked.

"I didn't at the time. I do now."

This immediately concerned[2] Bosch. Had the corporate minders[3] asked her about it?

"How do you know now?" he asked.

"Because after Mr. Vance passed[4] and his body was taken I was told to secure[5] his office," she said. "In doing so I noticed that his gold pen was missing. That was when I remembered the heavy object in that package he asked to be sent to you."

Bosch nodded with relief[6]. She knew about the pen. But if she didn't know about the will, then perhaps no one else did yet. That would give Haller an edge[7] when he made his move with it.

"What did Mr. Vance tell you when he gave you the package for me?"

"He told me to put it in my purse[8] and to take it home with me. He said he wanted me to take it to the post office and mail it the next morning before coming to work. I did as I was told."

1. confrontation

2. inquiéta

3. les boss de l'entreprise

4. le décès de M. Vance

5. on m'a demandé de sécuriser

6. soulagement

7. avantage

8. sac à main

"Did he ask you about it?"

"Yes, first thing when I came in that morning. I told him I had just been to the post office and he was pleased."

"If I showed you the envelope that was addressed and sent to me, do you think you could identify it?"

"Probably. It had his handwriting on it. I would recognize that."

"And if I write all of this as you have recounted it into an affidavit[1], would you be willing to sign it in front of a notary?"

1. déclaration sous serment

"Why would I do that? To prove that was his pen? If you're going to sell it, I would like the opportunity to buy it from you. I would pay above market price."

"It's not that. I'm not selling the pen. There was a document in the package that may become contested and I may need to prove, as well as I can, how it came into my possession. The pen, which was a family heirloom[2], will be helpful in that process but a signed affidavit from you would also be."

2. héritage

"I don't want to get mixed up with the board of directors, if that's what you're talking about. Those people are animals. They'll sell their own mothers for a piece of all that money."

"You wouldn't be pulled in any deeper[3] than you are already going to be, Ms. Forsythe."

3. Cela ne vous impliquera pas plus

She finally moved to one of the other chairs in the room and sat down.

"What do you mean by that?" she said. "I have nothing to do with all of that."

"The document in the package was a handwritten will," Bosch said. "It names you as a beneficiary[4]."

4. Vous êtes parmi les bénéficiaires

He studied her reaction. She seemed puzzled.

"Are you saying I get money or something?" she asked.

"Ten million dollars," Bosch said.

Bosch saw her eyes flare[1] for a moment at the realization that she was in line for some of the riches[2]. She brought her right arm up and held a fist against her chest[3]. Her chin came down but Bosch could still see her lips tremble as tears came. Bosch wasn't sure how to read it[4].

It was a long moment before she looked up at him and spoke.

"I didn't expect anything," she said. "I was an employee. I wasn't family."

"Have you been going to the house this week?" he asked.

"No, not since Monday. The day after. That was when I was informed that my services were no longer needed."

"And you were there Sunday when Mr. Vance died?"

"He called me and asked me to come in. He said he had some letters he wanted to write. He told me to come in after lunch and I did. I was the one who found him in his office when I got there."

"You were allowed to go back there unescorted?"

"Yes, I've always had that privilege."

"Did you call for an ambulance?"

"No, because he was clearly dead."

"Was he at his desk?"

"Yes, he died at his desk. He was slumped forward and to the side a little bit[5]. It looked like he went fast."

"So you called security."

"I called Mr. Sloan and he came in and called someone on staff who had medical training.

1. briller
2. allait recevoir sa part du gâteau
3. tint une main serrée contre sa poitrine
4. l'interpréter
5. tassé vers l'avant et de travers

They tried CPR[1] but it didn't work. He was dead. Mr. Sloan then called the police."

"Do you know how long Mr. Sloan worked for Vance?"

"A long time. At least twenty-five years, I would say. He and I were there the longest."

She dabbed at[2] her eyes with a tissue[3] that seemed to Bosch to have materialized out of nowhere[4].

"When I met with Mr. Vance he gave me a phone number and told me it was a cell phone," Bosch said. "He said to call him if I made any headway with[5] my investigation. Do you know what happened to that phone?"

She shook her head immediately.

"I don't know anything about it," she said.

"I called a few times and left messages," Bosch said. "And Mr. Sloan called me on it as well. Did you see him take anything from the desk or the office after Mr. Vance was dead?"

"No, he told me to secure the office after they removed the body. And I didn't see a cell phone."

Bosch nodded.

"Do you know what Mr. Vance hired me to do?" he asked. "Did he discuss it with you?"

"No, he didn't," she said. "Nobody knew. Everybody in the house was curious but he didn't tell anybody what you were doing."

"He hired me to find out if he had an heir. Do you know if he had anyone watching me[6]?"

"Why would he do that?"

"I'm not sure, but the will he wrote and had you send to me clearly assumes that I had found a living heir. But we never talked again after that day I visited him at the mansion."

1. de faire une réanimation cardio-pulmonaire
2. tamponna
3. mouchoir en papier
4. être sorti de nulle part
5. progressais dans
6. me faisait surveiller

Forsythe squinted her[1] eyes as though she had trouble tracking[2] the story.

"Well, I don't know," she said. "You said you called that number he gave you and left messages. What did you tell him?"

Bosch didn't answer her. He remembered now that he had left a carefully worded[3] message that could be ascribed[4] to the cover story of finding James Aldridge. But it could also have been taken as a message that Bosch had found an heir.

He decided to end the conversation with Forsythe.

"Ms. Forsythe," he said. "You should look into hiring[5] an attorney who will represent you in this. It's probably going to get nasty[6] when the will gets filed with the probate court[7]. You need to protect yourself. I'm working with an attorney named Michael Haller. Have whoever you hire[8] contact him."

"I don't know any lawyers I could call," she said.

"Ask your friends for a recommendation. Or your banker. Bankers probably deal with probate lawyers all the time."

"Okay, I will."

"And you never answered about the affidavit. I'll write it up today and bring it back tomorrow for you to sign. Will that be okay?"

"Yes, of course."

Bosch stood up.

"Have you actually seen someone watching you or the house?"

"I have seen cars out there that don't belong[9]. But I can't be sure."

"Do you want me to go out the back?"

"That might be best."

1. plissa les
2. du mal à suivre
3. formulé
4. attribué
5. devriez chercher
6. Ça risque de faire du vilain
7. aura été homologué au tribunal successoral
8. Demandez à celui que vous engagerez de
9. qui ne sont pas d'ici

"No problem. Let me give you my number. Call me if you have any difficulties or if anybody starts asking you questions."

"Okay."

Bosch handed her a business card and she led him to the back door.

39

From South Pasadena it was an easy drive up to the Foothill Freeway and then west toward San Fernando. Along the way Bosch called Haller to tell him he had completed[1] both the CellRight drop-off[2] and the interview with Ida Townes Forsythe.

"I just left[3] California Coding," Haller said. "They'll get back to us[4] next week with the results."

Bosch realized he was still in the car with Boyd driving and was playing to him[5], selling the decoy drop-off[6] DNA samples.

"You see any sign of surveillance?" Bosch asked.

"Not yet," Haller said. "Tell me about the interview."

Bosch recounted[7] the conversation with Forsythe and said he would write up a summary for her to sign the next day.

"You have a notary you like to use?" he asked.

"Yes, I can set you up[8], or I can witness it myself," Haller said.

Bosch said he would be in touch and disconnected. He got to the SFPD station shortly before 4 p.m. He expected the detective bureau to be deserted this late in the day[9] but he saw the light was on in the captain's office and the door was closed. He leaned his head to the doorjamb[10] to hear if Trevino was on the phone but heard nothing. He knocked on the door, waited, and Trevino suddenly opened it.

"Harry. What's up[11]?"

1. effectué
2. dépôt au labo
3. viens de quitter
4. nous recontactent
5. jouait la comédie
6. pour lui faire croire à leur ruse du dépôt des
7. relata
8. te mettre en contact avec lui
9. à une heure aussi avancée de la journée
10. montant
11. Qu'est-ce qui vous amène

"Just wanted to let you know I filed[1] on Dockweiler today. One twenty to one sixty years[2] in total if he goes down on all charges[3]."

"That's excellent news. What did they think about our case?"

"Said we're solid. The deputy gave me a list of things he wants me to put together[4] before the prelim[5] and I thought I'd get started[6]."

"Good. Good. So it was already assigned[7]?"

"Yes, Dante Corvalis was in it from the start. He's one of the best. He's never lost a case."

"Fantastic. Well, carry on. I'll be heading home in a few."

"How's Bella? You go to the hospital today?"

"I didn't go by today but I heard she's doing okay. They said they were going to try to send her home tomorrow and she's happy about that."

"It will be good for her to be with Taryn and their kid."

"Yeah."

They were both still standing at the door to Trevino's office. Bosch sensed that the captain had more to say but an awkward silence grew between them.

"Well, I've got some stuff to write up," Bosch said.

He turned toward his desk.

"Uh, Harry?" Trevino said. "You got a minute to come in?"

"Sure," Bosch said.

The captain stepped back into his office and moved behind his desk. He told Bosch to sit down and Harry took the one seat available[8].

"This about me using[9] the DMV computer on my private case?" he asked.

1. vous dire que j'avais présenté nos motifs de mise en examen
2. Entre 120 et 160 ans [de prison]
3. s'il en prend pour l'ensemble
4. que je réunisse
5. l'audience préliminaire
6. pensais m'y mettre
7. on a déjà désigné un procureur
8. seul siège disponible
9. C'est à propos du fait que j'ai utilisé

"Oh, no," Trevino said. "Far from it. That's water under the bridge[1]."

He gestured to the paperwork on his desk.

"I'm working on the deployment schedule[2] here," he said. "I do the whole department. In patrol we're fine but in detectives we're not. We are obviously down one[3] with Bella out[4] and there's no telling at this point[5] when or if she's coming back."

Bosch nodded.

"Until that unknown is known, we need to keep her position open[6]," Trevino said. "So I talked to the chief about this today and he's going to go to the city council with a temporary funding request[7]. We'd like to bring you on full-time[8]. What do you think?"

Bosch thought a moment before answering. He wasn't expecting the offer, especially coming from Trevino, who had never been sold on Bosch in the first place[9].

"You mean I wouldn't be a reserve? I'd get paid?"

"Yes, sir. Standard level-three[10] salary. I know you made more with L.A. but it's what we pay."

"And I'd handle all the CAPs[11] cases?"

"Well, for the most part I think you'd be doing prep on[12] Dockweiler, and we don't want to forget about cold cases[13]. But, yes, when things come up you'd handle crimes against persons. You'd work with Sisto on those, when you need to go into the field."

Bosch nodded. It was good to be wanted but he wasn't sure he was ready to commit to a full schedule[14] in San Fernando. He assumed the Vance case and his role as executor of his will would take up a lot of time in the near future, especially with a possible probate battle brewing[15].

Trevino took his silence for something else.

1. de l'histoire ancienne
2. calendrier de répartition
3. Il nous manque évidemment quelqu'un
4. en maladie
5. il n'est pas encore possible de savoir
6. son poste
7. faire une demande de financement provisoire auprès de la mairie
8. vous faire passer à plein temps
9. emballé par Bosch
10. normal d'inspecteur expérimenté
11. crimes contre les personnes
12. préparerez le dossier
13. les affaires non résolues
14. à s'engager pour un poste à temps plein
15. à venir

"Look," he said. "I know you and Sisto had that flare-up[1] in the Public Works office, but I think that was just a heat-of-the-moment sort of thing[2]. By the time you two were finding and rescuing Bella, it seemed like you were working together well. Am I wrong?"

"Sisto's all right," Bosch said. "He wants to be a good detective and that's half the battle right there. What about you? Was wanting to fire me that night a heat-of-the-moment sort of thing, too?"

Trevino raised his hand in a show of surrender[3].

"Harry, you know I've had trouble with this arrangement from the start," he said. "But I'll say it: I was wrong. Look at this case—the Screen Cutter. We got him all because of your work and I appreciate that. You and I are fine, as far as I'm concerned. And just so you know[4], this wasn't the chief's idea. I went to him and said I wanted to bring you on full-time."

"I appreciate that. So it would mean no more private work, right?"

"We can talk to the chief if you think you need to keep the private ticket going[5]. What do you say?"

"Well, what about the Sheriff's investigation of the shooting? Don't we need to wait until we get an official decision on that and it goes to the D.A.[6]?"

"Come on. We know it was a good shooting[7]. We may get dinged[8] on tactics but as far as the shoot or don't shoot question, nobody's going to bat a fucking eye[9]. On top of that, everyone understands that Bella's being out puts us in a personnel squeeze[10] and it's the chief's call[11]."

Bosch nodded. He had a feeling that he could keep asking questions and Trevino would say yes to anything.

1. altercation
2. dérapage dans le feu de l'action
3. geste de capitulation
4. pour votre information
5. vos missions dans le privé
6. procureur [District Attorney]
7. tir justifié
8. On peut se faire allumer
9. broncher
10. effectifs réduits
11. au chef de décider

"Cap, can I take the night to think about it and get back to you[1] tomorrow?"

"Sure, Harry, no problem. Just let me know."

"Roger that[2]."

Bosch left the captain's office, closing the door behind him, and moved into his cubicle. His real reason for coming to the station was to use the printer once he had written up the Forsythe affidavit. But he didn't want to start that document with the possibility that Trevino would come out of his office and see what he was doing. So he passed the time until Trevino left by going over the to-do list he had written[3] during the morning's meeting with Dante Corvalis.

Among other requests, the prosecutor wanted updated[4] and signed statements[5] from all of Dockweiler's known victims. He added specific questions he needed answered[6] in the statements. These would be entered into the record at the preliminary hearing[7] of the case against Dockweiler and would allow the victims to avoid having to testify. All that was required in a preliminary hearing was for the prosecutor to present a prima facie case[8] that supported the charges[9]. Proving guilt beyond a reasonable doubt[10] was a measure held for trial[11]. The burden[12] of delivering the case[13] at preliminary hearing would rest primarily on[14] Bosch, as he would testify about the investigation that led to Dockweiler. Corvalis said he wanted to avoid unless absolutely necessary having to put victims of rape on the witness stand[15] to publicly relive the horror of what happened to them. He only wanted that to happen once, and that was when it counted. At trial[16].

Bosch was halfway through creating a template[17] of questions to submit to the victims when

1. vous donner une réponse
2. Entendu
3. en relisant la liste de tâches qu'il avait écrite
4. actualisées
5. déclarations
6. auxquelles il voulait des réponses
7. versées au procès-verbal de l'audience préliminaire
8. des éléments préliminaires
9. étayant les accusations
10. Établir la conviction de la culpabilité
11. était un point qui attendait le moment du procès
12. charge
13. exposer l'affaire
14. reviendrait d'abord à
15. à la barre des témoins
16. Pendant le procès
17. avait commencé à élaborer un modèle

Trevino left and locked his office after snapping the light off.

"Okay, Harry, I'm out of here[1]."

"Have a good night and get some rest."

"You in[2] tomorrow?"

"Not sure yet. I'll either be here or I'll call you with my answer."

"Great."

Bosch watched over the cubicle wall as Trevino went to the attendance board and signed himself out. The captain didn't say a thing about Bosch having not signed it when he came in.

Soon the captain was gone and Bosch was alone in the bureau. He saved his work on the witness template and opened a new blank[3] document. He then typed out an affidavit beginning with the words "I, Ida Townes Forsythe …"

It took him less than an hour to complete a scant[4] two pages of basic facts, because he knew from years of dealing with witnesses, affidavits, and lawyers that the fewer facts he put into the document, the fewer angles of assault there would be[5] for attorneys from the opposition.

He printed two copies for Forsythe to sign, one to file with the court[6] and one to keep in a file containing copies of all the important case documents.

While he was at the printing station[7], he saw a sign-up sheet[8] on the unit bulletin board for sponsors of a bowl-a-thon[9] designed to raise funds for a fellow officer on injury leave[10]. The officer was referred to as 11-David, which Bosch knew was the radio call sign[11] used by Bella Lourdes. The flyer explained that while she would be receiving full pay while on leave[12], she was expected to incur[13] a variety of extra[14] expenses not covered by workmen's comp[15] and[16] the department's recently

1. je pars
2. Vous serez là
3. vierge
4. à peine
5. moins il y aurait d'angles d'attaque
6. à déposer au greffe du tribunal
7. imprimante
8. formulaire d'inscription
9. opération « bowling »
10. collègue en arrêt maladie pour accident du travail
11. signature radio
12. pendant son arrêt
13. encourir
14. supplémentaires
15. les indemnités pour accident du travail
16. ni par

trimmed-back medical plan[1]. Bosch guessed that those expenses most likely related to psychotherapy sessions no longer covered by department-provided insurance. Beginning Friday evening, the bowl-a-thon would go for as long as possible and the suggested sponsorship was for one dollar a game[2]—an estimated[3] four dollars an hour.

Bosch saw that Sisto was listed on one of the teams. He took a pen out of his pocket and signed his name below Trevino's name on the sponsorship list. The captain had put himself down for five dollars a game and Bosch matched that[4].

Once he returned to his desk Bosch called Haller. As usual, the lawyer was in the back of his Lincoln, being driven somewhere in the city.

"I have the affidavit ready and can go back any time you hook me up with[5] a notary," he said.

"Good," Haller said. "I'd like to meet Ida, so maybe we all go. What's your ten o'clock look like tomorrow[6]?"

Bosch realized he had failed[7] to ask Forsythe for a phone number. He had no way of contacting her to set up the appointment[8]. He doubted she was listed[9], considering her job had been working for one of the most reclusive men in the world.

"It works for me," he said. "We should meet at her house. I'll get there early and make sure she's home. You bring the notary."

"Deal," Haller said. "E-mail me the address."

"Will do. And one other thing. The original docs from the package I received? Do you need them tomorrow or when we go into court?"

"No, keep them wherever you have them, as long as they're safe."

"They are."

1. ni par les garanties de mutuelle de la police récemment revues à la baisse

2. la partie

3. ce qui revenait à peu près à

4. fit de même

5. dès que tu m'auras trouvé

6. Ça te va, 10 heures, demain matin

7. n'avait pas pensé

8. fixer le rendez-vous

9. qu'elle soit dans l'annuaire

"Good. We don't produce[1] originals until a court orders us to."

"Got it."

They ended the call. His business finished, Bosch collected[2] the copies of the Forsythe affidavit from the printer tray and left the station. He headed toward the airport over in Burbank, deciding it might be best to make one more change of transportation as he headed into what appeared to be some critical final steps[3] of the Vance case.

He pulled into the Hertz return lane[4], gathered his belongings[5], including the GPS jammer[6], and left the Cherokee there. He decided to change things up a little further by going to the Avis counter in the terminal to rent a replacement[7]. While he waited in line to rent, he thought about Forsythe and her accounting[8] of what had transpired in the days following his visit with Whitney Vance. She had a unique view and knowledge of the goings-on[9] inside the mansion on San Rafael. He decided he would prepare more questions for the intended meeting the next day.

It was dark by the time he got to Woodrow Wilson Drive. As he rounded the last curve he saw a car parked at the curb in front of his house and his headlights illuminated two figures[10] sitting inside it, waiting. Bosch drove by while he tried to figure out who it might be and why they would park directly in front of his house, giving their position away[11]. He quickly came to a conclusion and spoke it out loud[12].

"Cops."

He guessed they were Sheriff's detectives with follow-up[13] questions concerning the Dockweiler shooting. He turned around at the intersection at Mulholland Drive, drove back down to his house,

1. On ne présentera pas
2. récupéra
3. alors qu'il abordait ce qui semblait être le stade ultime et décisif
4. s'engagea dans le parking des retours Hertz
5. rassembla ses affaires
6. brouilleur
7. autre voiture
8. récit
9. était la mieux placée pour savoir ce qu'il se passait
10. silhouettes
11. trahissant leur position
12. le dit à voix haute
13. complémentaires

and pulled his rented Ford Taurus into his carport[1] without hesitation. After locking the car he walked out toward the street to check the mailbox—and to get a look at the sedan's license plate[2]. The two men were already getting out of the car.

Bosch checked the mailbox and found it empty. "Harry Bosch?"

Bosch turned to the street. He didn't recognize either of the men as part of the Sheriff's OIS team[3] that had worked the Dockweiler scene the other night.

"That's right. What's up, fellas[4]?"

In unison the men produced gold badges[5] that caught the reflection from the street lamp above them. They were both white, mid-forties, and wearing obvious cop suits, meaning off the rack at a two-for-one store[6].

Bosch noticed that one of them carried a black binder[7] under his arm. It was a little thing[8], but Bosch knew the standard-issue[9] binders used by the Sheriff's Department were green. LAPD used blue.

"Pasadena Police Department," one of them said. "I'm Detective Poydras and he's Detective Franks."

"Pasadena?" Bosch said.

"Yes, sir," Poydras said. "We are working a homicide case and would like to ask you a few questions."

"Inside, if you don't mind," Franks added.

Homicide. The surprises kept coming. A vision of Ida Townes Forsythe's fearful look when she said she was being watched crossed Bosch's mind. He stopped moving and looked at his two visitors.

"Who was murdered?" he asked.

"Whitney Vance," Poydras said.

1. sous son auvent

2. plaque d'immatriculation de la berline

3. faisant partie de la police des polices du comté [en cas de fusillade]

4. les gars

5. sortirent des insignes dorés

6. c'est-à-dire du prêt-à-porter au rabais

7. classeur

8. détail

9. réglementaires

40

1. fit asseoir
2. semblaient avoir
3. pouvoir
4. mâle dominant
5. pariait que
6. bicolore
7. front
8. bronzée
9. avait la quarantaine
10. correspondait bien aux
11. violon
12. partie
13. les pistonner pour jouer sur le parcours convoité

Bosch sat[1] the two Pasadena detectives down at the dining-room table and took the chair across from them. He didn't offer them water, coffee, or anything else. Franks had been carrying the binder. He placed it to the side of the table.

While the two detectives looked to be about[2] the same age, it remained to be seen who had the juice[3]—which one had seniority in the partnership, which one was the alpha dog[4].

Bosch was betting[5] it was Poydras. He was the one who spoke first and had been behind the wheel of the car. Franks may have been carrying the binder but those first two facts were clear signs that he was playing second to Poydras. Another was Franks's two-tone[6] face. His forehead[7] was as white as a vampire's but there was a clear line of demarcation where the lower half of his face was a ruddy tan[8]. It told Bosch that it was likely he frequently played either softball or golf. Since Franks was in his forties[9] Bosch guessed it was golf. It was a popular pastime among homicide detectives because it fit with the[10] obsessive qualities needed for the job. But sometimes, Bosch had noticed, golf became a greater obsession than the homicide work. You ended up with guys with two-tone faces playing second string[11] to an alpha dog because they were always thinking about the next round[12], and who could get them onto the next course[13].

Years ago, Bosch had had a partner named Jerry Edgar. He turned Bosch into a golf widow[1] because of his obsession with the game. Once they were working a case and had to go to Chicago to find and arrest a murder suspect. When Bosch got to LAX[2] for the flight, he saw Edgar checking[3] his golf clubs at the luggage counter. Edgar said he was planning to stay an extra day[4] in Chicago because he knew a guy who could get him onto[5] Medinah. Bosch assumed that was a golf course. The next two days, while looking for their murder suspect, they drove around with a set of golf clubs in the trunk of their rental[6].

Sitting across the table from the two men from Pasadena, Bosch decided it was Poydras who was the dog. He kept his eyes on him.

Bosch started with a question before they could.

"How was Vance killed?" he asked.

Poydras put an uneasy[7] smile on his face.

"We're not going to do it that way," he said. "We're here to ask you questions. Not the other way around[8]."

Franks held up a notebook he had taken from his pocket as if to show he was there to write information down.

"But that's the thing, isn't it?" Bosch replied. "If you want answers from me, then I want answers from you. We trade."

Bosch waved a hand back and forth between them[9] to signal equal and free trade.

"Uh, no, we don't trade," Franks said. "One call to Sacramento and we lift[10] your PI[11] license for unprofessional conduct. That's what we do. How would that be?"

Bosch reached down to his belt and pulled his San Fernando badge off it. He tossed it down[12] on the table in front of Franks.

1. Bosch s'était senti comme l'épouse délaissée d'un golfeur
2. l'aéroport [de Los Angeles]
3. qui enregistrait
4. jour de plus
5. le faire jouer à
6. voiture de location
7. gêné
8. l'inverse
9. alla de l'un à l'autre d'un geste de la main
10. on vous confisque
11. d'enquêteur privé [Private Investigator]
12. le jeta

"It would be okay," he said. "I've got another job."

Franks leaned forward and looked down at the badge, then smirked[1].

"You're a reserve officer," he said. "You take that and a dollar to Starbucks and they might give you a cup of coffee."

"I was just offered full-time today," Bosch said. "I'll be getting the new badge tomorrow. Not that what it says on a badge matters[2]."

"I'm real happy for you," Franks said.

"Go ahead and call Sacramento," Bosch said. "See what you can get done."

"Look, how about we stop the pissing match[3] right here?" Poydras said. "We know all about you, Bosch. We know about your LAPD history, we know about what happened in Santa Clarita the other night. And we also know you spent an hour with Whitney Vance last week, and we're here to find out what that was about. The man was old and he was terminal[4] but somebody sent him to Valhalla[5] a little early and we're going to figure out who and why."

Bosch paused and looked at Poydras. He had just confirmed that he had the juice in the partnership. He called the shots[6].

"Am I a suspect?" Bosch asked.

Franks leaned back in frustration and shook his head.

"There he goes with the questions again[7]," he said.

"You know the drill[8], Bosch," Poydras said. "Everybody's a suspect until they're not."

"I could call my lawyer right now and that would be the end of this," Bosch said.

"Yeah, you could," Poydras said. "If you wanted. If you had something to hide."

1. eut un petit sourire narquois
2. soit bien important
3. la guéguerre
4. en phase terminale
5. ad patres
6. C'est lui qui menait la danse
7. Et voilà qu'il recommence avec ses questions
8. comment ça marche

He then stared at Bosch and waited. Bosch knew Poydras was counting on his loyalty to the mission. He had spent years doing what these two were doing and he knew what they faced[1].

"I signed a confidentiality agreement with Vance," Bosch said.

"Vance is dead," Franks said. "He doesn't care[2]."

Bosch purposely[3] looked at Poydras when he next spoke.

"He hired me," Bosch said. "He paid me ten grand[4] to find someone for him."

"Who?" Franks asked.

"You know I can keep that confidential," Bosch said. "Even with Vance dead."

"And we can throw your ass in jail[5] for withholding information[6] in a homicide investigation," Franks said. "You know you'll beat it[7], but how long will that take? A day or two in the clink[8]? That what you want?"

Bosch looked from Franks to Poydras.

"I'll tell you what[9]," he said. "I only want to talk to you, Poydras. Tell your partner to go sit in the car. You do that and I'll talk to you, answer any question. I've got nothing to hide."

"I'm not going anywhere," Franks said.

"Then you're not getting what you came here to get," Bosch said.

"Danny," Poydras said.

His head tilted[10] toward the door.

"You're shitting me[11]," Franks said.

"Just go have a smoke," Poydras said. "Cool off[12]."

Franks got up with a huff[13]. He made a show of flipping closed his notebook[14], then grabbed the binder.

"You better leave that," Bosch said. "In case I can point out[15] things at the crime scene."

1. ce à quoi ils étaient confrontés
2. s'en fiche
3. exprès
4. mille dollars
5. vous foutre en taule
6. rétention d'informations
7. finirez par vous en tirer
8. au bloc
9. Écoutez
10. Il fit un signe de tête
11. te fous de moi
12. Déstresse
13. d'un air vexé
14. referma son carnet d'un air théâtral
15. montrer

Franks looked at Poydras, who gave a slight nod. Franks dropped the binder on the table like it was radioactive. He then left through the front door and made sure to slam it[1] behind him.

Bosch turned his head from the door to Poydras.

"If that was all a good-cop-bad-cop act[2], you guys are the best I've ever seen," Bosch said.

"I wish[3]," Poydras said. "But no act. He's just a hothead[4]."

"With a six handicap[5], right?"

"Eighteen, actually. Which is one reason he's pissed off all the time[6]. But let's stay on subject now that it's just us two talking here. Who did Vance hire you to look for?"

Bosch paused. He knew he was on the proverbial slippery slope[7]. Anything he told the police could get out into the world[8] before he wanted it to. But Vance's murder changed the landscape of things[9] and he decided it was time to give in order to get[10]—with limitations on the give[11].

"He wanted to know if he had an heir," he finally said. "He told me he got a girl pregnant at USC back in 1950. Under family pressure he more or less abandoned her. He felt guilty all his life about it and now wanted to know if she had the baby and whether he had an heir. He told me it was time to balance the books[12]. If it turned out that he was a father, then he said he wanted to set things right[13] before he died."

"And did you find an heir?"

"This is where we trade. You ask a question, I ask a question."

He waited and Poydras did the smart thing[14].

"Ask your question."

"What was the cause of death?"

"It doesn't leave this room."

"Fine with me[15]."

1. la claqua bien fort
2. le numéro du gentil et du méchant flic
3. Si seulement c'était le cas
4. soupe au lait
5. handicap de 6 [au golf]
6. pour lesquelles il est tout le temps furax
7. fameuse pente savonneuse
8. s'ébruiter
9. la donne
10. de donner pour mieux recevoir
11. mais en donnant avec parcimonie
12. dresser le bilan
13. remettre les choses d'aplomb
14. coopéra
15. Ça me va

"We think he was smothered[1] with a pillow off his office couch. He was found slumped at his desk and it looked like a natural[2]. Old man collapses at his desk. Seen it a hundred times before. Only Kapoor at the Coroner's Office takes the opportunity to grandstand[3] for the media and says there will be an autopsy. He does the cut[4] himself and finds petechial hemorrhaging[5]. Very slight, nothing on the face. Just conjunctival petechiae[6]."

Poydras pointed to the corner of his left eye to illustrate. Bosch had seen it in many cases. Cutting off oxygen[7] explodes the capillaries. The level of the struggle and the health of the victim were variables that helped define the extent of the hemorrhaging.

"How'd you keep Kapoor from holding a press conference?" Bosch asked. "He needs every bit of positive spin he can get[8]. Discovering a murder written off as a natural[9] is a nice story for him. Makes him look good."

"We made a deal[10]," Poydras said. "He keeps it quiet and lets us work and we cut him in on[11] the press conference when we break it open[12]. We make him look like the hero."

Bosch nodded approvingly. He would have done the same thing.

"So the case gets kicked over[13] to me and Franks," Poydras said. "Believe it or not, we're the A team. We go back out to the house. We don't say anything about it being a homicide. Just that we're quality control, doing a follow-up investigation, crossing all the *t*'s and dotting the *i*'s[14]. We take a few pictures and make a few measurements to make it look good, and we check the pillows on the couch and find what looks like dried saliva on a pillow. We sample it, get a DNA match to Vance,

1. étouffé
2. mort naturelle
3. en profite pour jouer le grand jeu
4. pratique la dissection
5. une hémorragie pétéchiale [des points rouges dans le derme]
6. au niveau de la conjonctive des yeux
7. Le manque d'oxygène
8. de tout ce qui peut lui faire de la pub
9. mort naturelle de prime abord
10. a passé un marché
11. on le fait participer à
12. rendra ça public
13. nous est confiée
14. qu'on fignole

and now we have the means of murder. Somebody took the pillow, came around behind him in his chair at the desk, and held it over his face."

"An old guy like that, not much of a struggle," Bosch said.

"Which explains the lack of obvious hemorrhaging. Poor guy went out like a kitten[1]."

Bosch almost smiled at Poydras calling Vance poor.

"Still," he said. "It doesn't feel like something planned in advance, does it?"

Poydras didn't answer.

"It's my turn," he said instead. "Did you find an heir?"

"I did," Bosch said. "The girl at USC had the baby—a boy—then gave him up for adoption. I traced the adoption and identified the kid. Only thing is, he went down in a helicopter in Vietnam a month before he turned twenty years old[2]."

"Shit. Did you tell Vance that?"

"Never got the chance[3]. Who had access to his office on Sunday?"

"Security people mostly, a chef and a butler type[4]. A nurse came in to give him a course of prescriptions[5]. We're checking them all out. He called his secretary in to write some letters for him. She's the one who found him when she got there. Who else knew what you were hired to do?"

Bosch understood what Poydras was thinking. Vance was looking for an heir. Somebody who stood to benefit[6] from his death if there was no apparent heir might have stepped in to hasten things along[7]. On the other hand, an heir might also be motivated to hasten the inheritance. Lucky[8] for Vibiana Veracruz, she was not identified as a likely inheritor until after Vance was dead. That was a pretty solid alibi in Bosch's book[9].

1. chaton
2. d'avoir 20 ans
3. l'occasion
4. genre de majordome
5. ses médicaments
6. espérait tirer profit
7. avait pu intervenir pour accélérer les choses
8. Heureusement
9. selon Bosch

"According to Vance, no one," Bosch said. "We met alone and he said no one was to know what I was doing. A day after I started the job, his security guy came to my house to try to see what I was up to. He acted as though he had been sent by Vance. I shined him on[1]."

"David Sloan?" Poydras asked.

"I never got the first name but, yeah, Sloan. He's with Trident."

"No, he's not with Trident. He was with Vance for years. When they brought in Trident he stayed on as the guy in charge of Vance's personal security and to liaison with Trident. He personally came to your house?"

"Yeah, knocked on the door, said Vance sent him to check on my progress. But Vance told me to talk to no one except the old man himself. So I didn't."

Bosch next showed Poydras the card with the phone number Vance had given him. He told the detective that he had called a couple times and left messages. And how Sloan had answered when Bosch called the number after Vance was dead. Poydras just nodded, taking the information in[2], and fitting it[3] with other case facts. He gave no indication if they had the secret phone and its call records[4]. Without asking if he could keep the card, Poydras put it in his shirt pocket.

Bosch too was fitting things Poydras had given up with the facts he knew. So far Bosch felt he had gotten more than he had given. And something bothered him about the new information when it was filtered through the sieve[5] of his existing case knowledge[6]. Something rubbed[7]. He could not quite place[8] what it was but it was there and it was worrisome.

1. l'ai envoyé paître

2. assimilant l'information

3. essayant de la faire coïncider

4. journal d'appels

5. l'eut passée au crible

6. ce qu'il savait de l'affaire

7. coinçait

8. déterminer

"You looking at the corporate side of this[1]?" he asked, just to keep the conversation going while he was grinding on the rub[2].

"I told you, we're looking at everybody," Poydras said. "Some people on the board[3] had been questioning Vance's competence and trying to oust him[4] for years. But he always managed to carry the votes[5]. So there was no love lost[6] with some of them. That group was led by a guy named Joshua Butler, who will probably become chairman now. It's always a question of who gains and who gains the most. We're talking to him."

Meaning they were looking at him as a possible suspect. Not that Butler would have done anything personally, but whether he was the kind of guy who could get it done[7].

"Wouldn't be the first time boardroom animosity leads to murder," Bosch said.

"Nope," Poydras said.

"What about the will? I heard they opened probate today."

Bosch hoped he had slid the question in casually[8], as a natural extension of the question regarding corporate motivation.

"They opened probate with a will filed with the corporate attorney[9] back in '92[10]," Poydras said. "It was the latest will on record[11]. Vance apparently had his first bout with[12] cancer then, so he had the corporate lawyer create a last will and testament to make the transition of power clear. Everything goes into the corporation. There was an amendment—I think *codicil* is the word—filed a year later that covers the possibility of an heir. But with no heir, it all goes to the corporation and is controlled by the board. That includes setting compensation[13] and bonus payouts[14]. There are

1. du côté de sa société
2. cherchait ce qui clochait
3. du conseil [d'administration]
4. le dégager
5. se faire réélire
6. Ce n'était donc pas le grand amour
7. le faire faire
8. amené la question le plus naturellement possible
9. signé devant le notaire de la boîte
10. en 1992
11. le plus récent connu
12. épisode de
13. les rémunérations
14. les versements de primes

now eighteen people remaining on the board and they're going to control about six billion bucks[1]. You know what that means, Bosch?"

"Eighteen suspects," Bosch said.

"Correct. And all eighteen of them are well heeled and insulated[2]. They can hide behind lawyers, behind walls, you name it[3]."

Bosch wanted to know exactly what the codicil regarding an heir said but thought that if he got more targeted[4] with his questioning, Poydras would start to suspect that his search for an heir didn't end in Vietnam. He thought Haller would at some point[5] be able to procure a copy of the 1992 will and get the same information.

"Was Ida Forsythe at San Rafael when you went there to visit Vance?" Poydras asked.

It was a turn in direction away from the idea of corporate murder. Bosch understood that a good interviewer never follows a straight line.

"Yes," he said. "She wasn't in the room when we talked but she led me back to the office."

"Interesting woman," Poydras said. "She'd been with him longer than Sloan."

Bosch just nodded.

"So have you talked to her since that day at San Rafael?" Poydras asked.

Bosch paused as he considered the question. Every good interviewer sets up a trapdoor[6]. He thought of Ida Forsythe saying she was being watched and about Poydras and Franks showing up on the day he visited her at her home.

"You know the answer to that," he said. "Either you or your people saw me at her house today."

Poydras nodded and hid a smile. Bosch had passed the trapdoor test.

"Yeah, we saw you," he said. "And we were wondering what that was about."

1. de dollars

2. armés et protégés

3. ce que vous voulez

4. se montrait trop précis

5. tôt ou tard

6. tend des pièges

1. gagner

2. C'est juste que je trouve que c'est

3. lui présenter

4. essayait de deviner

5. qu'elle en retire

6. dissimulait

7. d'en venir aux révélations

8. se sentait d'attaque

Bosch shrugged to buy[1] time. He knew that they might have knocked on Forsythe's door ten minutes after he left and that she could have told them what he had said about the will. But he guessed that if that were the case, Poydras would be coming at the interview from a different angle.

"It was just about me thinking she was[2] a nice old lady," he said. "She lost her longtime boss and I wanted to pay[3] my respects. I also wanted to know what she knew about what happened."

Poydras paused as he decided[4] whether Bosch was lying.

"You sure that's all it was?" he pressed. "When you were standing at the door she didn't look too happy to see you."

"Because she thought she was being watched," Bosch said. "And she was right."

"Like I said, everybody's a suspect until they're not. She found the victim. That puts her on the list. Even though the only thing she gets out of it[5] is being unemployed."

Bosch nodded. He knew at that moment that he was withholding[6] a big piece of information from Poydras—the will he had received in the mail. But things were coming together in Bosch's mind and he wanted time to think before giving up the big reveal[7]. He changed the subject.

"Did you read the letters?" Bosch said.

"What letters?" Poydras asked.

"You said Ida Forsythe was called in to write letters for Vance on Sunday."

"They never actually got written. She came in and found him dead at the desk. But apparently every Sunday afternoon, when Vance was feeling up to it[8], she came in and wrote letters for him."

"What kind of letters? Business? Personal?"

"I got the idea it was personal stuff. He was old-fashioned, liked to send letters instead of e-mails. Kind of nice actually. He had the stationery[1] out[2] on the desk, ready to go."

"So these were handwritten letters she was coming in to write for him?"

"I didn't ask specifically. But the stationery and his fancy pen[3] were there and ready to go[4]. I think that was the plan. Where are you going with this[5], Bosch?"

"You said a fancy pen?"

Poydras looked at him for a long moment.

"Yeah, you didn't see it? Solid gold pen in a holder[6] on his desk."

Bosch reached over[7] and tapped a finger on the black binder.

"You got a photo in there?" he asked.

"I might," Poydras said. "What's so special about the pen?"

"I want to see if it's the one he showed me. He told me it was made of gold that his great-grandfather prospected."

Poydras opened the binder and flipped through to a section of clear plastic sleeves[8] containing 8 × 10[9] color photos of the Vance death scene. He kept flipping[10] pages until he found a shot[11] he deemed appropriate[12] and then turned the book around to show Bosch. In the photo Whitney Vance's body was on the floor next to his desk and his wheelchair. His shirt was open, his ivory chest exposed, and it was clear the photo was taken after unsuccessful efforts had been made to revive him.

"Right here," Poydras said.

He tapped the top left side of the photo where the desk was in the background. On the desk was a sheaf[13] of pale yellow stationery that matched the[14]

1. papier à lettres
2. posé
3. beau stylo
4. à l'usage
5. Vous pensez à quoi
6. porte-stylos
7. tendit le bras
8. pochettes en plastique transparentes
9. d'env. 20 × 25 cm
10. à tourner
11. photo
12. qui lui parut convenir
13. bloc
14. semblable au

stationery Bosch had received in the package from Vance. And there was a gold pen in a holder that looked like the pen that had also been in the package.

Bosch leaned back and away from the binder. The pen being in the photo did not make sense because it had been sent to him before the photo was taken.

"What is it, Bosch?" Poydras asked.

Bosch tried to cover[1].

"Nothing," he said. "Just seeing the old guy dead like that … and the empty chair."

Poydras turned the binder to look at the photo himself.

"They had a house medical officer[2]," he said. "I use that term loosely[3]. On Sundays it was a security guard with EMT training[4]. He conducted CPR[5] but got no response."

Bosch nodded and tried to act composed[6].

"You said you went back after the autopsy and took more photos and measurements as cover," he said. "Where are those photos? You put them in the book?"

Bosch reached toward the murder book but Poydras pulled it back.

"Hold your horses[7]," he said. "They're in the back[8]. Everything's chronological."

He flipped further into the binder and came to a new set of photos of the office, at almost the same angle, but with no body of Whitney Vance on the floor. Bosch told Poydras to hold on[9] the second photo he turned to. It showed the full top of the desk. The pen holder was there but not the pen.

Bosch pointed it out.

"The pen's gone," he said.

1. se ressaisir
2. médecin à domicile
3. Au sens le plus large qui soit
4. formé au secourisme
5. a essayé de le réanimer
6. cacher son trouble
7. Minute !
8. à la fin
9. s'arrêter à

Poydras turned the binder so he could see it better. Then he flipped back to the first photo to make sure.

"You're right," he said.

"Where'd it go?" Bosch asked.

"Who knows? We didn't take it. We didn't seal[1] the office, either, after the body was removed. Maybe your pal[2] Ida knows what happened to the pen."

Bosch didn't say how close he thought Poydras was to the truth[3] with that suggestion. He reached over and pulled the binder across the table so he could look at the photo of the death scene again.

The appearance and disappearance of the pen was the anomaly, but it was the empty wheelchair that held Bosch's eyes[4] and told him what he had been missing all along[5].

1. scellé

2. copine

3. à quel point il pensait Poydras près de la vérité

4. retint l'attention de Bosch

5. ce qu'il n'avait pas vu depuis le début

41

The next morning Bosch was sitting in his car on Arroyo Drive by nine thirty. He had already called and talked at length[1] to Mickey Haller. He had already been to the evidence lockup[2] at the San Fernando Police Department. And he had already been to Starbucks, where he happened to notice that Beatriz Sahagun was back at work behind the brewer[3] as a barista.

He now sat and watched Ida Townes Forsythe's home and waited. He saw no activity at the house and no indication as to whether she was home. The garage was closed and the place was still[4], and Bosch wondered if she would be there when they knocked. He kept his eyes on the mirrors and saw no indications of police surveillance in the neighborhood either.

At nine forty-five Bosch saw Mickey Haller's Town Car enter his rearview mirror[5]. He was behind the wheel. He had told Bosch earlier that he had parted ways with[6] Boyd and no longer had a driver.

This time Haller got out of his car and came up to sit in Bosch's. He carried his own cup of coffee with him. "That was quick," Bosch said. "You just breezed into the courthouse[7] and they let you look at the probate file?"

"Actually, I breezed in[8] on the Internet," Haller said. "All case filings are updated online within twenty-four hours. The wonder[9] of technology.

1. longuement
2. casier où étaient enfermés les éléments de preuve
3. machine à café
4. silencieux
5. dans son rétroviseur
6. s'était séparé de
7. as débarqué au tribunal
8. ai plutôt débarqué
9. merveilles

Not sure my office needs to be in a car anymore. They've closed half the courthouses in L.A. County because of budget cutbacks[1], and most of the time the Internet gets me where I need to go."

"So, the codicil?"

"Your Pasadena Police friends were on the mark[2]. The will filed in '92 was amended[3] the following year. The amendment establishes standing for a[4] blood heir should one come forth[5] at the time of Vance's death."

"And no other will has surfaced?"

"Nothing."

"So Vibiana is covered."

"She's covered, but with an asterisk."

"Which is?"

"The amendment grants a blood heir standing as a recipient[6] of a share of the estate. It doesn't specify what or how much that share is. Obviously when he added this, he and his lawyer both thought that a blood heir was a long shot[7]. They added the codicil just in case."

"Sometimes long shots pay off[8]."

"If this is the will the court accepts, then we would declare Vibiana's standing[9] and that's when the fight begins. And it will be a hell of a[10] fight, because it's not clear what she's entitled to[11]. We're going to go in like gangbusters[12], say she gets it all[13], and then go from there[14]."

"Yeah, well, I called Vibiana this morning to tell her what was happening. She said she's still not sure she's up for this[15]."

"She'll change. It's like winning the lottery, man. Found money[16], more than she'll ever need."

"And I guess that's the point[17]. More than she'll ever need. You ever read those stories about people who win the lottery and how it ruins their lives? They can't adjust[18], they meet people

1. compressions budgétaires

2. avaient raison

3. modifié

4. impose de tenir compte d'un

5. au cas où il en apparaîtrait un

6. admet l'existence d'un héritier en tant que bénéficiaire

7. une éventualité hasardeuse

8. sont payantes

9. l'existence

10. sacrée

11. ce à quoi elle a droit n'est pas clair

12. On va y aller franco

13. prétendre qu'elle hérite de tout

14. on verra ce que ça donne

15. de vouloir tout ça

16. De l'argent tombé du ciel

17. Justement

18. n'arrivent pas à s'adapter

with their hands out[1] wherever they go. She's an artist. Artists are supposed to stay hungry."

"That's bullshit[2]. That's a myth invented to keep the artist down because art is powerful. You give an artist both money and power and they're[3] dangerous. Anyway, we're getting ahead of ourselves here[4]. Vibiana is the client and ultimately she makes the call[5]. Our job right now is to put her in the best position to make the call."

Bosch nodded.

"You're right," he said. "So you ready to proceed with the plan?"

"I'm ready," Haller said. "Let's do it."

Bosch pulled his phone and called the Pasadena Police. He asked for Detective Poydras and nearly a minute went by before he was connected.

"It's Bosch."

"I was just thinking about you."

"Yeah? Why's that?"

"Just thinking about how I know you're hiding something from me. You got more than you gave yesterday and that won't happen again."

"I don't expect it to. How's your morning looking[6]?"

"For you my morning's wide open. Why?"

"Meet me at Ida Forsythe's house in a half hour. You'll get the big give[7] then."

Bosch glanced over at Haller, who was spinning[8] a finger like he was rolling something forward[9]. He wanted more time.

"Make it[10] an hour, actually[11]," he said into the phone.

"An hour," Poydras said. "This isn't some kind of a game, is it?"

"No, no game. Just be there, and make sure you bring your partner."

1. qui viennent leur mendier des sous
2. des conneries
3. il devient
4. Mais n'anticipons pas
5. c'est à elle de décider
6. Qu'est-ce que vous avez prévu ce matin
7. Je lâcherai le morceau
8. faisait rouler quelque chose
9. faisait rouler quelque chose
10. Plutôt dans
11. en fait

Bosch ended the call. He looked at Haller and nodded. They could expect Poydras in an hour.

Haller grimaced.

"I really hate helping the cops," he said. "Goes against my religion."

He looked over and saw Bosch staring at him.

"Present company excluded[1]," he added.

"Look, if all goes well, you get a new client and a high-profile[2] case," Bosch said. "So let's go."

They got out of the Ford in unison, Bosch carrying a file containing the affidavit he had printed the day before, and crossed the street toward the Forsythe house. Bosch thought he saw a curtain move behind one of the front windows as they approached.

Ida Forsythe opened the front door before they had to knock.

"Gentlemen," she said. "I wasn't expecting you so soon today."

"Is this a bad time, Ms. Forsythe?" Bosch asked.

"No, not at all," she said. "Please come in."

This time she led the way to the front room. Bosch introduced Haller as the attorney representing a direct descendant and heir to Whitney Vance.

"Did you bring the affidavit?" Forsythe asked.

Bosch proffered[3] the file.

"Yes, ma'am," Haller said. "Why don't you take a few minutes to sit down and read it? Make sure you agree with the contents before you sign."

She took the file to the couch and sat down to read. Bosch and Haller took seats across a coffee table from her and watched. Bosch heard a buzz and Haller reached into his pocket for his phone. He read a text[4] and then handed the

1. Sauf celui en face de moi

2. médiatisée

3. lui tendit

4. SMS

phone to Bosch. The text was from someone named Lorna.

> Cal. Coding called. Needs new samples. Fire last night destroyed lab.

Bosch was stunned. He had no doubt that Haller had been followed to the lab and that the fire was an arson[1] designed to thwart[2] the effort to name[3] a DNA-matched[4] heir to the Vance fortune. He handed the phone back to Haller, who had a killer smile on his face, indicating he thought the same as Bosch.

1. incendie criminel
2. contrecarrer
3. pour établir
4. à l'ADN correspondant

"It looks correct to me," Forsythe said, drawing their attention back to her. "But I thought you said we would have to have a notary. I actually am a[5] notary but I can't witness[6] my own signature."

"It's fine," Haller said. "I'm an officer of the court[7] and Detective Bosch is a second witness."

5. suis moi-même
6. être témoin de
7. assermenté

"And I have a pen," Bosch said.

He reached into his inside coat pocket and pulled out the gold pen that had belonged to Whitney Vance. He watched Forsythe's face as she recognized the pen he handed her.

They were silent as she signed the document with a flourish[8], not realizing she was showing her familiarity with using the antique fountain pen[9]. She then capped it[10], put the document back in the file, and handed both back to Bosch.

8. élégant paraphe
9. vieux stylo plume
10. remit le bouchon du stylo

"It felt strange signing with his pen," she said.

"Really?" Bosch said. "I thought you'd be used to it."

"No, not at all," she said. "That was his special pen."

Bosch opened the file and checked the document and the signature page. An awkward[11]

11. gênant

silence ensued[1] with Haller just staring at Forsythe. She finally broke the sound barrier[2].

"When will you introduce the new will to the probate court?" she asked.

"You mean how soon will you get your ten million?" Haller asked back.

"That's not what I mean," she said, feigning offense. "I'm just curious about the process and when I might need a lawyer to represent my interests."

Haller looked at Bosch, deferring the answer[3].

"We won't be filing the will[4]," Bosch said. "And you could probably use a lawyer right now. But not the kind you're thinking of."

Forsythe was momentarily stunned.

"What are you talking about?" she said. "What about the heir you found?"

Bosch responded in a calm tone that was counterpoint to[5] the rising emotion in Forsythe's voice.

"We're not worried about the heir," he said. "The heir is covered. We're not filing the will because Whitney Vance didn't write it. You did."

"That's preposterous[6]," she said.

"Let me lay it out for you[7]," he said. "Vance hadn't written anything in years. He was right-handed[8]—I saw the photos of him signing his book to Larry King—but his right hand had become useless[9]. He didn't shake hands anymore, and the controller[10] on his wheelchair was on the left armrest[11]."

He paused there to allow Forsythe to register[12] an objection but she said nothing.

"It was important to him to keep this a secret," he said. "His infirmities were cause for concern[13] among members of the board of directors. A minority group on the board was constantly looking

1. s'ensuivit
2. rompit le silence
3. retardant la réponse
4. ne ferons pas homologuer le testament
5. contrastait avec
6. grotesque
7. vous expliquer
8. droitier
9. ne marchait plus
10. manette
11. accoudoir
12. d'exprimer
13. source d'inquiétude

for reasons to oust him[1]. He used you to write for him. You learned to imitate his handwriting and came in on Sundays, when fewer people were around[2], to write his letters and sign documents. That's why you felt comfortable writing the will. If there was a challenge[3] or a handwriting comparison, it was likely that the will would be compared to something else you had written."

"It's a good story," Forsythe said. "But you can't prove any of it."

"Maybe not. But the gold pen is your problem, Ida. The gold pen puts you in prison for a long, long time."

"You don't know what you're talking about. I think I want you both to leave now."

"I know that the real pen—the one you just signed your name with—was in my mailbox at the moment you supposedly found Vance dead. But the photos from the death scene show another pen on that desk. I think you realized that might be a problem so you got rid of it[4]. It wasn't there when the police went back for round two[5] with the camera[6]."

As previously planned, Haller came in[7] at that point[8] to play the big, bad wolf.

"It shows premeditation," he said. "The duplicate pen had to be made and that took time. And planning. Planning means premeditation and that means life without parole[9]. It means the rest of your life in a cell."

"You're wrong!" Forsythe yelled. "You're wrong about everything and I want you to leave. Now!"

She stood up and pointed toward the hallway leading to the front door. But neither Bosch nor Haller moved.

1. le démettre
2. il y avait moins de monde
3. récusation
4. vous en êtes débarrassée
5. la deuxième fois
6. leur appareil photo
7. intervint
8. alors
9. la perpétuité, sans possibilité de libération conditionnelle

"Tell us what happened, Ida," Bosch said. "Maybe we can help you."

"You need to understand something," Haller said. "You are never going to see a dime[1] of that ten million. It's the law. A murderer can't inherit from her victim's estate[2]."

"I'm not a murderer," Forsythe said. "And if you won't leave, then I will."

She maneuvered around the coffee table[3] and out of the seating arrangement[4]. She headed toward the hallway, intending to go out the front door.

"You smothered him with a pillow off the couch," Bosch said.

Forsythe stopped in her tracks[5], but didn't turn around. She simply waited for more and Bosch obliged[6].

"The police know," he said. "They're waiting out front[7] for you."

She still didn't move. Haller chimed in[8].

"You go out that door and we can't help you," he said. "But there is a way out in this[9]. Detective Bosch is my investigator. If I am representing you, everything we discuss in this room right now becomes confidential. We can work out a plan to go to the police and the district attorney and get the best possible solution."

"Solution?" she exclaimed. "Is that your way of saying *deal?* I make a deal and go to jail? That is crazy."

She abruptly turned and charged over to[10] one of the front windows. She split[11] the curtain to look out into the street. Bosch thought it was a little early for the arrival of Poydras and Franks but knew that the two detectives might have already shown up[12] to see if they could figure out what Bosch was up to[13].

1. centime
2. patrimoine
3. contourna la table basse
4. quitta le coin salon
5. s'arrêta net
6. s'exécuta
7. devant chez vous
8. poursuivit
9. moyen de vous en sortir
10. se précipita vers
11. écarta
12. pouvaient déjà être arrivés
13. manigançait

He heard a sharp intake of breath[1] and guessed that the detectives were indeed[2] parked out there, waiting for the appointed time[3] for them to come knock on the door.

"Ida, why don't you come back and sit down," Bosch said. "Talk to us."

He waited. He couldn't see her because she had gone to a window behind his chair. Instead, he watched Haller, who had an angle on her. When he saw Haller's eyes start tracking right[4] he knew she was coming back and that their strategy was working.

Forsythe came into Bosch's view and slowly returned to her place on the couch. Her face was distraught[5].

"You have it all wrong," she said after sitting down. "There was no plan, no premeditation. It was just a horrible, horrible mistake."

1. l'entendit retenir une exclamation
2. bien
3. heure convenue
4. à se diriger vers la droite,
5. Elle avait l'air éperdue

42

"Can you be one of the richest, most powerful men on the planet and still be a cheap and petty bastard[1]?"

Ida Forsythe said it with a distant look in her eyes. Bosch couldn't tell if she was looking at the past or a bleak[2] future. But it was how she began her story. She said that on the day after Bosch visited Whitney Vance the aging billionaire had told her he was dying.

"He had taken ill overnight[3]," she said. "He looked awful and he hadn't even gotten dressed. He came into the office around noon in his bathrobe[4] and said he needed me to write something. His voice was barely a whisper. He told me that he felt like things were shutting down inside[5], that he was dying and that he needed to write a new will."

"Ida, I told you, I'm your lawyer," Haller said. "There is no reason to lie to me[6]. If you lie to me I'm out[7]."

"I'm not lying," she said. "This is the truth."

Bosch held up a hand to halt Haller from pressing her. Haller was not convinced but Bosch believed that she was telling the story truthfully—at least from her perspective—and he wanted to hear it.

"Tell it," he said.

"We were alone in the office," she said. "He dictated to me the terms of the will and I wrote

1. être quand même un mesquin et un salaud

2. peu reluisant

3. était tombé malade dans la nuit

4. en peignoir

5. avait l'impression que tout s'éteignait en lui

6. de me mentir

7. je me retire

it in his hand[1]. He told me what to do with it. He gave me the pen and told me to send it all to you. Only … he left something out[2]."

"You," Haller said.

"All the years I worked for him," she said. "At his beck and call[3], keeping the facade of health intact[4]. All those years and he wasn't going to leave me anything."

"So you rewrote the will," Haller said.

"I had the pen," she said. "I took some of the stationery home and I did what was right and deserved[5]. I rewrote it to make it fair[6]. It was so little compared to all there was. I thought …"

Her voice trailed off and she didn't finish[7]. Bosch studied her. He knew that greed[8] was a relative term. Was it greedy, after thirty-five years of service, to scheme[9] a ten-million-dollar payout[10] from a six-billion-dollar fortune? Some might call it a drop in the bucket[11], but not if it cost a man the last months of his life. Bosch thought of the flyer for the movie that Vibiana Veracruz had put up in the lobby of her building. *See this place before the greed!* He wondered what Ida had been like before she decided that ten million dollars was her just reward[12].

"He told me that he had gotten a message from you," she said, beginning what appeared to be a new strand[13] of the story. "You said you had the information he was looking for. He said it meant that he'd had a child and there were heirs to his fortune. He said he would die happy. He went back to his room after that and I believed him. I didn't think I'd ever see him again."

She rewrote the will to include herself and put the package in the mail as instructed. She said that for the next two days, she came to work at the

1. avec son écriture
2. avait oublié quelque chose
3. À son entière disposition
4. sans jamais trahir son état de santé
5. mérité
6. le rendre plus juste
7. Elle n'acheva pas
8. la cupidité
9. de combiner
10. versement
11. goutte d'eau dans la mer
12. récompense
13. fil

mansion but she never saw Vance. He was sequestered in his room and only his doctor and a nurse were granted access[1]. Things looked grave around the mansion on San Rafael.

"Everybody was sad," she said. "It was clear that this was the end. He was dying. He was supposed to die."

Bosch surreptitiously[2] checked his watch. The detectives out front of the house were going to knock on the door in ten minutes. He hoped they wouldn't jump the gun[3] and ruin the confession.

"Then he called you Sunday," Haller said, trying to keep the story going.

"It was Sloan who called," Forsythe said. "Mr. Vance told him to call me in. So I got there and he was at his desk and it was like he had never even been sick. His voice was back and it was business as usual. And then I saw the pen. It was there on the desk for me to write with."

"Where did it come from?" Bosch asked.

"I asked him," she said. "He said it came from his great-grandfather, and I said, How can that be? I sent the pen to Detective Bosch. And he said the one on the desk was the original and what he had given me to send with the will was a copy. He said it didn't matter because only the ink was important. The ink could be matched to the will. He said it would be provenance to help prove the[4] will."

She looked up from the shining surface of the coffee table and directly at Bosch.

"He told me then that he wanted me to contact you and retrieve[5] the will," she said. "Now that he was better, he wanted to withdraw it and have a lawyer do it formally[6]. I knew if I brought it back to him, he would see what I had done, and it would be the end for me. I couldn't … I don't

1. autorisés à y entrer

2. discrètement

3. ne surgiraient pas prématurément

4. que l'origine de l'encre servirait à prouver l'authenticité du

5. pour récupérer

6. le faire refaire en bonne et due forme par un avoué

know what happened. Something broke inside[1]. I picked up the pillow and came up behind him ..."

She ended the story there, apparently not wanting to repeat the details of the actual murder[2]. It was a form of denial[3], like a killer covering the face of the victim. Bosch couldn't decide whether to buy in to the confession as[4] full and honest or to be skeptical. She could have been setting up a diminished-capacity defense[5]. She also could have been hiding the real motive—that Vance's plan to have a new will written by a lawyer would surely mean the ten million for her would disappear.

Vance's dying at his desk still gave her a shot at[6] the money.

"Why did you remove the pen after he was dead?" Bosch asked.

He knew it would be a detail that always bothered him.

"I wanted there to be only one pen," she said. "I thought if there were two, it would open up a lot of questions about the will you turned in. So after everyone was gone I went into the office and took the pen."

"Where is it?" Bosch asked.

"I put it in my safe deposit box[7]," she said.

A long silence followed and Bosch expected it to be broken by the arrival of the Pasadena detectives. It was time. But then Forsythe spoke in a tone that sounded like she was talking to herself rather than to Bosch and Haller.

"I didn't want to kill him," she said. "I had taken care of him for thirty-five years and he had taken care of me. I didn't go there to kill him ..."

Haller looked at Bosch and nodded, a signal that he would take it from here[8].

1. s'est brisé en moi
2. meutre lui-même
3. déni
4. s'il fallait croire à un aveu
5. projeter de plaider la responsabilité diminuée
6. lui laissait encore une chance de toucher
7. coffre-fort
8. prenait le relais

"Ida," he said. "I'm a deal maker[1]. I can make a deal with what you just told us. We go in, cooperate, work out a manslaughter plea[2], and then we shop for[3] a judge sympathetic to your story and your age."

"I can't say I killed him," she said.

"You just did[4]," Haller said. "But technically[5] you'll just plead nolo[6] in court—you say 'no contest' to the charges. Going any other way is not going to sell[7]."

"But what about temporary insanity[8]?" she asked. "I just lost it[9] when I realized he would know what I had done. I completely blanked out[10]."

There was a calculating tone to her voice now. But Haller shook his head.

"It's a loser[11]," he said bluntly[12]. "Rewriting the will and taking the pen—these are not the steps[13] of an insane person. To make the jump[14] that all of a sudden you lost the capacity to know right from wrong because you feared Vance would find out what you did? In a courtroom I can sell ice to Eskimos but no jury's going to buy[15] that."

He paused for a moment to see if he was getting through to her[16], then pressed it further.

"Look, a reality check here[17]," he said. "At your age we have to minimize your time inside[18]. What I've outlined is the way to go[19]. But it's your choice. You[20] want to go to trial on an insanity defense, that's what we'll do. But it's the wrong move."

Haller's statement was underlined by the sound of two car doors slamming out in the street. Poydras and Franks.

"That's the police," Bosch said. "They're coming to the door."

"How do you want to play it, Ida?" Haller asked.

1. du genre à conclure des accords
2. on plaide l'homicide involontaire
3. on cherche
4. venez de le faire
5. quant à la procédure officielle,
6. la non-contestation [*nolo contendere* ; par laquelle le défenseur n'admet ni ne conteste une accusation]
7. Le faire d'une autre manière ne passerait pas
8. la démence passagère
9. J'ai perdu la tête
10. ne savais plus ce que je faisais
11. perdu d'avance
12. sans ménagement
13. initiatives
14. Pour faire avaler
15. croire à
16. se faisait comprendre
17. soyons réalistes
18. durée d'emprisonnement
19. procéder
20. Si vous

Forsythe slowly rose to her feet. Haller did as well.

"Please invite them in," she said.

Twenty minutes later Bosch stood with Haller on the sidewalk[1] on Arroyo and watched as Poydras and Franks drove away with Forsythe in the backseat of their plain wrap[2].

"Speaking of looking a gift horse in the mouth[3]," Haller said. "They actually seemed pissed off[4] that we cleared their fucking case for them[5]. Ungrateful bastards[6]."

"They've been behind the curve on this one since the get-go[7]," Bosch said. "And they aren't going to look so good at the press conference when they have to explain that the suspect turned herself in[8] before they even knew she was the suspect."

"Oh, they'll find their way around that[9]," Haller said. "I have no doubt."

Bosch nodded in agreement.

"So, guess what?" Haller said.

"What?" Bosch said.

"While we were in there I got another text from Lorna."

Bosch knew that Lorna was Haller's case manager[10].

"Was it more info on California Coding?"

"No, she got the call from CellRight. There is a genetic match[11] between Whitney Vance and Vibiana Veracruz. She's the heir and in line for a big chunk[12] of money—if she wants it."

Bosch nodded.

"Okay," he said. "I'll talk to her and give her the news. See what she wants to do."

"I know what I would do," Haller said.

Bosch smiled.

"I know what you would do too," he said.

1. trottoir
2. voiture banalisée
3. À cheval donné on ne regarde pas les dents, tu parles !
4. avaient l'air furax
5. qu'on ait résolu leur foutue affaire à leur place
6. Quelle bande d'ingrats
7. ont pris du retard dès le départ
8. s'est rendue
9. sauront retomber sur leurs pattes
10. clerc
11. correspondance
12. en passe de toucher un gros paquet

"Tell her we could file it as a Jane Doe[1]," Haller said. "Eventually we would have to[2] reveal her to the court and opposing parties, but starting out[3] we could keep her name out of it."

"I'll tell her," Bosch said.

"Another option is to go to corporate counsel[4] and lay out[5] what we've got—the DNA, your tracing of the paternal lineage—and convince them that if we get into a fight we'll take it all. Then we negotiate a nice settlement from the estate[6] and we go away, leaving money and the corporation on the table."

"That's an idea, too. A real good idea, I think. You can sell ice to Eskimos, right? You could get this done[7]."

"I could. The board of directors will take that deal in a heartbeat[8]. So you talk to her and I'll do some more thinking on it[9]."

They checked both ways before crossing the street to their cars.

"So are you going to work on Ida's defense with me?" Haller asked.

"Thanks for saying 'with me' and not 'for me,' but I don't think so," Bosch said. "I think I just quit being[10] your investigator on this one. I'm taking a full-time gig[11] with San Fernando PD."

"You sure about that?"

"Yeah, I'm sure."

"Okay, my brother from another mother[12]. Keep in touch[13] about that other thing."

"Will do."

They parted ways in the middle of the street.

1. enclencher la procédure sous couvert d'anonymat
2. Il faudra bien finir par
3. pour commencer,
4. s'adresser aux conseillers juridiques de la société
5. de leur exposer
6. accord financier
7. peux certainement leur vendre ça
8. acceptera l'arrangement sans sourciller
9. vais creuser la question
10. viens de renoncer à être
11. boulot
12. demi-frère
13. Tiens-moi au courant

43

Bosch hated the Ford he was driving. He decided it was time to go back to LAX and retrieve[1] his own car after several days of vehicular subterfuge. From South Pasadena he took the 110 down through the center of the city, past the towers of downtown, and past USC[2] and the neighborhood where Vibiana Duarte had lived most of her short life. He eventually connected to[3] the Century Freeway and went west to the airport. He was handing[4] his credit card to the garage attendant[5] to cover[6] an enormous parking fee[7] when his phone buzzed with a 213 number he didn't recognize. He took the call.

"Bosch."

"It's Vibiana."

Her voice was a low but near hysterical whisper.

"What's wrong?"

"There's a man. He's been here all day."

"He's in your loft?"

"No, down on the street. I can see him from the windows. He's watching."

"Why are you whispering?"

"I don't want Gilberto to hear me. I don't want him to be scared."

"Okay, calm down[8], Vibiana. If he hasn't made any move to come up and get inside, then that's not his plan. You are safe as long as you stay inside."

"Okay. Can you come?"

1. reprendre
2. la fac Southern California
3. finit par rejoindre
4. tendait
5. surveillant
6. payer
7. facture
8. calmez-vous

Bosch grabbed his credit card and receipt from the attendant.

"Yes, I'm coming. But I'm at the airport. It's going to take me a while[1]. You need to stay inside and don't answer the door until I get there."

The parking gate was still down. Bosch covered the phone and yelled out the window at the attendant.

"Come on, open the gate! I gotta go!"

The gate finally started to rise. Bosch went back to the phone call as he powered through the exit[2].

"This guy, where exactly is he?"

"He moves around. Every time I look, he is somewhere else. I first saw him in front of the American[3] and then he moved down the street."

"Okay, try to track him[4]. I'll call when I get there and you give me his location[5]. What does he look like? What's he wearing?"

"He, uh, jeans, gray hoodie[6], sunglasses. He's a white guy and he's too old for the hoodie."

"Okay, and you think he's alone? You don't see anybody else?"

"He's the only one I can see but there might be somebody on the other side of the building."

"Okay, I'll check that when I get there. Just sit tight[7], Vibiana. Everything's going to be all right. But if something happens before I get there, call nine-one-one[8]."

"Okay."

"And by the way, the DNA came back. It's a match[9]. You are Whitney Vance's granddaughter."

She didn't respond. Only silence.

"We can talk about it when I get there," Bosch said.

He disconnected. He could have kept her on the phone but Bosch wanted both hands free for the drive. He retraced his path[10], jumping back

1. du temps
2. sortait en trombe
3. l'hôtel American
4. suivre ses mouvements
5. me direz où il est
6. un sweat à capuche gris
7. Surtout ne bougez pas
8. les secours
9. Ça correspond
10. rebroussa chemin

onto the Century and taking it to the 110. Midday traffic was light and he made good time[1] as he raced toward the looming[2] towers of downtown. Most prominent[3] of these was the U.S. Bank Tower and Bosch couldn't help but[4] think that whoever was watching Vibiana Veracruz had been dispatched[5] from the fifty-ninth floor.

He exited on 6th Street downtown and worked his way[6] into the Arts District. He called Vibiana and told her he was in the neighborhood. She said she was looking through the window as they spoke and could see the watcher under the scaffolding[7] that wrapped the front[8] of the building across the street, which was closed and under renovation. She said the scaffolding offered many places for him to watch from.

"That's okay," Bosch said. "What works for him will also work for me."

He told her he would call her back as soon as the situation was resolved.

Bosch found parking in a lot[9] by the river and then headed toward Vibiana's building on foot. He saw the structure wrapped in scaffolding and entered through a side entrance where several construction workers were sitting on stacks of drywall[10] during a break. One of them told Bosch he was in a hard-hat area[11] as he passed.

"I know," he said.

He followed a hallway toward the front of the building. The first floor was being prepared for commercial use and every unit had a garage-door-size opening to the street. No windows or doors had been installed yet. In the third unit he saw the back of a man in jeans and a gray hoodie. He was leaning against the right wall at the edge of the front opening and was well[12] under the scaffold. It was good cover from the outside, but on

1. put aller vite
2. imposantes
3. La plus marquante
4. s'empêcher de
5. envoyé
6. pénétra
7. échafaudages
8. couvraient la façade
9. à se garer dans un parking
10. Placoplâtre
11. zone à port du casque obligatoire
12. bien en retrait

the inside his back was to[1] Bosch and he was vulnerable. Bosch quietly pulled his gun from its holster[2] and started moving toward him.

Noise from an electric saw[3] being used on an upper level of the building covered Bosch's approach. He got all the way up on the man, then grabbed him by the shoulder and spun him around. He shoved him back[4] against the wall and jammed the barrel[5] of his pistol into the man's neck.

It was Sloan. Before Bosch could say a word, the man brought his arm up, knocked the gun away, and then spun Bosch into[6] the wall. Sloan pulled his own gun and it was now pressed into Bosch's neck. Sloan's elbows pinned Harry's arms[7] up and against the wall.

"What the fuck are you doing, Bosch?"

Bosch stared at him. He opened up his right palm in surrender and let his gun drop into his left until he was holding it by the barrel.

"I was going to ask you the exact same thing," he said.

"I'm watching out for her[8]," Sloan said. "Just like you."

Sloan stepped back. He withdrew his weapon and swung it behind his back and tucked it[9] under his belt. It left Bosch with the upper hand[10] but he knew he didn't need it. He holstered[11] his weapon.

"What's going on, Sloan? You work for them."

"I worked for the old man. The company on the paychecks[12] changed but I never stopped working for him. Including right now."

"He really sent you that day you came to my house?"

1. il tournait le dos à
2. étui
3. scie
4. le repoussa
5. enfonça le canon
6. envoya Bosch contre
7. De ses coudes, Sloan plaqua les bras de Harry
8. Je la surveille
9. avant de la coincer
10. laissait l'avantage à Bosch
11. rengaina
12. bulletins de paie

"That's right. He was too sick to call or talk. He thought he was dying and wanted to know who or what you'd found."

"You knew what I was doing."

"That's right. Just like I knew when you found her."

He jerked his head[1] in the direction of Vibiana's building.

"How?"

"They've got you wired,[2] Bosch. You and your lawyer. They're tracking your phones, your cars. You're old-fashioned. You never look up[3]."

Bosch realized Haller had nailed it[4]. They had watched him from a drone.

"And you're part of all of that?" he asked.

"I acted like I was[5]," Sloan said. "They kept me on[6] after Mr. Vance died. Until last night, when they burned out a DNA lab. I quit[7]. Now I'm going to watch over her. It's what he would have wanted and I owe him[8] that."

Bosch studied him. He could be a Trojan horse[9] sent in by Trident and the corporation. Or he could be sincere. Bosch reviewed the information that he had recently gathered on Sloan. That he had been with Vance for twenty-five years. That he had attempted to revive[10] Vance after he was already dead. That he had called the police to report the death instead of attempting to avoid an investigation. Bosch thought it added up to sincerity.

"Okay," he said. "If you want to watch over her, then let's do it right. This way."

They stepped through the open doorway and out from under the scaffolding. Bosch looked up at the windows of the lofts on the fourth floor. He saw Vibiana looking down. He pulled his phone

1. fit un brusque mouvement de tête
2. vous ont mis sur écoute,
3. en l'air
4. bien vu
5. J'ai fait comme si
6. m'ont gardé
7. les ai laissés tomber
8. lui dois
9. cheval de Troie
10. ranimer

and called her as he headed toward the entrance of her building. She skipped the greeting[1].

"Who is he?" she said.

"He's a friend," Bosch said. "He worked for your grandfather. We're coming up."

1. ne s'embarrassa pas de politesses

44

After Bosch left Vibiana in Sloan's capable hands, he headed north toward the Santa Clarita Valley. He had promised Captain Trevino that he would give him an answer on the job offer by the end of the day. As he had told Haller, he intended to take the job. He was excited about the idea of being a full-time cop again. It didn't matter if his turf was two square miles small or two hundred square miles large[1]. He knew it was about cases and about always being on the right side of things. He'd found both[2] in San Fernando and decided he would be there for as long as they would have him[3].

But before he could accept the offer, he needed to make things right[4] with Bella Lourdes and assure her he was not taking her job but only holding it[5] until she got back. He got to Holy Cross by 4 p.m. and hoped to catch Lourdes before she was released[6]. He knew that getting out of a hospital was sometimes a daylong process[7] and he believed he was on safe ground[8].

Once he got to the hospital, he retraced the path[9] he had taken before to the trauma floor. He located Lourdes's private room but entered to find the bed empty and unmade. There was still a bouquet of flowers on a chest of drawers[10]. He checked a small closet[11], and on the floor, there was a pale green hospital gown[12]. On the clothes bar[13], there were two metal hangers[14] that prob-

1. Peu importait la taille de son territoire
2. ces deux aspects
3. qu'ils voudraient bien de lui
4. mettre les choses au clair
5. qu'il le gardait
6. sa sortie
7. pouvait prendre la journée
8. qu'il avait toutes ses chances
9. refit le chemin
10. commode
11. placard
12. blouse
13. tringle à vêtements
14. cintres

ably once held the going-home outfit brought by Bella's partner, Taryn.

Bosch wondered if Bella had been taken for a medical test or if she had a last therapy session that had drawn her out of her room. He walked down the hall to the nursing station[1] and inquired.

"She hasn't left yet," a nurse told him. "We're waiting for the doctor to sign the paperwork and then she'll be ready to go."

"So where is she?" he asked.

"In her room, waiting."

"No, she's not. Is there a cafeteria around?"

"Just the one on the first floor."

Bosch took the elevator down and looked around the small and uncrowded[2] cafeteria. There was no sign of Lourdes. He knew he could have missed her. As he was going down in one elevator she could have been going up in another.

But a low-grade[3] feeling of panic started to creep[4] into Bosch's chest. He remembered Taryn being outraged[5] that Lourdes was suffering the indignity of being treated in the same hospital as her abductor[6] and rapist. Bosch had sought[7] to assure her that Dockweiler would be stabilized and moved downtown to the jail ward at[8] the county hospital. But he knew that no arraignment had been set yet for Dockweiler[9] because of his precarious health status. He realized that if Dockweiler's medical condition[10] was too critical for even a bedside arraignment[11] in the hospital jail ward, then it could also be too critical for a transfer from Holy Cross to County.

He wondered if Taryn had told Bella that Dockweiler was in the same medical center or if she had figured it out on her own[12].

He went to the information desk in the hospital's main lobby outside the cafeteria and asked

1. bureau des infirmières

2. déserte

3. léger

4. s'insinuer

5. s'indignant du fait

6. kidnappeur

7. cherché

8. l'aile carcérale de

9. Dockweiler n'avait pas encore été assigné à comparaître

10. état de santé

11. même pour une mise en examen au chevet de l'accusé

12. l'avait compris toute seule

if there was a specific ward for treatment of spinal injuries[1]. He was told spinal trauma was on the third floor. He jumped on an elevator and went back up.

The elevator opened on a nursing station that was located in the middle of a floor plan resembling an *H*. Bosch saw a uniformed Sheriff's deputy leaning over the counter and small-talking with the duty nurse[2]. Harry's anxiety kicked up another notch[3].

"This is the spinal trauma center?" he asked.

"It is," the nurse said. "How can I—"

"Is Kurt Dockweiler still being treated here?"

Her eyes made a furtive move toward the deputy, who straightened up off the counter[4]. Bosch pulled the badge off his belt and displayed it.

"Bosch, SFPD. Dockweiler's my case. Where's he at[5]? Show me."

"This way," the deputy said.

They headed down one of the hallways. Bosch could see an empty chair outside a room several doors down[6].

"How long have you been fucking off at the nursing station[7]?" he asked.

"Not long," the deputy said. "This guy's not going anywhere[8]."

"I'm not worried about that. Did you see a woman get off the elevator?"

"I don't know. People come and go. When?"

"When do you think[9]? Now."

Before the deputy could answer, they got to the room and Bosch put his hand out to his left to hold him back. He saw Bella Lourdes standing at the foot of the bed in Dockweiler's room.

"Stay here," he said to the deputy.

Bosch slowly entered the room. Lourdes gave no indication she had noticed him. She was

1. service de traumatologie spinale
2. en train de bavarder avec l'infirmière de service
3. monta d'un cran
4. se redressa
5. Dans quelle chambre est-il
6. plus loin
7. vous vous la coulez douce au poste des infirmières
8. ne peut pas bouger
9. À votre avis

staring intently down at Dockweiler, who lay in the elevated bed surrounded by all manner[1] of medical apparatus and tubes, including the breather[2] that went down his throat and kept his lungs pumping. His eyes were open and he was staring back at Lourdes. Bosch easily read his eyes. He saw fear.

"Bella?"

She turned at the sound of his voice, saw Bosch, and managed a smile.

"Harry."

He checked her hands for weapons[3]. There was nothing.

"Bella, what are you doing in here?"

She looked back at Dockweiler.

"I wanted to see him. Face him."

"You shouldn't be here."

"I know. But I had to be. I'm leaving here today, going home. I wanted to see him first. Let him know that he didn't break me like he said he would."

Bosch nodded.

"Did you think I came to kill him or something?" she asked.

"I don't know what I thought," Bosch said.

"I don't need to. He's already dead. Kind of ironic, don't you think?"

"What?"

"Your bullet cut his spine. He's a rapist and now he'll never be able to do that to anyone again."

Bosch nodded.

"Let me take you back to your room now," he said. "The nurse said the doctor has to see you before they can sign you out[4]."

In the hallway Bosch cut off[5] the deputy before he could speak.

1. toutes sortes
2. respirateur
3. vérifia qu'elle n'avait pas d'arme dans les mains
4. te laisser sortir
5. interrompit

"This never happened," he said. "You make a report and I report you for abandoning your post."

"Not a problem, never happened," the deputy said.

He remained standing by his chair and Bosch and Lourdes headed down the hall.

On the way back to her own room, Bosch told Lourdes about the offer from Trevino. He said he would only accept it if she approved and understood that he would drop back down to[1] part-time reserve officer as soon as she was ready to return.

She gave her approval without hesitation.

"You're perfect for the job," she said. "And maybe it will be a permanent thing. I'm not sure what I'm going to do. I might never come back."

Bosch knew that she had to be considering that she could easily and deservedly[2] receive a stress-related out from the job[3]. She could pick up[4] her entire salary and do something else with her life and her family, be away from the nastiness[5] of the world. It would be a tough choice but the specter of Dockweiler overshadowed it[6]. If she never came back, would it haunt her? Would it give Dockweiler a final power over her?

"I'm thinking you're going to be coming back, Bella," he said. "You're a good detective and you're going to miss it. Look at me, scratching and fighting[7] to keep a badge on my belt at my age. It's in the blood. You've got cop DNA."

She smiled and nodded.

"I kinda hope[8] you're right."

At the nursing station on her floor, they embraced and promised to keep in touch. Bosch left her there.

Bosch headed back down the 5 to San Fernando to tell Trevino he was in[9]—at least until Bella came back.

1. reprendrait son poste de

2. à juste titre

3. demander une rupture conventionnelle pour cause de souffrance au travail

4. garder

5. cruauté

6. prédominait

7. qui fais des pieds et des mains

8. D'une certaine manière, j'espère que

9. qu'il acceptait le poste

Along the way he thought about what he'd said to Lourdes about cop blood. It was something he truly believed. He knew that in his internal universe, there was a mission etched[1] in a secret language, like drawings on the wall of an ancient cave[2], that gave him his direction and meaning. It could not be altered and it would always be there to guide him to the right path.

1. tracée

2. grotte

It was a Sunday afternoon in spring. A crowd was gathered in the triangle created by the convergence of Traction Avenue and Rose and Third Streets. What for years had been a parking lot was now taking shape as the[1] first public park in the Arts District. Rows of folding chairs were lined in front of a sculpture twenty feet high[2], its shape and content only hinted at[3] by the contours of the massive white shroud[4] that draped it. A steel cable extended from the shroud to a crane[5] that had been used in the installation. The veil[6] would be dramatically lifted[7] and the sculpture revealed as the centerpiece of the park.

Most of the chairs were filled and videographers from two of the local news channels were on hand[8] to record the event[9]. Many in attendance[10] knew the artist who had created the sculpture. Some were meeting her for the first time even though they were bound by family ties if not by blood.

Bosch and his daughter sat in the back row[11]. Harry could see Gabriela Lida and Olivia Macdonald seated three rows in front of them. Young Gilberto Veracruz sat between them, his attention drawn to a handheld video game[12]. Olivia's grown children[13] were in the chairs to her right.

At the appointed start time of the unveiling[14], a man in a suit walked to the podium in front of the sculpture and adjusted the microphone.

1. prenait maintenant la forme du
2. de 6 m de haut
3. suggérés
4. drap
5. grue
6. voile
7. théâtralement levé
8. sur place
9. filmer l'événement
10. Beaucoup de personnes présentes
11. au dernier rang
12. captée par une console de jeux
13. Les enfants déjà grands
14. l'heure précise du début de l'inauguration

"Hello and thank you all for coming out on this wonderful spring day. My name is Michael Haller. I am legal adviser to[1] *the Fruit Box Foundation, which I am sure you have all learned about through the media in the past few months. Thanks to a very generous endowment*[2] *from the estate*[3] *of the late*[4] *Whitney P. Vance, the Fruit Box Foundation is dedicating this park today in honor of Mr. Vance. We are also announcing plans to purchase*[5] *and renovate four historic structures in the Arts District. These will be dedicated live-work complexes*[6] *offering affordable*[7] *housing and studio space for this city's artists. The Fruit Box—"*

Haller had to stop because of the applause from those seated in front of him. He smiled, nodded, and then continued.

"The Fruit Box Foundation has additional[8] *plans for the area as well. More structures containing affordable housing and studio space, more parks, and more consignment galleries*[9]*. They call this area the Arts District, and the Fruit Box Foundation—its very name*[10] *tied to the creative history of this neighborhood—will continue to strive*[11] *to keep it a vibrant community of artists and public art."*

More applause broke into[12] *Haller's speech and he waited it out*[13] *before continuing.*

"And finally, speaking of artists and public art, we are very proud today to dedicate[14] *this park with the unveiling of a sculpture created by Vibiana Veracruz, artistic director of the Fruit Box Foundation. Art speaks for itself. So, without delay*[15]*, I give you 'The Wrong Side of Goodbye'."*

In dramatic fashion[16] *the crane raised the shroud, revealing a sculpture of shining white acrylic. It was a diorama like Bosch had seen in Vibiana's loft the previous year. A multitude of*

1. le conseiller juridique de
2. dotation
3. ayants droit
4. de feu
5. des projets de rachat
6. Il s'agira de résidences « atelier-logement »
7. abordables
8. d'autres
9. dépôts-ventes
10. dont le nom même est
11. s'efforcer
12. interrompirent
13. qu'ils cessent
14. d'inaugurer
15. sans plus attendre
16. D'un mouvement théâtral,

1. personnages
2. déchiqueté
3. pale d'hélice
4. dressé comme une pierre tombale
5. silhouette
6. l'épave
7. était tendue, doigts écartés,
8. de mère avec sa fille dans les bras
9. au bout de l'allée centrale
10. sourire de travers

figures[1] and angles. The base of the sculpture was the mangled[2] fuselage of a helicopter lying on its side, a piece of a broken rotor blade[3] sticking up like a tombstone[4]. From the open side door of the craft rose hands and faces, soldiers looking and reaching up for rescue. The figure[5] of one soldier rose above the rest, his full body up and through the door, as if pulled from the wreckage[6] by the unseen hand of God.

One of the soldier's hands reached with splayed fingers[7] toward the heavens. From his angle Bosch could not see the face of the soldier but he knew who he was.

And standing next to the torso of the fallen helicopter was the figure of a woman holding a baby in her arms. The child was faceless but Bosch recognized the woman as Gabriela Lida and the mother-daughter[8] pose of the photo from the beach at the del Coronado.

Deep applause greeted the unveiling but at first there was no sign of the sculptress. Then Bosch felt a hand touch his shoulder and he turned to see Vibiana passing behind him on her way to the podium.

As she turned up the middle aisle[9], she glanced back at him and smiled. Bosch realized in that moment that it was the first time he had ever seen her smile. But it was a lopsided smile[10] he knew he had seen before.

La collection Yes you can!

Les faux débutants

Linwood Barclay	*Broken Promise*
M. C. Beaton	*Agatha Raisin and the Quiche of Death*
Harlan Coben	*The Stranger*
Michael Connelly	*The Black Box*
Michael Connelly	*The Burning Room*
Michael Connelly	*The Drop*
Michael Connelly	*The Wrong Side of Goodbye*
Ken Follett	*The Modigliani Scandal*
Mary Higgins Clark	*A Cry in the Night*
Mary Higgins Clark	*A Stranger is Watching*
Mary Higgins Clark	*Loves Music, Loves to Dance*
Mary Higgins Clark	*Where are the Children?*
Anthony Horowitz	*The House of Silk*
Ian Rankin	*Knots & Crosses*
Nicholas Sparks	*Message in a Bottle*

Les intermédiaires

Harlan Coben	*Caught*
Harlan Coben	*Play Dead*
Harlan Coben	*Stay Close*
Harlan Coben	*Tell No One*
Harlan Coben	*The Woods*
Ken Follett	*Paper Money*
Anthony Horowitz	*Moriarty*
P. D. James	*A Mind to Murder*
P. D. James	*Death Comes to Pemberley*
Douglas Kennedy	*The Big Picture*

Stephen King *Finders Keepers*

Stephen King *The Green Mile*

John le Carré *A Most Wanted Man*

Yann Martel *Life of Pi*

Les avancés

Paul Auster *Leviathan*

Paul Auster *Oracle Night*

Julian Barnes *The Sense of an Ending*

Michael Cunningham *By Nightfall*

Michael Cunningham *The Hours*

Helen Fielding *Bridget Jones's Diary*

Helen Fielding *Bridget Jones: The Edge of Reason*

Elizabeth George *A Great Deliverance*

Stephen King *Dolores Claiborne*

Stephen King *Misery*

Les classiques

Jane Austen *Pride and Prejudice*

G. K. Chesterton *The Innocence of Father Brown*

Arthur Conan Doyle *The Hound of the Baskervilles*

Francis Scott Fitzgerald *Tender is the Night*

Francis Scott Fitzgerald *The Great Gatsby*

Mary Shelley *Frankenstein*

Edith Wharton *The Age of Innocence*

Oscar Wilde *The Picture of Dorian Gray*

Virginia Woolf *To the Lighthouse*

HARRAP s'engage pour l'environnement en réduisant l'empreinte carbone de ses livres. Celle de cet exemplaire est de :
1,4 kg éq. CO_2
Rendez-vous sur www.larousse-durable.fr

PAPIER À BASE DE FIBRES CERTIFIÉES

Imprimé en Italie par Grafica Veneta
Dépôt légal : mai 2019
322471-02/11043983 - mai 2020